"NOBODY DOES SPACE OPERA BETTER THAN WEBER"

"Nobody does space opera better than Weber, and his heroine, Honor Harrington ... remains as engaging as ever.... The sweep of interstellar conflict contrasts with developments in Honor's personal life that ... succeed in being highly moving ... like a fusion of Horatio Hornblower, Robert A. Heinlein and Tom Clancy...."
—*Publishers Weekly* (starred review)

"Brilliant! Brilliant! Brilliant! ... unequivocally superb!"
—**Anne McCaffrey** on Weber's *Echoes of Honor*

"It's impossible not to be entertained, delighted, even enthralled by this splendid piece of storytelling."
—*Booklist* on Weber's *Honor Among Enemies*

"Space opera at its very best ... belongs in any collection."
—*Library Journal*

"Great stuff ... compelling combat combined with engaging characters for a great space opera adventure."   —*Locus*

"[David Weber's *On Basilisk Station*] spins a suspenseful and compelling yarn, whose slow buildup leads to a hair-raising climactic showdown.... The series' success is no mystery."   —*SFReviews.net*

"David Weber is one of the most popular authors of science fiction and fantasy ... *Off Armageddon Reef* is a fantastic read, utterly compelling ..."   —*SFFWorld.com*

IN THIS SERIES BY DAVID WEBER

The Star Kingdom:
A Beautiful Friendship
Fire Season, with Jane Lindskold (forthcoming)

Honor Harrington:
On Basilisk Station
The Honor of the Queen
The Short Victorious War
Field of Dishonor
Flag in Exile
Honor Among Enemies
In Enemy Hands
Echoes of Honor
Ashes of Victory
War of Honor
At All Costs
Mission of Honor
A Rising Thunder
Shadow of Freedom (forthcoming)

Honorverse:
Crown of Slaves, with Eric Flint
Torch of Freedom, with Eric Flint
The Shadow of Saganami
Storm from the Shadows

Edited by David Weber:
More than Honor
Worlds of Honor
Changes of Worlds
In the Service of the Sword
In Fire Forged

For a complete listing of Baen titles by David Weber,
please go to www.baen.com.

A BEAUTIFUL FRIENDSHIP

DAVID WEBER

A BEAUTIFUL FRIENDSHIP

Copyright © 2011 by Words of Weber, Inc.

An earlier version of "A Beautiful Friendship" copyright © 1998.

A Baen Books Original

Baen Publishing Enterprises
P.O. Box 1403
Riverdale, NY 10471
www.baen.com

ISBN: 978-1-4516-3826-4

Cover art by Daniel Dos Santos

First Baen paperback printing, September 2012

Distributed by Simon & Schuster
1230 Avenue of the Americas
New York, NY 10020

Library of Congress Control Number: 2011015815

10 9 8 7 6 5 4 3 2 1

Pages by Joy Freeman (www.pagesbyjoy.com)
Printed in the United States of America

A BEAUTIFUL FRIENDSHIP

UNEXPECTED MEETINGS

1518 Post Diaspora

Planet Sphinx,

Manticore Binary Star System

"I *MEAN* IT, STEPHANIE!" RICHARD HARRINGTON SAID. "I don't want you wandering off into those woods again without me or your mom along. Is that clear?"

"Oh, *Daaaddy*—!" Stephanie began, only to close her mouth sharply when her father folded his arms. Then the toe of his right foot started tapping lightly, and her heart sank. This wasn't going well at all, and she resented that reflection on her...negotiating skills almost as much as she resented the restriction she was trying to avoid. She was almost twelve T-years old, smart, an only child, and a daughter. That gave her certain advantages, and she'd become an expert at wrapping her father around her finger almost as soon as she could talk. Unfortunately, her mother had always been a tougher customer...and even her father was unscrupulously willing to abandon his proper pliancy when he decided the situation justified it.

Like now.

"We're not going to discuss this further," he said with

ominous calm. "Just because you haven't *seen* any hexa-pumas or peak bears doesn't mean they aren't out there."

"But I've been stuck inside with nothing to do all *winter*," she said, easily suppressing a twinge of conscience as she neglected to mention snowball fights, cross-country skiing, sleds, snow tunnels, and certain other diversions. "I want to go outside and *see* things!"

"I know you do, honey," her father said more gently, reaching out to tousle her curly brown hair. "But it's dangerous out there. This isn't Meyerdahl, you know." Stephanie closed her eyes and looked martyred, and his expression showed a flash of regret at having let the last sentence slip out. "If you really want something to do, why don't you run into Twin Forks with Mom this afternoon?"

"Because Twin Forks is a complete *null*, Daddy."

Exasperation colored Stephanie's reply, even though she knew it was a tactical error. Even above-average parents like hers got stubborn if you disagreed with them *too* emphatically, but *honestly!* Twin Forks might be the closest "town" to the Harrington freehold, but it boasted a total of *maybe* fifty families, most of whose handful of kids were a total waste of time. None of *them* were interested in xeno-botany or biosystem hierarchies. In fact, they spent most of their free time trying to catch anything small enough to keep as pets, however much damage they might do to their intended "pets" in the process. Stephanie was pretty sure any effort to enlist those zorks in her explorations would have led to words—or a fist in the eye—in fairly short order. Not, she thought darkly, that *she* was to blame for the situation. If Dad and Mom hadn't insisted on dragging her away from Meyerdahl just when she'd been accepted for the junior forestry program, she'd have been on her first internship field trip by now. It wasn't *her* fault she wasn't, and the least they could do to make up for it was let her explore their own property!

"Twin Forks is *not* a 'complete null,'" her father said firmly.

"Oh yes it is," she replied with a curled lip, and Richard Harrington drew a deep breath.

"Look," he said after a moment, "I know you had to leave all your old friends behind on Meyerdahl. And I know how much you were looking forward to that forestry internship. But Meyerdahl's been settled for over a thousand T-years, Steph, and Sphinx hasn't."

"I know that, Dad," she replied, trying to make her voice as reasonable as his. That first "Daddy!" had been a mistake. She knew that, and she didn't plan on repeating it, but his sudden decree that she stay so close to the house had caught her by surprise. "But it's not like I didn't have my uni-link with me. I could've called for help anytime, and I know enough to climb a tree if something's trying to eat me! I promise—if anything like that had come along, I'd've been sitting on a limb fifteen meters up waiting for you or Mom to home in on my beacon."

"I know you would have...if you'd seen it in time," her father said in a considerably grimmer tone. "But Sphinx isn't 'wired' the way Meyerdahl was, and we still don't know nearly enough about what's out there. We *won't* know for decades yet, and all the uni-links in the world might not get an air car there fast enough if you *did* run into a hexapuma or a peak bear."

Stephanie started to reply, then stopped. He had a point, she admitted grudgingly. Not that she meant to give up without a fight! But one of the five-meter-long hexapumas would be enough to ruin anyone's day, and peak bears weren't a lot better. And he was right about how little humanity knew about what was really *out* there in the Sphinx brush. But that was the whole point, the whole reason she wanted to be out there in the first place!

"Listen, Steph," her father said finally. "I know Twin

Forks isn't much compared to Hollister, but it's the best I can offer. And you know it's going to grow. They're even talking about putting in their own shuttle pad next spring!"

Stephanie managed—somehow—not to roll her eyes again. Calling Twin Forks "not much" compared to the city of Hollister was like saying it snowed "a little" on Sphinx. And given the long, dragging, *endless* year of this *stupid* planet, she'd almost be *seventeen T-years old* by the time "next spring" got here! She hadn't quite been ten and a half when they arrived . . . just in time for it to start snowing. And it hadn't *stopped* snowing for the next fifteen T-months!

"Sorry," her father said quietly, as if he'd read her thoughts. "I'm sorry Twin Forks isn't exciting, and I'm sorry you didn't want to leave Meyerdahl. And I'm sorry I can't let you wander around on your own. But that's the way it is, honey. And"—he gazed sternly into her brown eyes—"I want your word you'll do what your mom and I tell you on this one."

Stephanie squelched glumly across the mud to the steep-roofed gazebo. *Everything* on Sphinx had a steep roof, and she allowed herself a deep, heartfelt groan as she plunked herself down on the gazebo steps and contemplated the reason that was true.

It was the snow. Even here, close to Sphinx's equator, annual snowfall was measured in meters—*lots* of meters, she thought moodily—and houses needed steep roofs to shed all of that frozen water, especially on a planet whose gravity was over a third higher than Old Earth's. Not that Stephanie had ever seen Old Earth . . . or *any* world which wasn't classified as "heavy-grav" by the rest of humanity.

She sighed again, with an edge of wistful misery, and wished her great-great-great-great-whatever grandparents hadn't volunteered for the Meyerdahl First Wave. Her parents had sat her down to explain what that meant shortly after her eighth birthday. She'd already heard the word "genie," though she hadn't realized that, technically at least, it applied to her, but she'd only started her classroom studies four T-years before. Her history courses hadn't gotten to Old Earth's Final War yet, so she'd had no way to know why some people still reacted so violently to any notion of modifications to the human genotype... or why they considered "genie" one of the dirtiest words in Standard English.

Now she knew, though she still thought anyone who felt that way was silly. Of *course* the bio-weapons and "super soldiers" whipped up for the Final War had been horrible. But that had all happened over five hundred T-years ago, and it hadn't had a thing to do with people like the Meyerdahl or Quelhollow first waves. She supposed it was a good thing the original Manticoran settlers had left Sol before the Final War. Their old-fashioned cryo ships had taken long enough to make the trip for them to miss the entire thing...and the prejudices that went with it.

Not that there was anything much to draw anyone's attention to the changes the geneticists had whipped up for Meyerdahl's colonists. Mass for mass, Stephanie's muscle tissue was about twenty-five percent more efficient than that of "pure strain" humans, and her metabolism ran about twenty percent faster to fuel those muscles. There were a few minor changes to her respiratory and circulatory systems (to let her handle a broader range of atmospheric pressures without the nanotech pure-strainers used), and some skeletal reinforcement to cope with the muscles, as well. And the modifications had been designed to be dominant, so that all her descendants would have them. But her kind of genie was perfectly inter-fertile with pure-strainers, and as far as she could see all the changes put together were no big deal. They just meant that because she and her parents needed less muscle mass for a given strength they were ideally suited to colonize high-gravity planets without turning all stumpy and bulgy-muscled. Still, when she'd gotten around to studying the Final War and some of the anti-genie movements, she'd decided Dad and Mom might have had a point in warning her not to go around telling strangers about it. Aside from that, she seldom thought about it one way or the other... except to reflect somewhat bitterly that if they *hadn't* been genies the heavy gravities of the Manticore Binary System's habitable planets might have kept her parents from deciding they simply *had* to drag her off to the boonies like this.

She chewed her lower lip and leaned back, letting her eyes roam over the isolated clearing in which she'd been marooned by their decision. The tall green roof of the main house was a cheerful splash of color against the still-bare picketwood and crown oaks which surrounded it. But she wasn't in the mood to be cheerful, and it took very little effort to decide green was a stupid color for a roof. Something dark and drab—brown, maybe, or maybe even black—would've suited her much better. And while she was on the subject of inappropriate building materials, why couldn't they have used something more colorful than natural gray stone? She knew it had been the cheapest way to do it, but getting enough insulating capacity to face a Sphinx winter out of natural rock required walls over a meter thick. It was like living in a dungeon, she thought... then paused to savor the simile. It fitted her present mood perfectly, and she stored it away for future use.

She considered it a moment longer, then shook herself and gazed at the trees beyond the house and its attached greenhouses with a yearning that was almost a physical pain. Some kids knew they wanted to be spacers or scientists by the time they could pronounce the words, but Stephanie didn't want stars. She wanted . . . green. She wanted to go places no one had ever been yet—not through hyper-space, but on a warm, living, breathing planet. She wanted waterfalls and mountains, trees and animals who'd never heard of zoos. And she wanted to be the first to see them, to study them, understand them, protect them. . . .

Maybe it was because of her parents, she mused, forgetting to resent her father's restrictions for the moment. Richard Harrington held degrees in both Terran and xeno-veterinary medicine. They made him far more valuable to a frontier world like Sphinx than he'd ever been back home, but he'd occasionally been called upon by Meyer-dahl's Forestry Service. That had brought Stephanie into far closer contact with her birth world's animal kingdom than most people her age ever had the chance to come. And her mother's background as a plant geneticist—another of those specialties new worlds found so necessary—had helped her appreciate the beautiful intricacies of Meyer-dahl's flora, as well.

Only then they'd brought her way out here and dumped her on *Sphinx*.

Stephanie grimaced in fresh disgust. Part of her had deeply resented the thought of leaving Meyerdahl, but another part had been delighted. However much she might have longed for a Wildlife Management Service career, the thought of starships and interstellar voyages had been exciting. And so had the thought of emigrating on a sort of rescue mission to help save a colony which had been almost wiped out by plague. (Although, she admitted, *that* part would have been much less exciting if the doctors hadn't found a *cure* for the plague in question.) Best of all, her parents' specialties meant the Star

Kingdom had agreed to pay the cost of their transportation, which—coupled with their savings—had let them buy a huge piece of land all their own. The Harrington freehold was a rough rectangle thrown across the steep slopes of the Copperwall Mountains to overlook the Tannerman Ocean, and it measured twenty-five kilometers on a side. Not the twenty-five *meters* of their lot's frontage in Hollister, but twenty-five *kilo*meters, which made it as big as the entire city had been back home! And it backed up against an area already designated as a major nature preserve, as well.

But there were a few things Stephanie hadn't considered in her delight. Like the fact that their freehold was almost a thousand kilometers from anything that could reasonably be called a city. Much as she loved wilderness, she wasn't used to being *that* far from civilization, and the distances between settlements meant her father had to spend an awful lot of time in the air just getting from patient to patient.

At least the planetary data net let her keep up with her schooling and enjoy some simple pleasures—in fact, she was first in her class (again), despite the move, and she stood sixteenth in the current planetary junior chess competition, as well. Of course, that didn't mean as much here as it would have on Meyerdahl, given how much smaller the population (and pool of competitors) was. Still, it had kept her from developing a truly terminal case of what her mother called "cabin fever," and she enjoyed her trips to town (when she wasn't using Twin Forks' dinkiness in negotiations with her parents). But none of the few kids her age in Twin Forks were in the accelerated curriculum, which meant they weren't in any of her classes, and she hadn't gotten to know them on-line the way she'd known all her friends back on Meyerdahl. They probably weren't all *complete* nulls, but she didn't *know* them. Besides, she admitted, her "peer group inter-personal skills" (as the counselors liked to put it) weren't her strong suit. She knew she got frustrated quickly—*too* quickly, often enough—with people who couldn't keep up with her in an argument or who insisted on doing stupid things, and she knew she had a hot temper. Her mom said that sometimes accompanied the Meyerdahl modifications, and Stephanie tried to sit on it when it got out of hand. She really *did* try, yet more than one "interpersonal interaction" with another member of her "peer group" had ended with bloody noses or blackened eyes.

So, no, she hadn't made any friends among Twin Forks' younger population. Not yet, anyway, and the settlement itself was totally lacking in all the amenities of a city of almost three million people, like Hollister.

Yet Stephanie could have lived with all of that if it hadn't been for two other things: snow and hexapumas.

She dug a booted toe into the squishy mud beyond the gazebo's bottom step and scowled. Daddy had warned her they'd be arriving just before winter, and she'd thought she knew what that meant. But "winter" had an entirely different meaning on Sphinx. Snow had been an exciting rarity on warm, mild Meyerdahl, but a Sphinxian winter lasted almost *sixteen T-months*. That was over a tenth of her entire *life*, and she'd become well and truly sick of snow. Dad could say whatever he liked about how other seasons would be just as long. Stephanie believed him. She even understood (intellectually) that she had the better part of four full T-years before the snow returned. But she hadn't *experienced* it yet, and all she had right now was mud. Lots and lots and *lots* of mud, and the bare beginning of buds on the deciduous trees. And boredom.

And, she reminded herself with a scowl, she also had the promise not to do anything *about* that boredom which her father had extracted from her. She supposed she should

be glad he and Mom worried about her. But it was so...
so *underhanded* of him to make her promise. It was like
making Stephanie her own jailer, and he knew it!

She sighed again, rose, shoved her fists into her jacket
pockets, and headed for her mother's office. Marjorie
Harrington's services had become much sought after in
the seventeen T-months she'd been on Sphinx, but unlike
her husband, she seldom had to go to her clients. On
the rare occasions when she required physical specimens
rather than simple electronic data, they could be delivered
to her small but efficient lab and supporting greenhouses
here on the freehold as easily as to any other location.
Stephanie doubted she could get her mom to help her
change Dad's mind about grounding her, but she could
try. And at least she might get a little understanding out
of her.

Dr. Marjorie Harrington stood by the window and smiled
sympathetically as she watched Stephanie trudge toward
the house. Dr. Harrington knew where her daughter was
headed...and what she meant to do when she got there.
In a general way, she disapproved of Stephanie's attempts
to enlist one parent against the other when edicts were
laid down, but one thing about Stephanie: however much
she might resent a restriction or maneuver to get it lifted,
she always honored it once she'd given her word to do so.

Which didn't mean she'd *enjoy* it, and Marjorie's smile
faded as she contemplated her daughter's disappointment.
And the fact that she and Richard had no choice but to
restrict Stephanie didn't make it *fair*, either.

I really need to take some time away from the terminal,
she reflected. *There's no way I could possibly spend as many
hours in the woods as Stephanie wants to. There aren't
that many hours in even a Sphinxian day! But I ought to*

be able to at least provide her with an adult escort often enough for her habit to get a minimum fix.

Her thoughts paused and then she smiled again as another thought occurred to her.

No, we can't let Steph rummage around in the woods by herself, but there might just be another way to distract her. After all, she's got that problem-solver streak—the kind of mind that prints out hard copies of the Yawata Crossing Times *crossword so she can work them in ink instead of electronically. So with just a little prompting . . .*

Marjorie let her chair slip upright and drew a sheaf of hard copy closer as she heard boots moving down the hall towards her office. She uncapped her stylus and bent over the neatly printed sheets with a studious expression just as Stephanie knocked on the frame of the open door.

"Mom?" Dr. Harrington allowed herself one more sympathetic smile at the put-upon pensiveness of Stephanie's tone, then banished the expression and looked up from her paperwork.

"Come in, Steph," she invited, and leaned back in her chair once more.

"Can I talk to you a minute?" Stephanie asked, and Marjorie nodded.

"Of course you can, honey," she said. "What's on your mind?"

2

CLIMBS QUICKLY SCURRIED UP THE NEAREST NET-WOOD trunk, then paused at the first cross-branch to clean his sticky true-hands and hand-feet with fastidious care.

He *hated* crossing between trees now that the cold days were passing into those of mud. Not that he was particularly fond of snow, either, he admitted with a bleek of laughter, but at least it melted out of his fur—eventually—instead of forming gluey clots that dried hard as rock. Still, there *were* compensations to warming weather, and he sniffed appreciatively at the breeze that rustled the furled buds just beginning to fringe the all-but-bare branches. Under most circumstances, he would have climbed all the way to the top to luxuriate in the wind fingers ruffling his coat, but he had other things on his mind today.

He finished grooming himself, then rose on his rear legs in the angle of the cross-branch and trunk to scan his surroundings with sharp green eyes. None of the two-legs were in sight, but that meant little; two-legs were

14

full of surprises. Climbs Quickly's own Bright Water Clan had seen little of them until lately, but other clans had observed them for twelve full turnings of the seasons, and it was obvious they had tricks the People had never mastered. Among those was some way to keep watch from far away—so far, indeed, that the People could neither hear nor taste them, much less see them. Yet Climbs Quickly detected no sign that *he* was being watched, and he flowed smoothly to the adjacent trunk. Now that he was into the last cluster of net-wood, the pattern of its linked branches would at least let him keep his true-feet and hand-feet clear of the muck as he followed the line of cross-branches deeper into the clearing.

He slowed as he reached the final cross-branch, then stopped. He sat for long, still moments, cream and gray coat blending into invisibility against trunks and branches veiled in a fine spray of tight green buds, motionless but for a single true-hand which groomed his whiskers reflexively. He listened carefully, with ears and thoughts alike, and those ears pricked as he tasted the faint mind-glow that indicated the presence of two-legs. It wasn't the clear, bright communication it would have been from one of People, for the two-legs appeared to be mind-blind, yet there was something...nice about it. Which was odd, for whatever else they were, the two-legs were *very* unlike the People. That much had been obvious from the very beginning.

<*What are you listening for, Climbs Quickly?*> a mind-voice asked, and he looked back over his shoulder.

Shadow Hider was well named, for more than one reason, he thought. The other scout was all but invisible against the net-wood bark, even to Climbs Quickly, who knew exactly where he was from his mind-glow. Climbs Quickly had no fear that Shadow Hider would betray their presence to the two-legs, but that was unlikely to make him any more pleasant as a companion.

<*The two-leg mind-glow,*> he replied to the question, and tasted Shadow Hider's flicker of irritation at the tone of his own mind-voice. He'd made no attempt to hide the exaggerated patience of that tone, since Shadow Hider would have tasted the emotions behind it just as clearly.

<*Why?*> Shadow Hider asked bluntly. <*We already know they are as mind-blind as the burrow runners or the bark-chewers, Climbs Quickly.*>

Shadow Hider's disdain for any creatures who were so completely deaf and dumb was obvious in his mind-glow, and Climbs Quickly suppressed a desire to cross back over to the junior scout's position and cuff him sharply across the nose. He reminded himself that Shadow Hider was far younger than he, and that those who knew the least often *thought* they knew the most, but that made the other scout no less frustrating. And, of course, the People's ability to taste one another's emotions meant Shadow Hider knew exactly how Climbs Quickly felt, which made things no better.

<*Yes, they appear to be mind-blind, Shadow Hider,*> he replied after a moment. <*But do not make the mistake of thinking that means they are no more clever than a burrow runner! Can you do the things the People have seen the two-legs do? Can you fly? Can you gnaw down an entire golden-leaf tree in an afternoon? Because if you cannot, perhaps you should remember that the two-legs can . . . which is why we have been sent to keep watch on them in the first place!*>

He tasted Shadow Hider's flare of anger clearly, but at least the younger scout was wise enough not to snap back at him. Which was the *first* wise thing Climbs Quickly had seen from him since they'd left Bright Water Clan's central nest place this morning.

This is Broken Tooth's idea, Climbs Quickly thought disgustedly. The clan's senior elder had argued for some time now that Climbs Quickly was becoming too captivated by the two-legs. *If it were left up to him, Shadow Hider would have this task, not someone he fears is more interested in what the two-legs are and where they came from—and why—than in simply keeping watch upon them!*

Climbs Quickly had been the first scout to discover these two-legs' presence, and he admitted that he found everything about them fascinating, which was one reason Broken Tooth questioned his fitness to keep continued watch upon them. Clearly the elder believed Climbs Quickly was *too* fascinated with what he regarded as "his" two-legs to be truly impartial in his observations of them. Fortunately the rest of the clan elders—especially Bright Claw, the clan's senior hunter, and Short Tail, the senior scout—trusted Climbs Quickly's judgment and continued to believe he was the better choice to continue keeping watch upon them. In fact, though none of them had actually said so, from the taste of their mind-glows Climbs Quickly felt fairly certain that they agreed the task required someone with far more imagination than Shadow Hider had ever revealed. Unfortunately, it did make sense for more than one of the clan's scouts to have some experience with it, and Climbs Quickly was willing to admit that another perspective might prove valuable.

Even if it was Shadow Hider's.

He waited a moment longer, to see if Shadow Hider had something more to say after all, then turned back to the cross-branch and the clearing. The bright ember of Shadow Hider's anger faded with distance behind Climbs Quickly as he crept stealthily out to the last net-wood trunk, climbed easily to its highest fork, and settled down on the pad of leaves and branches. The cold days' ravages required a few repairs, but there was no hurry. The pad remained serviceable and reasonably comfortable, and it would be many days yet before the slowly budding leaves could provide the needed materials, anyway.

<*Come now!*> he called to Shadow Hider, then curled himself neatly to one side of the pad and allowed himself to savor the sun's gentle warmth.

In a way, he would be unhappy when the leaves did open and bright sunlight could no longer spill through the thin upper branches to caress his fur. His pad would have better concealment, which would undoubtedly make Shadow Hider happier, but if he had his way Shadow Hider wouldn't be here by that time, anyway.

Claws scraped lightly on bark as Shadow Hider swarmed up the last few People's lengths of trunk and joined him. The other scout looked around Climbs Quickly's pad, as if trying to find something with which to take fault. Climbs Quickly tasted his annoyance when he couldn't, but then Shadow Hider flirted his tail and settled down beside him.

<*This is a good scouting post,*> the younger scout acknowledged almost grudgingly after a few moments. <*You have an even better view than I thought you did, Climbs Quickly. And the two-leg nesting place is larger than I had thought.*>

<*It is large,*> Climbs Quickly agreed, reminding himself that size was one of the hardest things to judge from another scout's reports. The memory singers could sing that report perfectly, showing another of the People everything the original scout had seen, but for some reason, estimates of size remained difficult to share without some reference point. The only true reference point the two-legs had left in this case, however, was the towering golden-leaf whose massive boughs shaded their nest place, and golden-leaf trees tend to make *anything* look small.

<*Why should they need a nest place so large?*> Shadow Hider wondered, and Climbs Quickly flicked his ears.

<*I have wondered that myself,*> he admitted, <*and I have never found an answer that satisfies me. It required great labor by over a dozen two-legs, even with their tools,*

to build that living place. I watched them for many days, and when they were done, they simply went away. It was over three hands of days before the new two-legs came, and there are only three of them even now.>

<I know that was what you had reported, but now that I have seen how large their nest is it seems even stranger.>

Climbs Quickly gave a soft bleek of amusement at the perplexity in the other scout's mind-voice, but then that amusement faded.

<Unless I am mistaken, the smallest of the two-legs is only a youngling,> he said. *<I cannot be positive, of course, but if that is so, I wonder if perhaps something happened to its littermates. Could that be why their nest seems so vast? If they lost their other younglings to some accident only after they had planned their nest's size . . .>*

Shadow Hider said nothing, but Climbs Quickly tasted his understanding . . . and a glow of sympathy for the two-legs' loss which made Climbs Quickly think somewhat better of him.

<It is strange that they live so apart from one another,> Shadow Hider said after some moments. *<Why should a single mated pair and their young build a nest so far from any others of their kind? Surely it must deprive them of any chance to communicate with other two-legs! Assuming they* do *communicate, of course.>*

<I think they must communicate in some fashion,> Climbs Quickly replied thoughtfully. *<The two-legs who made this clearing and built the nesting place surely had to be able to communicate with one another in order to accomplish so many different tasks so quickly!>*

Shadow Hider considered that, recalling the memory song of Climbs Quickly's first glimpse of the two-legs in question.

The clan had not been too apprehensive when the first flying thing arrived and the two-legs emerged to create the clearing, for the clans whose territories had already been invaded had warned of what to expect. The two-legs could be dangerous, and they kept *changing* things, but they weren't like death fangs or snow hunters, who all too often killed randomly or for pleasure, and Climbs Quickly and a handful of other scouts and hunters had watched that first handful of two-legs from the cover of the frost-bright leaves, perched high in the trees. The newcomers had cut down enough net-wood and green-needle trees to satisfy themselves, then spread out carrying strange things—some that glittered or blinked flashing lights, and others that stood on tall, skinny legs—which they moved from place to place and peered through. And then they'd driven stakes of some equally strange non-wood into the ground at intervals. The Bright Water memory singers had sung back through the songs from other clans and decided the things they peered through were tools of some sort. Climbs Quickly couldn't argue with their conclusion, yet the two-leg tools were as different from the hand axes and knives of the People as the substance of which they were made was unlike the flint, wood, and bone the People used.

All of which explained why the two-legs must be watched most carefully...and secretly. Small as the People were, they were quick and clever, and their axes and knives and use of fire let them accomplish things larger but less clever creatures could not. Yet the shortest two-leg stood more than two People-lengths in height. Even if their tools had been no better than the People's (and Climbs Quickly knew they were much, much better) their greater size would have made them far more effective. And if there was no sign the two-legs intended to threaten the People, there was also no sign they did *not*, so no doubt it was fortunate mind-blind creatures were so easy to spy upon.

<Very well,> Shadow Hider said finally, his mind-glow grudging, <perhaps they *are* able to communicate...some-how. Yet as you yourself have reported, Climbs Quickly,

they truly do appear to be mind-blind.> The younger scout flattened his ears uneasily. *<I think that is the thing I find most difficult to understand about them. The thing that makes me ... anxious about them.>*

Climbs Quickly felt a flicker of surprise. That wasn't the sort of admission—or insight—he normally expected out of Shadow Hider. Yet the other scout had put his claw squarely upon it, for the two-legs were a new and frightening thing in the People's experience.

Yet they were not *entirely* new, which only made many of the People more nervous, not less. When the two-legs had first appeared twelve season-turnings back, the memory singers of every clan had sent their songs sweeping far and wide. They'd sought any song of any other clan which might tell them something—anything—about the strange creatures and whence they had come ... or at least why.

No one had been able to answer those questions, yet the memory singers of the Blue Mountain Dancing Clan and the Fire Runs Fast Clan had remembered a very old song—one which went back more than twelve twelves of turnings. The song offered no clue to the two-legs' origins or purpose, but it did tell of the very first time the People had seen two-legs, and how the long-ago scout who'd brought his report back to the singers had seen their egg-shaped silver thing come down out of the sky.

<I have often wished the Blue Mountain Dancing scouts had been a little less cautious when the two-legs first visited us,> Climbs Quickly admitted to Shadow Hider. *<Perhaps we might have been able to decide what the two-legs want—or what we should do about them—between then and now, when they have returned.>*

<And perhaps all of the People in the world would have been destroyed then,> Shadow Hider replied. *<Although,>* he added dryly, *<at least if that had happened, we would not be wondering what to do about them now.>*

Climbs Quickly was torn between a fresh desire to cuff Shadow Hider and a desire to laugh, but once again, he did have a point.

Personally, Climbs Quickly thought those first two-legs had been scouts, as he himself was. Certainly it would have made sense for the two-legs to send scouts ahead; any clan did the same thing when expanding or changing its range. Yet if that was the case, why had the rest of their clan delayed so long before following? And why *did* the two-legs spread themselves so thinly?

Shadow Hider was scarcely alone in wondering how—or if—the two-legs truly communicated at all. If they did, even Climbs Quickly was forced to admit that it must be in some bizarre fashion completely unlike the way in which the People did. That was one reason many of the watchers believed two-legs were unlike People in *all* ways, not just their size and shape and tools. It was the ability to taste their fellows' mind-glows, hear one another's mind-voices, which made People *people*, after all. Only unthinking creatures—like the death fangs, or the snow hunters, or those upon whom the People themselves preyed—lived sealed within themselves. So if the two-legs were not only mind-blind, but chose to *avoid* even their own kind, they could not be people.

But Climbs Quickly disagreed. He couldn't fully explain why even to himself, yet he was convinced the two-legs *were*, in fact, people—of a sort, at least. They fascinated him, and he'd listened again and again to the song of the first two-legs and their egg, both in an effort to understand what it was they wanted and because even now that song carried overtones of something he thought he'd tasted from the two-legs he spied upon.

Shadow Hider is wrong, he thought now. *Blue Mountain Dancing's scouts* should *have been less cautious*.

Yet even as he thought that, he knew he was being

unreasonable. Perhaps those long-ago scouts might have approached the intruders, but before any of them had decided to do so, a death fang attempted to eat one of the two-legs.

People didn't like death fangs. The huge creatures looked much like vastly outsized People, but unlike People, they were far from clever. Not that anything their size really *needed* to be clever. Death fangs were the biggest, strongest, most deadly hunters in all the world. Unlike People, they often killed for the sheer pleasure of it, and they feared nothing that lived... except the People. They never passed up the opportunity to eat a single scout or hunter if they happened across one stupid enough to be caught on the ground, but even death fangs avoided the heart of any clan's range. Individual size meant little when an entire clan swarmed down from the trees to attack.

Yet the death fang who'd attacked one of the two-legs had discovered something new to fear. None of the watching People had ever heard anything like the ear shattering "*Craaaack!*" from the tubular thing the two-leg carried, but the charging death fang had suddenly somersaulted end-for-end, crashed to the ground, and lain still, with a bloody hole blown clear through it.

Once they got over their immediate shock, the watching scouts had taken a fierce delight in the death fang's fate. But anything that could kill a death fang with a single bark could certainly do the same thing to one of the People, and so the decision had been made to avoid the two-legs until the watchers learned more about them. Unfortunately, the scouts were still watching from hiding when, after perhaps a quarter-turning, the two-legs dismantled the strange, square living places in which they had dwelt, went back into their egg, and disappeared once more into the sky.

All of that had been long, long ago, and Climbs Quickly

deeply regretted that no more had been learned of them before they left.

<I, too, often wish we had learned more when the two-legs first appeared so long ago,> Shadow Hider said, almost as if he had been reading Climbs Quickly's very thoughts, and not simply the emotions of his mind-glow. <Yet I also think we are fortunate Blue Mountain Dancing's scouts saw as much as they did, especially the ease with which they slew the death fang. For that matter, we are fortunate the memory singers were able even to recall the memory song from that long-ago time!>

<You are certainly right about that much, Shadow Hider,> Climbs Quickly agreed, although he did not agree with everything the younger scout had just said. In fact, he believed it was most *un*fortunate that the death fang's fate had frightened those long-ago People into avoiding closer contact. They *were* fortunate to retain a memory song from so long ago, however, especially when it was not one of the songs which had been important to the day-to-day lives of the People in all the weary turnings since it had first been sung.

Yet that very song's account only fueled Climbs Quickly's frustrated, maddening curiosity about the two-legs. He'd listened again and again to that song, both in an effort to understand what it was they wanted and because even now that song carried overtones of something he thought he had tasted for the two-legs *he* spied upon.

Unfortunately, the song had been worn smooth by too many singers before Sings Truly first sang it for Bright Water Clan. That often happened to older songs, or those which had been relayed for great distances, and *this* song was both ancient and from far away. Though its images remained clear and sharp, they had been subtly shaped and shadowed by all the singers who had come before Sings Truly. Climbs Quickly knew *what* the two-legs of the song had done, but he knew nothing about *why* they'd done it, and the interplay of so many singers' minds had blurred any mind-glow the long-ago watchers might have tasted.

Climbs Quickly had shared what he thought he'd picked up from "his" two-legs only with Sings Truly. It was his duty to report to the memory singers, and so he had. But he'd implored Sings Truly to keep his suspicions only in her own song for now, for some of the other scouts would have laughed uproariously at them, and they might well have strengthened Broken Tooth's suspicion that Climbs Quickly was not the best choice for his present duties. Sings Truly hadn't laughed, but neither had she rushed to agree with him, and he knew she longed to travel in person to the Blue Mountain Dancing or Fire Runs Fast Clan's range to receive the original song directly from their senior singers and not relayed over such a vast distance from one singer to another.

But that was out of the question. Singers were the core of any clan, the storehouse of memory and dispensers of wisdom. They were always female, and their loss could not be risked, whatever Sings Truly might want. Unless a clan was fortunate enough to have a surplus of singers, it must protect its potential supply of replacements by denying them more dangerous tasks. Climbs Quickly understood that, but he found its implications a bit harder to live with than the clan's other scouts and hunters did. There could be disadvantages to being a memory singer's brother when she chose to sulk over the freedoms her role denied her . . . and allowed *him*.

He bleeked softly with laughter at that thought.

<*What?*> Shadow Hider asked.

<*Nothing important,*> Climbs Quickly replied. <*Just a memory of something Sings Truly said to me. She was not happy at the time.*>

<*I am glad* someone *finds that humorous,*> Shadow Hider said dryly, and Climbs Quickly laughed again.

It was true that his sister had a formidable temper, and the entire clan still recalled the day a much younger Shadow Hider, but little removed from kittenhood, had accidentally dropped a flint knife. It had fallen perhaps a twelve of People's lengths and embedded itself in a net-wood limb...perhaps a double hand's width behind Sings Truly's tail.

It would not have been humorous if it had fallen any closer, of course. Short Tail had lost the last hand-width of *his* tail to a not dissimilar accident, and it could have injured Sings Truly seriously, even killed her. Shadow Hider's reaction most definitely *had* been humorous, however. Indeed, he'd received his name for the way he had vanished into the shadows when Sings Truly began her furious scold at the very top of a memory singer's mind-voice!

<*She would not truly have skinned you for a rug for her nesting place, younger brother,*> Climbs Quickly said now, feeling unusually fond of the other scout. <*And I do not think she will skin* me *for one, either. Although there are times I feel less certain of that!*>

<*Personally, I have no desire to find out whether or not you are correct about that,*> Shadow Hider replied with feeling.

<*A wise scout does not venture into the death fang's lair to see whether or not it is at home,*> Climbs Quickly agreed, stretching out on his belly with a sigh of pleasure. He folded his true-hands under his chin and settled himself for a long wait, and Shadow Hider settled down beside him.

Scouts learned early to be patient. If they needed help with that lesson, there were teachers aplenty—from falls to hungry death fangs—to drive it home. Climbs Quickly had never needed such instruction, which, even more than his relationship to Sings Truly, was why he was second only to Short Tail as Bright Water Clan's chief scout, despite his own relative youth.

So now he waited, motionless in the warm sunlight, and watched the sharp-topped living place the two-legs had built in the center of the clearing.

"SO WHY ARE YOU TURNING MY SHOP INTO A MESS *this* time?" Stephanie's dad inquired politely, leaning against his basement workshop's doorframe with a cup of coffee in one hand. His tone was one of weary resignation, but a laugh lurked in its depths, and Stephanie looked over her shoulder at him with a smile.

"I've been thinking about what Mom said about the celery thieves," she replied.

She opened one of his neatly labeled drawers and found the circuit chip she wanted. She also checked to make sure there was still at least one more t-chip in the drawer—one of the conditions for her free use of her father's tools and supplies was that she help keep track of inventory and tell him when it was time to reorder items—then turned back to the chassis of the device she was building.

"And that thinking led you to a conclusion which explains all this?" her father asked, raising an eyebrow and waving his coffee cup at the contraptions taking shape on the workbench.

"Well," Stephanie paused and turned around to face him fully, "in a way. It all seemed pretty silly right at first, of course. I mean, *celery?*" She rolled her eyes, and Richard snorted a laugh. Celery wasn't very high on Stephanie's list of edible foods. She'd eat it under parental duress (and if there was nothing better around) but that was about it. "Besides, according to all the reports, only a head or two at a time was missing, and who'd go to all that bother to steal that teeny an amount, right?"

"I can see where those thoughts might have occurred to you," he conceded.

It had been almost a full T-year since a mounting number of settlers had reported vanishing crops, but in the beginning, most people had been inclined to think it was some kind of hoax, especially since the only plant that was ever stolen was celery. And since, as Stephanie said, so few heads of celery were going missing each time the "thieves" struck.

"The first thing I thought when Mom told me about it was that some zork-brain was probably stealing the stuff and hiding it somewhere—or just getting rid of it, for that matter—as some kind of joke," Stephanie continued. "It wouldn't be any dumber than some of the other stuff I've seen kids in Twin Forks pull. In fact, it'd be *less* dumb than a lot of it!"

"You know," her father said after a moment, "not *all* the kids in Twin Forks are idiots, Steph."

"I didn't say they were," Stephanie replied. There might have been just a hint of insincerity in her response. "They sure *act* that way sometimes, though, don't they?"

"Not all of them," he said. "Still, I'll grant you that some of them do. Like that young hoodlum Chang."

"Stan Chang?" Stephanie cocked her head, surprised

at the noted genuine anger in her father's tone. It was unusual for her mild-mannered parent, and so was the curtness of his nod. "What did he do *this* time?" she asked a bit cautiously.

"He says he only meant it as a 'joke,' and that's his father's view of it, too," her father said. "It wasn't very funny for Ms. Steinman's Rottweiler, though. He set up a booby trap that was 'only' supposed to dump a five liter bucket of cold water on whoever walked into it. I guess we're all lucky it was Brutus and not another kid."

"How bad was it?" This time Stephanie's tone was resigned, not cautious.

"Let's just say he's not a very good carpenter, and the entire contraption collapsed when Brutus walked into it." Her father shook his head, his expression more resigned and sad than angry this time. "The whole thing came down on him. It crushed his entire right foreleg and he was trapped for over forty-five minutes before we could get him out. I spent better than two hours putting it back together again, and I'm not sure he's ever going to recover fully."

Stephanie nodded slowly. Her father cared—a lot—about his patients. Like he'd often said, they didn't have voices, so they couldn't explain what was wrong. And people couldn't explain it to *them*, either. No wonder she'd heard so much anger in his voice.

"I'll bet he wasn't real sorry about it, either, was he?" she said after a moment, and her father laughed harshly.

"Not so you'd notice," he agreed. "After all, Brutus is only an animal, right? And like Stan said, it's not like he got *killed*, is it?"

The two of them looked at one another for a moment, and Stephanie felt a warm surge of affection. It was so typical of her dad to take the dog's side, and she wondered just how her father's conversation with *Stan's* father might have gone. Under the circumstances, she was pretty darned sure there'd *been* one, at any rate!

Wish I could have been a fly on that *wall,* she thought with a mental smile. *I bet the sparks were just crackling off Dad's hair!*

"Well, I guess Stan's just proved they *can* do things dumber than stealing celery," she said out loud, winning an unwilling smile from her father. "But I did think at first that it was probably somebody stealing it because they thought it'd be funny to watch people run around in circles trying to figure out what was going on. Only then I did a search for every report about missing celery and plotted all of them on a map, and they're spread so wide every kid on the planet would have to be in on it!"

"You know," her father said, "when your mom mentioned this to me, it never even occurred to me to think about mapping them to see how widespread it actually was." He gave her a smile. "Of course, given my general all-around brilliance no doubt it *would* have occurred to me if I'd given the matter any *serious* thought."

"Yeah, sure," Stephanie said, rolling her eyes.

"It was a good notion, though," he said more seriously. "That puzzle-solver side of you coming to the surface again, I see."

"I guess," Stephanie agreed. "And you're not the only one who hasn't given it any 'serious thought,' either. It doesn't look like most people have noticed it at all. In fact, I wouldn't have if the farmers who've been losing the stuff weren't part of Mom's genegineering program."

Her lip curled, and her father tried to stifle his sigh.

Her father nodded thoughtfully.

Celery was one of the terrestrial plants which hadn't adapted well to the local planetary environment, and Stephanie's mom had taken over the project trying to do something about that. She'd had to restart it almost from zero, unfortunately, because the geneticist who'd originally started it had been one of victims of the Plague's final resurgence. In the end, she'd come up with an entirely new approach that was in the field test stage now, and the farmers' reports she was reading to assess its effectiveness were where she'd first heard about the mysterious thefts. None of the thefts had been very big, and they had been scattered pretty widely.

"They do cluster, though," Stephanie said, turning back to one of the contraptions on the workbench. "It's like there are maybe four or five areas where the celery's getting pinched, but there's an awful lot of separation between those areas. And I'm not sure it really started as recently as people seem to think it did, either."

"No?" Richard raised his eyebrows.

"People have had a lot on their minds, Daddy. First they were dealing with the Plague and just trying to stay alive, and since then everybody's been crazy busy trying to put everything back together again. I wouldn't be too surprised if a whole bunch of little, tiny 'celery raids' didn't just go completely unnoticed in the middle of all that, especially if whoever it is was just snatching them out of the field. *I* think the only reason anyone's noticed even now is that the stuff's been disappearing out of greenhouses during the winter months. Who knows how much of it might've gotten snatched out of outdoor gardens during the summer without anyone even noticing?"

"Point," he acknowledged.

"The thing is, though," she went on, "that however recently it started, it's not happening in just one place and nobody's been able to catch whoever's doing it."

"How hard have they tried?" he asked.

"Wellll..."

Stephanie looked up, forehead creased with thought as she considered the best way to answer her father's question. To her way of thinking, there was a difference between "how hard" and "how effectively" (or "how *intelligently*," for that matter). That wasn't exactly what he'd asked, though, and she shrugged.

"I think at first most people figured it *was* kids," she said, "and it's not like the amount of celery that's being taken is really hurting anyone that much. I mean, it's only *celery*, and it's not like there's a big market for stolen celery, right? So the truth is, no one put a whole lot of effort into it at first. Like I said, they've had other things to worry about.

"But it looks like whoever—or whatever—is behind it is starting to take more of it, and I think at least some people are worried the thieves might start branching out into stuff besides celery. Besides, like Mom says, an awful lot of it seems to be being taken out of the experimental greenhouses. In fact it looks like *most* of the reported incidents—the ones where people have actually noticed the celery disappearing—are coming out of the experimental plots. And if that keeps up or spreads to some of the other experimental farms' plots, it could screw up some of the long-term research projects. So in the last few T-months, people have been getting more serious about figuring out what's going on and stopping it. Besides, it's a challenge!"

"Getting more serious?" her dad repeated, and she shrugged.

"Well, they started out simple. Given where the celery's been disappearing from, most people figure whatever's taking it can't be *too* big, since it would have to squeeze into some pretty narrow places. A couple of people suggested setting traps, but the Forestry Service knocked that one on the head in a hurry because of the Elysian Rule."

Her expression sobered, and so did her father's. The Elysian Rule had been adopted over a thousand years before, after a disastrous clutch of mistakes had devastated the ecology of the colony world of Elysian. It absolutely forbade the use of lethal measures against a complete unknown without evidence that whatever it was posed a clear physical danger to humans, and no administration on a planet in the early stages of settlement would even consider its violation without a reason far more compelling than the minuscule economic loss thefts of *celery* represented.

"Since we don't know what's actually taking the celery, we can't be sure how to set a *non*lethal trap for it," Stephanie said. "That didn't keep some people from wanting to go ahead with traps, anyway, but Chief Ranger Shelton wasn't about to let them get away with that!"

She grinned in obvious approval of the chief ranger's stance, then continued.

"So they tried alarms and sensors. Since everybody figures we're dealing with some sort of local critter, they decided to try simple tripwires connected to lights and remote cameras first, but that didn't work. Whatever is actually snatching the stuff, either it doesn't spend a lot of time on the ground or else it's really good at spotting tripwires."

She paused, brown eyes narrowed thoughtfully, then looked back at her father.

"I think they're right that it's probably something local. Something small, I bet, and really, really *sneaky*. But what I can't figure out, is why something from Sphinx would be eating *celery* of all things."

"I can think of several possible reasons," her father replied. "Don't forget, one of the things that made the Manticore System so attractive to colonists despite Sphinx's gravity is how similar all three if its planetary biosystems are to the one humanity evolved in." His eyes darkened. "That's probably the only reason the Plague could evolve in it and hit us so hard."

He paused for a moment, then gave himself an almost apologetic shake and continued.

"Both Manticore and Sphinx use the same sugars our biochemistry does, and the local amino acids are pretty similar, as well. Sphinxian genes and chromosomes are actually a lot like terrestrial ones, too. I'm speaking in a general sense, of course, because there are at least as many differences as similarities. For example, the Sphinx equivalent of RNA forms double strands, not single, and it forms longer chains than anything we've found in terrestrial biology. Humans and the critters we tend to take with us when we colonize planets can eat Sphinxian plants and animals just fine, though—it just doesn't give us everything we need, like most of the essential vitamins, so we have to supplement it. Which is one reason your mom and I fuss at you about eating your vegetables, now isn't it?"

He glowered at her, and she grinned again.

"Anyway, my point is that there are quite a few things growing here on Sphinx that humans have decided are tasty. We like the way they *taste*, even if they don't have all the food values we need. So I don't see any reason to assume some Sphinxian animal wouldn't find celery a real delicacy."

"Um." Stephanie considered that for a moment, then shrugged. "Okay, I guess I can see that. Although the thought that anyone would feel that way about *celery* is kind of hard to accept.

"But what I was saying is that whatever it is, it's small and sneaky, and it doesn't go anywhere near tripwires. So they decided to try motion sensors, but that didn't work too well, either. There are so many small critters running around Sphinx, like the chipmunks, that the motion sensors kept going off all the time. They tried dialing their sensitivity down, so they'd only go off for something bigger than a chipmunk, but then whatever's stealing the celery started getting past them again. So then they tried setting infrared barriers just around the greenhouses themselves, but that isn't working either."

"I thought I remembered reading somewhere that at least a couple of alarms had gone off," her father said thoughtfully, and she nodded.

"Yes, but whatever's behind this, it seems to like bad weather. My data search couldn't nail down the weather conditions when *all* the robberies took place. For one thing, sometimes the people filing the report couldn't pin down the time any closer than a day or two. I mean, most people have better things to do than stand around in a greenhouse counting celery plants to make sure none of 'em have disappeared. No wonder they don't always notice immediately when one of them takes missing! But almost all the raids I *could* check the weather on took place when it was snowing, or during a thunderstorm, or at least when it was raining pretty heavily even for Sphinx. And *all* of them—all the ones I could nail down, at least—happened at night, too."

"So whatever it is, it's probably nocturnal, and it only comes out when it rains or snows? It's smart enough to use bad weather for cover?"

"That's what it looks like to me, anyway."

"And would it happen that you've shared this particular insight with any of the other investigators trying to figure out what's going on?" her father inquired politely.

"Gosh!" Stephanie widened her eyes at him. "I guess it must've slipped my mind, somehow."

"That's what I thought." Her father shook his head with a long-suffering expression, and Stephanie laughed.

"Anyway," she continued, "they have had a couple of cameras go off, and something tripped the alarms on one of the experimental farms over in Long Grass, but the weather was so bad they didn't get anything. Well, one of the cameras in Seaview got some really nice holos of *snowflakes*, but that wasn't much use. All of them were motion sensor-controlled, but with no pictures, all anyone's really sure about was that it was bigger than a chipmunk because that's where the filters were set."

Her dad nodded in understanding. Sphinxian "chipmunks" didn't look a lot like Meyerdahl's (or, for that matter, Old Terra's) chipmunks, although they filled much the same ecological niche. The burrow-dwelling marsupials were six-limbed and only a very little smaller than a terrestrial Chihuahua, and they were about as ubiquitous as a species got. Fortunately, they were also timid, unlike their slightly smaller arboreal cousin, the equally ubiquitous (and much more destructive) wood rat.

"But the thing I noticed about all of those," Stephanie went on in a satisfied tone, "was that even when one of the motion sensor alarms was set off, the celery thief still got through and got away with his celery *without* setting off any of the *infrared* alarms closer to the greenhouses themselves."

She paused, looking at her father expectantly, and he took a thoughtful sip of coffee, then nodded.

"You're thinking about what you and I discussed a couple of weeks ago, aren't you, Steph?" he said with a smile of approval.

"Yep." Stephanie smiled back at him. "I remembered what you said about that report about wood rats' eyes. If Dr. Weyerhaeuser's right and they do use a lot more of the lower end of the spectrum than human eyes do, then something like a wood rat might be able to actually *see* an infrared beam and stay out of it." Her smile turned into a grin. "You're always telling me to analyze a problem carefully before I jump into trying to solve it. Sounds to me like some other people should have been taking your advice, too!"

"Well, let's be fair here, Steph. Dr. Weyerhaeuser's report only came out in October. It's not like people have had a long time to think about it or put two and two together yet for something like this."

She nodded in agreement, but she'd also heard the approval in his voice for the way *she'd* put "two and two together."

"Anyway," she went on, waving at the partially assembled hardware spread down the workbench's length, "what I'm doing is putting together some *ultraviolet* sensors. We've got Mom's experimental greenhouse right here, and she's got some of the celery from that genetic development program growing in it. I figure we've already got the bait, so maybe we should try the other end of the spectrum and see if we don't get a little bit luckier than the folks in Long Grass and Seaview." She gave him her very best wheedling smile. "Wanna help?"

CLIMBS QUICKLY PERCHED IN HIS OBSERVATION POST
once more. He was relieved to be on his own again—Broken
Tooth had finally agreed, grudgingly, that Shadow Hider's
time could be more usefully employed elsewhere—but
the sunlit sky of three days earlier had turned to dark,
gray-black charcoal, and a stiff wind whipped in from
the mountains to the west. It brought the tang of rock
and snow, mingled with the bright sharpness of thunder,
but it also blew across the two-legs' clearing, and he
slitted his eyes and flattened his ears, peering into it as
it rippled his fur. There was rain, as well as thunder, on
that wind, and he didn't look forward to being soaked,
while lightning could make his present perch dangerous.
Yet he felt no temptation to seek cover, for other scents
indicated his two-legs were up to something interesting
in one of their transparent plant places.

Climbs Quickly cocked his head, lashing the tip of his
prehensile tail as he considered. Broken Tooth was correct

that he'd come to think of this clearing's inhabitants as "his" two-legs, but there were many other two-legs on the planet, most with their own scouts keeping watch over them. Those scouts' reports, like his own, were circulated among the memory singers of all the clans, and they included something he felt a burning desire to explore for himself.

One of the cleverest of the many clever things the two-legs had demonstrated to the People were their plant places, for the People weren't *only* hunters. Like the snow hunters and the lake builders (but not the death fangs), they ate plants as well, and they required certain *kinds* of plants to remain strong and fit.

Unfortunately, some of the plants they needed couldn't live in ice and snow, which made the cold days a time of hunger and death, when too many of the very old or very young died. Although there was usually prey of some sort, there was less of it, and it was harder to catch, and the lack of needed plants only made that normal hunger worse. But that was changing, for the eating of plants was yet another way in which two-legs and People were alike... and the two-legs had found an answer to the cold days, just as they had to so many other problems. Indeed, it often seemed to Climbs Quickly the two-legs could never be satisfied with a single answer to *any* challenge, and in this case, they had devised at least two.

The simpler answer was to make plants grow where they wanted during the warm days. But the more spectacular one (and the one that most intrigued Climbs Quickly) were their transparent plant places. The plant places' sides and roofs, made of yet another material the People had no idea how to make, let the sun's light and heat pass through, forming little pockets of the warm days even amid the deepest snow, and the two-legs made many of the plants they ate grow inside that warmth all turning long. Nor did they grow them only during the cold days. There were fresh plants growing in those plant places even now, for Climbs Quickly could smell them through the moving spaces the two-legs had opened along the upper sides of the plant places to let the breeze blow in.

The People had never considered making things grow in specific places. Instead, they'd gathered plants wherever they grew of their own accord, either to eat immediately or to store for future need. In some turnings, they were able to gather more than enough to see them through the cold days. In less prosperous turnings, hunger and starvation stalked the clans, yet that was the way it had always been and the way it would continue. Until, that was, the People heard their scouts' reports of the two-leg plant places.

The People weren't very good at it yet, but they, too, had begun growing plants in carefully tended and guarded patches at the hearts of their clans' ranges. Their efforts had worked out poorly for the first few turnings, yet the two-legs' success proved it was possible, and they'd continued watching the two-legs and the strange not-living things which tended their open plant places. Much of what they observed meant little or nothing, but other lessons were clearer, and the People had learned a great deal. They had no way to duplicate the enclosed, transparent plant places, yet this last turning Bright Water Clan had found itself facing the cold days with much more white-root, golden ear, and lace leaf than it had required to survive them. Indeed, there had been sufficient surplus for Bright Water to trade it to the neighboring High Crag Clan for additional supplies of flint, and Climbs Quickly wasn't the only member of the clan who realized the People owed the two-legs great thanks (whether the two-legs ever knew it or not).

But what made his whiskers quiver with anticipation

was something *else* the other scouts had reported. The two-legs grew many strange plants the People had never heard of—a single sharp-nosed tour of any of their outside plant places would prove that—yet most were *like* ones the People knew. But one wasn't. Climbs Quickly had yet to personally encounter the plant the other scouts had christened cluster stalk, but he was eager to do so. Indeed, he knew he was a bit *too* eager, for the bright ecstasy of the scouts who'd sampled cluster stalk rang through the relayed songs of their clans' memory singers with a clarity that was almost stunning.

It wasn't simply the plant's marvelous taste, either. Like the tiny, bitter-tasting, hard-to-find fruit of the purple thorn, cluster stalk sharpened the People's mind-voices and deepened the texture of their memory songs. The People had known the virtue of purple thorn for hundreds upon hundreds of turnings—indeed, People who were denied its fruit had actually been known to lose their mind-voices entirely—yet there had never been enough of it, and it had always been almost impossible to find in sufficient quantities. But the cluster stalk was even better than purple thorn (if the reports were correct), and the two-legs seemed to grow it almost effortlessly.

And unless Climbs Quickly was mistaken, that scent blowing from the two-legs' plant places matched the cluster stalk's perfume embedded in the memory songs.

He crouched on his perch, watching the sky grow still darker and heavier, and made up his mind. It would be full dark soon, and the two-legs would retire to the light and warmth of their living places, especially on a night of rain such as this one promised to be. He didn't blame them for that. Indeed, under other circumstances he would have been scurrying back to his own snugly-roofed nest's water-shedding woven canopy. But not tonight.

No, tonight he would stay—rain or no—and when the

two-legs retired, he would explore more closely than he'd ever yet dared approach their living place.

Stephanie Harrington pulled on her jacket, turned up its collar, and wiggled her toes in her boots as she gazed out of her bedroom's deep-set window at a night sky crosshatched with livid streaks of lightning. The planet of Sphinx had officially entered Spring, but nights were still cold (though far, *far* warmer than they had been!), and she knew she'd be grateful for her thick, warm socks and jacket soon enough.

She opened the tall casement window quietly, although the sudden earthquake rumble of thunder would have drowned just about any sound she could have made. The window swung inward in its deep embrasure, and chill dampness hit her in the face as she latched it back. Then she leaned forward, bracing herself on the broad windowsill, and smiled as she sniffed the ozone-heavy wind.

The weather satellites said the Harrington freehold was in for a night of thunder, lightning, rain, and violent wind, and cold or not Stephanie intended to savor it to the fullest. She'd always liked thunderstorms. She knew some kids were frightened by them, but Stephanie thought that was stupid. She had no intention of running out into the storm with a lightning rod—or, for that matter, standing under a tree—but the spectacle of all that fire and electricity crashing about the sky was simply too exhilarating and wonderful to miss... and this would be the first thunderstorm she'd seen in over a T-year.

Not that she'd mentioned her plans for the night to her parents. She figured there was an almost even chance they would have agreed to let her stay up to enjoy the storm, but she knew they would have insisted she watch it from inside. Thoughts of fireplace-popped popcorn and the hot chocolate Mom would undoubtedly have added to the experience had been tempting, but a little further thought had dissuaded her. Popcorn and hot chocolate were nice, but the only *proper* way to enjoy her first storm in so long was from out in the middle of it where she could feel and taste its power, and they weren't very likely to think that was a good idea.

And, of course, there was that other little matter.

She smiled in the dark and patted the camera in its case on her hip as thunder growled louder and lightning lashed the mountaintops to the west. She knew her mother had trolled the disappearing celery mystery in front of her as a distraction, but that hadn't made the puzzle any less fascinating. She didn't really expect to be the one to solve it, yet she could have fun trying. And if it just happened that she *did* find the answer, well, she was sure she could accept the credit somehow.

Her smile curled up in urchin glee at the thought, but she hadn't made her mother privy to *every* facet of her plan. Part of that was to avoid embarrassment if it didn't work, but most of it came from the simple knowledge that her parents wouldn't approve of her...hands-on approach. Fortunately, knowing what they would have said—had the occasion arisen—was quite different from actually hearing them say it when the occasion *hadn't* arisen, which was why she'd carefully avoided bringing the matter up at all.

She shoved the folded rain hat into her pocket, climbed up onto the deep, stone windowsill, swung her legs out, and sat there for a moment longer, feeling the wind whipping through her short, curly hair. She knew her mom expected her to be monitoring her carefully placed sensor net from her bedroom terminal, and she had a pretty shrewd notion that her parents Would Not Be Amused if they happened to wander into her room for some reason and she wasn't in it. She'd thought about stuffing pillows under her blankets just in case, but she'd decided against it. First, it wouldn't have fooled either of them. Second, they would be certain to notice the rope she'd anchored to the frame of her bed before dropping its free end out the window, anyway. But, third, it would have been cheating. It was one thing to set out on an adventure of which they might not approve; it was quite another to try to trick them into thinking she hadn't if they figured it out fair and square, and Stephanie didn't cheat. Of course, that didn't mean it wouldn't work out a lot better for all concerned if they *didn't* wander in. . . .

She twisted around to kneel on the window sill (which was more than half as deep as she was tall) while she tugged the casement closed. She couldn't close it *all* the way because of her climbing rope, but that was good. It would keep the window from closing and latching behind her, with her still outside, and she carefully hooked the length of cord she'd run from the window frame through the latching bracket. She pulled it taut and tied it to keep the window from slamming back and forth in the wind if the storm got as lively as it looked like it was getting, and tested it to make it was secure.

It was, so she slid down on her stomach, letting her legs dangle toward the ground, then lowered herself down to arms' length, and dropped the last half meter or so to the ground. She stood for a moment, looking back up, and gave the rope a tug to make sure it was still secure. Getting back into her bedroom unobserved was going to be trickier than getting out had been, but she felt confident she'd manage.

The wind roar in the massive crown oak closest to the house was louder than ever, with mighty branches creaking and swaying in the darkness far overhead or etched against the eye-blinding flash of lightning with almost painful clarity. All of Sphinx seemed to be alive, moving and swaying and lashing in the night, and she laughed in sheer delight as she scampered through the roaring, whispering prelude of a thunderstorm orchestra tuning its instruments.

Climbs Quickly clung to his pad while the net-wood's groaning branches lashed the night as if to protest the wind that roared among them. The rumbling thunder had drawn closer, barking more and more loudly, and lightning forks had begun to play about the mountain heads to the east. The storm was going to be even more powerful than he'd thought, and he smelled cold, wet rain on its breath. It would be here soon, he thought. Very soon, which meant it was time.

He climbed down the trunk more slowly and cautiously than was his wont, for he felt the sturdy tree quivering and shivering under his claws. It took him much longer than usual to reach the ground, and he paused—still a half-dozen People-lengths up the tree—to survey his surroundings. The People were quick and agile anywhere, but true safety lay in their ability to scamper up into places where things like death fangs couldn't follow. Unfortunately, Climbs Quickly's plans required him to venture into an area without handy net-woods, and while it was unlikely to hold any death fangs, either, he saw no harm in double-checking to be certain of that.

But scan the night though he might, he detected no dangers other than those of the weather itself, and he dropped the last distance to the ground. The mud, he noted, had begun to dry—on the top at least—but the rain would change that. He felt the faint, pounding vibration of rain drops through the ground, coming steadily nearer, and his ears flattened in resignation. If the reports about cluster stalk proved true, getting soaked would be small enough cost for this evening's excursion. That didn't mean he would enjoy it, though, and he flitted his tail and scurried quickly towards the nearest plant place.

Stephanie dipped into the stash she'd brought along and extracted a fruit bar. She might be willing to give up popcorn and hot chocolate, but she was still a growing girl with the Meyerdahl first wave's genetic modifications. That kind of accelerated metabolism had to be stoked regularly, and most Meyerdahl kids routinely packed along munchies for moments like this.

She settled back in her chair in the gazebo, camera in her lap, and her mind ran back over her checklist as she began to chew.

She'd been careful to leave the ventilation louvers open on the greenhouse which contained her mother's celery. In addition, she'd adjusted the greenhouse ventilation system to produce a slight overpressure, pushing whatever scent the celery might have out those open louvers. Her parents had known about that part of her plan, but somehow she hadn't gotten around to mentioning the fact that for tonight she'd disabled the audible alarm on her bedroom terminal and set up a silent relay from her sensor net to her camera, instead. Mom and Dad were smart enough to have guessed why she might have done that if they'd known about it, but since they hadn't specifically asked, she hadn't had to tell them. And that meant they hadn't gotten around to forbidding her to lurk in the gazebo tonight, which was certainly the most satisfactory outcome for all concerned.

If pressed, Stephanie would have conceded that her parents might have quibbled with that last conclusion, so it was probably just as well that they didn't know.

She giggled at the thought and took another bite of

fruit bar. The odds were against anything coming along to take advantage of the opportunity she'd provided, and she knew it. But it wasn't as if she had a lot of other things to do just now, and she smiled as the first spatters of rain began to tapdance on the gazebo's roof.

Climbs Quickly paused, head and shoulders rising as he stood high on his true-feet like—had he known—an Old Terran prairie dog to peer into the night. This was the closest he'd ever come to his two-legs' living place, and his eyes glowed as he realized he'd been right. He *had* been tasting a mind-glow from them, and he stood motionless in the darkness as he savored the texture.

It was unlike anything he'd ever tasted from another of the People...and yet it *wasn't* unlike. It was...was...

He sat down, curling his tail about his toes, and rubbed one ear with a true-hand while he tried to put a label on it. It *was* like the People, he decided after long, hard moments of thought, but without words. It was only the emotions, the feelings of the two-legs without the shaping that turned those into communication, and there was a strange drowsiness to it, as if it were half-asleep. As if, he thought slowly, the mind-glow rose from minds which had never even considered that anyone else might be able to taste or hear them and so had never learned to use it to communicate. Yet even as he thought that, it seemed impossible, for the glow was too strong, too powerful. Unformed, un-shaped, it blazed like some marvelous flower, brighter and taller than any of the People had ever produced in Climbs Quickly's presence, and he shivered as he wondered what it would have been like if the two-legs *hadn't* been mind-blind. He felt the brightness calling to him, tempting him closer like a memory singer's song, and he shook himself. This would be a very important part of his next report to Sings Truly and Short Tail, but he certainly had no business exploring it on his own *before* he reported it. Besides, it wasn't what he'd come for.

He shook himself again, stepping back from the mind-glow, but it was hard to distance himself from it. In fact, he had to make a deliberate, conscious decision not to taste it and then close his mind to it, and that took much longer to manage than he'd expected.

Yet he did manage it, eventually, and drew a deep breath of relief as he pulled free. He flipped his ears, twitched his whiskers, and began sliding once more through the darkness as the first raindrops splashed about him.

The rain came down harder, drumming on the gazebo roof. The air seemed to dance and shiver as incessant lightning split the night and thunder shook its halves, and Stephanie's eyes glowed as wind whipped spray in through the gazebo's open sides to spatter the floor and kiss her eyelashes and chilled cheeks. She felt the storm crackling about her and hugged herself, drinking in its energy.

But then, suddenly, a tiny light began to flash on the camera, and she froze. It couldn't be! But the light *was* flashing—*it really was!*—and that could only mean—

She tossed away the fruit bar—her third of the night—and pressed the button that killed the warning light, then snatched the camera up to peer through the viewfinder.

Visibility was poor through the rain cascading off the gazebo roof. There was too much water in the air for a clear view, even with the camera's light-gathering technology, and the lightning didn't help as much as one might have expected. The camera adjusted to changing light levels more quickly than any human eye, but the contrast between the lightning's split-second, stroboscopic fury and the darkness that followed was too extreme.

Stephanie had more than half expected that, so she wasn't really surprised not to see anything just yet. But what mattered at this particular moment was that something had just climbed through the open louvers. Whatever was stealing celery was inside the greenhouse right this minute, and she had a chance to be the very first person on Sphinx to get actual pictures of it!

She stood for a moment, biting her lip and wishing she had better visibility, then shrugged. If she ended up having to face the music, Mom and Dad wouldn't be a *lot* madder at her for getting soaked than they'd be over her having snuck out at all, and she needed to get closer to the greenhouse. She took a second to clip the rain shield onto the camera, then dragged her hat down over her ears, drew a deep breath, and splashed down the gazebo steps into the rain-whipped night.

Climbs Quickly dropped to the soft, bare earth of the plant place's floor. The rich smells of unknown growing things filled his nostrils, and his tail twitched as he absorbed them. The transparent material of the plant place seemed far too thin to resist the rain beating upon it, yet it did, and without a single drop leaking through! The two-legs were truly clever to design a marvel like that, and he sat for a moment luxuriating in the enfolding warmth that was somehow made even warmer and more welcoming by the furious splashing of the icy, lightning-laced rain.

But he hadn't come here to be dry, he reminded himself, and his true-hands untied the carry net wrapped about his middle while he followed his nose and resolutely ignored the background mind-glows of the two-legs.

Ah! There was the cluster stalk scent from Sings Truly's song! His eyes lit, and he swarmed easily up the side of the raised part of the plant place, then paused as he came face-to-face with cluster stalk for the very first time.

The growing heads seemed bigger than the ones from Sings Truly's song, and he wondered if the scout who'd first brought that song to his clan had sampled his first cluster stalk before it was fully grown. Whether that was true or not, each of *these* plants was two-thirds as long as Climbs Quickly himself, and he was glad he'd brought the carry net. Still, net or not, he would have to be careful not to take too much if he expected to carry it all the way home. He sat for another long moment, considering, then flipped his ears in decision. Two heads, he decided. He could manage that much, and he could always come back for more.

But even as he decided that, he realized he'd used the need to decide to distract him from the marvelous scent of the cluster stalk. It was like nothing he'd ever smelled before, and he felt his mouth water as he drew it deep into his lungs. He hesitated, then reached out and tugged gently on an outer stalk.

It responded with a springy resistance, like the top of a white-root, and he tugged harder. Still it held out, and he tugged still harder, then bleeked in triumph as the stalk came loose in his true-hands. He raised it to his nose, sniffing deeply, then stuck out his tongue.

Magic filled his mouth as he licked delicately. It was like hot, liquid sunlight on a day of frozen ice. Like cold mountain water on a day of scorching heat, or the gentle caress of a new mother, just ruffling her first kitten's delicate fur while her mind-glow promised him welcome and warmth and love. It was—

Climbs Quickly shook his head. It wasn't actually like any of those things, he realized, except that each of them, in its own way, was wonderful and unique. It was just that he didn't have anything else to which he could really compare that first blissful taste, and he nibbled gently at the end of the stalk. It was hard to chew—People didn't really have the right kind of teeth to eat plants—but it tasted just as wonderful as that first lick had promised, and he crooned in pleasure as he devoured it.

He finished the entire stalk and reached quickly for another, then made himself stop. Yes, it tasted wonderful, and he wanted more. But he was no ground burrower to gorge himself into insensibility on cluster stalk. He was a scout of Bright Water Clan, and it was his job to carry this home for Short Tail, Bright Claw, even Broken Tooth, and the memory singers to judge it for themselves. Even if they hadn't been the leaders of his clan, they were his friends, and friends shared anything this marvelous with one another.

It was actually easier to get an entire head out of the soft earth in which it grew than it had been to peel off that single stalk, and Climbs Quickly soon had two of them rolled up in his carry net. They made an awkward bundle, but he tied the net as neatly as he could and slung it onto his back, reaching up to hold the hand loops with his mid-limbs hand-feet while he used true-feet and true-hands to climb back down to the floor. Getting to the opening to the outer world would be more difficult with his burden than it had been coming in, but he could manage. He might not be very fast or agile, but not even a death fang would be out on a night like this!

Stephanie was glad her jacket and trousers were waterproof, and her broad-brimmed rain hat kept her head and face dry. But holding the camera on target required her to raise her hands in front of her, and ice-cold rain had flooded down the drain pipes of her nice, waterproof jacket sleeves. She felt it puddling about her elbows and beginning to probe stealthily towards her shoulders—just as her forearms were raised, her upper arms were parallel to the ground, providing an all-too-convenient channel for the frigid water—but all the rain in the world couldn't have convinced her to lower her camera at a moment like this.

She stood no more than ten meters from the greenhouse, recording steadily. Each of her camera's storage chips was good for over ten hours, and she had no intention of missing any of this for the official record. Excitement trembled inside as the minutes passed in the splashing, lightning-slivered darkness. Whatever it was had been inside the greenhouse for nine minutes now. *Surely* it would be coming back out pretty s—

Climbs Quickly reached the opening with a profound sense of relief. He'd almost dropped his carry net twice, and he decided to catch his breath before leaping down into the rain with his prize. After all, he had plenty of ti—

A whisker-fringed muzzle and prick-eared head poked out of the opening, green eyes glittering like emerald mirrors as lightning stuttered, and the universe seemed to stop as their owner found himself staring into the glassy eye of a camera in the hands of an eleven-T-year-old girl. Excitement froze Stephanie's breath even though she'd known this moment was coming, but Climbs Quickly *hadn't* known. His surprise was total, and he went absolutely motionless in astonishment.

Seconds ticked past, and then he shook himself mentally. Showing himself to a two-leg was the one thing he'd been most firmly instructed *not* to do, and he cringed inwardly at how Broken Tooth would react to this. He knew he could claim distraction on the basis of the storm and his first experience with cluster stalk, but that wouldn't change his failure into success, and he stared down at the two-leg while his mind began to work once more.

It was the youngling, he realized, for it was smaller than either of its parents. He didn't know what it was pointing at him, but from all reports he would have been dead already if the two-leg had intended to kill him. Yet deciding the thing aimed his way wasn't a weapon didn't tell him what it *was*. Those thoughts flashed through his brain in a heartbeat, and then, without really thinking about it, he reached out to the two-leg's mind-glow in an effort to judge its intentions.

He was totally unprepared for the consequences.

It was as if he'd looked straight up into the sun expecting to see only the glow of a single torch, and his eyes flared wide and his ears flattened as the intensity of the two-leg's emotions rolled over him. The glow was far brighter than before, and he wondered distantly if that was simply because he was closer and concentrating upon it, or if the cluster stalk he'd sampled might have something to do with it. But it didn't really matter. What mattered was the excitement and eagerness and wonder that blazed so brightly in the two-leg's mind. It was the first time any of the People had ever come face-to-face with a two-leg, and nothing could have prepared Climbs Quickly for the sheer delight with which Stephanie Harrington saw the marvelous, six-limbed creature crouched in the ventilation louver with the woven net of purloined celery slung over its back.

The representatives of two intelligent species—one of which had never even suspected the other's existence— stared at one another in the middle of a howling thunderstorm. It was a moment which could not last, yet neither wanted it to end. Triumph and excited discovery flooded through Stephanie like a fountain, and she had no idea that Climbs Quickly felt those emotions even more clearly than he would have felt them from another of his own kind. Nor could she have guessed how very much he wanted to *continue* feeling them. She knew only that he crouched there, gazing at her for what seemed like forever, before he shook himself and leapt suddenly down and outward.

Climbs Quickly pulled free of the two-leg's mind-glow. It was hard—possibly the hardest thing he'd ever done—yet he had his duty. And so he made himself step back from that wonderful, welcoming furnace. Or, rather, he stepped *away* from it, for it was too strong, too intense, actually to disconnect from. He could turn his eyes away from the fire, but he could not pretend it did not blaze.

He shook himself, and then he launched outward into the rain and darkness. He was slow and clumsy with the net of cluster stalk on his back, but he knew as surely as he'd ever known anything in his life that this young two-leg meant him no harm. The secret of the People's existence was already revealed, and haste would change nothing, so he sat upright in the rain for a moment, gazing up at the two-leg, who finally lowered the strange thing it had held before its face to look down at him with its own eyes. He met those odd, brown, round-pupilled eyes for a moment, then flipped his ears, turned, and scampered off.

Stephanie watched the intruder vanish with a sense of wonder which only grew as the creature disappeared. It was small, she thought—no more than sixty or seventy centimeters long, though its tail would probably double its body length. An arboreal, her mind went on, considering its tail and the well-developed hands and claws she'd seen as it clung to the lip of the louver. And those hands, she thought slowly, might have had only three fingers each, but they'd also had fully opposable thumbs. She closed her eyes, picturing it once more, seeing the net on its back, and knew she was right.

The celery snatcher might *look* like a teeny-tiny hexa-puma, yet that net was proof the survey crews had missed the most important single facet of Sphinx. But that was all right. In fact, that was *just* fine. Their omission had abruptly transformed this world from a place of exile to the most marvelous, exciting place Stephanie Harrington could possibly have been, for she'd done something tonight which had happened only eleven other times in the fifteen centuries of mankind's diaspora to the stars.

She'd just made first contact with a tool-using, clearly sentient, alien race.

CLIMBS QUICKLY LAY ON HIS BACK OUTSIDE HIS NEST, belly fur turned to the sun, and did his best to convince the rest of the clan he was asleep. He knew he wasn't fooling anyone who cared to taste his mind-glow, but good manners required them to pretend he was.

Which was just as well, for blissful as it was, the comfort of the drowsy sunlight was far too little to distract him from the monumental changes in his life. Facing his clan leaders and admitting he'd let one of the two-legs actually see him—and even worse, see him in the very process of raiding their plant place—had been just as unpleasant as he'd feared it would.

People seldom physically attacked other People. Oh, there were squabbles enough, and occasional serious fights—usually, though not always, limited to younger scouts or hunters. And there were even rarer situations in which entire clans found themselves feuding with one another, or fighting for control of their ranges. No one was particularly proud of such situations, but the ability to hear one another's thoughts and taste one another's emotions didn't necessarily make other People any easier to live with or fill a clan's range with prey when it was needed. A clan's leaders normally intervened before any-thing serious could happen *within* a clan, though, and it was rare indeed for one member of a clan to deliberately attack another unless there was something fundamentally wrong with the attacker.

Climbs Quickly himself could remember one occasion on which High Crag Clan had been forced to drive out one of its scouts, a rogue who *had* attacked other People. The exile had crossed into Bright Water's range, killing prey not just to live but for the sheer joy of killing, and raided Bright Water's storage places. He'd even attacked and seriously injured a Bright Water scout while attempting to steal a mother's kittens...for purposes Climbs Quickly preferred not to consider too deeply. In the end, the clan's scouts and hunters had been forced to hunt him down and kill him, a grim necessity none had welcomed.

So Climbs Quickly hadn't expected any of the Bright Water leaders to actually assault him, and they hadn't. But they *had* left him feeling as if they'd skinned him and hung his hide up to dry. It wasn't even the things they'd said so much as the way they'd said them.

Climbs Quickly's ears flicked, and he squirmed, trying to catch the sun more fully, as he recalled his time before Bright Water's leaders. Sings Truly had been present as the clan's second singer and the obvious heir to the first singer's position when Song Spinner died or surrendered her authority. But even Sings Truly had been shocked by his clumsiness. She hadn't scolded him the way Broken Tooth or Short Tail had, yet tasting his sister's wordless

reproach had been harder for Climbs Quickly to bear
than all of Broken Tooth's cutting irony.

He'd tried to explain, as clearly and un-defensively
as possible, that he'd never *meant* to let the two-leg see
him, and he'd suggested the possibility that somehow the
two-leg had known he was there in the plant place even
before seeing him, since it hadn't been surprised to see him
when he emerged from it. Some things about its reaction
had been surprised, but there'd been far more excitement,
almost delight. Indeed, he was virtually certain the two-
leg's surprise had been from seeing who (and what) he
truly was, not because the two-leg hadn't already known
that *someone* was in the plant place.

Unfortunately his suspicion rested on things he'd
tasted in two-leg's mind-glow, and although none of the
others actually said so, he knew they found it difficult
to believe a two-leg's mind-glow could tell one of the
People so much. He even knew why they thought that
way, for no other scout had ever come close enough
to—or concentrated hard enough upon—a two-leg to
realize how wonderfully, dreadfully powerful that mind-
glow truly was.

<*I believe that you believe the two-leg had some way
of knowing you were there,*> Short Tail had told him
judiciously, his mind-voice grave, <*yet I fail to see how it
could have. You saw none of the strange lights or tool things
the two-legs have used to detect other scouts, after all.*>

<*True,*> Climbs Quickly had replied as honestly as
possible. <*Yet the two-legs are very clever. I saw none of
the tool things I knew to look for, but does that prove the
two-legs have no tool things we have not yet learned of?*>

<*You hunt for ground runners in the upper branches,
little brother,*> Broken Tooth had put in sternly. <*You
allowed the two-leg not simply to see you but to see you
raiding its range! I do not doubt you tasted its mind-glow,*

but neither do I doubt that you tasted within that mind-glow that which was most important for you to taste.>

Much as Broken Tooth's charge had angered Climbs Quickly, he'd been unable to counter it effectively. After all, the feelings of the mind-glow were always easier to misinterpret, even among the People, than thoughts which were formed into deliberate communication. So perhaps it was only reasonable for Broken Tooth, who'd never tasted a two-leg mind-glow, to assume it would be even more difficult to interpret those of a totally different creature. Climbs Quickly knew—didn't think; *knew*—that the two-leg's mind-glow had been so strong, so vibrant, that he literally *could not* have read its excitement and eagerness wrongly. Yet he could hardly blame the clan's leaders for failing to accept that he'd interpreted those emotions accurately when they themselves had no experience at all with two-leg mind-glows. Nor could he fail to understand why they found it so difficult to accept the possibility that he could possibly have grasped, however imperfectly, what the two-leg was actually *thinking*.

Everyone knew there were messages within any mind-glow's feelings, yet even the strongest of those messages were only hints, suggestions that were frustratingly difficult to follow even at the best of times. It was as if meanings...leaked over into them like stream water trickling through the gaps in a thick, natural dam of fallen leaves. They got *through*, but without the clarity of deliberately formed thoughts, and it normally took turnings for one person to learn to read those leaks from another person with anything like reliability. As far as Climbs Quickly knew, no one had *ever* been able to read those scraps of meaning the very first time they met another person. No wonder they found his report so hard to accept!

And so, because they hadn't tasted the mind-glow for themselves and because he couldn't explain how *he* could have tasted it so strongly, he'd accepted his scolding as meekly as possible. The cluster stalk he'd brought home had muted that scolding to some extent, for it had proved just as marvelous as the songs from other clans had indicated. But not even that had been enough to deflect the one consequence he truly resented.

He had been relieved of his responsibility to watch over his two-legs, and Shadow Hider (who just happened to be a grandson of Broken Tooth) had been assigned to that task in his place. Broken Tooth hadn't said so in so many words, but he obviously believed Shadow Hider would do a better job of following instructions than Climbs Quickly had. Climbs Quickly believed that, too, although he personally thought it had more to do with Shadow Hider's natural lack of imagination and... timidity than his obedience to his grandsire.

And, truthfully, Climbs Quickly understood why the clan leaders insisted on such caution, however much he disliked it. The People had only to watch the two-legs cutting down trees with their whining tools that ate through the trunks of net-wood and golden-leaf trees large enough to hold whole clans of the People, or using the machines that gouged out the deep holes in which they planted their living places, to recognize the potential danger the two-legs represented. They need not decide to kill the People—or destroy a clan's entire range—to accomplish the same end by accident, and so the People had decided long ago, even before Climbs Quickly's birth, their only true safety lay in avoiding them entirely. The clans must stay undetected, observing without being observed, until they decided how best to respond to the strange creatures who so confidently and competently reshaped the world.

Unfortunately, Climbs Quickly had come to doubt the wisdom of that policy. Certainly caution was necessary, yet it seemed to him that many People—such as Broken

Tooth and those like him in the other clans—had become too aware of the potential danger and too *un*aware of the possible advantages the two-legs represented. Perhaps without even realizing it, they had decided deep down inside that the time for the two-legs to learn of the People's existence would never come, for only thus could the People be safe.

But though Climbs Quickly had too much respect for his clan's leaders to say so, the hope that the two-legs would never discover the People was foolishness. There were more two-legs at every turning now, and their flying things and long-seeing things (and whatever the young two-leg had used to detect his own presence) were too clever for the People to hide forever. Even without his own encounter with the two-leg, the People would have been found sooner or later. And when that happened—or perhaps more accurately, now that it *had* happened—the People would have no choice but to decide how they would interact with the two-legs . . . assuming that the two-legs allowed the People to make that decision.

All that was perfectly clear to Climbs Quickly and he suspected it was equally clear to Sings Truly, Short Tail, and Bright Claw, the clan's senior hunter. But Broken Tooth, Song Spinner, and Digger, who oversaw the clan's plant places, rejected that conclusion. They saw how vast the world was, how many hiding places it offered, and believed they *could* avoid the two-legs forever, even now that the two-legs knew the People existed.

He sighed again, and then his whiskers twitched with wry amusement as he wondered if the young two-leg was having as many difficulties as he was getting its elders to accept *its* judgment. If so, should Climbs Quickly be grateful or unhappy? He knew from its mind-glow that the youngling had felt only wonder and delight, not anger or fear, when it saw him. Surely if its elders shared its feelings, the People had nothing to fear. Yet the fact that one two-leg—and one perhaps little removed from kittenhood—felt that way might very well mean no more to the rest of the two-legs than *his* feelings meant to Broken Tooth.

Climbs Quickly lay basking in the sunlight, considering all that had happened—and all that still threatened to happen—and understood the fear which motivated Broken Tooth and his supporters. Indeed, a part of him shared their fear. But another part knew events had already been set in motion. The two-legs knew of the People's existence now. They would react to that, whatever the People did or didn't do, and all Broken Tooth's scolding could never prevent it.

Yet there was one thing Climbs Quickly hadn't reported. Something he had yet to come to grips with himself, and something he feared might actually panic Bright Water's leaders into abandoning their range and fleeing deep into the mountains. Perhaps that flight would even be the path of wisdom, he admitted. But it might also cast away a treasure such as the People had never before encountered. It was scarcely the place of a single scout to make choices affecting his entire clan, yet no one else *could* make this decision, for he alone knew that somehow, in a way he couldn't begin to understand, he and the young two-leg now shared something.

He wasn't certain what that "something" was, but even now, with his eyes closed and the two-legs' clearing far away, he knew *exactly* where the youngling was. He could feel its mind-glow, like a far off fire or sunlight shining red through his closed eyelids. It was too distant for him to taste its emotions, yet he knew it wasn't his imagination. He truly *did* know the direction to the two-leg, even more clearly than the direction to Sings Truly, who was no more than twenty or thirty People-lengths away at this very moment.

Climbs Quickly had no idea at all what that might mean, or where it might lead. But two things he did know. His connection, if such it was, to be young two-leg might—*must*—hold the key, for better or for worse, to whatever relationship People and two-legs might come to share. And until he decided what that connection meant in his own case, he dared not even suggest its existence to those who felt as Broken Tooth did.

STEPHANIE LEANED BACK IN THE COMFORTABLE CHAIR, folded her hands behind her head, and propped her sock feet on her desk in the posture which always drew a scold from her mother. Her lips were pursed in the silent, tuneless whistle that was an all but inevitable complement to the vague dreaminess of her eyes...and which would, had she let her parents see it, instantly have alerted them to the fact that their darling daughter was Up To Something.

The problem was that for the first time in a very long time, and despite a full T-month spent thinking about it from every angle she could come up with, she had only the haziest idea of precisely what she was up to. Or, rather, of how to pursue her objective. Uncertainty was an unusual feeling for someone who normally got into trouble by being too *positive* about things, yet there was something rather appealing about it, too. Perhaps because of its novelty.

She frowned, closed her eyes, tipped her chair further back, and thought harder.

She'd managed to evade detection on her way to bed the night of the thunderstorm. Oddly—though it hadn't occurred to her that it *was* odd until much later—she hadn't even considered rushing to her parents with the camera. Even now she still didn't know why she hadn't. Perhaps it was because the knowledge that humanity shared Sphinx with another sentient species was *her* discovery, and she felt strangely disinclined to share it. Until she did, it was not only her discovery but her secret, and she'd been almost surprised to realize she was determined to learn all she possibly could about her unexpected neighbors before she let anyone else know they existed.

She wasn't certain when she'd decided that, but once she had, it had been easy to find logical reasons for her decision. For one thing, the mere thought of how some of the kids in Twin Forks would react was enough to make her shudder. Even the ones with two brain cells to rub together (and she could count the ones who had even *that* many brain cells on the fingers of one hand, she thought sourly) would have been an outright threat to her little celery thief. Given their determination to catch everything from chipmunks to near-turtles as pets, they'd be almost certain to pursue these new creatures with even greater enthusiasm ... and catastrophic results.

She felt rather virtuous once she got that far, but it didn't come close to solving her main problem. If she didn't tell anybody, how did she go about learning more about them on her own? She might have been the *first* to come up with an answer to the mystery, but eventually someone else was going to catch another celery thief in the act. When that happened her secret would be out, and she was determined to learn everything she possibly could about them before that happened.

And, she thought, *at least I'm starting with a clean slate!*

Over the last several T-weeks, she'd accessed the planetary data net without finding a single word about miniature hexapumas with hands. She'd even used her father's link to the Forestry Service to compare her camera imagery to known Sphinxian species, only to draw a total blank. Whatever the celery snatcher was, no one else had ever gotten pictures of one of his—or had it been *her?*—relatives or even uploaded a verbal description of them to the planetary database.

And that's *as much evidence of their intelligence as that woven net of his,* she thought. *I know a planet's a big place, but from the pattern of the raids, they've got to be at least as widely distributed as our settlements and freeholds. And if they are, then the only way people could've missed spotting at least one of them for over fifty T-years, even with the Plague, would be for them to deliberately avoid humans. And that's a reasoned response. It means they had to actually* plan *to hide from us, and that kind of coordinated planning means they have to be able to talk to each other, and* that *means they must have a common language and some way to communicate over distances at least as widespread as we are!*

So they were not only tool-users, but language-users, and their small size made that even more remarkable. The one Stephanie had seen couldn't have had a body length of more than sixty centimeters or weighed more than thirteen or fourteen kilos, and no one had ever before encountered a sentient species with a body mass that low.

Stephanie got that far without much difficulty. Unfortunately, that was as far as she *could* get without more data, and for the first time she could recall, she didn't know how to get any more. That was a novel experience for someone who routinely approached most problems with complete confidence, but this time, she was stumped. She'd exhausted the available research possibilities, so if she wanted more information she had to get it for herself. That implied some sort of field research, but how did someone who'd just turned twelve T-years old—and one who'd promised her parents she wouldn't tramp around the woods alone—investigate a totally unknown species without even telling anyone it existed?

In a way, she was actually glad her mother had found herself too tied down by current projects to go for those nature hikes she'd promised to try to make time for. Stephanie had been grateful when her mother made the offer, but now her mother's presence would have posed a serious obstacle for any attempt to pursue her private research in secret.

It was perhaps unfortunate, however, that her father—in an effort to make up for her "disappointment" over her mother's schedule—had decided to distract her with the surprise gift of a brand-new hang glider for her twelfth birthday. She'd been touched by the thoughtfulness of the present, and even more by the way he'd rearranged his work schedule to free up time to resume the hang-gliding lessons their departure from Meyerdahl had interrupted. It wasn't that she didn't enjoy the lessons, either. In fact, Stephanie loved the exhilaration of flight, and no one could have been a better teacher than Richard Harrington. He'd made it into the continental hang-gliding finals on Meyerdahl three times, and she knew no one in the galaxy could have taught her more.

The problem is that every minute I spend on flight lessons is another minute I can't *spend doing what I really want to do . . . assuming I can figure out how to do it in the first place. And if I* don't *spend time on the lessons Mom and Dad are for sure going to figure out I've got something else on my mind!*

Worse, Dad insisted on flying in to Twin Forks for her lessons. That made sense, since unlike her mom he had to be "on-call" twenty-five hours a day and Twin Forks was the central hub for all the local freeholds. He could reach any of them quickly from town, and teaching the lessons there let him enlist the two or three other parents with gliding experience as assistant teachers. It let him offer the lessons to all the settlement's other kids, as well, which was one of the drawbacks in Stephanie's opinion, but exactly the sort of generosity she would have expected of him. But it also meant her lessons were not only eating up an enormous amount of her free time but taking her over eighty kilometers away from the place where she was more eager than ever to begin the explorations she'd promised her parents she wouldn't undertake.

She hadn't found a way around her problems yet, but she was determined that she *would* find one... and without breaking her promise, however much that added to her difficulties. But at least it hadn't been hard to give the species a name. It looked like an enormously smaller version of a "hexapuma," and like the hexapuma, there was something very (or perhaps inevitably) *feline* about it. Of course, Stephanie knew "feline" actually referred only to a very specific branch of Old Terran evolution. But it had become customary over the centuries to apply Old Terran names to alien species—like the Sphinxian "chipmunks" or "near-pine." Most claimed the practice originated from a sort of racial homesickness and a desire for familiarity in alien environments. Personally, Stephanie thought it was more likely to stem from laziness, since it let people avoid thinking up new labels for everything they encountered. Despite all that, however, she'd discovered that "treecat" was the only possible choice when she started considering names. She hoped the taxonomists would let it stand when she finally had to go public with their discovery. Usually the discoverer of the species did get to assign its common name, after all, though she suspected rather glumly that her age would work against her in that regard. Grown-ups could be so *zorky* sometimes.

And if she hadn't figured out how to go about investigating the treecats without breaking her promise—which was out of the question, however eager she might be to proceed—at least she knew the direction in which to start looking. She had no idea how she knew, but she was absolutely convinced that she would know exactly where to go when the time came.

She closed her eyes, took one arm from behind her head, and pointed, then opened her eyes to see where her index finger was aimed. The direction had changed slightly since the last time she'd checked, and yet she knew beyond a shadow of a doubt that she was pointing directly at the treecat who'd raided her mother's greenhouse.

And that, she reflected, was the oddest—and most exciting—part of the whole thing.

7

MARJORIE HARRINGTON FINISHED WRITING UP HER latest microbe-resistant strain of squash, closed the file, and sat back with a sigh. Some of Sphinx's farmers had argued that it would be much simpler (and quicker) just to come up with something to swat the microbe in question. That always seemed to occur to the people who faced such problems, and sometimes, Marjorie admitted, it was not only the simplest but also the most cost-effective and ecologically sound answer. But in this case she and the planetary administration had resisted firmly, and her final solution—which, she admitted, had taken longer than a more aggressive approach might have—had been to select the least intrusive of three possible genetic modifications to the *plant* rather than going after the microbe.

She knew even some of her colleagues back on Meyerdahl would have backed the "fast and aggressive" approach, but Marjorie had always regarded that as a last resort. Besides, her distaste for such methods lent a certain elegance to her work. There was something almost poetic about it, like the way she'd grafted the genetic resistance of native Sphinxian plants into terrestrial celery to defeat the blight which had threatened to destroy the plant. This one hadn't been quite as subtle as that one, but it still left her with a sense of profound satisfaction, very like the satisfaction she felt standing back from her easel to survey a finished landscape painting.

She smiled at the thought, looking remarkably like her daughter for a moment. Then her smile faded as she turned her mind from squash to other matters. Her workload had grown much heavier over the past weeks as Sphinx's southern hemisphere moved steadily towards planting time, and the press of priority assignments had kept her from finding the time for long hikes with Stephanie. She knew that, but she also knew she hadn't even been able to free up the time to help her daughter explore possible answers to the celery pilferage which had finally reached the Harrington freehold.

At least she'd responded enthusiastically to Richard's resumption of her hang-gliding lessons. In fact, she'd started spending hours in the air, checking in periodically over her uni-link—and despite the vocal worry of some of the Twin Forks parents whose kids were also learning to glide, Marjorie wasn't especially worried by the risks involved in her daughter's hobby. A certain number of bumps, scrapes, contusions, bruises, or even broken bones were among the inevitable rites of childhood, and while Marjorie Harrington didn't want her child running *stupid* risks, neither did she want Stephanie to grow up into an adult who was *afraid* to take risks.

Which, judging by Stephanie's personality at "twelve-but-I'll-be-thirteen-in-only-eight-months" wasn't very likely to happen, she reflected wryly.

Yet if Marjorie had no qualms over Stephanie's new interest, she was still unhappily certain Stephanie had

embraced it mainly as a diversion from other disappoint-
ments, and she rubbed her nose pensively. She had no
doubt Stephanie understood how important her own work
was, but the situation was still grossly unfair to her, and
although Stephanie seldom sulked or whined, Marjorie
had expected to hear quite a bit of carefully reasoned
commentary on the subject of fairness. And the fact
that Stephanie hadn't complained at all only sharpened
Marjorie's sense of guilt. It was as if Stephanie—

The hand rubbing Dr. Harrington's nose suddenly
stopped moving as a fresh thought struck her, and she
frowned, wondering why it hadn't occurred to her before.
It wasn't as if she didn't know her daughter, after all, and
this sort of sweet acceptance was very unlike Stephanie.
No, she *didn't* sulk or whine, but neither did she give
up without a fight on something to which she'd truly set
her mind. And, Marjorie thought, while Stephanie had
enjoyed hang gliding back on Meyerdahl, it had never
been the passion it seemed to have become here. It was
possible she'd simply discovered she'd underestimated its
enjoyment quotient on Meyerdahl, but Marjorie's abruptly
roused instincts said something else entirely.

She ran her mind back over her more recent conversations with her daughter, and her suspicion grew. Not
only had Stephanie not complained about the unfairness
of her grounding, but it was over two weeks since she'd
even referred to the mysterious celery thefts, and Marjorie scolded herself harder for falling into the error of
complacency. All the signs were there, and she should
have realized that the only thing which could produce
such a tractable Stephanie was a Stephanie who was Up
To Something and didn't want her parents to notice.

But what *could* she be up to? And *why* didn't she want
them to notice? The only thing she'd been forbidden was the
freedom to go wilderness hiking on her own, and however

devious she might sometimes be, Stephanie would never break a promise. Yet if she was using her sudden interest in hang gliding as a cover for something else, whatever she was up to must be something she calculated would arouse parental resistance. Which, unlike her promise to avoid woodland hikes, wouldn't stop her for a moment until they got around to catching her at it. Her daughter, Marjorie thought with affection-laced exasperation, was entirely too prone to figure that anything which hadn't been specifically forbidden was legal . . . whether or not the *opportunity* to forbid it had ever been offered.

On the other hand, Stephanie wasn't the sort to prevaricate in the face of specific questions. If Marjorie sat her down and asked her, she'd open up about whatever she was up to. She might not want to, but she'd do it, and Marjorie made a firm mental note to set aside enough time to explore the no doubt boundless possibilities.

Thoroughly.

8

STEPHANIE WHOOPED IN SHEER EXUBERANCE AS SHE rode the powerful updraft. Wind whipped through her birthday glider's struts, drummed on its fabric covering, and whistled around her helmet, and she leaned to one side, banking as she sliced still higher. The counter-grav unit on her back could have taken her higher yet—and done it more quickly—but it wouldn't have been anywhere near as much *fun* as this was!

She watched the treetops below and felt a tiny stir of guilt buried in her delight. She was safely above those trees—not even the towering crown oaks came anywhere near her present altitude—but she also knew what her father would have said had he known where she was. The fact that he *didn't* know, and thus wouldn't say it, wasn't quite enough for her to convince herself her actions weren't just a *bit* across the line. But she could always say—truthfully—that she hadn't broken her word. She wasn't walking around the woods by herself, and no hexapuma or peak bear could possibly threaten her at an altitude of two or three hundred meters.

For all that, innate honesty forced her to admit that she knew her parents would instantly have countermanded her plans if they'd known of them. For that matter, she'd taken shameless advantage of a failure in communication on their part, and she knew it.

Her father had been forced to cancel today's hang-gliding lesson because of an emergency house call, and he'd commed Mr. Sapristos, the Twin Forks mayor, who usually subbed for him in the gliding classes. Mr. Sapristos had agreed to take over for the day, but Dad hadn't specifically told him Stephanie would be there. The autopilot in Mom's air car could have delivered her under the direction of the planetary air-traffic computers, and he'd apparently assumed that was what would happen. Unfortunately—or fortunately, depending on one's viewpoint—his haste had been so great that he hadn't asked Mom to arrange transportation. (Stephanie was guiltily certain he'd expected *her* to tell her mother. But, she reminded herself, he hadn't actually *told* her to, had he?)

All of which meant Dad thought she was with Mr. Sapristos, but that Mr. Sapristos and Mom both thought she was with *Dad.* And that just happened to have given Stephanie a chance to pick her own flight plan without having to explain it to anyone else.

It wasn't the first time the same situation had arisen... or that she'd capitalized upon it. But it wasn't the sort of opportunity an enterprising young woman could expect to come along often, either, and she'd jumped at it. She'd had to, for the long Sphinxian days were creeping past, over two T-months had gotten away from her, and none of her previous unauthorized flights had given her big enough time windows. Avoiding parental discovery had always required her to turn back short of the point at which she *knew* her treecats lurked, and if *she* didn't find out more about them soon, someone else was bound to.

Of course, she couldn't expect to learn much about them just flying around overhead, but that wasn't really what she was after. If she could only pinpoint a location for them, she was sure she could get Dad to come out here with her—maybe with some of his friends from the Forestry Service—to find the physical evidence to support her discovery. And, she thought, her ability to tell them where to look would also be evidence of her strange link with the celery thief. Somehow she figured she'd need a *lot* of evidence of that before she got anyone else to believe it existed.

She closed her eyes, consulting her inner compass once more, and smiled. It was holding steady, which meant she was headed in the right direction, and she opened her eyes once more.

She banked again, very slightly, adjusting her course to precisely the right heading, and her face glowed with excitement. She was on track at last. She *knew* she was, just as she knew that this time she had enough flight time to reach her goal before anyone missed her, and she was quite correct.

Unfortunately, she'd also made one small mistake.

Climbs Quickly paused, one true-hand stopped in mid-reach for the branch above, and his ears flattened. He'd become accustomed to his ability to sense the direction of the two-leg youngling, even if he still hadn't mentioned it to anyone else. He'd even become used to the way the youngling sometimes seemed to move with extraordinary speed—no doubt in one of the two-legs' flying things—but this was different. The youngling *was* moving quickly, though far more slowly than it sometimes had. But it was also headed directly towards Climbs Quickly. In fact, it was already far closer than it had ever come since he'd been relieved of his spying duties—and he felt a sudden chill.

There was no question. He recognized exactly what the youngling was doing, for he'd done much the same thing often enough in the past. True, *he* usually pursued his prey by scent, but now he understood how a ground runner must have felt when it realized he was on its trail, for the two-leg was using the link between them in exactly the same way. It was *tracking* him, and if it found him, it would also find Bright Water Clan's central nesting place. For good or ill, its ability to seek out Climbs Quickly would result in the discovery of his entire clan!

He stood for one more moment, heart racing, ears flat with mingled excitement and fear, then decided. He abandoned his original task and bounded off along the outstretched net-wood limb, racing to meet the approaching two-leg well away from the rest of his clan.

Stephanie's attention was locked on the trees below her now. Her flight had lasted over two hours, but she was drawing close at last. She could feel the distance melting away—indeed, it almost seemed the treecat was coming to meet her—and excitement narrowed the focus of her attention even further. The crown oak had thinned as she'd left the foothills behind and begun climbing into the Copperwalls proper. Now the woods were a mix of various evergreens, dominated by shorter species of near-pine and the dark, blue-green pyramids of Sphinxian red spruce, and the crazy-quilt geometry of picketwood.

Of course they were, she thought, and her eyes brightened. The rough-barked picketwood would be the perfect habitat for someone like her little celery thief! Each picketwood system radiated from a single central trunk which sent out long, straight, horizontal branches at a height of between three and ten meters. Above that, branches might take on any shape; below it, they always grew in groups of four, radiating at near-perfect right angles from one another for a distance of ten to fifteen meters. At that point, each sent a vertical runner down to the earth below to establish its own root system and, in time, become its own nodal trunk. A single picketwood "tree" could extend itself for literally hundreds of kilometers in any direction, and it wasn't uncommon for one "tree" to run into another and fuse with it. When the lateral branches of two systems crossed, they merged into a node which put down its own runner.

Stephanie's mother was fascinated by the picketwoods. Plants which spread by sending out runners weren't all that rare, but those which spread *only* via runner were. It was also more than a little uncommon for the runner to spread out through the air and go down to the earth, rather than the reverse. But what truly fascinated Dr. Harrington was the tree's anti-disease defense mechanism. The unending network of branches and trunks should have made a picketwood system lethally vulnerable to diseases and parasites. But the plant had demonstrated a sort of natural quarantine process. Somehow—and Dr. Harrington had yet to discover how—a picketwood system was able to sever its links to afflicted portions of itself. Attacked by disease or parasites, the system secreted powerful cellulose-dissolving enzymes that ate away at connecting cross-branches and literally disconnected them at intervening nodal trunks, and Dr. Harrington was determined to locate the mechanism which made that possible.

But her mother's interest in picketwood meant very little to Stephanie at the moment beside her realization of the same tree's importance to treecats. Picketwood was deciduous and stopped well short of the tree line, abandoning the higher altitudes to near-pine and red spruce. But it crossed mountains readily through valleys or at lower elevations, and it could be found in almost every climate zone. All of which meant it would provide treecats with the equivalent of aerial highways that could literally run clear across a continent! They could travel for hundreds—thousands!—of kilometers without ever having to touch the ground where larger predators like hexapumas could get at them!

She laughed aloud at her deduction, but then her glider slipped abruptly sideways, and her laughter died as she stopped thinking about the sorts of trees beneath her and recognized instead the speed at which she was passing over them. She raised her head and looked around quickly, and a fist of the ice seemed to squeeze her stomach.

The clear blue skies under which she had begun her flight still stretched away in front of her to the east. But the western sky *behind* her was no longer clear. A deadly looking line of thunderheads marched steadily east, white and fluffy on top but an ominous purple-black below, and even as she looked over her shoulder, she saw lightning flicker.

She should have seen it coming sooner, she thought numbly, hands aching as she squeezed the glider's grips in ivory-knuckled fists.

Idiot! she told herself. *You should've checked the weather reports! You* know *you should have! Dad's pounded that into you every single time the two of you plan a flight!*

Yes, he had...and that, she realized sickly, was the point. She was used to having other people—*adult* people—check the weather before they went gliding, and she'd let herself get so excited, focus so intently on what she was doing, pay so little attention—

A harder fist of wind punched at her glider, staggering it in midair, and fear became terror. The following wind had been growing stronger for quite some time, a small logical part of her realized. No doubt she would have noticed despite her concentration if she hadn't been gliding in the same direction, riding in the wind rather than across or against it, where the velocity shift would *have* to have registered. But the thunderheads were catching up with her quickly, and the outriders of their squall line lashed through the air space in front of them.

Daddy! She had to com her father—tell him where she was—tell him to come get her—tell him—!

But there was no time. She'd messed up, and all the theoretical discussions about what to do in bad weather, all the stern warnings to avoid rough air, came crashing in on her. But they were no longer theoretical; she was in deadly danger, and she knew it. Counter-grav unit or no, a storm like the one racing up behind her could blot her out of the air as casually as she might have swatted a fly, and with just as deadly a result. She could die in the next few minutes, and the thought terrified her, but she didn't panic.

Yes, you have to com Mom and Dad, but it's not like you don't already know exactly *what they'd tell you to do if you did. You've got to get out of the air, get yourself down on the ground, now! And the last thing you need,* she thought sickly, *staring down at the solid green canopy below her, is to be trying to explain to them where you are while you do it!*

She banked again, shivering with fear, eyes desperately seeking some opening, however small, and the air trembled as thunder rumbled behind her.

Climbs Quickly reared up on true-feet and hand-feet, lips wrinkling back from needle-sharp white fangs as a flood of terror crashed over him. It pounded deep into him, waking the ancient fight-or-flight instinct which, had he but known it, his kind shared with humanity. But it wasn't *his* terror at all.

It took him an instant to realize that, yet it was true. It wasn't his fear; it was the two-leg youngling's, and even as the youngling's fear ripped at him, he felt a fresh surge of wonder. He was still too far from the two-leg. He could never have felt another of the People's mind-glow at this distance, and he knew it. But this two-leg's mind-glow raged through him like a forest fire, screaming for his aid without even realizing it could do so, and it struck him like a lash. He shook his head once, and then flashed down the line of net-wood like a cream-and-gray blur while his fluffy tail streamed straight out behind him.

Desperation filled Stephanie.

The thunderstorm was almost upon her—the first white pellets of hail rattled off her taut glider covering—and without the counter-grav she would already have been blotted from the sky. But not even the counter-grav unit could save her from the mounting turbulence much longer, and—

Her thoughts chopped off as salvation loomed suddenly before her. The black, irregular scar of an old forest fire had ripped a huge hole through the trees, and she choked back a sob of gratitude as she spied it. The ground looked dangerously rough for a landing in conditions like this, but it was infinitely more inviting than the solid web of branches tossing and flashing below her, and she banked towards it.

She almost made it.

Climbs Quickly ran as he'd never run before. Somehow he knew he raced against death itself, though it never occurred to him to wonder what someone his size could do for someone the size of even a two-leg youngling. It

didn't matter. All that mattered was the terror, the fear—
the danger—which confronted that other presence in his
mind, and he ran madly towards it.

It was the strength of the wind which did it.

Even then, she would have made it without the sudden downdraft that hammered her at the last instant.
But between them, they were too much. Stephanie saw it
coming in the moment before she struck, realized instantly
what was going to happen, but there was no time to avoid
it. No time even to feel the full impact of the realization
before her glider crashed into the crown of the towering
near-pine at over fifty kilometers per hour.

9

CLIMBS QUICKLY SLITHERED TO A STOP, MOMENTARILY frozen in horror. But then he gasped in relief.

The sudden silence in his mind wasn't—quite—absolute. His instant fear that the youngling had been killed eased, yet something deeper and darker, without the same bright panic but with even greater power, replaced it. Whatever had happened, the youngling was now unconscious, yet even in its unconsciousness he was still linked to it...and he felt its pain. It was injured, possibly badly—possibly badly enough that his initial fear that it had died would prove justified after all. And if it was injured, what could *he* do to help? Young as it was, it was far larger than he; much *too* large for him to drag to safety.

But what one of the People couldn't do, many of them often *could*, and he closed his eyes, lashing his tail while he thought. He'd run too far to feel the combined mind-glow of his clan's central nest place. His emotions couldn't reach so far, but his mind-voice could. If he cried out for help, Sings Truly would hear, and if she failed to, surely some hunter or scout between her and Climbs Quickly would hear and relay. Yet what message could he cry out *with*? How could he summon the clan to aid a two-leg—the very two-leg he had allowed to see him? How could he expect them to abandon their policy of hiding from the two-legs? And even if he could have expected that of them, what right had he to demand it?

He stood irresolute, tail flicking, ears flattened, as the branch behind him creaked and swayed and the first raindrops lashed the budding leaves. Rain, he thought, a flicker of humor leaking even through his dread and uncertainty. Was it *always* going to be raining when he and his two-leg met?

Strangely, that thought broke his paralysis, and he shook himself. All he knew so far was that the two-leg was hurt and that he was very close to it now. He had no way of knowing how bad its injuries might actually be, nor even if there were any *reason* to consider calling out for help. After all, if there was nothing the clan could do, then there was no point in trying to convince it to come. No, the thing to do was to continue until he found the youngling. He had to see what its condition was before he could determine the best way to help—assuming it required his help at all—and he scurried onward almost as quickly as before.

Stephanie recovered consciousness slowly. The world swayed and jerked all about her, thunder rumbled and crashed, rain lashed her like an icy flail, and she'd never hurt so much in her entire life.

The pounding rain's chill wetness helped rouse her, and she tried to move—only to whimper as the pain in her left arm stabbed suddenly higher. She'd lost her helmet somehow. That wasn't supposed to happen, but it had.

She felt a painful welt rising under her jaw where the helmet strap had lain, and her hair was already soaking wet. Nor was that all she had to worry about, and she blinked, rubbing her eyes with her right palm, and felt a sort of dull shock as she realized part of what had been blinding her was blood, not simply rainwater.

She wiped again and felt a shiver of relief as she realized there was much less blood than she'd thought. Most of it seemed to be coming from a single cut on her forehead, and the cold rain was already slowing the bleeding. She managed to clear her eyes well enough to look about her, and her relief vanished.

Her brand new glider was smashed. Not broken: *smashed*. Its tough composite covering and struts had been specially designed to be crash survivable, but it had never been intended for the abuse to which she'd subjected it, and it had crumpled into a mangled lacework of fabric and shattered framing. Yet it hadn't quite failed completely, and she hung in her harness from the main spar, which was jammed in the fork of a branch above her. The throbbing ache where the harness straps crossed her body told her she'd been badly bruised by the abrupt termination of her flight, and one of her ribs stabbed her with a white burst of agony every time she breathed. But without the harness—and the forked branch which had caught her—she would have slammed straight into the massive tree trunk directly in front of her, and she shuddered at the thought.

But however lucky she might have been, there'd been bad luck to go with the good. Like most colony world children, Stephanie had been through mandatory first-aid courses... not that any training was needed to realize her left arm was broken in at least two places. She knew which way her elbow was *supposed* to bend, and there was no joint in the middle of her forearm. That was bad enough, but there was worse, for her uni-link had been strapped to her left wrist.

It wasn't there anymore.

She turned her head, craning her neck to peer painfully back along the all too obvious course of her crashing impact with the treetops, and wondered where the uni-link was. The wrist unit was virtually indestructible, and if she could only find it—and *reach* it—she could call for help in an instant. But there was no way she was going to find it in that mess.

It was almost funny, she thought through the haze of her pain. *She* couldn't find it, but Mom or Dad could have found it with ridiculous ease... if they'd only known to use the emergency override code to activate the locator beacon function. Or, for that matter, if *she'd* thought to activate it when the storm first came up. Unfortunately, she'd been too preoccupied finding a landing spot to bring the beacon up, and even if she had, no one would have found it until they thought to look for it.

And since I can't even find it, I can't com anyone to tell them to start looking for it, she thought fuzzily. *I really messed up this time. Mom and Dad are going to be really, really pissed. Bet they ground me till I'm sixteen for this one!*

Even as she thought it, she knew it was ridiculous to worry about such things at a time like this. Yet there was a certain perverse comfort—a sense of familiarity, perhaps—to it, and she actually managed a damp-sounding chuckle despite the tears of pain and fear trickling down her face.

She let herself hang limp for another moment, but badly as she felt the need to rest, she dared do no such thing. The wind was growing stronger, not weaker, and the branch from which she hung creaked and swayed alarmingly. Then there was the matter of lightning. A tree this tall was all too likely to attract any stray bolt, and she had no desire to share the experience with it. No, she had to get herself down, and she blinked away residual pain tears and fresh rain to peer down at the ground.

For all its height, the near-pine into which she'd crashed wasn't a particularly towering specimen of its species, which could easily run to as much as sixty or even seventy meters, without a single branch for the lower third of its height. It was still a good twelve-meter drop to the ground, though, and she shuddered at the thought. Her gymnastics classes had taught her how to tuck and roll, but that wouldn't help from this height even with two good arms. With her left arm shattered, she'd probably finish herself off permanently if she tried. But the way her supporting branch was beginning to shake told her she had no option but to get down *somehow*. Even if the branch held, her damaged harness was likely to let go . . . assuming the even more badly damaged spar didn't simply snap first. But how—?

Of course! She reached up and around with her right arm, gritting her teeth as even that movement shifted her left arm ever so slightly and sent fresh stabs of anguish through her. But the pain was worth it, for her fingers confirmed her hope. The counter-grav unit was still there, and she felt the slight, pulsating hum that indicated it was still operating. Of course, she couldn't be certain how long it would go *on* operating.

Her cautiously exploring hand reported an entire series of deep dents and gouges in its casing. She supposed she should be glad it had protected her back by absorbing the blows which had left those marks, but if the unit had taken a beating anything like what had happened to the rest of her equipment, it probably wouldn't last all that long. On the other hand, it only had to hold out long enough to get her to the ground, and—

Her thoughts chopped off as something touched the back of her head, and she jerked back around, in a shock spasm fast enough to wrench a half-scream of pain from her bruised body and broken arm. It wasn't that the touch *hurt* in any way, for it was feather-gentle, almost a caress.

Only its totally unexpected surprise produced its power, and all the pain she felt was the result of her *response* to it. Yet even as she bit her pain sound back into a groan, the hurt seemed far away and unimportant as she stared into the treecat's slit-pupilled green eyes from a distance of less than thirty centimeters.

Climbs Quickly winced as the two-leg's peaking hurt clawed at him, yet he was vastly relieved to find it awake and aware. He smelled the bright, sharp scent of blood, and the two-leg's arm was clearly broken. He had no idea how it had managed to get itself into such a predicament, but the bits and pieces strewn around and hanging from its harness straps were obviously the ruin of some sort of flying thing. The fragments didn't look like the other flying things he'd seen, yet such it must have been for the two-leg to wind up stuck in the top of a tree this way.

He wished fervently that it could have found another place to crash. This clearing was a place of bad omen, shunned by all of the People. Once it had been the heart of the Sun Shadow Clan's range, but the remnants of that clan had moved far, far away, trying to forget what had happened to it here, and Climbs Quickly would have much preferred not to come here himself.

But that was beside the point. He was here, and however little he might like this place, he knew the two-leg had to get down. The branch from which it hung was not only thrashing with the wind but trying to split off the tree—he knew it was, for he'd crossed the weakened spot to reach the two-leg. And that didn't even consider the way green-needle trees attracted lightning. Yet he could see no way for a two-leg with a broken arm to climb like one of the People, and he was certainly too small to carry it!

Frustration bubbled in the back of his mind as he realized how little he could do, yet it never occurred to him not to try to help. This was one of "his" two-legs, and he knew that it was the link to *him* which had brought it here. There were far too many things happening for him to begin to understand them all, yet understanding was strangely unimportant. This, he realized with a dawning sense of wonder, wasn't "one" of his two-legs after all; it was *his* two-leg. Whatever the link between them was, it reached out in both directions. They weren't simply linked; they were *bound* to one another, and he could no more have abandoned this strange-looking, alien creature than he could have walked away from Sings Truly or Short Tail in time of need.

Yet what could he *do*? He leaned out from his perch, clinging to the tree's deeply furrowed bark with hand-feet and one true-hand, prehensile tail curled tight around the branch, as he extended the other true-hand to stroke the two-leg's cheek. He crooned to it, and he saw it blink. Then its hand came up—so much smaller than a full-grown two-leg's, yet so much bigger than his own—and he arched his spine and crooned again—this time in pleasure—as the two-leg returned his caress.

Even in her pain and fear, Stephanie felt a sense of wonder—almost awe—as the treecat reached out to touch her face.

She'd seen the strong, curved claws the creature's other hand had sunk into the near-pine's bark, but the wiry fingers which touched her cheek were moth-wing gentle, claws retracted, and she pressed back against them. Then she reached out her own good hand, touching the rain-soaked fur, stroking its spine as she would have stroked an Old Terran cat. The outer layer of that fur, she realized, was an efficient rain shedder. The layers under it were dry and fluffy, and the creature arched with a soft sound of pleasure as her fingers stroked it. She didn't begin to understand what was happening, but she didn't have to. She might not know exactly what the treecat was doing, yet she dimly sensed the way it was soothing her fear— even her pain—through that strange link they shared, and she clung to the comfort it offered.

But then it drew back, sitting higher on its four rear limbs. It cocked its head at her for a long moment while wind and rain howled about them, and then it raised one front paw—no, she reminded herself, one of its *hands*— and pointed downward.

That was the only possible way to describe its actions. It *pointed* downward, and even as it pointed it made a sharp, scolding sound whose meaning was unmistakable.

"I *know* I need to get down," she told it in a hoarse, pain-shadowed voice. "In fact, I was working on it when you turned up. Just give me a minute, will you?"

Climbs Quickly's ear shifted as the two-leg made noises at him.

For the first time, thanks to the link between them, he had proof the noises were actually meant to convey meaning, although just what their meaning might be was more than he could have said. While the two-leg's emotions themselves were almost painfully sharp and clear at this short range, the echoes, the hints of meaning, which infused the emotions of any mind-glow were far too strange and unfamiliar for him to sort out any sort of specific meaning. Yet it was obvious the youngling was *trying* to communicate with him, and he felt a stab of pity for it and its fellows. Was that the *only* way they knew to communicate with one another? But however crude and imperfect the means might be compared to the manner in which the People spoke, at least he could now prove they *did* communicate. That should go a long way towards convincing the clan leaders the two-legs truly were People in their own fashion. And at least the noises the hurt youngling was making coupled with the taste of its mind-glow were proof it was still thinking. He felt a strange surge of pride in the two-leg, comparing its reaction to how some of the People's younglings might have reacted in its place, and bleeked at it again, more gently.

"I know, I know, *I know!*"

Stephanie sighed and reached back to the counter-grav's controls. She adjusted them carefully, then bit her lower lip as a ragged pulsation marred its smooth vibration.

She gave the rheostat one last, gentle twitch, feeling the pressure of the harness straps ease as her apparent weight was reduced to three or four kilos. But that was as far as it was going. She would have preferred an even lower level—had the unit been undamaged, she could have reduced her apparent weight all the way to zero or even a negative number, in which case she would actually have had to pull herself down against its lift. But the rheostat was all the way over now. It wouldn't go any further... and the ragged pulsation served notice that the unit was likely to pack up any minute, even at its current setting.

Still, she told herself, doggedly trying to find a bright side, maybe it was just as well. Any lighter weight would have been dangerous in such a high wind, and getting her lightweight self smashed against a tree trunk or branch by a sudden gust would hardly do her broken arm any good.

"Well," she said, looking back at the treecat. "Here goes."

The two-leg looked at him, made another mouth noise, and then—to Climbs Quickly's horror—it unlatched its harness with its good hand and let itself fall.

He reared up in protest, ears flattened, yet his horror vanished almost as quickly as it had come, for the youngling didn't actually *fall* at all. Instead, its good hand flashed back out, catching hold of a dangling strip of its broken flying thing, and he blinked. That frayed strap looked too frail to support even *his* weight, yet it held the two-leg with ease, and the youngling slid slowly down it from the grip of that single hand.

The counter-grav's harsh, warning buzz of imminent failure clawed at Stephanie's ears.

She muttered a word she wasn't supposed to know and slithered more quickly down the broken rigging stay. It was tempting to simply let herself fall, but any object fell at over thirteen meters per second in Sphinx's gravity. She had no desire to hit the ground at that speed with an arm which was so badly broken, no matter how little she "weighed" at the moment of contact. Besides, although the stay's torn anchorage would never have supported her normal weight, it was doing just fine with her *current* weight. All it had to do was hold for another minute or two and—

She was only two meters up when the counter-grav unit decided to fail. She cried out, clutching at the stay as her suddenly restored weight snatched at her, but it disintegrated in her grip. She plummeted to the ground, automatically tucking and rolling as her gym teacher had taught her, and she would have been fine if her arm hadn't been broken.

But it *was* broken, and her scream was high and shrill as her rolling weight smashed down on it and the darkness claimed her.

10

CLIMBS QUICKLY LEAPT DOWN THROUGH THE GREEN-needle branches with frantic haste. His sensitive hearing had detected the sound of the counter-grav unit, and though he'd had no idea what it was, he knew its abrupt cessation must have had something to do with the youngling's fall. No doubt it had been another two-leg tool which, like the youngling's flying thing, had broken. In an odd sort of way, it was almost reassuring to know two-leg tools *could* break. But that was cold comfort at the moment, and his whiskers quivered with anxiety as he hit the ground and scuttled quickly over to the youngling.

It lay on its side, and he winced as he realized its fall had ended with its broken arm trapped under it. He tasted the shadow of pain even through the murkiness of its unconscious mind-glow, and he dreaded what the youngling would experience when it regained its senses. Worse, he sensed a new pain source in its right knee. But aside from the arm, the knee, and another bump swelling on its forehead, the young two-leg appeared to have taken no fresh damage, and Climbs Quickly settled back on his haunches in relief.

He might not understand what had happened to forge the link between him and his two-leg, but that was no longer really important. What mattered was that the link existed and that for whatever reason the two of them had somehow been made one. There was an echo to it much like that in the mind-glows of mated couples, but this was different, without the overtones of physical desire and bereft of the mutual communication of ideas. It was a thing of pure emotion which only one of them could truly perceive, not the two-way flow and exchange which two of the People would have shared. And yet he felt frustratingly certain that he had touched the very edge of the youngling's actual thoughts a time or two. It could not shape and send them as one of the People did, yet he had *almost* captured those echoes of meaning and made them his, and he wondered if perhaps another of the People and another two-leg might someday reach further than that. For that matter, perhaps he and *his* two-leg would manage that someday, for if this was in fact a permanent link, they would have turnings and turnings in which to explore it.

That prompted another thought, and he groomed his whiskers with a meditative hand while he wondered just how long two-legs lived. The People were much longer lived than large creatures like the death fangs and snow hunters. Did that mean they lived longer than two-legs? The possibility woke an unexpected pain, almost like a presentiment of grief for the loss of the youngling's—*his* youngling's—glorious mind-glow. Yet it *was* a youngling, he reminded himself, while he was a full adult. Even if its natural span was shorter than his, the difference in their ages might give them an equal number of remaining turnings. That thought was oddly comforting, and he shook himself and looked around.

The battering rain had already eased as the squall line passed through, and much of the wind's strength had died away, as well. He was glad his two-leg had gotten down before the wind could knock it out of the tree, yet every instinct insisted that the ground was not a safe place to be. That was certainly true for the People, but perhaps the youngling had one of the weapons with which its elders sometimes slew the death fangs which threatened them. Climbs Quickly knew those weapons came in different shapes and sizes, but he'd never seen the small ones some two-legs carried, and so he had no way to tell if the youngling had one.

Yet even if it did, its injured condition would leave it in poor shape to defend itself, and it certainly couldn't follow him up into the trees if danger threatened. Which meant it was time to scout around. If there *was* danger here, best he should know about it now. Once the young two-leg reawakened, it might have ideas about how to proceed; possibly it even had some way to let the other two-legs know where it was and summon them to its aid. Until then he would simply have to do the best he could on his own.

He turned away from the two-leg and began to circle it, moving out in an ever-widening spiral while nose and ears probed alertly. There was normally little undergrowth to obscure one's line of sight under the thick canopy of the mature forest, but there was far more of it here in the old forest fire's scar, where sunlight could reach the ground. Low-growing scrub and young trees—future giants like the one from which the two-leg had fallen—were beginning to reclaim the clearing, and even this early in the season, they were putting out thick coverings of new leaves. He could see little enough through that riotous explosion of green, but at least the rain had not been hard enough or fallen long enough to wipe away scents. Indeed, the moist air actually made them sharper and richer, and his muzzle wrinkled as he tested them.

But then, suddenly, he froze, whiskers stiff and fluffy tail flattened out to twice its normal width. He made himself take another long, careful scent, yet it was no more than a formality. No clan scout could *ever* mistake the smell of a death fang lair, and this one was close.

He turned slowly, working to fix the location clearly in his mind, and his heart fell. The scent came from the clearing, where the undergrowth would offer the lair's owner maximum concealment when it returned and scented the two-leg. And it *would* return, he thought sinkingly, for he smelled something more now. The death fang was a female, and it had recently littered. That meant it must be out hunting food for its young... and that it would be back sooner rather than later.

Climbs Quickly stood a moment longer, then raced back to the two-leg. He touched its face with his muzzle, willing it to awaken with all his might, but there was no response. It would wake when it woke, he realized. Nothing he did would speed that moment, and that left but one thing he *could* do.

He sat upright on his four rearmost limbs, curling his tail neatly about his true-feet and hand-feet, and composed his thought carefully. Then he sent it soaring out through the dripping forest. He shaped and drove it with all the urgency in him, crying out to his sister, and somehow his link to the two-leg lent his call additional strength.

<Climbs Quickly?> Even from here he tasted the shock in Sings Truly's mind-voice. *<Where are you? What's wrong?>*

<I am near the old fire scar to sun-setting of our range,> Climbs Quickly replied as calmly as he could, and felt a surge of astonishment from his sister. No one from Bright Water Clan would soon forget the terrible day Sun Shadow Clan had lost control of the fire and seen

its entire central nesting place—and all too many of its kittens—consumed in dreadful flame and smoke.

<*Why?*> she demanded. <*What could possibly take you there?*>

<*I—*> Climbs Quickly paused, then drew a deep breath. <*It would take too long to explain, Sings Truly. But I am here with an injured youngling ... and so also is a death fang lair filled with young.*>

Sings Truly knew her brother well, and the oddness in his reply was obvious to her. But so was the unusual strength and clarity of his mind-voice. He'd always had a strong voice for a male, but today he reached almost to the strength of a memory singer, and she wondered how he'd done it. Some scouts and hunters gained far stronger voices when they mated, as if their mates' minds somehow harmonized with theirs at need, but that couldn't explain Climbs Quickly's new power. Yet those thoughts were but a fleeting background for the chill horror she felt at the thought of any injured youngling trapped so near a death fang.

She started to reply once more, then stopped, tail kinking and ears cocking in sudden consternation and suspicion. No, surely not. Not even Climbs Quickly would dare *that*. Not after the way the clan elders had berated him! Yet try as she might, she could think of no way any Brightwater youngling would have strayed so far, and no other clan's range bordered on the fire scar. And Climbs Quickly had named no names, had he? But—

She shook herself. There was, of course, one way to satisfy her curiosity. All she had to do was ask ... but if she did, then she would know her brother was violating the edicts of his clan heads. If she didn't ask, she could only suspect—not *know*—and so she kept that particular question to herself and asked another.

<*What do you wish of me, Brother?*>

<*Sound the alarm,*> he replied, sending a burst of gratitude and love with the words. He knew what she'd considered, and her choice of question told him what she'd decided.

<*For the "injured youngling."*> Sings Truly's flat statement was a question, and he flicked his tail in agreement even though she could not see it.

<*Yes,*> he returned simply, and felt her hesitation. But then her answer came.

<*I will,*> she said with equal simplicity—and the unquestionable authority of a memory singer. <*We come with all speed, my brother.*>

Stephanie Harrington awoke once more. A weak, pain-filled sound leaked from her—less words than the mew of an injured kitten—and her eyelids fluttered. She started to sit up, and her mew became a breathless, involuntary scream as her weight shifted on her broken arm. The sudden agony was literally blinding, and she screwed her eyes shut once more, sobbing with hurt as she made herself sit up anyway. Nausea knotted her stomach as the anguish in her arm and shoulder and broken rib vibrated through her, and she sat very still, as if the pain were some sort of hunting predator from whom she could hide until it passed her by.

But the pain didn't pass her by. It only eased a bit, and she blinked on tears, scrubbing her face with her good hand and sniffling as she smeared mud and the blood from her mashed nose across her cheeks. She didn't need to move to know she'd smashed her knee, as well as her bad arm, and she felt herself shuddering, quivering like a leaf as hopelessness and pain crushed down on her. The immediacy of the need to get out of the tree had helped carry her to this point, but she was on the ground now. That gave her time to think—and feel.

Fresh, hot tears brimmed, dripping down her face, and she whined as she made herself gather her left wrist in her right hand and lifted it into her lap. Just moving it twisted her with torment—she wasn't sure whether she'd broken it in yet a third place or not—but she couldn't leave it hanging down beside her like it belonged to someone else. She thought about using her belt to fasten it to her side, but she couldn't find the energy—or the courage—to move that shattered bone again. It was too much for her. Now that the immediate crisis was over, she knew how much she hurt. She knew how totally lost she was, how desperately she wanted—needed—her parents to come take her home. How *stupid* she'd been to get herself into this mess...and how very little she could do to get herself *out* of it.

She huddled there at the foot of the tree, crying hopelessly for her mother and father. The world had proved bigger and more dangerous than she'd ever quite believed, and she wanted them to come find her. No scold they could give her, however ferocious, could match the one she gave herself, and she whimpered as the sobs she couldn't stop shook her broken arm and sent fresh, vicious stabs of pain through her.

But then she felt a light pressure on her right thigh and blinked furiously to clear her eyes. She looked down, and the treecat looked back. He stood beside her, one hand resting on her leg, his ears flattened with concern, and she heard—and felt—his soft, comforting croon. She gazed down at him for a moment, her mouth quivering in exhaustion, despair, pain, and physical shock. And then she held out her good arm to him, and he didn't even hesitate. He flowed up her leg to stand on his rearmost limbs in her lap and place his hands—those strong, wiry, long-fingered hands with those carefully sheathed claws—on either side of her neck. He pressed his whiskered muzzle to her cheek, the power of his croon quivering through him as if he were a dynamo, and she locked her right arm around him. She held him close, almost crushing him, and buried her face in the dampness of his soft, outer fur, sobbing as if her heart would break. And even as she wept, she felt him somehow taking the worst hurt, the worst despair and helplessness, from her.

Climbs Quickly accepted the two-leg's tight embrace.

People's eyes didn't shed water as the two-leg's did, but only the mind-blind could possibly have mistaken the grief and fear and pain in the youngling's mind-glow, and he felt a vast surge of protective tenderness for it. For *her*, he realized now, though he wasn't quite certain how he knew. Perhaps it was just that he was becoming more accustomed to the taste of her mind-glow. One could almost always tell whether one of the People was male or female from no more than that, after all. Of course, this youngling was totally unlike the People, but still—

He pressed more firmly against her, stroking her cheek with his muzzle and patting her good shoulder with his left true-hand while he settled more deeply into fusion with her. It wasn't as it would have been with another of his own kind, for she was unable to anchor the fusion properly from her end. But it was enough to let him draw off the worst of her despair. He felt the burden of her fear and pain ease and sensed her surprised awareness that he was somehow responsible, and a deep buzzing purr replaced his croon. He nudged her cheek more firmly, then pulled back just far enough to touch his nose to hers. He stared deep into her eyes, and her good hand caressed his ears. She said something—another of those mouth-sounds which so far meant nothing—but he felt her gratitude and knew the meaningless sounds thanked him for being there.

She leaned back against the tree, easing her broken arm carefully, and he settled down in her lap, wishing with what he hoped was concealed desperation that there was some way to get her away from this place. He knew she remained confused and frightened, and he had no desire to undo all the soothing he'd achieved, yet the scent of the death fang seemed to clog his nostrils. If not for her injured knee, he would have done his best to get her on her feet despite her broken arm. But the tough covering she wore over her legs had torn when she hit the ground, and the knee under it was swollen and purpling around a deep, obviously painful gash. He didn't know if it was actually broken, but he needed no link to know she could move neither fast nor far, and he turned his mind once more towards his sister.

<*Does the clan come?*> he asked urgently, and her reply astonished him.

<We *come,*> Sings Truly repeated with unmistakable emphasis, and he blinked. Surely she didn't mean—?

But then she sent him a brief burst of her own vision, and he realized she did. She was leading every male adult of the clan herself. A *memory singer* was leading the clan's fighting strength into battle with a death fang! That wasn't merely unheard of—it was *unthinkable*. Yet it was happening, and he poured a flood of gratitude towards her.

<*There is no choice, little brother,*> she told him dryly. <*The clan may protect your "youngling" from the death fang, but without me, there will be no one to protect* you *from Broken Tooth and Digger . . . or Song Spinner! Now leave me in peace, Climbs Quickly. I cannot run properly with you nattering at me.*>

He pulled in his thought, basking in his sister's love and trying not to think about the implications of her warning. From the glimpse he'd shared through her eyes, she and the others were making excellent speed. They would be here soon, and only a very stupid death fang would risk attacking anything with an entire clan of People perched protectively in the trees above it. It would not be long until—

Stephanie had fallen into a half-doze, leaning back against the tree. But her head snapped up instantly as the treecat came to his feet in her lap with a harsh, rippling sound like shredding canvas. She'd never heard anything like it, yet she knew instantly what it meant. It was as if the link between them transmitted that meaning to her, and she felt his fear and fury . . . and fierce determination to protect her.

She looked around wildly, trying to find the danger, then gasped, eyes huge in a parchment face, as the hexapuma flowed out of the undergrowth like a great, six-legged shadow of death. It was five meters long, black as night, with its coat seamed with the scars of old combats, and it must have weighed six or seven hundred kilos—as much as a good-sized Old Earth horse. Its lips wrinkled back, baring bone-white canines at least fifteen centimeters long, and its ears flattened as it sent its own rippling snarl—this one voiced in basso thunder—to meet the treecat's.

Terror froze Stephanie, but the treecat leapt from her lap. He sprang up onto a low-growing limb and crouched there, threatening his gargantuan foe from above, and his claws were no longer sheathed. For some reason, the hexapuma hesitated, twisting its head around them, staring up at the trees, almost as if it were afraid of something. But that couldn't last, and she knew it.

"No," she heard herself whisper to her tiny protector. "No, it's too big! Run away. Oh, *please*—please! *Run away!*"

But the treecat ignored her, his green eyes locked on the hexapuma, and despair mixed with her terror. The hexapuma was going to get them both, because she couldn't run away . . . and the treecat *wouldn't*. Somehow she knew, beyond any possibility of question, that the only way the hexapuma would reach her would be through him.

There was very little to sense in the death fang's brain, but Climbs Quickly understood its hesitation. This was an old death fang, and it had not lived this long without learning some hard lessons. Among those lessons must have been what a roused clan could do to its kind, for it had the wit to look for the others who should have been there to support him.

But Climbs Quickly knew what the death fang couldn't. There *were* no other People—not yet. They were coming, tearing through the treetops with frantic, redoubled speed, but they would never arrive in time.

He glared down at the death fang, sounding his challenge, and knew he couldn't win. No single scout or hunter could encounter a death fang and live, yet he could no more abandon his two-leg youngling than he could have abandoned a kitten of the People. He felt her desperate emotions urging him to flee and save himself despite her own terror, even as he felt his sister's mind-voice screaming the same. But it didn't matter. It didn't even matter that the death fang would kill the two-leg the moment he himself was dead. What mattered was that his two-leg—his *person*—must not die alone and abandoned. He would buy her every moment of life he could, and perhaps, just perhaps, it would be long enough for Sings Truly to arrive. He told himself that firmly, fiercely, trying to pretend he didn't know it was a lie.

And then the death fang charged.

Stephanie watched the motionless confrontation as treecat and hexapuma glared and snarled at one another, and the tension tore at her like knives. She couldn't stand it, yet neither could she escape it, and the treecat's utter, hopeless gallantry ripped at her heart. He could have run away. He could have escaped the hexapuma *easily*. But he'd refused, and deep inside, under the panic of an exhausted, hurt, terrified child face-to-face with a murderous menace she should never have encountered, his fierce defiance touched something in *her*. She didn't know what it was. She didn't even realize what was happening. Yet even as the treecat was determined to protect her, she felt an equally fierce, equally unyielding determination to protect *him*.

Her right hand fell to her belt and closed on the hilt of her vibro blade survival knife. It was only a short blade—barely eighteen centimeters long, which was nothing compared to the sixty-centimeter bush knives Forestry Service Rangers carried. But that short blade had a cutting "edge" less than a molecule wide, sharp enough to whittle old-fashioned steel as if it were wood, and it whined to life in her hand as she somehow shoved herself to her feet. She leaned back against the trunk, left arm dangling while terror rose like bile in her throat, and knew her knife was too puny. It would slice through the hexapuma effortlessly, cutting bone as easily as tissue, yet it was too short. The huge predator would tear her apart before she could cut it at all. And even if she somehow did manage to cut it as it charged—even inflict a mortal wound—it was so big and powerful it would kill her before it died. She knew that. But the knife was all she had, and she stared at the hexapuma, hardly daring to breathe, waiting.

And then it charged.

Climbs Quickly saw the death fang move at last. He had time to send out one more urgent message to Sings

Truly. A moment to feel her raging despair and fury at the knowledge she would come too late. And then there was no more time to think. There was no time for anything but speed and violence and ferocity.

Stephanie couldn't believe it. The hexapuma was terrifyingly quick for so huge a creature, yet the treecat sprang from his perch, catapulting through the air in a cream-and-gray streak that somehow evaded the hexapuma's slashing forepaws. He landed on the back of its neck, and it screamed as centimeter-long claws ripped at thick fur and tough skin. It whirled, both rear pairs of limbs planted firmly, forequarters rising as it twisted to snap and claw at the treecat, but its furious blow missed. The treecat had executed his flashing attack only to race further down his enemy's spine and fling himself back up onto the trunk of a near-pine. Then he turned, clinging head-down to the rough bark, snarling his war cry into the teeth of the hexapuma's rage.

The hexapuma forgot about Stephanie. It wheeled, charging the tree in which the treecat waited, rising up on its rear legs and spreading its front and mid-limbs wide to claw at the thick trunk. It dragged itself as high as it could, slashing and snarling, and Stephanie suddenly understood what the treecat was trying to do.

He was *distracting* the hexapuma.

He knew he couldn't kill it or even truly fight it. His attack had been intended to hurt it, to make it angry and direct that anger at *him* and away from her, and it was working. But it was a desperate, ultimately losing game, for he must keep up the attack, keep stinging the hexapuma, and he couldn't be lucky forever.

Climbs Quickly felt a fierce exultation, unlike anything he'd ever imagined.

This was a fight he couldn't win, yet he was eager for it. He *wanted* it, and the blood-red taste of his own fury filled him with fire. He watched the death fang lunge up the green-needle tree and timed his response perfectly. Just as the death fang reached the very top of its leap, he dropped to meet it, claws slashing, and the death fang howled as he shredded its muzzle and tore an ear to pieces. But again its counter-striking forepaws missed him as he sprang away once more.

It charged after him, and he came to meet it yet again. He danced in and out of the trees, pitting blinding speed, skill, and intelligence against the death fang's brute power and cunning. It was a dance which could have only one ending, yet he spun it out far longer than even he would have believed possible before it began.

"*No!*"

Stephanie screamed in useless denial as the treecat finally made a mistake. Perhaps he slipped, or perhaps he'd simply begun to tire at last. She didn't know. She only knew she'd felt a wild, impossible hope as the fight raged on and on. Not that he could win, but that he might not *lose*. Even as she'd let herself hope, she'd known it was in vain, but the suddenness of the end hit her with the cruelty of a hammer.

The treecat was a fraction of a second too slow, lingered to slash at the hexapuma's shoulders for just an instant too long, and a mid-limb paw flashed up savagely. Ten-centimeter claws flashed like scimitars, and she heard—and *felt*—the treecat's scream of agony as that brutal blow landed.

It didn't hit squarely, but it came close enough. It stripped him away from the hexapuma's neck, flicking him aside like a toy, and he screamed again as he slammed into the trunk of a tree. He tumbled down it in a broken, bloody ball of fur, and the hexapuma rose on its rearmost limbs. It hovered there, howling its rage and triumph, and then it lowered all six feet to the ground and crouched to spring and rend and tear and crush its tiny enemy.

Stephanie saw it. She understood it, knew what it intended...and that she couldn't possibly stop it. But the treecat—*her* treecat—had known he couldn't stop it from killing *her*, either, and that hadn't kept him from trying. A part of her knew it was only a pathetic gesture, no more than the hiss and spit of a kitten in the instant before hungry jaws closed on it forever, but it was a gesture she simply could not *not* make.

She lunged, ignoring her snapped rib, the agony in her wounded knee and broken arm. In that moment, she wasn't just a twelve-T-year-old girl. There was no time for her to fully grasp all that was happening, but something inside her had changed forever when the treecat offered his life to save hers, and her scream was a war cry as she brought the vibro blade slashing forward and offered *her* life for his.

The hexapuma shrieked as the high-tech blade sliced into it.

It had forgotten about Stephanie, narrowed all its attention to Climbs Quickly, and it was totally unprepared for the unadulterated agony of that blow. The blade of immaterial force caught it on its right flank, so "sharp" that even a twelve-T-year-old's arm could drive it hilt-deep. The creature's own frantic lunge to escape the pain did the rest, and blood sprayed across the fallen leaves of winters past as its movement dragged the unstoppable blade through muscles, tendons, arteries, and bone.

Stephanie staggered and almost fell as the huge predator squirmed frantically away. Her hand and arm were soaked in its blood, more steaming blood had gouted across her face and eyes, and if she'd had the time for it, she would have been nauseated. But she didn't have time, and she staggered further forward, putting herself between the treecat and the hexapuma.

It was all she could do to stay on her feet. She shook like a leaf, her blood-coated face streaked with tears, while terror yammered within her. Yet somehow she stayed upright and raised the humming blade between them as the hexapuma stared at her in animal disbelief. Its right leg trailed helplessly while blood pulsed from the huge, gaping wound in its flank. But the very sharpness of the vibro blade worked against Stephanie in at least one respect: that wound was fatal, but the hexapuma didn't know it. It would take time to bleed out, and the knife was so sharp, the wound inflicted so quickly, that the creature had no idea of the catastrophic damage it had just received. It only knew it was hurt. Knew that the injured prey it had expected to take so easily had inflicted more agony than any enemy it had ever faced, and it howled its fury.

It paused for just a moment, hissing and spitting. The ears Climbs Quickly had shredded were flat to its skull, and Stephanie knew it was going to charge. She had no more idea than the hexapuma that she'd already inflicted a mortal wound, and she tried to hold her knife steady. It was going to come right over her, but if she could get the knife up, stick it into its chest or belly and let its charge do there what its lunge away had done to its hind quarters, then maybe at least the treecat would—

The hexapuma howled again, and Stephanie wanted desperately to close her eyes. But she couldn't, and she saw it lunge—saw it spring forward in the first of the two leaps it would take to reach her, dragging its crippled leg, fang-studded maw agape.

Only it never completed that lunge.

Stephanie's head jerked up as a dreadful noise filled the forest. She'd heard a single echo of that sound from the treecat who'd fought to protect her, but this wasn't the defiant cry of one hopelessly gallant defender. This was the rippling snarl of dozens—scores—of treecats, filled with hate and vengeance, and its challenge pierced even the hexapuma's rage. Its head snapped up, as Stephanie's had done, and its yowl was filled with as much panic as fury as the trees exploded above it.

A cream-and-gray avalanche thundered down with a massed, high-pitched scream that seemed to shake the forest. It engulfed the hexapuma in an unstoppable flood of slashing ivory claws and needle-sharp fangs, and Stephanie Harrington collapsed beside a dreadfully wounded Climbs Quickly as the scouts and hunters of his clan literally ripped their foe to pieces.

"I'M HOME!" RICHARD HARRINGTON CALLED OUT AS he walked into the living room.

"About time," Marjorie replied from her office. She was at the end of the section anyway, so she hit save and closed the report, then rose and stretched.

"Hey, don't give me a hard time," her husband told her severely as he walked down the short hallway and poked his head in her door. "*You* may be able to do a full day's work without going anywhere, but some of us have patients who require our direct, personal attendance. Not to mention a superb bedside manner."

"'Bedside manner,' right!" Marjorie snorted, and Richard grinned as he leaned close to kiss her cheek. She put an arm around him and hugged him briefly.

"Did Steph have a good day with Mayor Sapristos?" she went on.

"What?" Richard pulled back with a strange expression, and she cocked an eyebrow.

"I asked if Stephanie had a good day with Mayor Sapristos," she said, and Richard frowned.

"I didn't drop her off in Twin Forks," he said. "I didn't have time, so I left her home. Didn't I tell you I was going to?"

"Left her home?" Margie repeated in surprise. "Here? On the freehold?"

"Of course! Where else would I—" Richard broke off as he recognized his wife's incomprehension. "Are you saying you haven't seen her all day?"

"I certainly haven't! Would I have asked you about Mr. Sapristos if I *had*?"

"But—"

Richard broke off again, and his frown deepened. He stood for a moment, thinking hard, then turned and half-ran down the hall. Marjorie heard the front door open and close—then it opened and closed again, seconds later, and Richard was back.

"Her glider's gone," he told Marjorie grimly.

"But you said you didn't take her to town," Marjorie protested.

"I didn't," he said even more grimly. "So if her glider's gone, she must've gone off on a flight of her own... without telling either of us."

Marjorie stared at him, her own mind filled with a cascade of chaotic thoughts and sudden, half-formed fears. Then she took a firm mental grip on herself and cleared her throat.

"If she went out on her own, she should be back by now," she said as calmly as she could. "It's getting dark, and she would've wanted to be home before that happened."

"Absolutely," Richard agreed, and the tension in their locked gazes was just short of panic. An inextricable brew of fear for their daughter, guilt for not having watched her more closely, and—hard though they tried to suppress it—*anger* at her for evading their watchfulness flowed through them. But there was no time for that. Richard shook himself, then raised his uni-link and tapped the key that brought up the communicator interface. It blinked, and he cleared his throat.

"Screen Stephanie," he said in a voice he *made* come out clear and crisp.

Then he waited, right forefinger and second finger drumming anxiously on the com's wristband, and his face went bleak as the seconds oozed past with no reply. He waited a full minute, a minute in which his eyes became agate and the last expression leached from his face, and Marjorie caught his upper right arm. She squeezed tightly, but she said nothing, for she, too, understood what that lack of reply meant.

It took a painful act of will for Richard Harrington to accept the silence, but then his forefinger moved again. He keyed another combination, and inhaled sharply as a red light began to flash almost instantly on the uni-link display. In one way, the light was almost worse than the total lack of response had been; in another, it was an enormous relief. At least it gave them a beacon to track—one which would guide them to their daughter. But if her emergency beacon was working, the rest of the unit should also be functional. And if it was—if it had produced the high-pitched buzz which was guaranteed to be audible from a distance of thirty meters—then Stephanie should have answered it. If she hadn't, there had to be a reason, and neither Harrington had the courage to voice what that reason might well be.

"Grab the emergency med kit," Richard said instead, his voice harsh. "I'll get my car back out of the garage."

Stephanie Harrington couldn't hear the signal from the lost uni-link that hung on the stub of a limb in the middle of a wreckage trail more than fifty meters above her and almost a hundred meters behind her. Nor was she even thinking about uni-links, for she was surrounded by over two hundred treecats. They perched on branches, clung to trunks, and crouched with her on the wet leaves. Two actually sat pressed against her sides, and they—like all the rest—crooned a deep, soft harmony to the bloody, mauled ball of fur in her lap.

She was grateful for their presence, and she knew those scores of guardians could—and would—protect her from any other predators. Yet she had little thought to spare them, for every scrap of her attention was fixed with desperate strength on *her* treecat, as if somehow she could keep him alive by sheer force of will. The pain of her arm and knee and ribs and her residual, quivering terror still filled her, but those things scarcely mattered. They were there, and they were real, but nothing—literally *nothing*—was as important as the treecat she cuddled with fierce protectiveness in the crook of her good arm.

Her memory of what had happened after the other treecats poured down from the trees was vague. She recalled switching off the vibro knife, but she hadn't gotten it back into its sheath. She must have dropped it somewhere, but it didn't matter. All that had mattered was getting to her treecat.

She'd known he was alive. There was no way she could *not* know, but she'd also known he was desperately hurt, and her stomach had knotted as she fell to her good knee beside him. Her own pain had made her whimper whenever she moved, yet she'd hardly noticed that as she touched her protector—her *friend*, however he'd become that—with fearful fingers.

Blood matted his right side, and she'd felt fresh nausea as she saw how badly his right forelimb was mangled. The blood flow was terrifying—without the spurt of a severed artery, but far too thick and heavy. She had no idea how his internal anatomy was arranged, but her frightened touch had felt what had to be the jagged give of broken bones, and his mid-limbs' pelvis was clearly broken, as well. She'd cringed at the thought of the damage all those broken bones could have done inside him, but there was nothing she could do about them. That shattered forelimb needed immediate attention, however, and she plucked the drawstring from the left cuff of her flying jacket. Tying it into a slip noose with only her teeth and one working hand was impossibly difficult, yet she managed it somehow, and slipped it up the broken, bloodsoaked limb. She settled it just above the ripped and torn flesh and drew it tight, bending close to use her teeth again. Then she worked a pocket stylus under the improvised tourniquet and tightened it carefully. She'd never done anything like this herself, but she knew the theory, and she'd once seen her father do the same thing for an Irish setter who'd lost most of a leg to a robotic cultivator.

It worked, and she sagged in relief as the blood flow slowed, then stopped. She knew that cutting off all blood from the damaged tissues would only damage them worse in the long run, but at least he wouldn't bleed to death now. Unless, she thought, fighting a suddenly resurgent panic, there *was* internal bleeding.

She didn't really want to move him, but she couldn't leave him lying on the cold, wet ground. He had to be in shock after such traumatic injuries. That meant he needed warmth, and she lowered herself to the ground to sit beside him and lift him as carefully as she could with only one hand. She flinched when he twisted with a high-pitched sound, like the mewl of a broken kitten, but she didn't put him back down. Instead, she tucked him inside her unsealed flying jacket and tugged the loose flaps closed around him as well as her single working arm could manage. Then she leaned back against the tree he'd been flung against, whimpering with her own pain, holding him against her and trying to fight his shock and blood loss with the warmth of her own body.

She didn't think about her missing uni-link, or her parents, or her own pain. She didn't think of anything. She only sat there, cuddling her defender's broken body against her own, and thought of nothing at all.

That was all she had the strength to do.

The elders of Bright Water Clan sat in a circle about the young two-leg. All of them, even Song Spinner, who had come after the others for the sole purpose of berating Sings Truly for her incredible folly in risking herself in such a fashion. But no one was berating anyone now. Instead, the other elders watched in confusion and uncertainty as Sings Truly and Short Tail crept closer to the two-leg. The chief scout and the clan's second-ranking memory singer crouched on either side of the two-leg, quivering noses scarcely a handspan's distance from it. They sniffed it carefully, and then reached out to touch the link between it and Climbs Quickly.

Sings Truly's ears went flat in shock that, even for her—even now—was honed by disbelief. Despite the alienness of the two-leg, Climbs Quickly's link to it was *at least* as strong as that of any mated pair she'd ever encountered. More than that, the link clearly had yet to reach its maximum strength. It couldn't possibly happen—not with a creature as obviously and completely mind-blind as the two-leg. Yet it *had* happened, and Sings Truly's mind whirled as she tried to imagine the ramifications of that simple fact.

The rest of her clan's adult fighting strength sat or crouched or hung behind and above and all about her and the two-leg. As she, they'd watched the youngling, tasting its pain like their own as it dragged its gravely injured body to Climbs Quickly. As Sings Truly, they had tasted its fear for him, its tenderness and frantic concern. Its . . . love. And, as Sings Truly, they had watched the youngling—surely no more than a kitten itself—tighten the string which had stopped Climbs Quickly's bleeding before he died. And then they'd watched the two-leg gather him against itself, hugging him, giving of its own body heat to him, and the music of the clan's soft, approving croon had risen about the two-leg.

The clan had reached out, able to touch the two-leg—albeit indirectly—through its link to Climbs Quickly, and their massed touch had calmed the youngling's fear and pain and eased it tenderly into a gentle mind haze. The People of Bright Water took its hurt upon themselves and soothed it into something very like sleep, and it was safe for them to do so, for nothing that walked the world's forests could threaten or harm Climbs Quickly or his two-leg through their watchful ring of claws and fangs.

Sings Truly saw all that, understood all that, and deep inside, wanted—as she had never wanted anything before—to hate the two-leg. Climbs Quickly might live. His mind-glow was weak, yet it was there, and even now she felt his awareness creeping slowly, doggedly back towards the surface. But he was terribly hurt, and those hurts were the two-leg's fault. It was the two-leg which had drawn him here. It was the two-leg for which he'd fought his impossible battle, risked—and all too probably lost—his life. And even if he lived, he would have only one true-hand, and that, too, was the two-leg's fault.

Yet badly as Sings Truly wished to hate the two-leg, she knew Climbs Quickly had *chosen* to come. Or perhaps not. Perhaps the strength of his link to this alien creature had left him no choice *but* to come. Yet if that was true, it was equally true that the two-leg had been given no choice, either. They were one, as tightly bound as any mated pair, and Sings Truly knew it . . . just as she knew her brother, as she herself, would have fought to the death to protect his mate.

And so would this two-leg. Youngling or no, despite broken bones and legs which would scarcely bear it, this barely weaned kitten had attacked a *death fang* single-handed. Climbs Quickly had done the same, but he had been an adult—and uninjured. The two-leg had been neither, but it had risen above its wounds, above its broken bones and terror, to fight the same terrible foe for Climbs Quickly. No youngling of the People, and all too few of the People's adults, could have done that. And without the two-leg, Climbs Quickly would already be dead, so—

<How shall we untangle this knot, Sings Truly?>

The question came from Short Tail, and though it was directed to Sings Truly, the chief scout had thought it loudly enough to be certain all of the elders heard him.

<We should leave while we still can!> Broken Tooth replied sharply, before Sings Truly could. *<The danger of this is far too great! Sooner or later, this two-leg's fellows will come seeking it, and we must not be here when they do.>*

<And Climbs Quickly?> Short Tail asked bitingly, and the People's ability to taste one another's emotions was not a useful thing at the moment. Broken Tooth felt the scout's searing contempt as clearly as if Short Tail had shouted it aloud—which, indeed, he had in a way—and his own mind-voice was hot when he replied.

<Climbs Quickly chose *to come here!>* he snapped. *<He was told to stay away from the two-legs—that Shadow Hider would have that duty—yet he disobeyed. Not content with that, he summoned the clan to save the two-leg from a death fang, despite the danger. Many of us might have been killed or hurt by such an enemy, and you know it!*

I am sorry for his wounds, and I wish him no evil, but what has happened to him stems from his own decisions. Our task is to safeguard our entire clan, and to do that we must be far away when the other two-legs arrive. If that requires us to leave Climbs Quickly to his fate, it cannot be helped.>

<*It was not Climbs Quickly who summoned the clan,*> Song Spinner observed with frigid disapproval. <*Or not directly. It was you, Sings Truly, and you knew he was trying to protect the two-leg!*>

<*It was, and I did.*> The calmness of Sings Truly's reply surprised even her. <*Oh, I did not* know, *but that was only because I had declined to ask him. So, yes, senior singer. I knew what Climbs Quickly desired. Perhaps I was even wrong to give it to him. But even if I was wrong,* he *most certainly was not.*>

The other elders stared at her in consternation, and she turned from her contemplation of the young two-leg and her brother to face them.

<*Climbs Quickly and this two-leg are linked,*> she told them. <*I have tasted that link, and so can any of you, if you doubt me. He was defending... not his "mate," precisely, but something very close to it. This is his two-leg, and he is its. He could no more have failed to protect it than he could have failed to protect me or I him.*>

<*Prettily said,*> Song Spinner said acidly when none of the males would meet Sings Truly's eyes or refute her words. <*Perhaps even true... for Climbs Quickly. But Broken Tooth speaks for the rest of the clan. We have no link to this two-leg, and surely this is only fresh proof of the danger of hasty contact with them. Look at your brother, memory singer, and tell me risking further contact with these creatures is not the path of madness!*>

<*Very well, senior singer,*> Sings Truly said, still with that same astounding calm and clarity of mind-voice.

<If you wish, I will tell you exactly that. Indeed, what has happened here is the clearest proof that we must seek out more *contact with the two-legs, for we must learn if more of the People can establish such bonds with them.>*

<More *bonds?*> Broken Tooth gasped.

He and Digger gawked at her in horror, but Song Spinner stared at her in shock too profound for any other emotion. Short Tail, on the other hand, crouched beside her radiating fierce agreement, and they were joined—albeit with less certainty—by Fleet Wind, the elder charged with the instruction of young scouts and hunters, and by Stone Biter, who led the clan's flint shapers.

<More bonds,> Sings Truly replied levelly, and Broken Tooth hissed—not in anger, for no male would ever show challenge to a senior memory singer, whatever the provocation, but in utter rejection.

<No, hear me out!> Sings Truly commanded. *<Right or wrong, I* am *a singer. You* will *hear me, and the clan— the* clan, *Broken Tooth, not simply the elders—will* judge *between us on this!>*

Broken Tooth reared back in astonishment, and Song Spinner twitched in even greater shock. As the clan's second-ranking singer, Sings Truly had every right to make that demand. Yet by making it, she had in effect challenged Song Spinner's own position. She'd appealed to the entire clan, seeking the judgment of the majority of its adults, when all knew Song Spinner opposed her. If the clan chose to support Sings Truly, *she* would become Bright Water's senior singer, while if the clan chose to reject her, she would be stripped of all authority.

But the challenge had been issued, and the clan adults drew closer.

<What my brother has done, the bond he has formed with this two-leg, was not of his choice,> Sings Truly said quietly but clearly. *<It could not have been his choice, for*

none of the People even guessed such a thing was possible. Nor could he—or any of us—have known how to establish such a link with a two-leg even had we desired to do so. But he did establish the link, and though the two-leg is mind-blind and clearly fails to understand what has happened, it shares the link. It is as linked to him as he is to it. Is that not true, senior singer?>

Sings Truly looked directly at Song Spinner, and Bright Water's senior singer could only flick her ears in curt agreement, for it was obvious to all—singer and non-singer alike—that it *was* true.

<Very well,> Sings Truly continued. *<We did not know— then—that such links were possible. We do know now, however, just as all of us have seen proof of the link's depth and power. Climbs Quickly fought the death fang for his two-leg, but the two-leg also fought the death fang for* him, *and by the standards of its own kind, this two-leg is but a kitten. We dare not judge all two-legs by its actions, yet we dare not reject its example, either. We must learn more about them and their tools and their purpose in being here. They are too dangerous, and there are too many of them, and their numbers increase too quickly for us* not *to learn those things. Climbs Quickly was right in that . . . and the very things which make them so dangerous could also make them powerful* allies.*>*

Not a whisper rose among her listeners. Every eye was fixed upon her, and even Broken Tooth's tail had stopped its lashing, for it had never occurred to him to consider what the two-legs could do *for* the People. He'd been too aware of all the threats the intruders posed *to* them, and Sings Truly felt her hope rise higher as she tasted the shifting emotions of his mind-glow.

<If others of the People can—and choose to—form such links, we will learn much. If they go with those with whom they link to live among the two-legs, they will see far more than we can ever see spying upon them from the shadows.

They can report to us, tell us of all they learn, help us to understand the two-legs. And remember the nature of such links. The two-legs do, indeed, appear to be mind-blind. Certainly this one is. Yet for all its blindness, it senses the link. It feels and recognizes Climbs Quickly's love for it . . . and returns that love. I think it is clear from Climbs Quickly's original report that this two-leg thought him no more clever than the ground runners or lake builders when first it met him. It knows better now, yet it cannot know how much more clever the People are. Perhaps it would be as well if we do not let it or its elders know just how clever we are, for it is always wise to let those we do not know well underestimate us. But let us also build more links with the two-legs, if such we can. Let us learn, and let those of the People who share such links with them teach them that we do not threaten them. There is much room in the world. Surely enough for us to share it with the two-legs if we can make them our friends.>

The mental silence lingered, hovering in the wet, rapidly darkening woods. And then, in the way of the People, it was broken by mind-voices in ones and twos, choosing their course.

RICHARD HARRINGTON'S FACE WAS WHITE AS THE AIR car's powerful lights picked the wreckage trail from the darkness.

The icon of Stephanie's emergency beacon glowed in the dead center of his air car's HUD, indicating that it lay almost directly below him, but he didn't really need it. Bits and pieces of the mangled hang glider were strewn through the tops of three different trees, and the continued silence from his daughter's end of the com link was suddenly even more terrifying.

He didn't know what Stephanie had been doing out here, but she'd clearly been trying to reach the clearing ahead when she went down, and he sent the air car scudding forward. Marjorie sat tense and silent beside him, twisting the control that swept the starboard spotlight in a wide half-circle on her side of the car. Richard was just reaching for the control to the port light when Marjorie gasped.

"Richard! *Look!*"

His head snapped around at his wife's command, and his jaw dropped.

Stephanie sat huddled against the base of a huge tree, clasping something against her with one arm. Her clothing was torn and bloody, but her head rose as he looked at her. She stared back into the lights, and even from his seat in the air car, he saw the bottomless relief on her bruised and bloody face. Yet even as he recognized that, and even as his heart leapt to a joy so sharp it was anguish, stunned surprise held him frozen.

His daughter was not alone.

A grisly ruin of white bone and mangled tissue lay to one side. Richard had done enough anatomical studies of Sphinxian animal life to recognize the half-stripped skeleton of a hexapuma. But neither he nor any other naturalist had ever seen or imagined anything like the dozens and dozens and *dozens* of tiny "hexapumas" who surrounded his daughter protectively.

He blinked, astonished by his own choice of adverb, yet it was the only one which fitted. They were *protecting* Stephanie, watching over her. And he knew—as if he'd seen it with his own eyes—that *they*, whatever they were, had killed the hexapuma to save her.

But that was all he knew, and he touched Marjorie's arm gently.

"Stay here," he said quietly. "This is more my area than yours."

"But—"

"Please, Marge," he said, still in that quiet voice. "I don't think there's any danger—now—but I could be wrong. Just stay here while I find out, all right?"

Marjorie Harrington's jaw clenched, but she fought

down her unreasoning surge of anger, for he was right. He was the xeno-veterinarian. If the problem had been plant life, he would have deferred to *her* expertise; in this case she must defer to his, however her heart raged at her to rush to her daughter's side.

"All right," she said grudgingly. "But you be careful!"

"I will," he promised, and popped the hatch.

He climbed out slowly and walked very carefully towards his daughter, carrying the emergency medical kit. The sea of furry, long-tailed arboreals parted about his feet, retreating perhaps a meter to either side and then flowing back in behind him, and he felt their watchful eyes as he stepped into the small clear space about Stephanie. A single creature crouched by her side—smaller and more slender than the others, with a dappled brown-and-white coat instead of their cream and gray—and he felt its grass-green eyes bore into him. But despite the unnerving intelligence behind that scrutiny, his attention was on his daughter. This close, the bruises and blood stains—few of the latter hers, thank God!—were far more evident, and his stomach clenched at the evidence of her injuries. Her left arm hung beside her, obviously badly broken, and her right leg was stretched stiffly before her, and he had to blink back tears as he dropped to his knees.

"Hello, baby," he said gently, and she looked at him.

"I messed up, Daddy," she whispered, and tears welled in her own eyes. "Oh, Daddy! I messed *everything* up! I—"

"Hush, baby." His voice quivered, and he cupped the right side of her face in his palm. "We'll have time for that later. For now, let's get you home, okay?"

She nodded, but something in her expression told him there was more. He frowned speculatively—and then his eyebrows shot up as she opened her jacket to reveal another of the creatures hovering all about them.

He stared at the brutally mauled animal, then jerked his eyes to his daughter's.

Stephanie read the question in her father's gaze. There wasn't time to explain everything—that would have to come later, when she also accepted whatever thoroughly merited punishment her parents decided to levy—but she nodded.

"He's my friend." Her voice trembled, heavy with tears—the voice of a child begging her parents to tell her the problem could be fixed, the damage mended... the friend saved.

"He...he saved me from the hexapuma," she went on, fighting to keep that fraying voice steady. "He *fought* it, Daddy—fought it for *me* all by himself—until the others came, and he got hurt so *bad*. I—"

Her voice broke at last, and she stared at her father, white-faced with exhaustion, pain, fear, and grief. Richard Harrington looked back, his own heart broken by her distress, and cupped her face between both his hands.

"Don't worry, baby," he told his daughter softly. "If he helped you, then I'll help *him* any way I can."

Climbs Quickly floated slowly, slowly up out of the blackness.

He lay on his left side on something warm and soft, and he blinked. He felt the pain of his hurts and knew they were serious, yet there was something strange about the *way* they hurt. The pain was distant and far away, as if something were making it less than it should have been, and he turned his head. He looked up, seeking what he already knew was there, and made a soft sound—a weak parody of his normal, buzzing purr—as he saw the face of his two-leg.

She looked down quickly, and the brilliant flare of her

joy and relief at seeing him move blazed through the odd, pleasantly lazy haziness which afflicted his thoughts. She touched his fur gently, and he realized the blood had been cleaned from her face. White bits of something covered the worst of her cuts and scratches, and her broken arm was sheathed in some stiff, equally white material. He tasted an echo of pain still coloring her mind-glow, but the echo was almost as muted as his own. She opened her mouth and made more of the sounds the two-legs used to communicate, and he rolled his head the other way as another, deeper voice replied.

His person was seated on one of the two-legs' sitting things, he realized, but it took several more breaths to realize the sitting thing was inside one of the flying things. He might not have realized even then, without his link to his person. But that same link—and the haziness—kept him from panicking at the thought of tearing through the heavens at the speed at which the flying things regularly moved.

Two more two-legs—his two-leg's parents—sat in front of them. One looked back at his two-leg, and he blinked again as their link helped him to recognize her as *his* two-leg's mother. But it was the other adult—his two-leg's father—who spoke. The deep, rumbling sound still meant nothing, and Climbs Quickly wondered vaguely if he would ever really learn to understand these strange creatures.

"He looked at me, Daddy!" Stephanie cried. "He opened his eyes and *looked* at me!"

"That's a good sign, Steph," Richard replied, putting as much encouragement as he could into his voice.

"But he looks awfully weak and groggy," Stephanie went on in a more worried tone, and Richard turned his head to exchange glances with Marjorie.

Despite the painkillers, Stephanie still had to be suffering fairly extreme discomfort, but there was no concern at all for herself in her voice. Every bit of it was for the creature—the "treecat"—in her lap, and it had been ever since they'd found her. She'd insisted that her father examine the "treecat" even before he set her arm, and given the vast, silently watching audience of *other* treecats—and the fact that Stephanie, at least, was in no immediately life-threatening danger—he'd agreed. Neither he nor Marjorie could make much sense of the bits and pieces of explanation they'd so far heard, but they'd already concluded that Stephanie was right about one thing. Whatever else they might be, these treecats of hers were another sentient species.

God only knew where *that* was going to end, and, at the moment, Richard and Marjorie Harrington didn't much care. The treecats had saved their daughter's life. That was a debt they could never hope to repay, but they were quite prepared to spend the rest of their lives trying to, and he cleared his throat carefully.

"He looks weak because he *is*, honey," he said now, turning back to his HUD as the air car sped towards the Twin Forks infirmary and his own veterinary office. "He's hurt pretty badly, and he lost a lot of blood before you got that tourniquet on him. Without that, he'd be dead by now, you know."

Stephanie recognized the approval in his voice, but she only nodded impatiently.

"The painkiller I used is probably making him look a little groggy, too," he went on. "But we've been using it on Sphinxian species for over forty T-years without any dangerous side effects."

"But will he be *all right*?" his daughter demanded insistently, and he gave a tiny shrug.

"I'm pretty sure he's going to live, Steph," he promised.

"I don't think we'll be able to save his forelimb, and he'll have some scars—maybe some that show even through his fur—but he should recover completely except for that. I can't *guarantee* it, baby, but you know I wouldn't lie to you about something like this."

Stephanie stared at the back of his head for a moment, then swiveled her eyes to her mother. Marjorie gazed back and nodded firmly, backing up Richard's prognosis, and a frozen boulder seemed to thaw in Stephanie's middle.

"You're *sure*, Dad?" she demanded, but her voice was no longer desperate, and he nodded again.

"Sure as I can be, honey," he told her, and she sighed and stroked the treecat's head again. It blinked wide, unfocused green eyes at her, and she bent to brush a kiss between its triangular ears.

"Hear that?" she whispered to it. "You're gonna be all right. Daddy said so."

Yes, Climbs Quickly thought fuzzily, he really did have to start learning what the two-legs' sounds meant. But not tonight. Tonight he was simply too tired, and it didn't matter right now, anyway. What mattered was the mind-glow of his two-leg, and the knowledge that she was safe.

He blinked up at her and managed to pat her leg weakly with his good arm. Then he closed his eyes with a sigh, snuggled his nose more firmly against her, and let the welcome and love of her mind-glow sing him to sleep.

WITH FRIENDS LIKE THESE...

1520–1521 Post Diaspora

Planet Sphinx,

Manticore Binary Star System

13

"YOUR FOURTEEN-HUNDRED APPOINTMENT IS HERE, Chief," Chief Ranger Gary Shelton's desk terminal announced. It would have been unfair to say he grimaced as he turned from his office window's view of the sun-drenched sidewalks of Twin Forks, but he definitely rolled his eyes before he walked back around to his desk and seated himself.

"Thank you, Francine," he said with scarcely a wince.

"You're welcome," Francine Samarina, his longtime secretary and the official chief receptionist and general all-around manager of the Sphinx Forestry Service, replied from the terminal's display. Shelton looked at her a bit suspiciously, but he decided he couldn't really accuse her of grinning at him. No, that was probably just his imagination. *Surely* she wouldn't find the thought that her boss was being stalked remorselessly by a thirteen-and-a-half-year-old girl *amusing*.

Of course not, he thought sourly. *And if I did accuse*

*her of it, she'd only put on her best "Who, me?" expression
and deny it, anyway.*

"Send them in, please," he said instead, and rose to
stand in courteous greeting as his office door opened.

A man, a woman, a child, and a . . . treecat came through
the door.

The man was tall and probably in his late thirties, with
dark hair just starting to silver and dark eyes. His wife
was about the same age, with a fairer complexion and eyes
that hovered somewhere between brown and hazel. The
child looked to be about thirteen or fourteen T-years old,
with her father's dark brown eyes and a riotously curly
version of her mother's more carefully controlled hair.

And looking around alertly from her shoulder was a
treecat, a representative of the native Sphinxian species
whose discovery just over a T-year ago had done so much
to complicate Shelton's life.

At first, no one had paid much attention to the possibility that the creatures might actually be sentient. In
fact, there'd been a pronounced tendency to scoff at the
entire notion. After all, as some had pointed out, the
Harringtons had only migrated to Sphinx less than three
T-years earlier. Who could honestly believe that such
newcomers (some, like Jordan Franchitti, leaned towards
the use of less complimentary terms) could possibly have
discovered a *sentient species* of which no one else had ever
caught so much as a glimpse? And that nonsense about
their having "rescued" the girl from a hexapuma (and what
kind of idiot family let a twelve-T-year-old *encounter* a
hexapuma, in the first place?) was downright ridiculous!

Shelton had been inclined to doubt the stories of sentience himself, but only until Scott MacDallan and then
Arvin Erhardt had encountered them as well. Of course,
Dr. MacDallan was another "newcomer" as far as someone
like Franchitti was concerned, but Erhardt's family had

arrived aboard the colony ship *Jason*. Even Franchitti had
to take him seriously when he insisted treecats not only
existed but were extraordinarily smart.

Of course, there could still be a huge gap between a
"smart" animal and a genuinely sentient species. Which
was why Sphinx was now finding itself inundated by such
a plethora of scientists—busybodies making all sorts of
trouble for his chronically understaffed rangers. Which,
in turn, was the reason he regarded the creature on the
girl's shoulder with decidedly mixed feelings.

Even without its tail, the treecat was was over a third
as long as the girl was tall, which (Shelton thought) made
her look just a bit silly carrying him around on her back.
She'd rigged a light harness with a tough fabric pad on
top of her right shoulder, and the six-limbed treecat had
sunk the curved claws of his mid-limb feet lightly into
the padding for balance. Most of his weight, however,
was supported by his rearmost feet, which were dug
into a second protective pad just below the girl's right
shoulder blade. His head and shoulders stuck up above
that shoulder, and his tail curved up and over, draping
its very tip across the top of her left shoulder where it
brushed very gently against her cheek.

There were peculiar streaks, almost shadows, through
his thick, silken pelt of cream and gray fur. Places where
the fur didn't lie quite the way it should because of the
fierce scars underneath it. And while the long fingers of
his left forepaw rested lightly on the girl's head, there was
no right forepaw to match it, for only a short stub of his
amputated right forelimb remained.

"Good afternoon, Doctors," Shelton said, holding out
his hand to the parents. They shook it in turn, and he
looked at the girl.

"And good afternoon to you, Ms. Harrington," he said.
"Why don't we all be seated?"

Stephanie was on her very best behavior.

She let both of her parents and the chief ranger sit before she settled into her own chair, and then Lionheart (her father had suggested the name, since however small he was, he obviously had a lion's heart) swarmed down from her shoulder into her lap. Had the chair back been a little wider, he would have stretched out along it lengthwise and lain against the back of her neck; instead, he settled on his rear limbs, sitting upright and leaning back against her while he cocked his head and regarded Chief Ranger Shelton with bright green eyes.

Stephanie didn't know how well Lionheart was going to follow today's meeting. It was pretty obvious Standard English was still going right past him. He did seem to have become increasingly adroit at figuring out what she was trying to get across in day-to-day life, but trying to explain something like this by gesture and pantomime had been well beyond her abilities. On the other hand, if he was understanding her at all he was doing better than she was at understanding him. His vocal apparatus was hopelessly ill-suited for producing the sounds of any human language, which meant he couldn't possibly speak to her even if he ever learned to understand her, and the best she could say was that she was beginning to be able to interpret his body language with a fair degree of certainty.

Or at least I think I am. I guess it's always possible I'm still getting all of it wrong.

She didn't think she was, though. And if she *was* reading him correctly, whatever he was picking up from Chief Ranger Shelton wasn't very hopeful.

"Thank you for seeing us, Chief Ranger," her father said. "I know there's always more going on than you have time to deal with. I hope we won't have to take up a lot more of your time with this."

"I am busy," Shelton acknowledged, and allowed himself to grimace. "The Plague hammered all of us, but I sometimes think the Forestry Service got hammered even harder than the rest of the star system." He shook his head, his expression tightening further. "I lost better than half my uniformed personnel, and over a third of my clerical and support staff. We're trying to rebuild, but with so many other crying needs for manpower, well—"

He shrugged, and all three Harringtons nodded in sober understanding.

"Actually," he continued with the air of a man taking the bull firmly by the horns, "that shortage of manpower is one of the reasons why I'm afraid I'm not going to be able to meet your request."

Stephanie felt her face lose expression, but she couldn't really pretend that answer came as a surprise. Her parents were firmly in her corner on this one, yet they'd all recognized that it would be an uphill fight...and that not all the reasons it was going to be so hard were bad ones.

And some of those reasons are going to change in the next T-year or so, too, she reminded herself firmly. *Which is why the last thing we need is for me to start kicking up a fuss about it now. But, darn it, it's hard to remember "it's better to live to fight another day," even if Dad is right about it!*

"I know that's not what you wanted to hear, Stephanie," Shelton said, at least doing her the courtesy of speaking to her directly. "I'm sorry about that. But I'm afraid my decision is final."

"Can I ask why?"

She kept her voice as level as she could, but she knew there was an edge of anger in it. He obviously heard it, but he only nodded to her, as if he were acknowledging her right to feel it.

"There are several reasons," he told her. "First, the Sphinx Forestry Service has never had an internship program, and especially not a *junior* internship program. We weren't set up for one even before the Plague hit, much less now. You have to understand, Stephanie. This entire star system's been colonized for only about one T-century. The first colonists didn't land on Sphinx for fifty T-years after that, so there's only *been* a Sphinx Forestry Service for about thirty-five T-years. Then the Plague came along and killed sixty percent of our total population. Both my parents died, and so did my older brother, and most of the survivors of the first wave could tell pretty much the same story. You know all that, I know. The only reason I'm mentioning it is that as pleased as I am whenever I find anyone who wants to be a ranger," (he sounded as if he truly meant that, she thought), "Sphinx isn't Meyerdahl. We're badly understaffed, we're especially short of the kinds of specialists we need, we've got a lot more wilderness area—like, oh, ninety-nine-point-nine percent of the planet—to take care of, and that wilderness is *real* wilderness. The Sphinx bush isn't like Meyerdahl's nature preserves. We haven't even begun to survey it properly yet, and to be brutally honest, it's a lot more dangerous."

He held her eyes for a moment with the last two words, then let his own eyes flick sideways to the scarred, maimed treecat in her lap.

"The fact is that you're lucky to be alive, young lady," he said quietly. "I'm not condemning you for having done anything wrong when I say that, either. I mean it. You're alive because you were lucky, but also because you were smart and capable, and because you had some... unexpected help. But if all of that hadn't broken exactly right, you'd be dead. You realize that, don't you?"

"Yes, sir," Stephanie said softly. The memory of that horrible afternoon washed through her on the heels of the chief ranger's words, and she wrapped her arms tightly around Lionheart. The treecat leaned back against her, buzzing a gentle purr, and patted her forearm gently with a true-hand.

"Well, that's the bottom line," Shelton said, turning back to her parents. "I don't have a program I could insert your daughter into. However much I might *like* to, I just don't have the manpower or the funding to set one up, either. And, to be frank, Stephanie's discovery of the treecats only makes that worse. We're beginning to be flooded by out-system xeno-anthropologists and xeno-biologists, and I'm afraid most of them are a lot less adept at surviving in the bush than your daughter's demonstrated *she* is. The Interior Ministry's insisting I have to provide nursemaids to look after them, and at the same time, I have to protect the treecats *from* them." He shook his head. "Governor Donaldson keeps promising me more budget and more personnel, and I believe she's doing her best. But I also know I'm going to see the budget before I see the warm bodies, and that's just making bad worse. I don't see any way I could possibly justify setting up any sort of intern-ship/training program at this point, because I simply don't have the personnel to divert to it. And I'm not about to sign off on any kind of 'intern' arrangement that isn't closely supported and monitored by fully trained, *adult* rangers. The bush is simply too dangerous for me to even consider anything like that."

14

"I WISH I COULD SAY ANY OF THAT HAD COME AS A surprise," Richard Harrington said as the family air car headed back towards the Harrington freehold.

"*I* wish he wasn't so darned . . . *reasonable* about it all," Stephanie replied.

"Well, he makes a lot of sense, too, Steph," Marjorie Harrington pointed out. "It's hard not to sympathize with him, you know."

"That's what I meant." Stephanie sighed, gazing out the side window and stroking Lionheart where he lay across her lap. "I still think he's wrong, but I think he's being as reasonable about it as he thinks he can be. Lionheart thinks that, too."

Her parents glanced at one another. It was hard to remember sometimes that Lionheart had come into their lives barely sixteen T-months ago. In fact, it often seemed he'd always been part of their family. Yet other times they were forcibly reminded of how short sixteen months truly were, and seldom more so than when Stephanie said something like that. There seemed to be absolutely no doubt in her mind that she was correctly interpreting Lionheart's emotions. For that matter, having watched the two of them together, Richard and Marjorie were of the opinion that she usually *did* interpret them correctly. But was that simply because she was getting better at reading his body language? Or was... something else at work?

Stephanie was aware of what her parents were thinking, and she fully understood the reasons for the skepticism of many of the adults she and Lionheart had encountered. Despite which, she *knew* she was reading the treecat's emotions correctly.

Exactly how treecats communicated with one another was only one of the countless unanswered questions about the newly discovered species. No one had paid them a lot of attention at first (since no one had really seemed to believe her story in the first place) but then, over the next four or five T-months, Dr. MacDallan and Mr. Erhardt had encountered treecats as well.

Even then, belief had been slow to grow, but the rest of the galaxy had made up for that in a hurry over the last few T-months. Stephanie had more motivation than most to keep up with the published speculation of the xeno-anthropologists and xeno-biologists beginning to swarm to study them, and because of her relationship with Lionheart, her family was under constant pressure to allow those same xeno-anthropologists and xeno-biologists to study *her*. In fact, they'd hounded her so persistently—with the very best of intentions, of course—that her parents finally laid down the law and strictly limited their access to her and Lionheart. Richard and Marjorie Harrington wanted to understand treecats just as badly as anyone else possibly could, but (as they'd pointed out rather acidly to the more persistent members of the scientific community) Stephanie wouldn't even be fourteen for another five T-months, and they had no intention of allowing the scientific community to drive her crazy before she got there.

Stephanie had breathed a huge sigh of relief when that parental ruling came down. She also had to admit that her parents' decision to ground her—in every sense of the word—for three entire T-months following her ... excursion had actually been surprisingly welcome. Even with quick-heal, a shattered arm and an all-but-broken leg (not to mention the two ribs she hadn't realized she'd broken) would have pretty much grounded her anyway, of course. They hadn't stopped with confining her to the freehold, though. Or, rather, they'd taken the restriction to the next level. Aside from her studies and her virtual classroom, she'd been denied all electronic excursions, as well.

She couldn't pretend it hadn't been deserved, although she'd discovered long ago that knowing a punishment was deserved (and most of hers were) didn't make it any less a punishment. As her father had explained to her when she'd been much younger and full of indignation, punishments were *supposed* to be unpleasant; that's why they were called "punishment."

The good side of it had been that it had given her and Lionheart time to explore their relationship without a bunch of outside intrusion. Time not simply to recover from their physical injuries, but also to come to some sort of grips with the bond which had sprung up between them. She was certain, now, that Lionheart was able to read—probably actually *feel*—anything she felt, and she felt vaguely cheated by the fact that she couldn't sense his emotions in return. And yet ... and yet there *were* those times, those fleeting moments, when for just an *instant* she was almost certain she truly had felt something from him.

She hadn't mentioned those times to anyone, even her parents, and she had no intention of doing so. She strongly suspected that it was one reason she was able to "read his body language" so well, but she was determined not to throw that particular bit of information out where anyone else might hear of it. She and Lionheart were dealing with too much intrusion into their lives already, and it would only have turned up the flame under the already heated debate over the treecats' means of communicating.

Most (although not all) of the xeno-anthropologists who accepted their sentience agreed with Stephanie that the treecats' success in hiding from humanity for so long could only have been the result of a concerted, planned strategy executed by all treecats. That clearly implied some fairly sophisticated means of communication, because they couldn't have coordinated that kind of strategy without one.

But *how* did they communicate? And how *clearly* did they communicate? There was general agreement (based on observing her and Lionheart... when her parents had still been allowing scientists to watch them) that the treecat had some sort of special bond with her. But what sort of bond? *Did* he actually feel her emotions? Had humanity finally encountered a species with a true sense of empathy? A true ability to feel and share the emotions of others? And if treecats were telempathic, able to sense emotions with their minds (or some other way), was it possible they were also tele*pathic?* Could they actually *speak* to one another with their minds? And if they communicated telepathically, did they use words? Or did they simply send images to one another, like moving pictures or videos, perhaps? Or did they send thoughts directly somehow, without any need to break them up into words *or* images? And how much complexity could they communicate with one another? They were tool-users, but only of very simple tools. Was it possible they were communicators, but only of very simple *concepts?*

Obviously, no one knew...yet.

At the moment, skepticism was in first place. The scientists seemed unwilling to leap to any conclusions. Which, in Stephanie's opinion, was just another way of saying they were unwilling to go where the evidence seemed to point because they were afraid people would think they were crackpots, making wildly extravagant claims on the treecats' behalf. Still, there did appear to be a sort of emerging agreement that the treecats were *at least* telempathic and that there *might* be evidence of telepathy as well.

Even that limited acceptance was electrifying. Despite literally thousands of years of effort, humanity had never managed to demonstrate the existence of any measurable, controllable "psionic" talents. Until she'd met Lionheart, Stephanie hadn't had much of an opinion either way, but she'd been plowing through every source she could reach since, and she come to the conclusion that there was way too much evidence of at least individual cases of what might be considered "rogue talents" to ignore. Despite that, no one had ever figured out how to quantify and measure them. And perhaps even more to the point, no one had ever figured out how to reproduce such abilities or teach them to someone else. Or how to "awaken them" in someone who might have a natural potential for them, either. And no one had ever encountered an *alien* species with such abilities. For that matter, the treecats were only the twelfth alien tool-using species humanity had ever encountered, period.

Which meant everyone was very much in unexplored territory.

"Should we take it you're not ready to give up on the chief ranger yet, though, honey?" her father asked after a moment, and she turned from the window to smile at the back of his head.

"You've always said I'm stubborn, Dad," she pointed out.

"One of my more infallible statements, I see," he replied, and she giggled.

"Well, yeah," she acknowledged.

"I'm not sure what else we can do at this point, Steph." Her mother sounded thoughtful, not dismissive. "Chief Ranger Shelton is the head of the Sphinx Forestry Service. I don't know if even the Interior Minister has the authority to give him orders about something like this—assuming she'd have any interest in doing it in the first place."

Stephanie nodded soberly. She'd gone with her parents to meet Idoya Vázquez, the Star Kingdom of Manticore's Minister of the Interior, and she liked the minister. She was pretty sure Vázquez was on their side, too—as much as anyone could be "on their side," anyway. But her mom had a point about Shelton's authority. The Star Kingdom's present Constitution was still less than forty T-years old, and it had completely changed Manticore's *old* constitution. She understood—mostly—why the survivors of the original colonists had made the changes. *She* would have wanted to make sure her family wasn't going to find itself completely overwhelmed by a whole flood of newcomers, too—especially by newcomers whose passage to Manticore the government had helped finance. So she guessed it made sense to establish a monarchy and turn the original settlers into nobles as a way to protect their political power, although at the moment that meant there were an awful lot of "barons" or even "earls" out there with work-callused hands while they and their families weeded the tomatoes or milked the cows.

But that meant some of the details were still a bit vague. Exactly who was in charge of what, for instance, and exactly who was qualified to vote for Parliament, was still being worked out. And that was even more true in the case of Sphinx, which—as Chief Ranger Shelton had pointed out—had only seen its first colonists arrive barely fifty T-years ago . . . just in time to get decimated by the Plague. They were *really* working things out as they went along where Sphinx was concerned, and that didn't even *consider* Gryphon, the Manticore Binary System's *third* habitable planet! Some of the Star Kingdom's "great nobles" already held title land on Gryphon, but as far as she knew, nobody actually *lived* there yet.

The thought of a habitable planet with no one at all living on it seemed awfully strange to someone who'd been born on Meyerdahl, whose population had been just over six billion when Stephanie's family departed for the Star Kingdom. Even with the current influx of new colonists, Sphinx's population was still less than two *million*. That was barely one three-hundredth of a percent of Meyerdahl's population—in fact, it was barely two-thirds of the population of Hollister, alone!—and it was hard for her to really get a handle on the thought of having that much planet with that few people living on it. When she thought about it that way, though, it sort of put Chief Ranger Shelton's comment about how little of Sphinx had really been explored so far—and of how terribly understaffed he was—into perspective. And as Mom had just said, it also helped to underscore the question of just how much authority to override Shelton the royal government truly had at this point.

"If Minister Vázquez doesn't have the authority to give him orders now, that can always be . . . clarified by Parliament," Richard Harrington said a bit more grimly.

"Richard, you're not seriously suggesting we try to get the Crown to take over the Forestry Service just so Stephanie can have her internship, are you? I mean, you know I'm on her side on this. But doesn't that strike you as just a *bit* extreme?"

Marjorie Harrington looked at her husband quizzically, and he snorted.

"Put that way, I guess it does," he acknowledged, then turned to wink over his shoulder at Stephanie before returning his attention to the air car's HUD. "On the other hand, that wasn't the *only* thing I had in mind, Marge."

"No?"

"No." His tone had turned much more serious. "The thing is, I've been thinking about this ever since word got out, and especially since people seem to have begun seriously considering the possibility that treecats really might be more than just cuddly little woodland creatures. I'm afraid the presence of another sentient species here on Sphinx has the potential to cause all kinds of problems. Don't forget what happened on Barstool."

Stephanie drew a sharp breath at his reminder. The original settlers of the planet Barstool hadn't been aware there was a native sentient species on their new home world, either. In their case, it was because the amphibian natives built their settlements underwater for defensive reasons, given the nasty predators who prowled the planet's land masses. From what she'd been able to read about it, the predators of Barstool weren't as bad as hexapumas or peak bears, but that was partly because Barstool's gravity had been only seventy-five percent of Old Earth's, so they hadn't been as strong or as fast.

But the colonists of Barstool hadn't reacted well when they discovered that "their" planet already belonged to another intelligent species. The fact that the Amphors, as the natives had finally been named, were clearly not as intelligent as humans (at least not as intelligent as *humans* ranked intelligence, at any rate) had only made things worse. According to the articles Stephanie had read, the xeno-anthropologists' ultimate conclusion was that the Amphors had probably ranked only about point-seven on the sentience scale, which would have put them considerably behind Old Terran dolphins. There wasn't much way to know now, though. The government of Barstool had legally declared the Amphors animals, not sentients, and the species had been virtually exterminated in the space of less than thirty T-years.

As her father had once bitterly remarked when she asked him about it, it had not been "humanity's most shining moment."

And it was also the reason why, although treecats were the twelfth tool-using species to be discovered, they were only the *eleventh* to be studied.

So far, at least.

"Do you really think that could happen here, Dad?" she asked now, anxiously, hands tightening protectively on Lionheart. The treecat stirred, rolling over onto his back and wrapping all five of his remaining limbs around her right arm in a reassuring hug, and she smiled down at him, but her eyes were dark.

"I don't know. I don't *think* so, honey, but I don't know," Richard replied unflinchingly. "That's one reason your mom and I have been in favor of not pushing the case for how smart they are any harder than we have. It could turn into a real can of worms."

He glanced over his shoulder to meet her gaze for a moment, and she nodded to show her understanding. One thing about her parents: they never lied to her. They might not always be *comfortable* about answering her questions, but they were always honest when they did.

"Barstool still hasn't recovered from how bitterly almost every other inhabited world condemned its decision where the Amphors were concerned," he continued then, soberly, as he turned back to the controls. "The entire planet's still got a terrible reputation, and at least some star systems continue to boycott it completely. They won't do business with anyone from Barstool, won't lend them money, won't sell them anything or buy anything from them, won't invest there.... Their actions have even been condemned by an official resolution of the Solarian League Assembly." He shook his head. "Given all that, I doubt anybody else is really going to want to follow in their footsteps. But human beings can do some pretty ugly things, Stephanie. We can do some pretty *wonderful* things, too, and I happen to think the good things we do ultimately outnumber the bad ones, but there's always someone out there ready to do some more of those ugly things if other people don't stop them.

"In this case, the only people in any kind of position to take the treecats' side are us—the people who think like us and Chief Ranger Shelton's Forestry Service personnel. But the Forestry Service works for the Sphinx planetary government, not for the entire *star system's* government. It's a *local* agency, not a national one. So if the planetary Parliament should decide to allow the exploitation of the range the treecats need to survive, or if the planetary Parliament should decide to support more... intrusive means of study, there's no one higher up who could overrule it. That's why your mom said we're not sure if Minister Vázquez even has the authority to give the chief ranger orders. And, you know, there aren't that many people here on Sphinx right now, and a lot of them are zero-balancers who still don't have the vote yet."

He was starting to get into waters Stephanie still understood only imperfectly, but she knew where he was headed. In order to encourage immigration following the Plague's dreadful death toll, the new Manticoran Parliament had offered land credits to people who would move to Manticore or Sphinx from another star system. The land they'd offered was equal in value to the cost of a starship ticket to the Star Kingdom, and they'd offered bonuses for people with special skills, like her own parents. Those who could afford to buy their tickets on their own received their full land credit when they arrived, and those who could afford part of the price of their tickets received a land credit equal to the amount of their tickets which they'd been able to pay. Those who couldn't afford tickets at all without the government's help were known as "zero-balancers," because they'd arrived having expended their full land credit simply getting there.

Her own parents had been able to pay almost the full cost of their passage. They'd used a little more of their land credit to finance the construction of their home and invest in the equipment their professions required, but they'd still had a comfortable balance, which they'd taken in the land that made up their freehold. They weren't like some of what were already being called the "second-wave aristocrats"—people who'd not only been able to pay for their tickets but to buy huge chunks of additional land on arrival—but they had solid "yeoman" status, which meant they'd received the right to vote one Manticoran year (roughly twenty-one T-months) after their arrival. Zero-balancers, however, wouldn't receive the franchise until they'd become well enough established to pay taxes for five consecutive Manticoran years. Which meant that at the moment perhaps as much as forty or even fifty percent of the total population of Sphinx was nonvoting and had no voice in the policies of their planetary or system governments.

"I don't know how the first-wave colonists are going to feel about all this, especially if it turns out there are even more treecats out there than anyone thinks at this point," her father continued. "What I do know is that right this minute, if it's left solely up to the local government to decide what happens, what kind of long-term policy is set where the treecats are concerned, we're talking about a relatively small number of people. It wouldn't take a lot of them deciding to get together to push policy in the direction they want it to go. That's why it's so important we get off on the right foot with them from the very beginning."

15

"DO I REALLY HAVE TO GO, DAD?" STEPHANIE ASKED somberly, and Richard Harrington turned to look at her thoughtfully.

"You don't want to? I thought you sounded pretty enthusiastic when Mayor Sapristos first suggested the idea."

"Yeah, but that was then, and..."

Stephanie's voice trailed off, and Lionheart made a soft, distressed sound from her shoulder. She reached up to touch his ears, radiating apology for the bleakness of her mood, but she couldn't help it. It was less than three T-weeks since Arvin Erhardt's body had been found in a crashed air car. That would have been bad enough, but then had come the shattering news that it hadn't been an accident. That Erhardt had been murdered...by the same person who had done her best to kill off an entire group of treecats just to cover up some stupid mistake! The Forestry Service and the Crown investigators had finally released their preliminary report yesterday, and it was even worse than she'd thought it was.

In fact, it made her physically sick to her stomach just thinking about it. It would have been horrible enough if the treecats really were "only animals." Only they weren't. She *knew* that, but how did she make everyone *else* understand it? At the moment, she didn't seem to be able to work up a whole lot of enthusiasm even for hang gliding.

"I'm not going to try to make you do something you don't want to," her father said. "You're fourteen now, and that's certainly old enough to make your own mind up about something like this. I would like to point out two things, though. First, you told Mayor Sapristos you'd be there, and you're one of the people he was counting on as a flight leader. Second, you don't spend a lot of time with other kids your age to begin with. This would be an opportunity for you to do that...and also for Lionheart to spend some time 'in public.'" He met her eyes levelly. "After what's happened, getting him out where he can make a good impression on other people probably won't hurt when everyone starts debating how the government and the Forestry Service should respond to it."

Stephanie nodded, although the truth was that the reason she didn't "spend a lot of time" with other kids her age was because she didn't get along very well with most of them. Especially not with two or three whose names came readily to mind. On the other hand, her father had a point. In fact, a pretty good one, she admitted grudgingly.

"All right, Dad. You're right. Let me go get my glider."

"And don't get into trouble," Richard Harrington said sternly as Stephanie climbed out of the air car and opened the cargo compartment to get at her hang glider.

"Get into trouble? *Me?*" Stephanie looked up with her very best wide-eyed "butter-wouldn't-melt-in-my-mouth" look. Lionheart did his best to radiate the same total innocence as he sat on her shoulder, but her father wasn't fooled.

"Yes, you. *Both* of you, as a matter of fact." He shook his head, then waved an index finger under Lionheart's nose. "I realize you're actually a moderating influence on this young terror, but I don't have the liveliest faith in either of you when it comes to finding trouble to get into. I haven't forgotten the way you two *met*, you know!"

Despite her intention to maintain the image of dutiful daughter meekly absorbing parental decrees, Stephanie rolled her eyes. By her current estimate, she'd be forty-two before her parents stopped using that particular phrase. Fortunately, her father only snorted in amusement when he saw her expression. Then his own expression sobered.

"Seriously, Steph," he said, resting one hand on the shoulder not occupied by Lionheart. "Remember people are watching you and Lionheart and don't—"

"And don't forget they still haven't made their minds up about whether or not treecats are 'safe,'" Stephanie finished for him, and nodded. "I understand, Dad. And so does Lionheart."

"I know you do," her father said. "But just remember that that's even more important than usual. Whether or not you're going to be allowed to take Lionheart all the places you want to take him is going to depend mostly on how other human beings—and especially *adult* human beings, I'm afraid—regard him. If they decide he's just some kind of a pet, or even worse, that he's some kind of *dangerous* pet, there's no telling what kind of restrictions the two of you could end up facing. Not to mention what it could mean for getting treecats genuinely accepted as a sentient species. Clear?"

"Clear," Stephanie replied in a considerably more serious tone, and he gave her a smile.

"Good! In that case," he climbed back into the air car

and waved in the general direction of the people on the far side of the grassy field, "have fun."

The truth was, Stephanie reflected as the Harrington air car lifted away and she and Lionheart started across the field towards the others, that even though she was genuinely looking forward to showing off her new hang-glider, she *wasn't* looking forward to this little effort, after all. Or not to the guest list, at least. *All* the other invitees weren't that bad, but there were some, like Trudy Franchitti and Stan Chang...

Unfortunately, there was no way to back out of it without its looking like that was exactly what she'd done. And Dad was right about all the reasons it was important to win acceptance for Lionheart. So when Mayor Sapristos invited her to join the flying club being organized by the graduates of the hang-gliding lessons he and Dr. Harrington had been teaching for the last T-year or so, she'd agreed with the proviso that she'd like to bring Lionheart along. To his credit, Mr. Sapristos hadn't even hesitated, although Stephanie wouldn't have been surprised if he'd really wished she hadn't brought the treecat up.

"Well," she told Lionheart quietly as they approached the others, "I guess we're about to find out whether it was a good idea or not, aren't we?"

"Bleek," Lionheart replied, equally quietly, and she chuckled as she reached up to rub his ears.

Climbs Quickly wasn't certain exactly why he and his two-leg were here, and that made him feel fidgety inside. She was carrying her folding flying thing over her free shoulder, but that didn't worry him any longer. It *had* made him more than a little nervous, whether or not he'd wanted to admit it, the first time she'd taken him flying with her. The last time she'd gone flying before that—without benefit of her parents' bigger, metal flying thing, at least—hadn't worked out all that well, after all.

Yet any concern he might have cherished had long since disappeared, and it was obvious her earlier, disastrous flight wasn't causing *her* any qualms. Which was interesting, because she definitely did have qualms about *something*. He knew where the darkness he'd tasted within her mind-glow for the last few hands of days had come from, and a fresh wave of grief flowed through him, as well, as he thought about what had happened to Bright Heart Clan. Yet that had become a familiar taste, and this sense of... trepidation was different. Sharper and more distinct. From the frustratingly fragmented echoes of thought filtering through her mind-glow to him, a lot of it was bound up somehow with the other younglings waiting for them. For some reason, she clearly felt it was important for both of them to win those others' acceptance... despite which, she seemed to have profound reservations about her ability to do so. That puzzled him, and he felt his ears pricking as he reached out to sample *their* mind-glows.

He couldn't taste them as completely as he could *his* two-leg's mind-glow. But what he could taste was... different. Just as bright as hers, in many ways, but not as strong. Not as... powerful. Or was the concept he was truly reaching for "focused"? He couldn't have described it any more clearly than that even to another of the People, but the difference was as pronounced as it was subtle. Yet even as he thought that, he tasted a sudden swirl in his two-leg's emotions and their normal brilliance took on a distinctly muddy tinge. If "focus" *was* the right concept, it was as if her mind-glow was becoming *un*focused, for some reason.

Why are we here, I wonder, if she dislikes these other

younglings so much? But, no, that is not exactly it, either. She is ... uncomfortable with them. Climbs Quickly considered that as the two of them approached the others. *It is more than just discomfort,* he decided. *She is* uncertain. *Even afraid, perhaps?*

The thought surprised him. One thing his two-leg very seldom was was uncertain. In fact, Climbs Quickly had come to the conclusion that while she might occasionally be *wrong,* she would *never* be uncertain. In that respect, at least, she was still very, very young, which he actually found rather endearing, all things considered. In this case, though, there was no other way to describe what she felt. Which confused him more than a little. It was almost as if she doubted her ability to function with these other younglings, and that was silly. She was clearly more capable than they, and from the taste of their mind-glows, *they* realized she was, as well. In fact, there was more than a little resentment from some of them. Well, that wasn't unheard of among the People, either, especially among the young, but—

But she is mind-blind, he thought suddenly. He'd known that all along, and he'd thought he'd considered its implications. Now he realized he hadn't really come close to truly considering them. *She cannot taste their mind-glows, which means she must fumble towards understanding them like one trying to run along a cross-branch when he cannot even see the sun, far less where he is going.* The sheer bizarreness of that inability made him abruptly and jarringly aware of the differences between the People and the two-legs in an entirely new way. *How do the poor things manage even to* survive, *much less grow up?*

He understood now—partly, at least—why his two-leg's father had seemed so concerned before he sent them off. Just as the People had been worried, even frightened, by the two-legs, the two-legs might be worried about the People. The idea seemed ridiculous, given the difference in their sizes and the many marvelous tools the two-legs had developed, yet as he considered what the People had done to the death fang he'd fought, he could see how these poor clawless, fangless two-legs might be excused for feeling at least a little nervous. And if his two-leg got into a quarrel with one of these other younglings—a distinct possibility, judging from the taste of their mind-glows and hers, he thought glumly—they might well be worried about what could happen if *he* took a hand in it. Not that Climbs Quickly would ever dream of harming one of them . . . unless he actually *threatened* Climbs Quickly's two-leg, that was.

Still, he wasn't tasting any special fear from the younglings—yet, at least. The older two-leg who was obviously in charge didn't taste *fearful*, either, although there was a tart, sharp-tasting edge of wariness in his mind-glow. What Climbs Quickly tasted most clearly from the younglings, however, was a confused, bubbling mixture of curiosity, fascination, envy, desire, jealousy, and wonder. The stew of emotions was impossible for him to sort out, yet there seemed to be nothing immediately threatening about it, and he reminded himself to be on his best behavior.

"Stephanie! Glad you could make it!" Mr. Sapristos said.

"Thank you, sir," Stephanie replied. "Sorry I haven't been around for classes lately. But what with everybody who wants to ask questions about Lionheart and everything, especially in the last couple of weeks . . ."

She shrugged, and Sapristos nodded.

"Well, as you can see, we've added a few new faces since the last time you were here. I don't think you've met Jake Simpson or Allison Dostoevskaya yet. And Toby here is another newcomer. He and his family only relocated from the Balthazar System a couple of T-months ago."

"Hi," Stephanie said, smiling at the newcomers and trying not to notice how everyone else's eyes seemed to be glued to Lionheart.

The others nodded or waved or whatever, and Mr. Sapristos smiled.

"We've got enough warm bodies now that we can actually think about organizing into teams," he said, addressing all of them this time, "and I've set up a point system based on your demonstrated skill levels. And using those points, I've come up with a proposed roster for a Blue Team and a Red Team that ought to be fairly evenly matched. What I'd like to do today is let you guys look at my suggestions and maybe spend a few hours in the air getting a feel for how well they might work out. Nothing's set in stone at this point, so don't fret if it doesn't seem to be a perfect fit. Just take it as a suggested starting point. Once we're comfortable with the roster for each team, we'll be setting up competitions. We'll be going for individual achievements, but also for group records for duration, altitude, formation flying and aerobatics, all that kind of thing. And Trudy here"—he nodded at dark-haired, blue-eyed Trudy Franchitti—"has suggested we think about relay races and team distance marathons, as well."

Heads nodded all around, Stephanie's among them, and she felt herself perking up. She did love hang gliding, and she knew she was stronger in the air than most—if not all—the gathered kids. On the other hand, one of the reasons she loved hang gliding as much as she did was that it was basically a solo sport. She didn't have to put up with all the petty squabbling that seemed so much a part of other kids her age. It would be interesting to see just how well this notion of teams worked out, though. She wasn't going to start jumping up and down with enthusiasm, but given the way it would combine team activities with solo performance, it might not be *quite* as bad as she'd expected.

Might not.

"All right," Sapristos said. "In that case, let's get our gliders assembled, and as soon as we can complete our checklists, we'll get into the air."

It had been obvious to Stephanie that Lionheart had been more than a little nervous the first time she'd taken him gliding, and she hadn't really blamed him for that, under the circumstances. He'd been brave, though. He'd watched her father constructing the new glider, with its considerably more powerful counter-grav generator, and he'd cooperated (obviously not without some misgivings) as Richard Harrington carefully installed the treecat-sized safety harness. It was anchored to the glider frame, just behind the main spar, which put Lionheart in the most crash-survivable location. That wasn't a minor consideration, since they still hadn't been able to figure out how to make a safety helmet that would fit a treecat. It also put Lionheart's head just behind her own, where she could listen to his comments when they flew.

One thing she'd already discovered about treecats was that (judging by Lionheart, at least) they used an amazingly wide set of vocalizations for creatures who obviously had no spoken language. She didn't *think* any of the sounds she'd heard him make had a specific meaning, but they certainly seemed to be an effective barometer for his emotions. In fact, she'd come to the conclusion (so far, at least) that they were basically simply a form of emphasis, like the way a human might wag an index finger at someone to underscore a point or stamp her foot if she was angry about something.

Whether Lionheart's comments had any meaning beyond

that was yet one more of the many puzzles waiting to be solved, but they'd sounded decidedly nervous on their first flight. Still, he'd gotten over it quickly. In fact, he was even more enthusiastic about it than she was now, and he leapt eagerly into place for her to buckle him up.

She laughed and made very certain he was carefully secured, then buckled her own harness, pulled on her helmet, and toggled the heads up display on the inside of its visor. She powered the counter-grav generator, although she left their weight adjusted to one Sphinxian gravity, then looked at Mayor Sapristos and raised her right hand to signal her readiness.

One or two people had completed their preflight checks before her, thanks to the need to be sure Lionheart was properly secured, but she was still ahead of most of the others. Mayor Sapristos had already finished his own checks, as well, and he nodded to acknowledge her readiness, then waited patiently for the others. Toby Mednick, the new arrival, was the last to complete his preparations, and it looked as if he was flushed with embarrassment by the time he was done. His complexion was dark enough she wasn't certain, but she flashed him an approving thumbs-up, and he returned the gesture gratefully.

"All right," Mayor Sapristos said over their helmet coms. "I know there's not much wind here at ground level, but once we clear the trees at the edge of the field, it's going to pick up pretty sharply out of the southwest. I want you guys to spread out before you bring up your counter-grav—let's make sure there's enough spacing we don't get any mid-airs before we're able to build speed-over-ground. Shoot for about seventy meters for your initial altitude."

He waited for each glider's individual response, then nodded.

"Let's go!"

Stephanie put her black and orange, tiger-striped glider into a steeply diving left bank, listening to wind drum across the taut fabric and whistle around her helmet, and laughed as she heard Lionheart's high-pitched, gleeful bleek. This was the first time she'd *really* put her glider through its aerobatic paces, and she was sure she could literally feel his delight as they soared cleanly across the heavens.

No one was trying for any personal records today, but she was actually surprised by how much she'd enjoyed jockeying to maintain formation with the others. Maybe this idea of team hang gliding actually had something to recommend it after all! And after an hour or so of that, Mayor Sapristos had cleared them for a half-hour's free flight. Stephanie was uncomfortably aware that she'd proceeded to succumb to the opportunity to "show off" in front of the other kids, but she didn't really care. She'd spiraled up to several times their initial altitude—more than high enough to make her grateful for her heavy jacket, despite the season—and spent almost twenty minutes dancing with the wind.

They'd drawn quite a crowd, too, she realized, looking down. In fact, for a dinky little place like Twin Forks it amounted to a *huge* crowd. There must be thirty or forty people down there, shading their eyes with their hands while they watched the hang gliders swooping and dancing above them.

Well, if they'd come out to see the show, maybe she and Lionheart should go ahead and give them one!

She steepened her dive, simultaneously tightening her turn, and swooped towards the athletic field from which they'd launched like a stooping, four-winged Sphinxian mountain eagle. She was going to have to flare soon to lose the velocity she was building, but she found herself whooping in exhilaration as the ground swept dizzily around below them.

Climbs Quickly slitted his eyes against the buffeting wind as they went slicing across the sky and he heard his two-leg's joyous mouth-sounds mingling with his own high, ringing bleek of excitement. To think he'd once been nervous about this! It was wonderful—almost as wonderful as cluster stalk! No, maybe it *was* as wonderful as cluster stalk!

He knew he'd flown much faster and higher in the metal flying thing, but this—! This must be what a bird experienced, one of the great hunting birds of the upper peaks! He felt his tail streaming behind him, felt the wind whipping through his fur and plastering back his whiskers, and understood exactly why his two-leg took such joy from moments like this.

She shifted her weight again, and Climbs Quickly could see how that adjusted the angle of their flying thing. He had little idea yet why any particular angle adjustment affected their flight, but he'd quickly figured out *how* she controlled their course, and he wasn't surprised when their speed fell off abruptly. They slowed still further, and he saw the ground reaching up for them. Then they were scarcely moving—compared to their earlier speed, at least—and her feet dropped down and found the grass. She ran forward, laughing and breathless, until she could absorb the last of their velocity and come, at last, to a stop, and he leaned forward, patting the back of her helmet with his remaining true-hand.

Stephanie laughed again as she felt Lionheart patting her helmet. She heard a spatter of applause from the spectators who'd gathered while they were aloft, but it was that pat on her helmet and the sheer joy behind it that she truly treasured.

"Not so bad, huh?" she asked, stripping off her helmet and turning her head to smile at him as she went to one knee and rested the glider frame on the ground. "Liked that, did you?"

"Bleek! Bleek, bleek, *bleek!*" he replied, and she laughed yet again as she tucked the helmet under her left arm and reached up to stroke him with her right hand.

"Oh, he's adorable!" another voice said. *Squealed*, really, Stephanie thought as she turned her head and saw Trudy Franchitti standing there.

Trudy and Stephanie were the two best female hang-gliders of the group. In fact, Stephanie thought they were both better than Stan Chang, who obviously thought he was *the* hotshot glider of all Sphinx. And equally obviously thought Trudy was as deeply smitten by his manly accomplishments as *he* was.

For all Stephanie knew, Trudy was, too. They spent enough time hanging around (and sneaking off) with each other. And their personalities, she thought darkly, were a perfect match for each other.

The fact that she and Trudy were both good hang-gliders and happened (for now, at least) to be assigned to the same team didn't necessarily translate into any glowing friendship. Nor was it likely to. Despite Trudy's undeniable proficiency in at least some areas of athleticism, Stephanie had come to the conclusion that she'd been badly shortchanged in terms of neural synapses. Hers just didn't seem to *work* very well. Although Trudy was almost a full T-year older than Stephanie, Stephanie was three semesters ahead of her in terms of coursework. Of course, looking at the two of them side by side, Trudy looked like she was at least two (or even three, Stephanie thought glumly) T-years older, judged by her steadily—one might almost have said explosively—blossoming figure. Stephanie wasn't prepared to admit just how much she resented that, since she figured it was a pretty silly thing to be resenting. Didn't feel that way sometimes, though. And she *really* hated the way Trudy had taken to standing artfully posed to emphasize her new...attributes.

Especially when there was any even marginally attractive male of the species in the vicinity.

And double-especially when the male in question actually fell for it, she thought, glancing in Stan's direction. The absolute mindlessness behind his eyes was almost frightening. Not that there really *was* that much mind behind them, now that she thought about it. And not that she would have wanted *Stan*—yuck!—looking at *her* that way, but still...

Despite that, Stephanie thought she could probably have actually liked Trudy if she'd only had a functioning brain. Or something remotely resembling a sense of maturity. Or (little though Stephanie wanted to consider the possibility) if Trudy had been just a little less popular with the "in crowd."

Not that Stephanie cared anything about the "in crowd's" opinion, of course. She had more useful things to do with her time than worry about *that*.

"He's so *cute*, Stephanie!" Trudy gushed, coming closer as Stephanie began unbuckling her harness. "Oh, I've *got* to get one of my own! Doesn't he—Lionheart, I mean—doesn't he have, you know, a friend you could introduce me to?"

She batted her eyes with a giggle. Undeniably, it was a *giggle*, Stephanie thought disgustedly. And wasn't it amazing how all of a sudden Trudy had gotten so friendly? Or perhaps what was truly amazing was that Trudy could think for an instant that Stephanie was stupid enough not to realize why the other girl had so unexpectedly developed a desire to be her friend.

"I don't think so," Stephanie replied as pleasantly as she could. "I mean, I'm sure he's got friends, but I don't think most of them are as eager as he seems to be to 'take up with humans,' as my Mom puts it. Personally, I think that just shows they've got better sense than he does!"

She said the last sentence as humorously as she could, hoping to turn it off as a joke, but Trudy wasn't prepared to be diverted.

"Oh, come on," she said. "Nobody's ever seen one of them before, and the very first one you meet decides he does want to 'take up' with you?" She pouted and shrugged her shoulders. "How hard can it be, really? Once you get the opportunity, I mean."

"I'm afraid it's not quite that simple, Trudy." Stephanie tried—she really *tried*—to keep the exasperation out of her tone. She'd *known* how the null wits like Trudy were going to react to this, she'd just known. "Just finding them is tough enough, unless you luck into it by accident the way I did. And nobody knows exactly why Lionheart decided to hang around with me in the first place. Not yet."

"Well, I *know* that," Trudy said a bit tartly. "But now that we all know they're out there, I expect we'll be seeing more of them around town."

"Trust me," Stephanie laughed, "nobody's going to see a treecat unless he *wants* them to see him!"

"Oh?" Trudy cocked her head and her smile took on a slightly fixed look as she watched Stephanie finish unbuckling.

"Oh," Stephanie said with a nod. She shucked off her own harness and began unbuckling Lionheart, who reached out to her with his remaining true-hand and both hand-feet. He swarmed into her arms as she finished unstrapping him, then whisked around to take his proper position on her shoulder.

"*You* seem to have found them," Trudy observed with what sounded remarkably like a hint of petulance.

"Maybe." Stephanie shrugged. "On the other hand, like

I already said, it was sheer luck I met Lionheart here the first time. And the *second* time...well, let's just say I'd recommend a less traumatic way of making friends with somebody."

"Yeah, we've *all* heard about you and the hexapuma." Trudy rolled her eyes. "My dad says anybody who really ends up face-to-face with a hexapuma's gonna get eaten."

"He said that, did he?" It was Stephanie's turn to cock her head, and she realized her own tone had become cooler.

This wasn't the first time she'd heard similar remarks, although it was the first time someone had said them directly to her...and deliberately implied that it hadn't really happened. It was the first time they'd come from someone her own age, too, and she was surprised by how much more infuriating that made it. Why in the world was she letting *Trudy Franchitti*, of all people, get to her?

"He's hunted hexapuma, you know," Trudy said, and if Stephanie's tone had cooled, Trudy's had sharpened. "*He* says anybody a hexapuma catches on the ground without a gun or something is dead meat."

There was a certain undeniable relish in the way he Trudy said the last two words, and Stephanie made herself pause before she fired back at the other girl.

She supposed she couldn't blame people for being astonished by her survival. For that matter, *she* was still astonished by it, and she knew Lionheart and the other treecats were the only reason she was alive today. Still, she wasn't accustomed to people doubting her honesty. Besides, the Forestry Service had been out and photographed the carcass exactly where her parents had told them they'd find it. So just how did Ms. Trudy Franchitti think that hexapuma had ended up dead?

"Well, *I* didn't have a gun," she said after a moment. "Guess I was lucky Lionheart and his friends came along when I needed them, wasn't I?"

"I guess," Trudy said a bit snippily, then shook herself. "But that's my point. If they 'came along' for you, then why shouldn't they come along for somebody else?"

"Like you?" Stephanie could have bitten her tongue as soon as the two-word question was out of her mouth, but it was too late, and Trudy's blue eyes flashed.

"I don't see why *not*. I mean, I've made lots of pets. I've got two chipmunks and a near-otter right now!"

Stephanie's jaw muscles tightened. It was moments like this when she was convinced Trudy was really only about nine T-years old, whatever her birth certificate (or physical assets) might claim. She knew all about that near-otter of Trudy's, and if she could have figured out a way to liberate the poor creature, she'd have done it in a heartbeat. And she also knew Trudy hadn't captured the beast in the first place; that had been her older brother, Ralph, who ranked even lower on the intellectual food chain than she did.

Hard as it was at this moment to believe that *anyone* could plumb such deep and dark ocean depths.

"Lionheart isn't a *pet*, Trudy," she said as calmly as she could.

She began collapsing her glider, hoping Trudy would take the hint and go elsewhere. She didn't expect to be that lucky, though, and her heart sank as she realized most of the others had landed by now and quite a few of them seemed to be gathering around her and Trudy. Stan Chang, Becky Morowitz, and Frank Câmara had ranged themselves behind Trudy, which was hardly surprising, given Stan's attitude where Trudy was concerned and the fact that all four of them were buddies. Chet Pontier and Christine Schroeder were trying to pretend they weren't eavesdropping on the conversation, as well, but they weren't very good actors. Worse, at least some of the spectators seemed to be edging closer to listen in as well.

"Oh, sure, we *all* know he isn't a *pet*," Trudy said, rolling her eyes much more dramatically than before. "He just *looks* like a pet, right?"

Walk away, Stephanie, a little voice which sounded remarkably like her mother's said in the back of Stephanie's brain. *Walk away. The last thing you need is to get into this kind of a discussion with a mental featherweight like Trudy.*

"Really?" she heard herself say instead, glancing up from the glider she was folding in upon itself. "That's what he looks like to you, is it?"

"Of course it is!" Trudy grimaced. "*My* dad was *born* on Sphinx, you know, just like me. We've been here *forever*...unlike some people. And *he* says it's ridiculous to think anything as small as *that*"—she jabbed her hand in Lionheart's direction—"has enough body mass to support a real *brain*. Everybody knows *that*."

"Then I suggest your dad point that out to all of the xeno-biologists and xeno-anthropologists who're lining up to meet Lionheart," Stephanie replied. "I don't think most of them share his opinion."

"Are you calling my father *stupid*?" Trudy demanded with one of those dazzling shifts of subject Stephanie had never understood. "Is that what you're saying? That my father doesn't know what he's talking about?"

"No, I'm not calling your father stupid," Stephanie said. After all, her parents had always taught her to be polite. "I'm just saying he hasn't had the opportunity to actually meet Lionheart. If he's relying on what other people have told him, they might've gotten some of it mixed up."

"They certainly did *not*!" Trudy snapped. "We've talked to the rangers, too, you know. And if they're so smart, why did so many of them get killed last month? Didn't sound very '*smart*' to me!"

A flash of pure, distilled rage went through Stephanie. She felt it singing in her blood, quivering in her muscles.

"It wasn't the *treecats* who weren't smart, Trudy," she heard herself say. "It was humans. It was that Dr. Ubel and her *stupid* experiment! If she'd had—"

Stephanie chopped herself off, shaking her head sharply, and Trudy sneered.

"If she'd had as many brains as *you* do? Is *that* what you were going to say?" she demanded, and laughed scornfully. "You *do* think you're such hot stuff, don't you? You think everybody thinks you're so *special*, you and 'Lionheart.' Well, you're not. My dad says he'll be happy to get me a treecat of my *own* if I want one!"

"And just how does he plan to accomplish that?" Stephanie demanded, turning on Trudy with a fierce frown. The anger Trudy had already managed to fan roared suddenly higher, fanned into a furnace by the suggestion of a threat to the treecats.

"Wouldn't you like to *know*?" Trudy shot back with a nasty smile. "Let's just say he and Ralph have been hunting here on Sphinx longer than your entire *family's* been on Sphinx."

"And never even *saw* a treecat in all that time, did they?" Stephanie fired back with a sweet smile that was even nastier than Trudy's. "Doesn't say much for their tracking skills, does it?"

"They'll find them now that they know what to look for!" Trudy's eyes glittered. "Now that *you've* found them, I'm sure other people can, don't you think?"

A torrent of pure, white fury boiled up inside Stephanie, and she felt her right hand balling into a serviceable fist. The possibility that someone who wanted to hurt the treecats might follow up her own experience, figure out where to find them from some clue *she* provided, was her worst nightmare.

"After all," Trudy continued, not even trying to hide her pleasure at having provoked Stephanie's anger, "a real hunter knows how to find any dumb animal he's hunting for. I guess the trick would be figuring out how to bring one back alive instead of just shooting or poisoning it. But practice makes perfect, and I'm sure they'll get it right . . . eventually."

Climbs Quickly tasted the red-fanged fury as it boiled up in his two-leg's mind-glow. His inability to make any sense out of the mouth-sounds going back and forth was maddening, but he didn't have to be able to understand the sounds to realize from the echoes that at least part of them concerned him, somehow. Or that much of his two-leg's anger stemmed from her desire to protect him. Yet there was more to it, as well, and he didn't have to understand *everything* to know at least generally what was going on.

The People were no strangers to the sudden, often irrational anger to which younglings of a certain age were prone. In fact, it was almost reassuring to discover the same thing happened among two-legs. It made them seem less alien and strange, somehow. Of course, two-legs were mind-blind, and he realized now that that could be an advantage, as well as a weakness. It wasn't unheard of for two of the People in a confrontation like this one to find themselves trapped in the other Person's mind-glow. Fury could feed on fury, and being able to taste the feelings behind someone else's anger often only made one's own, answering anger even worse. When that happened among the People the result was almost always ugly, sometimes even deadly, unless someone else (usually one of the clan's memory singers) managed to separate them first.

That wasn't likely to happen to the two-legs, at least, although they obviously didn't need to be able to taste each other to recognize anger. Worse, because they were mind-blind, neither of the younglings in this confrontation were even trying to mute the waves of anger they were projecting, which meant Climbs Quickly found himself taking the brunt of *both* two-legs' wrath.

He felt his own fury trying to rouse in response, beating against his control. It was even harder to keep it leashed, he discovered, because all of the poisonous passion pouring out of the other two-leg was directed not at him, but at his two-leg. He felt his claws creeping out of their sheaths in an instinctive reaction to protect her, yet he knew that was the last thing he needed to be doing at this moment. It wasn't as if the other two-leg truly meant to physically attack—or not yet, at least—but he wasn't at all certain *his* two-leg wasn't about to attack the other one. In fact, he could taste something welling up within her which was very like what happened when People got trapped in one another's mind-glows.

Climbs Quickly was no memory singer, but he'd seen Sings Truly and Song Spinner separate younglings and even the occasional adult scout or hunter. He knew how they did it; it was simply something he'd never attempted himself, and he found himself wishing he'd been able to practice ahead of time.

No doubt Sings Truly felt the same way the first time it happened to her, he thought, and flung himself into the fray.

Stephanie knew the instant Lionheart took a hand.

She didn't know exactly what he was doing, far less how he was doing it, but she knew *she* wasn't responsible for the sudden break in the rising tide of her fury.

She'd always known she had a dangerous temper. Although it didn't get away from her all that often—or *she* didn't think it did, at least; her mom seemed to have a somewhat different view—she'd figured out long ago that it was likely to get her into a great deal of trouble someday. Someday, she realized suddenly, like today.

Except that something new had been added. It was like . . . like a sheet of bulletproof glass pushed between her and her own wrath. It wasn't that she was any less angry. It was just that . . . just that she was suddenly able to stand back from that anger. To *feel* it without being *driven* by it. She'd never imagined anything like it, but whatever Lionheart was doing, and however he was doing it, she felt a sudden surge of gratitude.

She also felt the tip of his tail sweep forward and wrap itself around her throat. It was a *protective* gesture, she realized, and also a comforting one. One that helped her more than she would have imagined was possible as she made her fist unclench and drew a deep breath, then looked Trudy square in the eye.

"I'm sorry you feel that way, Trudy," she heard herself say in a suddenly calm tone. "Of course, the fact that you do probably explains why no treecat in his right mind is going to have anything to do with you. And while I'm sure your father and Ralph are great hunters, believe me, they're not going to be catching any treecats who don't decide to be caught. I don't imagine the treecats are going to be much happier about the thought of ending up with them than they'd be about the thought of ending up with *you*, either, so don't hold your breath waiting for it to happen. In the meantime, I've got better things to do with my time than stand here and listen to you being stupid."

She smiled, rather enjoying the way Trudy's jaw dropped. She'd never realized it could actually be more satisfying to watch the other person being reduced to gobbling incoherence than to simply punch the idiot out, and she filed the thought away for future consideration.

"You—you—!" Trudy spluttered, and Stephanie shook her head.

"Mighty impressive vocabulary you've got there, Trudy. Do you practice it in front of the mirror, or does it come naturally?" she asked dryly, then bent to gather up her hang glider.

"Think you're such a smart ass, don't you?" another voice asked harshly, and Stephanie looked up, less surprised than she might have been to see Stan Chang glaring at her. "You and your damn treecat."

"I didn't pick this fight, Stan," she said, still leaning on that plate of bulletproof glass. "Trudy did. If she doesn't like the way it's turning out, maybe she shouldn't have."

"Listen, you—!" Stan began, stepping forward and half-raising one fist.

Stephanie straightened and turned to face him. She raised her eyebrows, cocking her head ever so slightly, and Stan paused. At a hundred and eighty centimeters, he was a good forty-five centimeters taller than she was, and broadshouldered and muscular, to boot. Yet there was something about her expression. She didn't look angry, and she certainly didn't look *frightened* by him. In fact, she looked . . . calm. Almost *amused*, and she smiled ever so slightly as she shook her head.

"I don't think you want to do that, Stan," she said simply.

He hovered, irresolute, but something inside him seemed to shrivel before the armor plating of that smile. Then he darted a look past her shoulder, where Mayor Sapristos had finally landed and was striding in their direction.

"Looks like the mayor just saved your butt, Harrington," he hissed. "Yours and that furry little freak of yours. For *now*, at least." He gave her one last, hot-eyed glare, then turned away. "Come on, Trudy."

He twitched his head and the two of them turned and walked away before Sapristos could get there.

"Is there a problem?" the mayor asked a moment later, looking around as Stephanie bent once again to gather up her hang glider.

"No, sir," she replied as she straightened.

He looked at her sharply, obviously not deceived by her response, but she only looked back calmly. After a moment, he nodded.

"Good," he said, then surprised her by reaching out and resting one hand on her treecat-less shoulder. "Good," he repeated.

"I guess I'd better be going," Stephanie said then, glancing at her chrono. "Dad's going to be waiting for me. Bye, Mayor Sapristos. Guys."

She nodded to the other teenagers, who'd watched the entire confrontation goggle-eyed, then shouldered the hang glider and headed away.

The spectators—who, she reflected, had gotten to witness rather more than they'd probably expected to—parted before her. Several of them seemed to be watching Lionheart a bit warily, but she only nodded politely to them, thanking them for getting out of her way. One of the ones she'd never met—a dark-haired boy, at least four or five centimeters taller than Stan, who looked to be a T-year or so older than she was—met her eyes squarely for a moment. Then he grinned, raised his right hand in an approving thumbs-up, and stepped aside.

Wonderful, she thought. *Not only the entire town of Twin Forks but even people I've never even* seen *before are going to hear all about this. I can just imagine how that's going to help convince people to listen to what I've got to say about the treecats.*

Yet somehow even that thought didn't make her feel one bit less satisfied by the memory of Trudy's spluttering.

"DR. HOBBARD SCREENED THIS MORNING," MARJORIE Harrington said as Stephanie came thundering into the dining room for lunch with Lionheart in her arms. "She asked if she could come by and talk to you tomorrow. I told her"—her mom looked Stephanie in the eye—"yes."

"Awwww, *Mom!*" Stephanie groaned, rolling her eyes.

"That's enough of that, young lady," her mom said firmly. "Dr. Hobbard is only doing her job—a job *somebody* has to do, which you know perfectly well. The least you can do is be polite to her."

Stephanie glowered down at the floor for a moment, her shoulders tight with resentment. Then Lionheart made a soft, slightly scolding sound, and she shook herself. The treecat turned his head to look into her eyes, and after a moment, Stephanie drew a deep breath and nodded.

"Sorry, Mom," she said contritely. "You're right. It's just . . . just . . ."

"Just that you're sick and tired of people asking questions

about Lionheart and his family." Marjorie nodded. "That's exactly why your father and I have laid down the law about access to the two of you. To be honest, honey, I wish we could just tell all of them you're permanently 'unavailable,' but we can't. This is too important. Besides, if you don't talk to them at all, they're just going to go rummaging around out there on their own, and you know how well *that's* likely to work out!"

Personally, and despite her own experience, Stephanie wouldn't have minded too much if some of the noisier (and nosier) "scientists" making her life a misery encountered a hexapuma. Or maybe a peak bear, although they'd have to go higher up into the mountains for that, and the peak bears were nowhere near as territorial as the hexapumas were. Still, one could hope....

"Bleek!" Lionheart said, and this time it was clearly a laugh, not a scold.

"I know, Mom," she said out loud, looking up at her mother. "And the truth is, I don't really mind talking to Dr. Hobbard as much as I do some of the others. At least I'm pretty sure she's on the treecats' side!"

"Only '*pretty* sure'?" Marjorie asked quietly.

"Well, that's sort of the problem, isn't it?" Stephanie replied, and her mother nodded. "And I guess part of it is that Lionheart and I were planning on spending tomorrow visiting his family," Stephanie went on. "If Dr. Hobbard's coming to visit, there won't be time for that."

"No, there won't." Her mother nodded. "On the other hand, one reason I went ahead and invited her to come out and talk tomorrow is that I don't really like the weather forecast. I think it would probably be a good idea for you to stay home, anyway, which means we can kill two birds with one stone this way. And without costing you a day you *could* go visit them."

It was Stephanie's turn to nod. She hadn't personally

checked the weather forecasts yet today, but she wasn't about to argue with her mother's judgment. Not after what had happened the day she first met Lionheart! And she knew how lucky she was that her parents had not only decided she could use her hang glider—her *new* hang glider—to visit Lionheart's family group, but actually encouraged her to do it.

With Lionheart to provide navigational input by the simple expedient of sitting upright in the air car's front seat and pointing in the right direction, it hadn't been difficult for them to locate his clan's central settlement, and it wasn't far from the freehold by air car. On the other hand, Stephanie had been worried from the very outset about leading other humans to them. Her exchange with Trudy had only sharpened that concern, and her parents were more than half-afraid she might have a point. They knew the Franchitti family, and her mom and dad didn't care for them any more than Stephanie did. Unfortunately, the Franchittis weren't as unique as the Harringtons might have wished. So until they had some sort of regularized, formal protection in place to guard the treecats against human interlopers and interference, keeping them as far below the radar as possible struck them as a very good idea. Which was the real reason her father had helped customize her replacement glider (once she was un-grounded again). With its upgraded counter-grav to boost their combined weight to a higher altitude, she could reach the clan's settlement in no more than an hour or so, and a single hang glider was almost impossible for anyone to track without a direct visual lock.

She knew her parents had felt a qualm or two at the thought of allowing her to fly back and forth by herself, especially in light of her original venture in that direction. She also knew there were several reasons they hadn't, including the fact that they would never have been cruel—or stupid—enough to try to keep her away from the rest of Lionheart's family. She *had* been sternly forbidden to set foot on the ground between the freehold and her destination, and she was absolutely required to file flight plans before departure—and to demonstrate that *this* time she'd checked the weather carefully—for each trip, but after her unfortunate earlier experience, she was fine with that.

"I understand, Mom," she said now, crossing to let Lionheart flow out of her arms and onto the sturdy perch her father had built for him.

The treecat stretched himself out along the artificial "limb," and Stephanie grinned as his ears pricked and he sniffed happily. Lionheart approved of ham and cheese sandwiches. Despite his clearly carnivorous teeth, he even liked the thick slabs of homemade bread—most of the time, anyway. There were days when he peeled the bread away to get at the sandwich stuffings, instead. Not as many of them, anymore, since her mom disapproved of wasting food. She was just as capable of folding her arms and looking sternly at treecats as she was at daughters.

He didn't care too much for the mustard Stephanie liked to slather thickly into her own sandwiches, and he was no great fan of sliced tomatoes, either. But he was very fond of onion—he liked his slices thick—and he'd almost swooned in ecstasy the first time he encountered Swiss cheese. They were still exploring human foods with him, and they were being a little cautious about it. Richard Harrington, in particular, was monitoring his health closely, trying to make sure he was getting what he actually needed, not just what he liked. Fortunately, treecats' digestion seemed highly . . . adaptable, and Lionheart was willing to try almost anything at least once. Of course that inexplicable passion of his for celery posed its own problems. Adaptable or not, his essentially carnivorous digestion objected to processing that much cellulose, with predictable consequences. Fortunately it wasn't something that couldn't be handled with a little laxative, and her father had discovered that a local fish extract did the trick nicely. Lionheart even liked the way it tasted, although Stephanie was none too delighted by the way it made his breath smell.

Now she worked quickly to put his sandwich together. He watched attentively, head cocked and eyes bright with interest, but he didn't offer to help. They were still working on his sandwich-constructing skills, and Marjorie Harrington had informed her daughter that they could practice on their own time—preferably during one of her picnic meals with his family. Given the messiness of his current culinary attainments, Stephanie didn't really blame her mother for that.

Besides, cleaning up after their experiments wasn't exactly her own favorite thing to do in all the world.

She finished assembling Lionheart's meal, and he bleeked his thanks, then waited while she slid into her chair at the table and began building her own sandwich. The bread smelled wonderful, fresh and still ever so slightly warm from the bread machine her father filled with dough every morning. Mayonnaise, a thick layer of shaved ham, onions, mustard, tomato, slice of Swiss cheese, more ham, and a layer of lettuce to finish it off. A huge, juicy kosher dill pickle on the side, along with a hefty serving of potato salad, a spoonful or two of baked beans, and a glass of milk, and she was ready to say grace.

Some people might have considered the towering sandwich and the more-than-adult-sized serving of potato salad (not to mention the baked beans . . . with plenty of brown sugar) a bit much for a small-framed fourteen-T-year-old girl, but not if they knew about her genetically modified metabolism. It took a *lot* of fuel to keep her going, and she could put away an impressive load of calories when she put her mind to it.

Besides, she *really* liked potato salad!

"So you still don't have any idea whether or not they use some sort of written language or recordkeeping, Stephanie?" Dr. Sanura Hobbard asked.

"No, ma'am," Stephanie said politely, and shook her head, her expression studiously intent. "I mean, I haven't *seen* anything like that, but that doesn't really prove anything, does it? One way or the other, I mean." She waved one hand around the living room in which she and Hobbard had been seated for the last three hours or so, indicating the old-fashioned bookcases on either side of the fireplace. "If somebody didn't know what *books* were, they might not realize we're sitting in a whole roomful of written records, right?"

"A valid point," Hobbard acknowledged with a nod.

The xeno-anthropologist was a pleasant-faced woman in her late forties, with dark brown eyes and brown hair that verged on auburn. There was a lot of intelligence in those eyes, and Stephanie saw more than a little frustration to keep it company as she sat back in her chair.

That frustration made her feel a bit guilty. She *liked* Dr. Hobbard. She also respected her, and she knew only someone a lot stupider than Hobbard could possibly have failed to realize Stephanie wasn't telling her everything she could have. Stephanie knew she could get away with holding back a lot by falling back on her "just a kid" persona, but that didn't mean she liked doing it. For that matter, she was pretty sure Dr. Hobbard knew what she was doing—maybe even why—even as she continued to pretend she didn't...and treated Stephanie and Lionheart courteously, as equals, anyway.

None of which was going to change Stephanie's mind at this point.

It's not that I don't trust her, anyway, she thought. *Or not mostly, anyway. But given who she is and why she's here, we've almost got to be more careful with her than with anyone else!*

Dr. Hobbard's area of specialization, the study of nonhuman societies, had been hugely understaffed here in the Star Kingdom when Stephanie's discovery of the "treecats" (and at least Stephanie's name for them seemed to be standing up) had burst upon the scene. In fact, Hobbard was the only qualified xeno-anthropologist on Landing University's faculty . . . which was how she'd ended up heading the Crown commission charged to explore and study this brand-new species.

Hobbard hadn't migrated to the Star Kingdom because of her interest in xeno-anthropology, of course, since no one had even suspected the Manticore Binary System might have a native sentient species. Stephanie knew that she and her husband, like Stephanie's own family, were part of the new wave of colonists, although they'd arrived on the planet of Manticore—the most Earthlike of the Star Kingdom's three habitable planets, orbiting ten light-minutes closer than Sphinx to the binary system's G0-class primary star—twenty-three T-years ago.

The Star Kingdom had originally started subsidizing immigration in 1489, although it hadn't been easy to attract new settlers at first, even with the subsidies. The Plague had first appeared in 1464 Post Diaspora, but its threat hadn't been recognized until its first mutation, sixteen T-years later. When *that* happened, people had begun dying within T-months. Worse, the Plague virus had entered a period of rapid, frequent mutations, which had complicated the vaccine researchers' task horribly. It had taken almost four more dreadful years, until 1484, to come up with a vaccine that worked, and by then the Manticore System's population had been reduced to a level which threatened the colony's very survival.

That was when aided immigration was first proposed, bringing in a tide of new settlers over the next three T-years... until the Plague the doctors had thought they'd defeated mutated yet again. The new mutation had been even deadlier than the original, in many ways, and fatalities had been heaviest among the newest arrivals, who lacked the resistance the original population had gradually built up.

Immigration (understandably, Stephanie thought) had fallen sharply as the heartbreaking procedure to create a new vaccine began all over again, and it had taken *another* nine T-years—until 1496—to find another effective treatment. In those nine T-years, well over half of the new immigrants had died, and it had taken several more years for immigration rates to slowly increase once more.

The Hobbards had arrived in 1497, in the vanguard of that second wave of immigrants, because Jerome Hobbard was a city planner who specialized in designing entire human cities to fit into alien biospheres with a minimum of negative environmental impact. He'd been exactly the sort of specialist Manticore needed, and he'd been heavily recruited by the Ministry of Immigration. And while no one had been actively recruiting anthropologists, Landing University's faculty had been just as devastated by the Plague as everyone else. Since Sanura Hobbard held a second doctorate in *human* anthropology, she'd ended up the chairwoman of a brand-new Anthropology Department and settled down to a satisfying academic career, even if it hadn't been in her own primary *nonhuman* area of interest.

Until Lionheart and I came along, anyway, Stephanie thought wryly. *We even got her to come all the way out here to Sphinx, and I* know *how much she just loves* that!

Despite how much Stephanie had come to love Sphinx herself over the last couple of T-years, she understood why Hobbard didn't much care for the planet. Sphinx was almost three times as far from its sun as Old Earth was from Sol, which explained its enormously long planetary year. It was also the reason why, even though the system primary was a bit warmer than Sol, Sphinx probably wouldn't have been habitable at all if it hadn't possessed an abnormally active carbon dioxide cycle, which boosted its surface temperature. Despite that, even summer on Sphinx was decidedly on the cool side, whereas Manticore's average temperature was just as decidedly on the warm side for inhabitable planets. And Stephanie was sure Dr. Hobbard vastly preferred Manticore's gravity, which was barely one percent higher than Old Earth's. Hobbard didn't have any of the genetic modifications Stephanie did, and even with the nanotechnology which helped her lungs cope with Sphinx's air pressure and the personal belt-mounted counter-grav generator she always wore, she had to feel much heavier than she ought to feel.

"I don't suppose Lionheart's done anything which might suggest that *he's* keeping some sort of record of his experiences with you?" she asked now.

"No, ma'am." Stephanie shook her head gravely, and Hobbard smiled a bit crookedly.

"Have you been able to decide whether or not he knows how to count?" she went on.

"Not really," Stephanie said, after considering the question for a moment. "It's kind of hard to tell when we can't talk to each other, you know. I *think* we're making some progress in his learning to understand me when I talk to him, but I can't even be *positive* about that. And even if we are, *he* can't talk to me, no matter what we do. So I don't know if he can actually count, but I do think he understands the difference between 'some' and 'more.'"

"Maybe something along the lines of 'one, two, three, many,' you mean?"

"Something like that. Maybe," Stephanie agreed, and Hobbard nodded with a broader, warmer smile.

Stephanie smiled back, pleased there was an answer she'd felt comfortable giving. And the truth was, she wasn't totally unwilling to share any information about the treecats. In fact, she *wanted* to share everything she safely could, but that was the problem. How did she decide what would actually help the treecats' case, and how did she decide what might be *dangerous* to them? One thing she was determined upon though, and her parents agreed with her.

"I don't suppose you've made any more progress on locating the rest of Lionheart's clan, have you?" Hobbard asked now, and Stephanie winced inside. That question was a perfect example of the sort of information she was afraid might endanger her new friends. A part of her—the part that liked Hobbard as a person and not the head of the Crown Commission on Treecats—*wanted* to tell the xeno-anthropologist, but...

"I'm afraid there's still not anything much I can say about that, Dr. Hobbard," she replied. She was a little uncomfortable with that response, but it wasn't actually a lie. She hadn't said she didn't *know* where the rest of Lionheart's clan lived; she'd only said she couldn't tell *Dr. Hobbard* where they lived. Which she couldn't. Or wouldn't, at any rate. She wasn't telling *anyone* that if she could help it.

"I see," Hobbard replied, and Stephanie felt the very tips of Lionheart's claws prick gently at her skin. If she'd worked out her signals with him as accurately as she thought she had, that meant he thought Dr. Hobbard didn't really believe her, and she concentrated on looking as sincerely helpful—and as young—as she possibly could.

Dr. Hobbard's lips twitched in what might have been a tiny smile, and there was a gleam deep in those brown eyes. As far as Stephanie was concerned, that was all the proof she needed that Hobbard was perfectly well aware of the game they were playing. She was tempted—again—to be more forthcoming, but she suppressed the temptation. It wasn't *Hobbard* she mistrusted in the first place. No, what worried her were the *other* people who would inevitably end up reading Hobbard's reports. The xeno-anthropologist worked for the government, and that meant anything Stephanie told her would eventually end up part of the public record, where just anyone—including people who didn't like treecats (the name "Franchitti" came to mind)—could get at it.

"In that case," Dr. Hobbard went on, "let's talk about that carry net of his. We've been able to observe the clan that got displaced after that BioNeering accident, you know. We're keeping our distance, as much as we can—they're in a pretty distressed state right now, and we don't want to make that worse. In fact, the Forestry Service's refused to tell anyone—even me—exactly where that clan's been relocated to. That's a little frustrating, but overall, I have to say I think it's a wise decision on Chief Ranger Shelton's part.

"In the meantime, though, I've been studying the video from the Forestry Service's long-range cameras, watching them work, and it looks to me like there's a very set pattern for the way they weave their nets. They aren't all the same size, but as nearly as I can tell trying to scale from the images, the *meshes* of their nets *are* all the same size, regardless of how big or small the net itself is. And they seem to use exactly the same knots. But the nets *they* make don't match the pattern of the one Lionheart was carrying when the two of you met the hexapuma. That's one of the first real differentiating factors we've noticed between that clan and his—wherever his is." She smiled again, faintly. "I don't suppose you could try to communicate with him and ask him if he could either make some more nets for us himself or possibly go home to visit his own clan and bring us some we could study comparatively?"

"I might be able to," Stephanie said after a moment. "I can certainly try, anyway."

"Thank you!" Hobbard said with a much broader smile, and Stephanie smiled back, a bit surprised herself to realize how much the prospect of being able to give the xeno-anthropologist *something* appealed to her.

"Well, I guess that's about it for today," Hobbard said, glancing over the deplorably sparse notes on her minicomp. "Thank you, and please thank your mom for letting me visit this morning, too."

"Sure," Stephanie said, climbing out of her chair to walk the xeno-anthropologist out to her waiting air car. *And thank* you, *Dr. Hobbard,* she added silently, *for suggesting who else I should be talking to . . . even if you* didn't *realize you were doing it.*

"Yes?" the voice at the other end of the com link said.

It wasn't the voice Stephanie had expected, since it was a woman's, not a man's. It also sounded a bit . . . wary. Which, given the events of the last month and a half or so, didn't exactly surprise Stephanie. Assuming that the voice belonged to somebody who was friendly with the person she was actually trying to reach. anyway.

"Excuse me," she said, sounding as much like an adult as she could. "I'm trying to reach Dr. MacDallan."

"May I ask why?" The other voice *definitely* sounded wary now, Stephanie decided. Probably because its owner had been helping to fend off newsies and scientists. "I'm afraid he's not available right this minute, anyway," the woman at the other end of the link went on. "He's been quite busy lately, as I'm sure you understand."

"Oh, believe me, I *do* understand," Stephanie said feelingly. "In fact, that's why I'm screening. My name is Stephanie Harrington, and I think Dr. MacDallan and I need to talk."

17

"ARE YOU TWO FINALLY READY TO KNOCK OFF FOR lunch? Or should Karl and I go ahead and eat without you?" Irina Kisaevna demanded.

Dr. Scott MacDallan looked up from the deep, green pool where his lure swam beguilingly along at the end of his fishing line, dancing its way seductively through the water in an effort to entice one of Sphinx's leopard trout onto its hook.

So far, he'd had precious little luck in that regard. In fact, his expensive rod, his painstakingly hand-tied lure, and all his decades of crafty experience had failed to catch a single fish. Which was particularly irritating for a confirmed fishing fanatic such as himself when the still-slightly-damp treecat currently sunning himself on a flat rock a few meters away had done quite well for himself. In fact, at that very moment, Irina was ready to plop Fisher's cleaned and scaled fish—all *five* of them—into the skillet as lunch's star attraction.

"I'm sure it's only a matter of a few more minutes—a *very* few more minutes—before I catch a veritable monster of the deeps to put Fisher's miserable little fishies into proper perspective," he replied, raising his voice to carry across the rush, chatter, and roar of the white-water cataract just upstream.

"*Sure* you will," Irina shot back. "I'm sure you'll manage that around the time my personal invitation to high tea with the king arrives."

"Your lack of faith wounds me, woman!" MacDallan shook his head mournfully. "Betrayed! That's what I am—betrayed by those closest to me!"

"Well, Mr. Betrayed, if you want to go on fishing, that's fine with me. But poke Fisher awake. It wouldn't be fair for Karl and me to eat up all of his fish while he sleeps right through lunch."

MacDallan glowered at her, then laughed and conceded defeat. He reeled in his line and gathered up his tackle box, then crossed to the rock the treecat had turned into a comfortable snoozing spot.

"Hey, Fisher," he said softly, reaching down and gently stroking the soft, sun-warmed, cream-colored belly fur. "Time to wake up, little guy."

The treecat named "Fisher" by his adopted human opened green eyes, blinked sleepily, then stretched and yawned.

"Come on," MacDallan said with a grin. "Certain parties are about to put your fish on to cook, and if you and I don't get a move on, they aren't saving any for us."

Fisher—he seldom thought of himself as "Swift Striker," the name the People had given him, when he was among the two-legs—tasted the amusement in his two-leg's mindglow. He'd been working hard at understanding how the two-legs communicated, and it was obvious the mouthsounds they made were the equivalent of the People's mind-voices. But it was such a *bizarre* equivalent he was beginning to despair of the possibility of any Person ever truly wrapping his mind about it, though he had at least learned to recognize the sounds of the name his two-leg had given him. That didn't mean he couldn't understand his two-leg's general meaning, though. There was enough contiguity through their bond for that ... and since what his two-leg was radiating right this moment was more than enough to remind him his middle felt excessively empty, he bleeked a laugh and rolled to his feet.

"That's right," MacDallan said. "Go ahead. Rub it in. But you know, for us humans, fishing isn't supposed to be a full contact sport."

He scooped the treecat up, draping him comfortably around the back of his neck like a thick, silken muffler, then picked up his tackle box again and waded carefully across the roaring rapids to join Irina on the far bank. He took his time, checking his footing with each stride, remembering the day, just over nineteen T-months ago, he and Fisher had met. He'd slipped and fallen in rapids much like these that day, and struck his head, then landed face down in the water with a concussion. If the treecat hadn't been there, hadn't swarmed down out of the tree from which he'd been watching the human fish, and used his carry net to hold MacDallan's mouth and nose out of the water until he regained consciousness, he would have died that day.

Not a bad way to make someone's acquaintance, the doctor thought now, mouth quirking in a smile. *Little hard on the skull, maybe, but it sure does tend to cement a friendship in a hurry.*

Actually, as Scott MacDallan knew better than anyone else on the planet of Sphinx, his relationship with Fisher was more than just a "friendship." Even he didn't know exactly how *much* more, yet he had direct, personal experience that the furry little arboreals were more intelligent—and more capable of sophisticated communication—than even their most ardent champions among the xeno-anthropologists and xeno-biologists were prepared to suggest.

The problem was what to do about it.

He waded clear of the water on the other side of the river, and Fisher sprang down from his shoulders. The treecat flowed across the rough ground, head up and ears pricked, and MacDallan heard another delighted "Bleek!" of pleasure as Fisher saw the skillet and the cleaned fillets of his catch.

"Aren't you just a *little* put out"—Irina held up her right hand, thumb and forefinger about two centimeters apart—"that he managed such a haul when you and all that fancy equipment you carry around didn't manage to catch a thing?"

"Not really," he said. "Oh, it's always a little frustrating if you don't catch anything, but most fishermen will tell you the fishing itself is the real reward. When you actually hook one of the real monsters, when you spend half an hour fighting until you manage to land it, that's *great*. But those are the high points. What really brings you back again and again is just spending the time out here—you and the river. That's what it's really all about."

Irina Kisaevna cocked her head, considering him sidelong, and knew he meant it. Not that she intended to let him off the hook that quickly. She and MacDallan had known one another ever since his arrival on Sphinx twelve T-years ago as a brand new doctor, fresh out of medical school and brimming with dedication. The assisted immigration policies had helped pay his way, but he'd come more because of the Star Kingdom's desperate need for doctors than for any incentives its government might have offered.

By the time he arrived, the researchers had finally broken the Plague's back, but it had died hard, with periodic flare-ups which had required constant tweaking of the vaccines. The situation had still been pretty horrible, the need for trained doctors still acute, and he'd dived straight into it fearlessly, despite the fact that new immigrants, without the resistance the survivors had built up, were far more vulnerable to the Plague. Not that it had killed *only* the newcomers. In fact, Irina had met him because her husband had been one of the pandemic's last native-born victims. MacDallan had done everything anyone could have done to save Stefan Kisaevna, but Stefan had been one of the patients who'd had an especially severe response to the Plague. Despite everything MacDallan could do, his own immune system had killed him, trying to fight off the disease.

Irina had taken his death hard, but she'd seen a lot of death by then. It had never occurred to her for a moment to blame MacDallan, and as the weeks, and then the months, and finally the T-years had passed, she'd realized that what she'd come to feel for him was much too strong to call "friendship" any longer. Which was why the two of them were getting married in about six T-months. As far she was concerned, they could have tied the knot tomorrow, but he wanted his mother to be there for the wedding, and given the interstellar distances involved...

She'd also discovered that for all his naturally warm, empathic personality, there was a darkness deep inside Scott MacDallan. A...melancholy, perhaps. He *felt* things, she thought. Felt them too deeply, sometimes. He *cared*— that was one of the things she loved about him, one of the things which had brought him to Sphinx in the first place—but sometimes he cared too much. Which was why he needed someone to give him a hard time, keep him focused on the here and now.

That was *her* job, she'd decided. So—

"Yeah, sure!" She rolled her eyes at him. "I can't think of anything *I'd* rather do than stand up to my waist in ice-cold water for four or five hours at a time without hooking a single fish! I *love* nature!" She threw back her head and flung her arms wide. "Nothing *I* like more than freezing my behind off without catching a thing! Unless, maybe, it's standing in the *rain* freezing my behind off without catching a thing." She frowned thoughtfully, then nodded firmly. "Yes, now that I think about it, that's probably even *more* fun. And if I could only get to cut a hole in the *ice* in the middle of a blizzard, then I'm sure—"

"All right. All right!" He laughed and threw one arm around her. "So, maybe actually catching something *is* a little more important than I might have implied."

"Maybe, huh?" She regarded him skeptically. Then she shrugged. "Well, at least you don't fling yourself bodily into the water the way Fisher does. No wonder he spends so much time sunning on warm rocks. He's thawing out from all those swims of his!"

MacDallan laughed again, although she probably had a point. Fisher's technique consisted of lying very still on an overhanging limb or shelf of rock, staring down into the water until he spotted a fish, then pouncing on his unsuspecting victim with all claws spread. MacDallan had watched him doing it and been deeply impressed by the treecat's blinding speed and skill, but it was undeniably a wet, cold way to fish. A technique that probably did help explain why sun-warmed rocks were so high on his list of favorite things.

"Anyway," Irina continued, waving one hand in the direction of her nephew, Karl Zivonik, "Karl and I have been loyally preparing provisions as our share of this expedition."

Karl looked up and grinned from where he was cutting fresh lemons into wedges. The old-fashioned cast-iron skillet his mother had sent along sat ready by the fire, oiled and awaiting the salted fish fillets Irina had dredged

with flour and fresh-ground black pepper. The outsized
bread pan at his elbow was filled with fresh, golden cornbread; he'd just taken the snap-on top off a huge bowl
of coleslaw; and the plastic tumblers were waiting beside
the thirty-liter thermos of tea.

The doctor felt his mouth watering as he smelled the
mingled scents of woodsmoke and cornbread. Right off the
top of his head, he couldn't think of anything better than
fresh-caught and fried fish, garnished with fresh-squeezed
lemon juice, and Evelina Zivonik's homemade cornbread
and coleslaw. Especially not eaten outside with friends.

"Well, in that case, by all means, let's eat!" he said.

Much later that evening, MacDallan and Irina sat in
an old-fashioned glider on the veranda of Aleksandr and
Evelina Zivonik's sprawling farmhouse.

As the son of one of the colony's first-shareholders,
Aleksandr Zivonik was technically entitled under the
new Constitution to call himself "Baron Zivonik." One
of these days, MacDallan thought, that title was probably
going to have some genuine meaning. For the moment,
it was simply an indication that the Zivoniks had been
on Sphinx as long as anyone else. The steadily expanding
farmhouse was additional evidence of that. He'd delivered
Aleksandr's youngest child in this house little more than
a T-month ago, and its core was already fifty T-years
old. He wondered how many more generations of hands
were going to add on to it, how many more generations
of children's feet were going to run and play and work
under its roof, in the fullness of time.

It was a soothing sort of thought, one that consoled
the heart of someone who'd seen far too many people
die of the Plague.

"Comfortable?" he asked quietly as Irina nestled her

head down on his shoulder while he used one foot to move the glider gently back and forth.

"Oh, yes," she murmured, looking up past the edge of the veranda's roof at the stars beginning to creep shyly into the darkening cobalt blue of the sky. "I love this place," she continued softly. "Hard to remember sometimes—like when it snows for fifteen T-months without a break. But then we get fifteen months of spring and another fifteen months of *this*."

She swept one hand in a gesture at the near-pines and enormous crown oaks towering over the farmhouse and the night sky settling above them like clear, clean velvet, and MacDallan nodded.

"And don't forget the surprises," he said wryly. "I guess we should've remembered how little of the planet we've actually explored, but still—!"

"And the surprises," she agreed. Then she sat up a bit, leaning back so she could look directly into his eyes. "*All* the surprises," she added in an even softer voice.

MacDallan looked back at her. He knew what she meant. In fact, she was the only person on the planet he'd trusted with the full truth, and it hadn't been easy even with her.

He'd spent most of his life hiding his "oddity." He was lucky he hadn't had as much of the "gift" as his grandmother had, but it had always been there, always threatening to rear its head, especially in moments of stress. And people still didn't understand. In fact, he sometimes thought people were even less understanding about little personal "quirks" like that now than they'd been before the Diaspora carried humanity to the stars. The prejudice against "genies" could extend itself to almost anything someone found peculiar or different, whether or not the difference in question really had anything at all to do with actual genetic manipulation. And the fact that people who allowed themselves to be prejudiced that way were seldom exactly mental giants didn't mean they couldn't do a lot of damage.

But here on Sphinx, with Fisher and the other treecats, he'd finally found that his "oddity" truly was a *gift*. It still had its dark sides, of course, he thought, remembering the night—had it really been only three T-months ago?—when the treecats had proved to him they truly were telepaths. The night they'd made him see what one of *them* had seen, shown him the devastation one of his own kind had unleashed upon the forests of Sphinx, and begged him to do something about it.

He still had nightmares about that entire adventure. Nightmares about how close he'd come to dying...and of a treecat who *had* died to save his life. But more important than the nightmares, he knew—*knew*, beyond a shadow of a doubt—that the treecats were far more than anyone else, with one possible exception, had even begun to guess.

"You need to talk to her, you know," Irina said. "She's probably the only person on the planet who knows as much—if not more—about treecats than you do. And I think you can safely assume you can trust her. She and her parents certainly aren't ever going to do *anything* that could hurt them, you know."

"But she's still only a kid, Irina," MacDallan protested. "Only—what? Thirteen? Fourteen, now?" He shook his head. "This is an awful lot to dump on a kid that age."

"That 'kid' single-handedly discovered that we share this planet with another sentient species," Irina pointed out a bit tartly. "And in case you haven't noticed it yet, Scott MacDallan, 'kids' tend to grow up pretty quick here on Sphinx. You've noticed my nieces and nephews, perhaps?"

"Point," he acknowledged. "Definitely a point."

"Well, what you may not be aware of is that Karl's

actually met Ms. Harrington. In a manner of speaking, at least."

"Huh?" MacDallan blinked and looked at her sharply.

"That's one of the things I love most about you," Irina said dryly. "That wonderful vocabulary of yours, I mean."

"Stop criticizing my vocabulary and tell me about Karl and young Harrington," he said with a grin.

"It was when he went in to Twin Forks for that trip to the main ranger station Frank Lethbridge arranged for him last month. He didn't actually talk to her, but she and a bunch of other kids around her age were hang gliding. Karl says they're organizing a formal hang-gliding club, and he wishes we were closer. I think he'd really love to learn how to float around the sky himself. Anyway, they were flying around for at least a couple of hours, and he and Frank ended up going down to their landing field to watch. And it seems young Harrington had a bit of a set-to with one of the other kids. Two of them, actually, if Karl got it right. One of them was a guy, quite a bit bigger than Harrington, and I think Karl figured he might have to take a hand if it got physical. But he says Harrington faced both of them down. 'Kicked both of them right in the butt without ever actually laying a finger on them,' I believe was his elegant summation of what happened." She smiled and shook her head. "From the way he said it, I think he rather admires her."

"Which wouldn't have anything to do with the fact that she's not only about his own age but already has a treecat of her own, would it?" MacDallan asked with a chuckle.

"Oh, it might," Irina conceded. "On the other hand, you know he's got his head fairly well screwed on. I think his judgment's usually pretty good."

"You're right about that," MacDallan agreed, and frowned up at the stars—brighter now, as the sky continued to darken—for several minutes, then shook his head again.

"You're probably right about the maturity quotient of Sphinxian teenagers," he said. "On the other hand, if I talk to her and anyone finds out about it, they're going to assume—correctly—that it was about the treecats. I mean, what *else* is anyone going to think when two of the three—really the *only* two, I guess, now that Erhardt and the Stray are dead—humans known to have adopted treecats get together for a little chat?"

"So?"

"So they're going to wonder just why I wanted to talk to her. What have I discovered that I want to check with her? Or what has *she* discovered that she wants to share with *me*? And the people who wonder things like that are going to remember that whole BioNeering catastrophe. They're going to be trying to put two and two together, and I'm afraid too many of them really will get 'four' this time. You know how much trouble I'm having with people like Hobbard, despite the fact that I've been stonewalling on this whole thing from the very beginning. You really think I want to bring that down on *her*, too?"

"Um." Irina frowned.

He had a point, she reflected. Irina actually thought quite highly of Dr. Hobbard, but she was like a bloodhound on a particularly marvelous scent, and she obviously suspected that MacDallan was concealing something from her.

On the other hand, she was a lot better than some of the other "scientists" beginning to swarm around Sphinx (and one Dr. Scott MacDallan) to investigate the newly discovered species. She might suspect that MacDallan wasn't telling her everything, but she seemed deeply and sincerely concerned with protecting the treecats, as well as studying them.

"All right, I agree that exposing a fourteen-year-old to that kind of intrusiveness wouldn't exactly be a good thing," she said finally. "At the same time, the way she talked makes me think she's probably the only person on the planet who's already being pestered more by people like Hobbard—or the rest of them—than *you* are! You may be the one who kept that lunatic Ubel from getting away with murder—*more* murders, anyway—and worse, but she's the one who discovered the treecats in the first place. And don't forget just *how* she discovered them! I doubt that your going to have a talk with her is likely to make things any worse in that regard."

"Maybe not, but how much *good* would it do? I don't want to sound like I'm putting her down because she's a kid, but she *is* only fourteen, Irina. It's not just a question of how mature she is. It's a question of how much she understands about what's going on. For that matter, it's a question of how much someone her age *can* do to keep things from sliding entirely out of control."

"Granted." Irina nodded. "On the other hand, *I* think this is something you need to do, if only to find out if she knows something you ought to find out about. And if you have any qualms about her...capabilities, let's say, why don't you discuss them with Frank? He's probably in a position to give you a better feel about that than I possibly could."

"Scott! Fisher!" Frank Lethbridge waved an enthusiastic greeting as MacDallan walked into his office with Fisher on his shoulder. "I didn't know you two were coming clear out here today."

"Well, we were in the neighborhood," MacDallan replied.

"Just in the neighborhood, huh?" Lethbridge raised a skeptical eyebrow, then looked out the office window. His isolated Sphinx Forestry Service ranger station was over six hundred kilometers from MacDallan's Thunder River medical office. Even for a counter-grav air car, that was a fair trip.

"As it happens, we were in the neighborhood because I wanted to talk to you . . . privately," MacDallan admitted, and Lethbridge's expression sobered as the doctor's tone registered.

"Talk to me about what?" the ranger asked a bit cautiously. "And why in person instead of by com?"

"Partly because I wanted a chance to get a feel—a personal feel—for what you might have to say," MacDallan told him levelly. "But also, to be honest, because I don't want to take a chance on anybody overhearing us."

"You're starting to make me a little nervous here, Scott."

"Sorry." MacDallan grimaced. "It's not really anything sinister, Frank. It's just . . ." He paused. "It's just that I'm worried. About the treecats."

He reached up, stroking Fisher's head, and the treecat butted his palm gently.

"What about the treecats?" Lethbridge asked, eyes narrowing intently.

"First, let me be up front about this," MacDallan said. "I'm talking to you as my *friend*, not as a Forestry Service ranger. I'm not going to ask you to violate any professional codes, and I'm not going to ask you to do anything you shouldn't be doing. But if what I'm about to say to you gets to the wrong set of ears, it could have some pretty unfortunate repercussions."

Something like a hint of anger sparked in Lethbridge's gray eyes, and MacDallan shook his head quickly.

"I'm not saying I think you'd betray any confidences, Frank! I just want to be sure you understand how serious my worries are. And, to be honest, I'm a lot more concerned with protecting Fisher and the other treecats than I am with helping those busybodies poking and prying around them."

Lethbridge's expression cleared, and he snorted harshly.

"Don't think I don't agree with you about *that*!" He shook

his head in disgust. "Hobbard and her crowd aren't too bad, but I wouldn't trust some of these other . . . scientists as far as I could spit upwind in a hurricane! And most of them would make some hungry hexapuma really happy if we let them go wandering around all by themselves in the bush like a herd of Old Terran elephants! For that matter, I'm scheduled to take a half dozen of them out to 'observe the treecats in the wild' next week. The only thing I can think of right off hand that I'd enjoy more would be regrowing a broken tooth without quick-heal."

MacDallan chuckled.

"Somehow I'm not too surprised to hear you say that," he said. "Anyway, are you okay with talking to me?"

"Sit down and we'll see," Lethbridge said, pointing at the chair on the far side of his desk. "If you start saying anything that makes me uncomfortable, I can always tell you to stop, can't I?"

"I guess you can."

MacDallan took the indicated chair, urged Fisher down into his lap, and tipped back comfortably.

"The thing is, Frank," he said quietly after a moment, "more went on with that BioNeering business than I ever officially admitted. I don't want to go into the details even with you, for a lot of reasons—some of them purely personal. But what it comes down to is that I've got what I think is pretty darned convincing personal evidence the treecats are a lot smarter than most people are guessing even now. Not only that, but I'm pretty sure I've got proof they really are telepaths."

Lethbridge pursed his lips in a silent whistle and leaned back in his own chair, folding his arms across his chest. He looked at his friend—both his friends—for several seconds, then nodded to himself.

"I wondered about that," he said simply. "You went awfully straight to the heart of things, and I never did buy all that business about your 'playing a hunch.' So it was Fisher here who spilled the beans to you?"

"No, not really. Oh, he helped—he was part of it. But it was the Stray. Erhardt's treecat."

Lethbridge's expression hardened into something like cold, hammered iron, and Fisher made a soft sound of distress. MacDallan scooped him up, hugging him, pressing his face against the soft fur in apology for taking all three of them back to that horrible day when the half-starved, emaciated treecat MacDallan had known only as "the Stray"—Erhardt had never shared *his* name for his friend, if he'd ever given him one—had led MacDallan and Aleksandr Zivonik to the crashed air car and the three dead bodies.

One of those bodies had been Arvin Erhardt's. Erhardt had been a cargo pilot, hired by the BioNeering research group and assigned to their research facility here on Sphinx...and he and the other two men aboard his air car had been murdered by Dr. Mariel Ubel, the facility's lead scientist. She'd sabotaged the air car's flight computers to ensure that it would crash on its way back to civilization in an effort to keep them from revealing the fact that she'd released a deadly pathogen into the planetary environment, poisoning and destroying the very heart of a treecat clan's home range. It had apparently been an accident, but it was the sort of accident *competent* scientists didn't have, and her career would have been over if the news had gotten out. For someone like Ubel, that had been more than sufficient reason to casually murder three human beings.

She'd darned near murdered MacDallan, too, when he turned up at the research facility following up on the "hunch" he'd offered to the authorities as his official reason for being there. In fact, she *would* have killed him...if the Stray hadn't flung himself directly onto the muzzle of her rifle just as she fired and deflected her shot at the cost of his own life.

"The Stray, huh?" Lethbridge said after a moment. "Poor little guy. Bad enough to lose Erhardt, but then..."

The ranger sat silent for several more seconds, then shook himself and drew a deep breath.

"Okay," he said more briskly, "I'm not going to ask you about what kind of 'proof' of treecat telepathy you've got. Mind you, I *would*, but it seems pretty obvious you *really* don't want to talk about it. All right, I can accept that. But in that case, what is it you *do* want to talk about?"

"I've been thinking about this a lot, Frank. And I've been discussing it with Irina; she's the only other person—two-footed person, anyway—who really knows about all of it. And it's occurred to me that I need to find out everything I *can* find out about treecats as quickly as I can. I've got sort of an inside track here, and whether I like it or not, I think I've got a responsibility to look out for Fisher and his relatives. I don't know that it'll do any good in the end, but I'd rather stay at least a couple of steps in front of those 'scientists' of yours. Not Hobbard—although, to be honest, I'd just as soon not tell *her* anything I don't have to—but the others."

"And?" Lethbridge prompted when he paused again.

"And I'm thinking that probably the only person who knows as much or more about them than I do right this minute is Stephanie Harrington," MacDallan admitted. "There's a part of me that really wants to know what she may have turned up on her own. And from everything I've heard, she's a pretty remarkable kid. But I may have heard *wrong* about that, and even if I haven't, I don't see how I can go and start asking her about what *she* knows without being willing to tell her about what *I* know. Which brings up the question of just how much I can trust her discretion. I think it's pretty likely she's already keeping her mouth shut about quite a few things—that's why I want to talk to her in the first place—but will she keep her mouth shut about what *I've* found out?"

"That depends," Lethbridge said, regarding him very steadily across the desk.

"Depends on what?"

"Depends on whether or not she thinks she can trust *you* to keep *your* mouth shut," Lethbridge said flatly. "I think you're absolutely right that she's not beginning to tell everything she knows or suspects at this point. But I'll tell you this—if she doesn't think you're every bit as determined to protect the treecats as she is, she's not going to tell you a single solitary thing."

"No?" MacDallan was more than a little surprised by Lethbridge's certitude. He knew it showed in his tone and his expression, and Lethbridge chuckled. It was not a sound of amusement.

"Did Karl tell you about the two of us running into her, in a manner of speaking, on that Twin Forks trip?"

"Not me, no, but he has discussed it with Irina," MacDallan said. "To be honest, what he said to her is one of the things inclining me towards going ahead and getting in contact with her."

"Really? I'm not surprised," Lethbridge said. "And I've always sort of trusted Karl's judgment, too. He does see more than a lot of 'adults' do, doesn't he? For example, I've talked to Shelton about her, and to be honest I think the Boss is underestimating her quite a bit. He doesn't think she's your typical fourteen-year-old, mind you, but I don't think he's even begun to guess just *how* atypical she is. And I know absolutely that there's nothing—nothing in this world—that girl won't do to protect her treecat. Lionheart, she calls him."

"You sound pretty positive," MacDallan said slowly, and his friend nodded.

"That's because I am. You know the story—her hang glider crashed, a hexapuma came after her, and Lionheart fought it off until the rest of his tribe or clan or whatever we end up calling them got there. Right?"

MacDallan nodded.

"Well, that's the official story. The only one she's ever told, as a matter of fact. But Ainsley was the first ranger on the spot, you know."

MacDallan nodded again. Ainsley Jedrusinski was Lethbridge's partner. There were so few rangers, especially since the Plague, that even official "partners" often operated solo, but the doctor had become well acquainted with Jedrusinski since his arrival on Sphinx. He had considerable respect for her competence and judgment.

"Her parents had already lifted the girl and Lionheart out by air car," Lethbridge continued, "so there was no rush, but Ainsley got the coordinates from the father and went out to take a look. By the time she got there, there wasn't a lot left of the hexapuma. You know what the scavengers are like out there. But she found something very interesting when she examined the skeleton."

"What?" MacDallan asked.

"The treecats may've pulled that hexapuma down, Scott," Lethbridge said quietly, "but Stephanie Harrington had already killed it."

"*What?*" MacDallan repeated in a very different tone, his eyes wide.

"Ainsley's sure of it. She found the girl's vibro blade where she'd dropped it. And examining the hexapuma's skeleton, she also found where she'd *used* it before she dropped it. She got it into that hexapuma, Scott. Must've buried it all the way to the hilt, and she cut right through the left mid-limb pelvis. From the angle of the cut, she had to have gone straight through the major artery there. I don't doubt that critter was still on its feet. I don't doubt it could still have killed her and Lionheart without the *other* treecats, but it was already dead—it just didn't know it yet. And Ainsley said it was pretty clear from the angle and the way the ground laid out that she hit it from *behind*—probably when it was ready to finish off Lionheart. How many twelve-year-olds do you know who're going to go after a flipping *hexapuma* with nothing but an eighteen-centimeter vibro blade? You think somebody willing to do that, with an arm broken in two places and a leg she could barely stand on, to protect a treecat who might already have been dead for all she knew, won't do *whatever it takes* to protect that treecat now?"

18

<*YOU LOOK WELL, CLIMBS QUICKLY,*> SINGS TRULY said quietly, lying stretched out beside her brother on the net-wood limb fifteen meters below her nest place.

<*I feel well,*> he replied, never taking his eyes from his person as she lay laughing in a deep patch of moss, covered in a pile of joyous kittens. The clan's younglings found the two-leg's mind-glow—and the welcoming delight which filled it—irresistible. <*I will not pretend I do not sometimes miss my true-hand,*> he continued, <*but compared to what would have happened without my two-leg's sire's healing place...*>

Sings Truly radiated her agreement, yet there was a hint of reservation in it, and he turned his head to look at her questioningly. He didn't actually voice the question, but there was no need for one of the People to be that explicit. Especially not with another of the People who knew him as well as Sings Truly did.

<*Some of the other clans' elders are less than delighted*

with our decision to mingle so with the two-legs,> she admit-ted. <*What happened to Bright Heart Clan has frightened them. It seems to some of them to prove how dangerous the two-legs are, and they would rather move their ranges entirely, flee ever deeper into the forest and farther away from the two-legs, lest still worse befall them.*>

<*If such is their desire, it only proves their foolishness!*> Climbs Quickly said sharply. <*Yes, what happened to Bright Heart Clan is terrible. And, yes, it was a two-leg who caused it. But the* other *two-legs punished the guilty one, just as the People have punished those guilty of evil acts.*>

<*So far as I know, no one has ever claimed the other two-legs did* not *punish the guilty one,*> Sings Truly replied. <*I do not think that is their point, Climbs Quickly. They know now that there can be truly evil two-legs, like the terrible one who slew True Stalker's two-leg to try and hide the evil she had done from her fellows. That is frighten-ing enough, and reason for some of the clans to wish to withdraw further from the two-legs, at least until they have fully considered that proof. But more of them are concerned by Swift Striker's report that what first happened was an* accident. *Bad enough that the evil two-leg was willing to do murder to conceal its actions, yet all of that destruction, all that terrible wounding of Bright Heart's range, was not* even *intentional. There are not yet that many two-legs on this world, Climbs Quickly, but some of the other elders fear that as they become more numerous, there will be more such accidents, and they have no desire to find their own clans caught up in such terrible mischances.*>

Climbs Quickly lay silent for several long, thoughtful breaths. Then he twitched his ears.

<*I suppose there is at least some reason in that,*> he said, <*but it is not the reason of foresight. Those who fear the consequences of such actions should recall how swiftly the two-legs moved to help Bright Heart when they learned of*

the disaster. Their flying things carried food to the clan that very same day, and my two-leg's sire personally traveled to tend to the hurts of those who had been injured. And do not forget the axes and the knives the two-legs gave to the People of Bright Heart! They are far better than anything the People have ever made of stone or wood, and the People of Bright Heart have already nearly completed their new central nesting place with their assistance.>

<Agreed,> Sings Truly acknowledged. *<And I have made the same point to the other clans' messengers. Even those who are most frightened acknowledge that the two-legs who are not evil did all those things to undo the harm which had been done to Bright Heart. But there are those who would prefer to stay far enough from the two-legs that they do not* require *two-leg assistance in undoing harm. And even many of those who do not wish to run deeper into the forest and hide believe it may be rash to actually encourage others of the People to form the sort of bond you have formed with Death Fang's Bane.>*

Climbs Quickly's eyes dropped once more to his two-leg, and a soft, possessive purr buzzed deep in his chest. He hadn't given her that name; it had been bestowed upon her by the rest of Bright Water Clan, and it was well deserved. He might have been unconscious at the moment she earned it, but others of the clan had been close enough to see what she had done, and Sings Truly had sung the memory song of her actions to him. He had seen as if with his own eyes that wounded, frightened youngling attack the death fang to save his life. And if there could have been any doubt as to the reason she had attacked, he'd seen her stumble forward on her wounded leg to stand *between* him and the death fang. More than that—Sings Truly had been close enough to taste her mind-glow when she did it, and so Climbs Quickly knew his two-leg had fully expected to die...and that her only hope, the only thing for which she had fought, had been that she might kill the death fang before it could kill *him*, as well.

How often, even among the People, he wondered, *can one truly* know *that another will die for one?*

Now he listened to Death Fang's Bane's laughter, tasted her delight as one of the kittens burrowed its way up under her shirt while two more stalked the wind-blown curls of her brown hair. It was so good to taste her so, without the frustration and the worry which seemed to afflict her mind-glow so often of late. Climbs Quickly was frustrated by his complete inability—so far, at least—to learn the meanings of her mouth-sounds, especially when she tried to explain what was worrying her so and he found it impossible to fully understand. Yet he understood enough from what he tasted in her mind-glow to understand that much of her worry was similar to that of the clan leaders who feared to approach the two-legs too closely.

<*I do not like to admit it, even to myself,*> he said finally, slowly, to Sings Truly, <*yet I suspect from some of what I have tasted in Death Fang's Bane's mind-glow that she, too, has some…reservations about revealing too much of ourselves to the other two-legs. I do not know why she feels that way, but I do know there are those among the two-legs who are as eager to learn more about the People as the People are to sample cluster stalk. Indeed, they plague Death Fang's Bane and her parents with endless questions they cannot answer, and I think some of them would desire nothing more than to take me away from Death Fang's Bane so they might study me more fully in their own ways.*>

<*Indeed?*> Sings Truly rolled two-thirds of the way onto her back, turning her belly fur to the sun while she swivelled her head to keep her eyes on her brother. <*That is disturbing news, Climbs Quickly.*>

<I may be wrong about it,> Climbs Quickly pointed out. *<I am still only beginning to understand two-legs. It is easy enough to taste their mind-glows—indeed, who can not taste them if he comes close enough?—but it is far more difficult to understand how their minds work. If only we could hear their mind-voices, or they could hear ours! Things would be so much simpler.>*

<Would they truly? Or would it simply mean we would learn that much faster that coming close to the two-legs was a serious mistake?>

Climbs Quickly blinked. It was unlike Sings Truly to question her own decisions after the fact. On the other hand, this was the first time one of her decisions could have such far-reaching consequences for every Person alive or yet to be born, and he felt a sudden surge of sympathy for her. And a flicker of guilt, as well, since all of this stemmed from his own first, completely unauthorized encounter with Death Fang's Bane.

<Do not feel guilty,> his sister's mind-voice chided him gently. *<You did not do it intentionally, and my decision to challenge Song Spinner and Broken Tooth was my own, not yours. Besides, I still believe it was the right one. It is simply that I understand why those who question it have concerns.>*

<No, it was not intentional,> he agreed, *<but it was still my action which began all this. And while I, too, understand why some of the other clans—or their elders, at least—may be concerned, even fearful, I agree that your decision was the right one. If those other two-legs might wish to take me away from Death Fang's Bane to study, neither she nor her parents will permit any such thing. And if the evil two-leg who destroyed Bright Heart Clan's nest place did not care that she might have slain an entire clan of the People, it was Swift Striker's two-leg, Darkness Foe, who stopped her. It is clear the two-legs have come*

to this world to stay, Sings Truly. All among the People must surely understand that! And as you told Song Spinner and Broken Tooth, the world is not big enough for us to hide from them forever. I have come to the conclusion that your suggestion that we form still more bonds with the two-legs was even wiser than you realized at the time. Yes, we must learn more about them. But perhaps even more importantly, we must make allies among them. We must find those of the two-legs with whom any Person might be proud to bond—the ones like Death Fang's Bane and Darkness Foe. And one of the reasons we must do that is so that when an evil one among the two-legs might harm the People, we will have our own allies, our own friends among the other two-legs who will defend us. I think that is the message you should send back to those clan leaders who doubt the wisdom of the course you have proposed.>

Stephanie Harrington sat up, spilling treekittens off her chest and shoulders, as her uni-link warbled. One of the treekittens, ears pricked in delight, pounced on the fascinating new plaything, and she laughed as she gently shooed it away.

She was careful about how she did it. She'd discovered the hard way that treekittens' claws had needle-sharp points, but at least they weren't the ivory scimitars of an *adult* treecat, like Lionheart.

Her father found everything about the treecats endlessly fascinating. Stephanie was pretty sure there were at least two dozen xeno-biologists who would cheerfully have murdered Richard Harrington just to get their hands on the notes he was compiling, and one of the things he'd found especially fascinating was the structure of Lionheart's claws.

They were very unlike the claws of a terrestrial cat. For one thing, they were extraordinarily dense, more like stone than horn. In fact, her father had told her they were more like a shark's tooth than anything else he could think of from terrestrial biology. They were only between a centimeter and a centimeter and a half in length, but they were sharply curved, and the inner surface—the drawing surface—was scalpel-sharp. The claws retracted into wells that were lined in the same stonelike material to protect the treecats from their own claws' sharpness, but it certainly helped explain how such diminutive, almost dainty creatures had shredded a massive hexapuma. And they had four of them on each hand and foot—two dozen naturally evolved razor blades at their fingertips, one might say. When it came down to it, Stephanie thought, a treecat was far better (and more lethally) armed than anyone might ever think simply looking at one of them.

Fortunately, developing that sort of armament apparently took time. Which probably explained how treekittens lived to grow up! It certainly helped Stephanie's clothing (and skin) survive their onslaught, anyway.

Now she managed to reclaim her uni-link from the curious treekitten and checked the caller ID. It was her father's, and she accepted the call.

"Hi, Dad!"

"Hi yourself," Richard Harrington responded. "Would it happen you've been keeping an eye on the time, young lady?"

"You know I have," she replied. "I'm sure not going to mess up and get myself grounded! Again, I mean," she added, and sitting in his office back at the freehold, Richard grinned.

"Well," he said, "I've been monitoring the forecast, and it looks to me like that storm center's moving in on the coast faster than anyone expected. I don't think it's going to cause any problems with your original schedule, but we're going to be in for a lot of rain, and you're probably going to be meeting stronger headwinds on the way back."

"Yes, sir," Stephanie responded. "I'll pull in a direct weather feed on my uni-link and keep an ear on it, Dad."

"Good," he said. Then it seemed to Stephanie that he hesitated for a moment before going on. "You might want to think about heading back in a little earlier, anyway," he told her. "We're going to have dinner guests."

"Not more *scientists*!" Stephanie didn't quite groan, but it was close, and Richard chuckled.

"Nope, not tonight," he said sympathetically. "We did promise Dr. Hobbard she could come out and talk to you and Lionheart on Thursday, though."

"Oh, *Dr. Hobbard* isn't all that bad," Stephanie replied. "At least she's polite. Lionheart likes her, too. And she doesn't act like I'm some stupid kid who doesn't have a clue, either."

No, she doesn't, her father thought. *On the other hand, young lady, you've done quite a job of convincing almost all of her colleagues you* are *"a stupid little kid." Or that you really don't have a clue, anyway. One of these days there are going to be some really . . . irritated xeno-anthropologists when they realize you've been systematically playing dumb with them.*

"I've noticed that," he said out loud. "But it's not scientists tonight. In fact, I think you'll probably be glad to see them."

"I will?" Stephanie frowned suspiciously at her uni-link. She recognized that tone of voice. It was his "Dad's up to something" tone.

"Yep." He chuckled. "Seems we're going to be visited by a couple of folks from over near Thunder River."

"Thunder River?" Stephanie repeated, frown deepening. Thunder River came roaring out of the high Copperwalls close to a thousand kilometers north of the Harrington freehold.

"The person who called is an Irina Kisaevna. She says

she talked to you on the com last week, and she's coming over with a friend of hers—fellow named Scott MacDallan. Maybe you've heard of him?" Richard Harrington's tone could not possibly have sounded more innocent. "I think *I* heard something about him, anyway, around—what, a couple of months or so ago? Something about him and his treecat, wasn't it?"

19

STEPHANIE WATCHED THEIR VISITORS' ARRIVAL WITH mixed feelings.

Her father had been right about how much more rapidly the stormfront was moving in off the Tannerman Ocean, and the air car came sliding down out of a sky of increasingly angry-looking black clouds. There were occasional flashes of lightning off to the west, and wind thrashed the branches of the picketwood and crown oaks around her parents' home. Stephanie had often wondered what bad weather would be like on a planet with gravity closer to that of Old Earth's, where rain and other things fell a bit more . . . sedately. She'd never seen that, but she was well accustomed to the kind of heavy gravity Sphinx boasted, and there was a reason Sphinxian homeowners kept a careful eye on overhead branches. Nobody wanted a four- or five-meter crown oak branch crashing down on her head (or her roof) in a 1.35-gravity field, and tree surgeons were a well-paid specialty here on Sphinx.

Tonight's storm promised to be a doozy even by Sphinx's standards, though. The weather forecasters had been warning everyone about it for the better part of a week, but it had veered farther south as well as speeding up, which meant it was going to make landfall less than eighty kilometers from the Harrington freehold. It was also going to track directly across the central settlement of Lionheart's clan (she'd decided she liked Hobbard's term for the extended treecat family groups), and worry over her friends burned in the back of her mind, distracting her from her anticipation of the upcoming visit.

Still, she was a little surprised to discover there was another element tempering that anticipation. One she felt despite the fact she'd been the one who set this meeting in motion in the first place...and one she didn't much care for when she recognized it, either.

It was jealousy. She was actually *jealous* of all the newsies' recent stories about Dr. MacDallan and Fisher, and that made her feel...ashamed.

You ought *to feel ashamed*, she scolded herself. *What? Is it really all that important for* you *to be the only heroine where the treecats are concerned? You think* you *need to get all the credit? And if you're so envious about all the news coverage and all the congratulations Dr. MacDallan got, then why don't you make it a point to spend a little more time with all those xeno-anthropologists and xeno-biologists making sure* your *name gets into all their reports instead of his?*

She didn't like feeling that way, and she didn't just feel ashamed. She felt *disappointed* in herself...and she knew her parents would have felt the same way if they'd known.

"*Bleek!*" Lionheart said softly into her ear, and she felt him stir on her shoulder. His remaining true-hand reached out, touching her lightly on the side of the head, and somehow she sensed his gentle reprimand. Not for what she'd just realized she was feeling about Dr. MacDallan but for blaming herself for feeling it. And even though she thought he was wrong to let her off so easily, she had to admit that it wasn't as if she'd *set out* to envy the doctor. She hadn't even realized she did, and as she reached up to caress Lionheart's ears, she promised herself she was going to stamp out that envy just as soon as she possibly could.

"Bleek!" the treecat said again, more cheerfully, as he sensed the shift in her emotions, and she chuckled.

"All right," she whispered to him as the air car grounded. "All right, I'll behave. You be sure you do, too!"

Lionheart buzzed a purr, pressing warmly against the side of her neck, and they watched the air car hatch open.

Scott MacDallan, Stephanie decided, was just about the reddest redhead she'd ever seen in her life. His hair looked like you could light campfires with it, and his skin was so liberally dusted with freckles she was surprised it didn't glow.

Irina Kisaevna was shorter than he was, with a definitely feminine yet considerably more stocky build. Her hair was as dark as his was fiery, and she had big brown eyes that looked like they were designed to laugh a lot. She had a strong nose, too, and high cheekbones.

But it was the cream-and-gray colored treecat riding in the crook of Dr. MacDallan's arm that truly drew her attention. It didn't seem to be quite as large as Lionheart, and it had fewer dark bars circling its tail, but aside from that and Lionheart's missing arm, the two of them could have been twins, and the other treecat's head came up, green eyes bright as he looked in their direction.

<*Greetings, Swift Striker!*> Climbs Quickly called. <*Welcome to Death Fang's Bane Clan's range.*>

<I thank you for the greeting, elder brother,> Swift Striker replied. *<I had not realized Death Fang's Bane and her parents had become a full* clan, *though.>*

<If they have not yet, they soon will,> Climbs Quickly said. *<And Bright Water Clan has decided they are surely entitled to clan status. They have already taught us much, not to mention—>*

He raised his truncated right arm slightly, and felt Swift Striker's acceptance of his point. Then his eyes narrowed as he and the Laughing River Clan scout sampled one another's mind-glows. It was the treecat equivalent of what a human might have called "getting acquainted," except that it was far quicker—and far more thorough—than any pair of humans could have managed. Of course, neither of them was a memory singer, so there were depths they couldn't plumb, but in the time it took Swift Striker and his humans to climb out of their air car and cross to the waiting Harringtons, he and Climbs Quickly had become something very like old friends.

With that out of the way, they each turned to sampling the mind-glows of the humans they hadn't previously met. It was an interesting experience, since both MacDallan's and Stephanie's mind-glows had been included in the memory songs passed from clan to clan over the previous few months. The memory songs had made it clear to every listener that the two humans had exceptionally powerful mind-glows even for two-legs, yet it was obvious now that the songs had done them less than full justice.

<Your two-leg's mind-glow is even stronger than I expected,> Swift Striker said. *<I think it may burn even brighter than Darkness Foe's, in some ways!>*

<Darkness Foe's mind-glow is very powerful, too,> Climbs Quickly replied respectfully. *<I do not think either of them is truly* brighter *than the other, though. They are just . . . different.>*

He flirted the tip of his tail, thinking hard, trying to find a way to express what he felt.

<*I think,*> he said a moment later, <*that the difference is in the way in which each of them senses our bond. Death Fang's Bane is mind-blind, and Darkness Foe is not mind-blind ... entirely. I hear almost ... almost an echo of a mind-voice from him. Yet I think Death Fang's Bane may actually taste my feelings more strongly than he tastes yours. It is as if ... as if each of them has half of a Person's skill to taste a mind-glow, but neither has all.*>

<*I think you are right,*> Swift Striker replied. <*I had not thought of it in quite that way, but it makes sense now of the way in which Clear Singer was able to make him hear True Stalker's memories of what the evil one had done.*>

<*This is good!*> Climbs Quickly said. <*Already we are learning more about the two-legs—and especially about our own two-legs! I hope they are learning as much about us.*>

"Dr. MacDallan, Ms. Kisaevna—Fisher," Richard Harrington said, extending his hand to each of the humans in turn and nodding a greeting to the treecat. "Welcome! Now come inside before the rain starts!"

"That," Scott MacDallan said in a deep, pleasant baritone, "sounds like a *very* good idea, Dr. Harrington."

"Amen," Irina Kisaevna echoed, then looked across at Stephanie with a grin. "And you must be Stephanie." She winked. "Glad to actually meet you in person. Especially since you and I seem to be the only non-doctors present this evening!"

Stephanie laughed and came forward to hold out her own hand.

"Yeah," she said, shaking her head. "I get a lot of that around these two." She tilted her head in her parents' direction, and Marjorie Harrington smacked her gently on the top of that same head.

"Just remember who's handing out the hot chocolate later tonight," she told her daughter in an ominous tone, and it was Irina's turn to chuckle.

She had a nice laugh, Stephanie decided. And a nice face, too.

The Harringtons' guests accompanied them inside and into the big, comfortable living room, where a fire crackled and popped in the huge stone hearth. That hearth wasn't entirely a relic from the distant past, either. One thing Sphinx had plenty of was firewood. And if the house were to lose power in the middle of a Sphinx winter, that anachronistic fireplace (and the ones like it in almost every other room) might well make the difference between survival and freezing to death.

Tonight, though, the fire was simply for friendliness, and the five humans found themselves gathering around it in a shallow half-circle as the hiss of burning wood exercised its ancient, welcoming magic.

"I love those paintings," Irina said, looking at a trio of old-fashioned oils on the living room wall.

She stepped closer, studying the painting at the right end of the line with obvious pleasure and admiring the play of sunlight and shadow, the deep greens and the gray, black, and brown of the tree trunks, in the summer landscape. The painting to its left showed the same landscape, but in the earth tones, pale green, and robin's-egg-blue skies of spring. And the painting at the extreme left end of the row showed the same landscape yet again, this time clad in the sun-sparked whiteness of snow and embellished with the crystalline daggers of icicles. All of them were filled with a very different sense of the vibrant, ongoing life of Sphinx as the planet swept through the slow, stately march of its seasons. It was almost as if the viewer could reach into the pictures, actually touch the seasons they portrayed, and there was a bare patch of wall to the right of the summer landscape. It was clearly waiting for autumn, she thought, and turned back to the Harringtons.

"I thought I knew most of the artists here on Sphinx," she said, "but I certainly don't recognize this one's work. I'd love to get whoever did these to come out to my brother's place and do the same kind of series for him!"

"I think that might be arranged," Richard Harrington said with a slow smile, and nodded in his wife's direction. "I happen to know the artist pretty well."

"*You* did these?" Irina looked at Marjorie. "They're wonderful!"

"Well, I've still got to wait another T-year or so before I can add autumn to the wall," Marjorie responded. "It's not exactly something you can do in a rush here on Sphinx. But if your brother doesn't mind investing four or five T-years in the project, I can probably manage to squeeze him into my busy schedule."

The two women smiled at each other, and MacDallan shook his head.

"We're doomed, you know," he said to Richard and Stephanie. Stephanie arched her eyebrows at him, and he shrugged. "Your mom paints. Well, Irina sculpts—not just clay, either. She really likes bronze, too. She's already done three life-size studies of Fisher, and as if that weren't bad enough, she's a potter, too. Her place is littered with bowls, goblets, vases, plates, platters, saucers, pitchers, bowls, mugs, carafes, salad plates—did I mention *bowls*? And she gives them away at the drop of a hat, too. Fills all her friends' platter rails and cupboards with stuff. I did mention *bowls*, didn't I?"

"All the better for breaking over your thick skull," Irina told him sweetly, then looked at Marjorie with a chuckle. "All the same, though, I'm sure we could work

out a little trade in kind, if you're interested. I'd love to
do a sculpture of Lionheart." Her expression turned more
serious as she looked at Stephanie. "I think the way he
wears his honor scars says a lot about him."

"So do I," Stephanie said softly, reaching up to the
treecat on her shoulder.

"And on that note," Richard Harrington said firmly,
"let's get washed up and eat."

Supper was a decided success.

Both Harringtons were excellent cooks, and neither
MacDallan nor Irina had ever experienced Meyerdahl-style
cuisine. It reminded MacDallan of a sort of cross between
Old Earth Oriental and Iberian cooking, combining elements of each in ways which would never have occurred
to him but worked beautifully. It began with a starter
course of mushrooms sautéed in olive oil, garlic, scallions,
and parsley, accompanied by a salad with what his aunt
from Nueva Madrid would have called romescu sauce—a
tangy, tomato-based sauce with garlic, almonds, and hazel
nuts. The almonds were the original Old Terran version,
although the "hazel nuts" were from a local tree which
offered its own variation on the original theme. The same
was true of the "anchovies" in the salad, which had come
from a fish which filled very much the same ecological
niche on Sphinx's sister planet Manticore, although the
Bibb lettuce and endive were the original Old Terran
article, courtesy of Marjorie Harrington's gardens and
greenhouses right here on Sphinx. The olives, like the
"anchovies," had come from Manticore, whose orbital
position closer to the system primary gave it a climate
better suited to things like olive trees and orange groves.

The main course consisted of chicken thighs with
sage, rosemary, and thyme, but served over rice in a

coconut milk-based sauce with just a hint of curry, and accompanied by spinach with small slivers of pineapple and orange. Home baked bread completed the menu... aside from the homemade coconut milk and red bean ice cream which followed for dessert.

"That," MacDallan said with a sigh of repletion, sitting back from the table with an after dinner cup of coffee, "was delicious."

"Are you sure you wouldn't like a little more?" Marjorie Harrington offered with a smile, nodding at the sadly depleted serving dishes still mounting guard at the center of the table.

"Couldn't," he said. "Not after all that."

"It was delicious," Irina agreed. "And I'm stuffed, too."

She had not, Stephanie noticed, eaten nearly as much as the other humans at the table. Which, coupled with her stockier figure, suggested that, unlike Stephanie's own family, her metabolism and muscles hadn't been genetically engineered for a heavy-gravity environment. She was obviously accustomed to Sphinx's gravity, but Stephanie wondered what it must be like for an unmodified human to live day in and day out in a gravity thirty-plus percent higher than the one in which mankind had originally evolved.

The treecats, on the other hand, weren't done yet. Stephanie suspected that treecat notions of cuisine were very...basic. She'd been a little surprised, actually, to discover that they preferred their food cooked at all, although they were perfectly capable of eating it raw if they had to. But Lionheart had almost tried to dive right into the serving bowls and *wallow* there in pure delight the first time he'd encountered her parents' cooking, and Fisher seemed equally taken by it. He was currently working on his fifth chicken thigh, at any rate.

He hadn't cared much for the *spinach*, though, she reflected. Maybe if they'd spiked it with a little celery...

"In that case, if everyone's done, why don't we migrate back into the living room?" Marjorie suggested.

"Only if you let Scott and me help you clean up, first," Irina responded.

"If you're sure," Marjorie said, and Irina chuckled.

"Oh, I'm sure, believe me! I don't want him developing any bad habits just because we're not at home."

"All right," Marjorie agreed, and the human members of the party descended upon the table, hauling the wreckage off to the kitchen to be stored in the refrigerator, scraped into the compost bag, sorted into the trash, or scoured by the dishwasher's sonic emitters, as the case might be.

Some time later, they sat in a comfortable, conversational ring around the fireplace once more, listening to the thunderous waterfall-beat of rain on the roof and the roar of wind. Thunder rumbled—still distant, but coming steadily closer—and Richard Harrington shook his head.

"I think you guys better plan on spending the night here," he said.

"If we won't be putting you out, I think that's probably a good idea," MacDallan said ruefully, smiling as he reached up to gently touch the thoroughly stuffed treecat stretched sleepily across the back of his armchair. "The first time Fisher and I met, I wound up flying with him through the middle of a thunderstorm with a concussion. I think that's probably going to do both of us for a while where bad-weather flying is concerned."

"I can see how that might be," Richard said, then cocked his head slightly and arched an eyebrow. "Of course, bringing up the way you two met also offers the opportunity for a segue into the reason you're visiting us in the first place, doesn't it?"

"I guess it does," MacDallan acknowledged, and looked

at Stephanie. "I have to admit the possibility of comparing notes with you had crossed my mind—crossed it quite a few times, as a matter of fact—before you actually screened, Stephanie. I was a little...nervous about the possibility, though. And I don't suppose it's going to come as any great surprise to anyone that one reason I was nervous was the fact that I feel really protective where Fisher is concerned."

"I think you can safely assume we'd understand that, yes," Marjorie said dryly, and MacDallan chuckled. It was a curiously strained chuckle, Stephanie thought, and felt Lionheart raising his head from his perch on the back of her own chair to gaze at the visiting doctor.

"I've really wanted to sit down and talk with you—all of you, but especially with *you*, Stephanie—ever since Fisher came into my life, though," MacDallan continued. "Obviously, we've all been awfully busy. And then there was that BioNeering business."

His mouth tightened, and he reached out to take Irina's hand in his as shadows flickered behind his blue eyes.

"That was pretty bad, really," he said quietly. "And if I thought people had been pestering me about trying to 'figure out' the treecats *before* it happened—!" He shook his head. "Trust me, it got a lot worse."

He sat gazing silently into the fire for a few moments, then shook himself and looked back at Stephanie.

"I'm pretty sure they've been after you at least as much as they've been after me," he told her. "From what I've heard, your mom and dad have been pretty firm about laying down limits, and I think that was a really good idea. Most—well, a lot—of these people don't actually seem to mean any harm, but they're enough to drive Fisher crazy. I think their emotions are like some kind of feeding frenzy as far as he's concerned, and I don't think he's far wrong about that, either."

He paused, and Stephanie shrugged.

"Lionheart and I have met a few like that," she admitted. "Dr. Hobbard—you know her, right?" MacDallan nodded, and Stephanie went on, "She's not so bad. In fact, we kind of like her. But even she keeps—"

She stopped suddenly, and MacDallan's eyes narrowed.

"Even she keeps asking you questions you don't really want to answer," he said softly. "That's what you started to say, wasn't it, Stephanie?"

Stephanie only looked at him. She was surprised she'd started to say even that to a pair of complete strangers. She'd contacted MacDallan in the first place specifically because she wanted to discuss the situation with him, yet she'd planned on going more slowly. On getting a better feel for his personality, judging where *he* stood on the question of protecting treecats, before she jumped straight into it, anyway. But there was something about MacDallan—something more than the fact that he, too, had been adopted by a treecat. Something that made her want to trust him.

She looked at her parents, eyes silently questioning, and after a moment, her father gave a very small nod.

"Actually, she keeps on asking questions *none* of us want to answer," she said then, turning back to MacDallan. "Not yet, anyway."

"That's what I thought."

MacDallan leaned back in his own chair, still holding Irina's hand. His eyes swept the Harringtons' faces while the storm battered at the house, and then he inhaled deeply.

"That's what I thought," he repeated. "I know how excited I've been learning things about Fisher, and I was pretty sure you had to be at least equally excited, Stephanie. But you weren't going on and on about it to anyone who'd listen, the way a lot of kids would have, and that suggested to me that you were keeping your mouth shut on purpose. You're worried about how humans and treecats are going to get along in the long run, aren't you?"

"Yes," she admitted quietly, her eyes dark. "I think there was a reason they were hiding from us for so long, and I'm not sure they were wrong to worry about us. I know a lot of the other kids in Twin Forks are all going crazy trying to figure out how to catch themselves a treecat for a 'pet.'" Her eyes hardened and her lips thinned. "I wouldn't trust most of them with an Old Terran hamster, and treecats aren't *pets*! I can't seem to get any of those idiots to figure that out, either! They're all too busy being jealous, too busy thinking I'm just trying to keep Lionheart all for myself. They don't have a *clue* what he did for me—not really—and they all think he's so cute, so *cuddly*—!"

She chopped off what she was saying and gave herself a shake.

"Sorry about that. It just really, really makes me mad sometimes. And it scares me, too. Because if the *kids* can feel that way, why can't the grown-ups? And Dad and I have spent a lot of time talking about what happened on Barstool to the Amphors. I don't want that happening to the treecats!"

"You have no idea how delighted I am to hear you say that," MacDallan said. "That's exactly the same sort of thing I've been afraid of. And I didn't feel a lot better about the possibility after seeing the way Ubel was willing to let an entire clan die just to cover her own... posterior, either. So when you screened, it occurred to me that you had a pretty good point. I think it *would* be a good idea for any of us who have been adopted by one of these little guys," he reached up to caress Fisher's soft fur again, "to get together and see if we can't all arrange to be singing from the same sheet of music."

"You mean concentrate on figuring them out for ourselves?"

"That's part of what I mean—a *big* part, really. But more than that, I think you're right that the treecats are going to need us to protect them just as much as you needed Lionheart's clan to help you deal with that hexapuma and I needed Fisher to keep me from drowning. And, to be honest, I'm pretty sure they're a lot smarter than anybody else suspects, even now, and that they really are telepathic."

"I think they're a lot smarter than anybody else thinks—except maybe Dr. Hobbard—too," Stephanie agreed. "I'm not sure about her. But most of those other 'scientists' keep acting like the treecats are maybe a couple of steps up from a golden retriever." She grimaced. "I think maybe part of it's because they're so small. It's bad enough when you run into *anyone* who thinks that way, but I had one xeno-biologist who insisted on explaining—and explaining and *explaining*—to me that treecats just don't have enough body mass to sustain genuine intelligence. Their brains can't be big enough for 'advanced cognitive functions,' anybody knows that! So of course there's no point in finding out whether or not what 'anybody knows' is *accurate!*" She rolled her eyes. "The idiot was standing there holding Lionheart's flint knife and looking at his cargo net, and he was insisting treecats couldn't possibly be 'truly intelligent' however cleverly they 'mimicked' sapient behavior. I thought he was going to pat me on the head and tell me to run along and play with my dolls like a good little girl while the real, qualified, properly skeptical *scientists* got on with straightening out everything *I'd* obviously gotten wrong!"

"I've run into some of those myself," MacDallan told her with a wry grin. "And speaking about big enough brains, people like that make you sort of want to unscrew their heads from the rest of their bodies to see if there's anything actually inside *their* skulls, don't they?"

"Yeah, but I'm not *big* enough!" Stephanie told him with a broader grin of her own.

"For which the rest of the human race can only be grateful," her father observed. "I'm afraid a temper kind of like the one popular legend assigns to people with your hair color runs in the Harrington family, Scott."

"Actually, you know, there really is a link between red hair and enhanced adrenal function." MacDallan chuckled. "I think that's the reason redheads tend to get into trouble so much."

"And a very convenient excuse it is, too," Irina said dryly.

"But getting back to the subject at hand," MacDallan said in dignified tones, "I think in some ways the idiots you've just been describing, Stephanie, are almost our secret weapon at the moment. Personally, I think it may be better—initially, at least—for the treecats to be *under*estimated instead of overestimated."

"Are you sure about that, Scott?" Richard asked quietly. MacDallan looked at him, and he shrugged. "I can't get Barstool out of my mind. If the powers that be here on the Sphinx decide treecats are really only slightly more clever animals, they could be in a lot of trouble. I'd hate to have some fool with more political clout than brain power decide the proper policy is to institute game control laws and bag limits rather than give them protected status!"

"I agree entirely. I just don't want us rushing into anything, Richard. The way I see it, we can always admit treecats are smarter than people have been thinking they are if we have to. It'd be a lot harder to convince humanity in general that they *aren't* as smart as people think, assuming that turns out to be a good idea, if we rush this."

"Dr. MacDallan's right, Dad," Stephanie said soberly. "I've been thinking about this a lot, especially since you and I started talking about Barstool, and I think there are three things we need to be doing, if we can, really."

"Which three things?" MacDallan asked, watching her intently.

"First, I think you're right. No matter what we do, most people—especially those who haven't actually *met* a treecat—are going to think of them like those null wits in Twin Forks. They're going to think 'Oh, what cute, fluffy little pets!' I think that's probably dangerous for *individual* treecats, given the lengths some people are already going to trying to catch them. But as far as *all* treecats are concerned, I think you're right that it would be better for them to be underestimated, instead of overestimated, at least at first.

"So I think we want people to realize they are intelligent, they *are* tool-users, but to think of them . . . well, to think of them as kind of permanent, cute *kids*, if you know what I mean. An intelligent species that needs to be *protected*, not exploited, but which nobody could think of as a real *threat*."

She paused, watching MacDallan until he nodded slowly, then went on.

"At the same time, though, I think we do need to make it clear they *are* an intelligent species. Not only that, they're the *native* intelligent species of Sphinx. They were here first—this is *their* world, not ours—and we need to make sure nobody tries to take it away from them.

"And finally, as part of that first thing I was talking about, we need to convince people here on Sphinx, at least, that the treecats who adopt people are more than just pets. Treecats like Lionheart and Fisher have to be . . . ambassadors, I guess. I've seen what they can do when they're angry." She shivered, remembering a huge hexapuma shrieking in agony as it was literally torn apart by a tidal wave of "cute, fluffy" treecats. "Sooner or later, other people are going to figure it out, too. I mean, Dr. Hobbard already has, and I kind of suspect the Forestry Service rangers have been thinking in the same direction. Well, it's all well and good to convince people they're 'permanent kids' who need to be looked after, but at the same time, we have to convince the people around us

that no treecat is just going to suddenly take it into his
head to eat somebody's Pekingese or pet parakeet...or
rip out somebody's throat!"

She came to a halt, staring at MacDallan, and the doctor looked back at her. Then he looked at her parents.

"Remarkable daughter you have here," he told them.

"We think so," Marjorie replied, smiling at Stephanie,
and MacDallan returned his attention to her.

"I agree with everything you've said," he told her,
"but I think we might want to go a little slower on your
second point."

"But they *were* here first!" Stephanie protested. "We can't
just let people take their whole planet *away* from them!"

"No, we can't. And if I have anything to say about it,
we won't. But, to be honest, one of the reasons I think
it would be a good idea to have them underestimated, at
least initially, is that what really happened to the Amphors
was that they got in the way. The colonists who'd settled
Barstool had already divided up the planet and its mineral
rights. For that matter, they'd already committed some
of the rights to exploit the planet to off-world investors
in return for the capital they'd needed to get their own
colony up and running. So when the Amphors turned
up all of a sudden, there were groups—factions—who
stood to lose an awful lot of land...and money. All they
had in some cases, if it turned out the *Amphors* owned
the planet and not the humans. You know, back on Old
Earth more than one bunch of *humans* got exterminated
or chased into exile by other humans who wanted what
they had. I'm afraid what happened to the Amphors suggests it's even easier to do that if the people you're taking
it away from aren't even shaped the same way you are."

"Exactly! That's why it's so important to make sure
nobody can do that to the treecats!"

"I agree. But right now, there aren't a lot of humans

on Sphinx, which means there aren't going to be that many people suddenly worrying about what happens to the land they're actually living on. Most of the planet is still public domain, too, which means it belongs to the Star Kingdom as a whole, not to individual people. *Except* that there are land speculators over in Landing and here in Yawata Crossing, who've already acquired options on some of it."

"Options?" Stephanie repeated.

She didn't have a clue what he was talking about, but the City of Landing on the planet of Manticore was the Star Kingdom's capital. Yawata Crossing was the current planetary capital here on Sphinx, though there was talk of moving the Planetary Parliament to the more central city of Tillingham. But anyone living in either of those places right now would have ready access to their system or planetary parliaments. And that, she thought sinkingly, meant politics were going to be involved somehow. She didn't know a lot about politics—yet—but she'd learned enough in her history classes to know politics could always be counted on to make a bad situation worse.

"It was an idea the government came up with during the worst of the Plague," Irina explained. "Before the colonists ever left Old Earth, Roger Winton took everything the expedition had managed to scrape together and hadn't spent on the cryo ship and supplies and invested it. It wasn't all that much compared to what they'd already invested, but since it took better than six hundred and forty T-years for the ship to get here, that investment had a *lot* of time to earn interest. By the time *Jason* got to Manticore, that 'minor' investment had grown into an enormous sum. Most of the colonies hadn't bothered with anything like that, since the whole object was to leave Old Earth (and everything on it) behind forever. Besides, it would have taken centuries for light-speed ships in normal-space to make the trip back to the Sol System to *do* anything with money invested there, anyway. But King Roger—only he wasn't king then, of course—suspected that somebody might make a breakthrough into a practical commercial hyper-space drive that made faster-than-light travel practical for *everybody*, not just survey ships, while his expedition was on its way. In that case, money back on Old Earth might come in handy, after all."

She shrugged.

"Obviously, he was right about that, and Manticore wound up a whole lot better off than the vast majority of colonies because of that. And it helped a lot when the Plague hit, too—helped pay to bring in doctors and researchers, helped fund the immigration program and the land credits. But even with the Star Kingdom's investments back on Old Earth, we were really strapped for funds at the height of the Plague. We needed cash to pay for supplies, medicines, all kinds of stuff, from people out *here*, and it's five and a half T-months from here to Old Earth one-way, even for a high-speed courier boat in hyper-space. Some of the people we needed things from weren't real eager to wait around for eleven T-months until money could be requested from the Sol System and then transported out here to pay them, so the government decided to raise cash locally by selling options on public lands."

"But what *kind* of options?" Stephanie asked. "You mean they sold off public lands? That's not what they told me in school!"

"Because that's not exactly what they *did*," Irina said. "Some of the land and mineral rights here on Sphinx have already been assigned, even if no one's tried to develop them yet. They're *not* public lands anymore; they were deeded over to first-shareholders from the original colony fleet.

"Of course, some of those people died without heirs

during the Plague Years, and their lands and rights have reverted to the Crown, so those are back in the public lands category. Other first-shareholder grants are like my brother's land—or my husband's and mine. Or like the land that's been distributed under the immigration incentive program, like your parents' freehold, for that matter. It's already been settled, claimed, and proved, so that's not public land anymore, either.

"But what *does* still come under the 'public lands' heading is the better than ninety-nine-point-nine percent of the planet that hasn't been distributed or sold yet. What the Crown *did* sell was the option to be first in line to buy public lands when they *are* sold. The idea was always that, ultimately, except for a modest wilderness reserve, most of the land on all three habitable planets here in the Manticore system would end up in private hands, you know, Stephanie. Given their climates—and gravity wells—Manticore itself is the obvious first prize, which is why something like seventy percent of its land and mineral rights have already been distributed. Sphinx is attractive, too, but mostly to people like your family and Scott's, who are ... particularly well-suited to heavy-gravity planets, let's say. Gryphon's generally considered the consolation prize, though, since it orbits the system's other stellar component which puts it a long way from Manticore and Sphinx. And then there's its climate."

She made a face, and MacDallan chuckled. Stephanie hadn't really paid that much attention to Gryphon, yet, but what she'd seen about its seasons—exceptionally violent, thanks to its extreme axial tilt—suggested Irina was right about that!

"Anyway," Irina resumed, "Sphinx is where most of the *desirable* undistributed land is located. So everybody's figured all along that eventually the public lands here would mostly be sold, probably at pretty good prices when the time finally comes. What the government did to raise cash during the emergency was to allow people to put down a relatively tiny payment—only about four or five cents on the dollar, actually—for chunks of land so that they'd be guaranteed the *first* chance to buy that land whenever it finally goes on the market. There's a little more to it than that, including a provision that the government agrees to discount the price for option-holders—by up to forty percent of the current market value, in some cases—at the time it goes up for sale. So, especially since the option prices were based on the land's *current* value, not what it's going to be worth when there are hundreds of thousands or even millions of people ready to bid against each other for it, the people holding those options stand to make a *lot* of money on their initial investment."

"But at the rate people are settling on Sphinx, most of the people who bought the options will be *dead* by the time the government gets around to selling all that land!" Stephanie protested.

"Of course they will. But in the meantime, the options can be sold and traded just like any other property or investment, and they have been. Not only that, but their value can be expected to do nothing but increase over the long term. So what Scott is getting at is that if the government decides the entire planet belongs to the tree-cats, there are going to be people—quite a lot of them, in fact—who will suddenly find that the options they've invested in are worthless. And since options like that tend to end up in the hands of professional speculators, the people that could happen to are likely to already have a lot of money...and a lot of political influence. If the government wants to give Sphinx back to the treecats, they aren't going to like it very much, and it's possible some of them will decide to use that money and influence of theirs to keep it from happening."

Stephanie's eyes widened in horrified understanding, and Lionheart reared up on the back of her chair, hissing, ears flattened as he sensed her distress.

"I don't think anyone's going to really believe the Crown's likely to declare the entire planet off limits to everybody else, no matter how intelligent it decides treecats are, Stephanie!" MacDallan said quickly. "And it'd probably take something that radical to start any organized effort to turn them into more Amphors anytime soon."

"But if people start thinking they *are* that smart, then some of those option holders you're talking about *are* liable to think that!" Stephanie protested. "You know they are!"

"Maybe," MacDallan agreed, "but they're going to try to limit the damage first—restrict how *much* of the planet might be set aside for the treecats—not go directly to an all-out 'exterminate the little monsters' campaign. And that would probably be a more workable approach for them in the first place. Just like there aren't all that many two-legged people on Sphinx yet, there aren't all that many *treecats* here, either, unless I'm sadly mistaken. If I've understood what Hobbard's been telling me correctly, she's thinking they're only just beginning to make the transition from a basically hunter-gatherer society to one that grows its own food, and that means their population can't be anywhere near as dense as a human population might be. So I doubt they're going to need the entire planet no matter what happens. I imagine the government's going to see it that way, anyway. And let's be fair, here, the people who traveled all the way out here to build new homes for themselves, new lives for their families, do have a legitimate interest in what happens to the land here on Sphinx. So I doubt most of the speculators Irina's talking about are likely to find themselves really desperate when the time comes.

"That doesn't mean there won't be *any* opposition to setting a good-sized chunk of the planet aside for the treecats, though. That's what I think we need to be concerned about. What we want to happen—what I think we need to be working for—is to see to it that when those public lands we've been talking about are finally sold, the treecats are guaranteed enough of the planet for them and their children and their children's children."

"But how do we do that?" Stephanie asked, gathering Lionheart into her arms as she—and the treecat—calmed down again.

"I'm not sure about that," MacDallan admitted. "Not yet. It's going to be tricky, especially since the original colonization charter gave most of the authority to the local planetary governments when it comes time to deal with this particular question. And if the planetary administrations exercise that authority, then two-thirds of the revenue generated from the sale of the lands go to the *planetary* governments, not to the system government. That's going to make a lot of planetary administrators feel mighty greedy, and I'm not sure where that provision stands under the new Constitution. I'm inclined to doubt that anyone really wants to push real hard to find out at the moment, either.

"But the point I was trying to make is that there probably are people who are going to feel economically threatened if somebody suddenly starts making noises about handing the entire planet over to its 'indigenous intelligent species.' At this point, no one's really worried about those 'cute, fluffy' little treecats of yours. Or, at least, I don't think they are. And we need to keep it that way as long as we can, because no matter what we do, sooner or later, the people who stand to lose all that money are going to wake up to the fact that they do. I think we need to keep them from realizing that long enough for us to get as many protections—and as much good publicity—as possible for the treecats in place before anybody does start organizing a political campaign to turn them into Sphinx's Amphors."

Stephanie looked at him for several more seconds, then nodded slowly and looked at her parents.

"That's what you and Mom have been thinking about, isn't it, Dad?"

"More or less," Richard admitted, glancing at Marjorie. "It sounds to me like Scott's been giving it a lot of thought, too, though, and I'm inclined to agree with him. On the other hand," he looked back at MacDallan, eyes narrowing slightly, "I'm also inclined to wonder about something you said earlier, Scott. Something about *knowing* the treecats are even smarter than anyone else thinks. Would it happen that however it is you come to know that has you particularly worried?"

"In a way," MacDallan admitted.

Then he paused, visibly steeling himself, and Fisher raised his head. He put his triangular chin on his person's shoulder, leaning his whiskered muzzle against MacDallan's cheek, and crooned encouragingly. MacDallan's expression eased slightly, and he pressed his cheek back against the treecat and looked back at Richard.

"The thing is, I'm afraid that if the people who might worry about treecats staking a claim to all of Sphinx realized how smart they *really* are, they might be panicked into taking some kind of... preemptive action after all. Or worse." His expression tightened again, although not as much as it had before. "It's bad enough to think about having xeno-anthropologists poking and prodding at them in their native environment, but if anyone ever *confirms* that they're genuine telepaths—extremely *capable* telepaths—then every black-ops genetic lab in the galaxy is going to want treecat *specimens* so they can figure out how it works. And that doesn't even consider how the 'fear factor' could play into the hands of anyone who wants to sweep them out of his way here on Sphinx. Your family's from Meyerdahl; mine's from Halakon. We know how much prejudice there is against human genies, how many times stupid people have started rumors about genies' 'sinister powers.' You think that kind of crap wouldn't be used against 'evil telepathic treecats' if it worked to get them out of someone's way?"

"And you're saying it *would* work?" Richard asked slowly. "That they really are—what was it you called them? 'Extremely *capable* telepaths'?"

"Yes, they are."

"And you know this because—?"

"I know it because I've got 'the sight,'" MacDallan sighed. He managed a particularly crooked smile. "Runs in my family—Highland Scots, you know." He shrugged. "My grandmother, God rest her soul, could be five thousand kilometers away when one of her kids or grandkids broke an arm, and it would turn out she'd already been in the air headed for the hospital before he did it. That kind of thing."

"So you were speaking from personal experience about people talking about 'genies' sinister powers,'" Marjorie Harrington said gently, her eyes soft with sympathy.

"Oh, yes." MacDallan smiled at her, and this time the expression was a little more natural looking. "And, to be honest, I'd just as soon not hear them talking about it again where my family or I are concerned. Which is one reason I've kept my mouth very firmly shut about what *really* happened when the Stray turned up."

"But you trust us enough to tell us about it?" Marjorie asked in that same gentle voice.

"Well," MacDallan reached up and stroked Fisher. "As far as I can see, you come pretty highly recommended."

"So do you, Dr. MacDallan," Stephanie said with a smile of her own, and pointed at Lionheart, who had leaned forward to mimic Fisher, pressing against the side of her neck and purring.

"Go ahead and tell them, Scott," Irina said quietly, still holding the hand that wasn't stroking Fisher.

"All right."

He let his gaze circle his hosts' faces and settled himself visibly in the chair.

"After the Stray and Fisher led me to Erhardt's air car, I called the Twin Forks tower to get a search and rescue crew out to recover the bodies. Since I was already on site, Wylie Bishop—he had the tower watch that day— asked me to go ahead and conduct the field autopsies. It wasn't very pleasant.

"I'd completed my preliminary exams before the accident investigation guys had finished with the air car, though, and Fisher wanted me to head off into the woods for some reason. I wasn't real crazy about that, since it was already after dark and that was hexapuma country, but he was insistent. So I went with him. And when I did, he and the Stray led me right to a tiny campfire completely surrounded by treecats."

He was watching Stephanie as he spoke, and he saw her eyes when he mentioned the campfire. Clearly the fact that the treecats were fire-users as well as tool-users was no surprise to her, although he knew she'd never mentioned anything of the sort to Sanura Hobbard or the other scientists. He nodded to her slightly, putting down another plus mark on his mental ledger under the heading of "Harrington, Stephanie, Good Things about."

"I didn't know what they had in mind at first," he continued, "but it didn't take them long to show me. One of them, a female from her coloring and markings, I think, was obviously in charge, and she obviously wanted something from me. I didn't know what, but then she looked into my eyes and—"

20

"HI, SCOTT," RICHARD HARRINGTON SAID CHEERFULLY.
"Didn't expect to hear from you again quite so soon."

Dr. MacDallan grinned from the com screen. He and
Irina had ended up spending two nights, not one, as
the Harringtons' guests. The weather had been partly to
blame, but the real reason had been that they'd simply
discovered how much they liked the Harrington family.
Besides, Fisher and Lionheart had clearly taken a real shine
to each other, and Stephanie had wanted to take Fisher
home to meet Lionheart's clan. From Fisher's response
when he got back to the freehold with Stephanie and
Lionheart, the visit had been a great success.

Of course, that *might* have been because he'd gotten to
go hang gliding for the first time in his life, too.

On the other hand, MacDallan hadn't realized Stephanie
was traveling back and forth between the freehold and

the treecats' central range by herself. When he did figure that out, he was horrified. The fact that she was making the trip by air mollified his concerns a little, but still...

Which, after all, was the reason he'd screened this morning.

"Well, I hadn't really expected to be screening you this soon, either," he said, "but I've been thinking about something. I hope I'm not going to be...intruding on anything, but the truth is I'm a little worried about the way Stephanie's getting back and forth to the treecats."

"I could be happier myself," Richard said, his expression sobering. "I think it's probably the best compromise when it comes to keeping their location secret, though. And, trust me, the counter-grav unit I put into *this* glider would keep her up at three hundred meters for the better part of sixteen hours without a bit of airfoil lift! If she runs into any kind of trouble, she knows she's supposed to go straight up, com us, and then *stay* there until one of us comes and collects her." He shrugged. "I can't say I'm delighted with the arrangement, but we can't keep her wrapped up in cotton forever, and this whole situation with Lionheart's making that even truer than it would have been otherwise."

"I agree," MacDallan said. "For that matter, Halakon's only been settled for about three hundred years. We're probably still closer to a 'frontier mentality' where I come from than you folks on Meyerdahl were. And from what I've seen of Stephanie, that's one capable kid you've got there. But I'm still worried. The best equipment in the world malfunctions occasionally, and I've always been a big believer in the belt-and-suspenders approach."

"Meaning what?" Richard asked in a slightly puzzled tone.

"Well, what I'm thinking is that if she goes down in the bush again, it might be a good idea for her to have something just a bit better than a vibro blade if a hexa-puma or a peak bear comes calling."

"I don't know, Richard."

Marjorie Harrington and her husband stood facing each other across the kitchen's central island. She was chopping carrots and shredding lettuce for a salad while Richard carefully seasoned the steaks waiting to go onto the broiler. Stephanie was keeping careful watch on the baking potatoes... and trying (unsuccessfully) to conceal her intense interest in their conversation.

Now Marjorie glanced in her daughter's direction and found herself wishing this particular conversation wasn't being listened to by that particular set of ears. More than one other conversation had fallen into that category in the past, though, and they'd survived those. She imagined they'd survive this one, and given how deeply it concerned Stephanie, she deserved to hear it.

"To be honest, I don't much like the idea myself," Richard said, then shrugged. "Still, he's got a point. More than one, really. And I think you and I might've considered it ourselves if we hadn't grown up on Meyerdahl."

"I know Meyerdahl wasn't still some rough, wild-frontier colony planet," Marjorie said just a bit tartly. "The planetary constitution did guarantee the right of self-defense, though, you know!"

"Of course it did. It just wasn't something that came up all that often—at least where anything besides our fellow humans was concerned."

Marjorie nodded. That nod looked unwilling, but her expression was thoughtful.

"Would it really be practical, though?" she asked. "Stephanie's never going to be all that big, you know. Tall, I mean," she added, turning to smile at her daughter before Stephanie could take umbrage.

"Scott seems to've factored that into his calculations," Richards said. "I think that's one reason he wants her to learn to handle a rifle, too. In fact, he's suggested—and I think it would be a good idea—that you and I learn, too. Neither of us has spent any time traipsing around the bush yet, but that's certain to change eventually. And when it does, it's always possible *we* could run into a hexapuma, you know."

Marjorie made a small face, but she also nodded.

"What he's really thinking about, though, is that if she's gliding back and forth, what she'd probably really need is something she can carry fairly easily. Something powerful enough to at least . . . discourage the biggest predators while she sits in a tree or something and coms for help. He says what he had in mind would be something like, oh, a ten or eleven-millimeter handgun."

"Ten or eleven-millimeter!" Marjorie looked at him. "A gun that size would be as long as *she* is, Richard!"

"Not quite," he disagreed with a smile. "Close, I'll grant you, but she could probably keep the muzzle from dragging if she carried it in a shoulder holster instead of on her belt."

"Very funny." Marjorie's tone was deflating, but the corners of her own mouth twitched in an unwilling half-smile.

"Look," Richard said, "this isn't my area of expertise, so I'm sort of having to take Scott's word for it. He says one of the friends he mentioned to us—Frank Lethbridge—is a Forestry Service and law enforcement-certified firearms instructor. He says Lethbridge has already volunteered to teach her, and as Scott points out, it wouldn't be a bad idea for her to be making friends—gathering allies, if you like—in the Forestry Service. Lethbridge's willing to train you and me, too, and he's talking about rifles all around, as well as handguns if we want to learn those, as well.

As far as a handgun for Steph is concerned, Scott says Lethbridge would probably be the best person to ask for recommendations. He says Lethbridge is a pretty good gunsmith, too. Apparently he's the one who customized Scott's own pistol for him."

"I don't know," Marjorie repeated. "I mean, it all sounds perfectly logical, but...she's my little girl!" She looked at Stephanie again. "Sorry, honey, but there it is. You *are* my little girl. I know you're growing up fast, but there's still a part of me that *worries* about you. And something like this—"

She shook her head, and Richard touched her lightly on the shoulder.

"I know exactly what you're saying," he said, "and I'm pretty sure Stephanie understands, too." He smiled at their daughter, who was wise enough to recognize that this was not a time to insist she was all grown up. "For that matter, I think Scott was a bit hesitant about...pushing the idea. But you saw how he and Stephanie got on. He's genuinely worried about her, and to be honest, he's right. I think we've been guilty of a serious blind spot in not considering this ourselves, Marge. Especially after we already almost lost her to a hexapuma once."

His voice was much more somber with the final sentence, and Marjorie's facial muscles tightened as she remembered that terrible night.

"Scott says Irina's nephew, Karl, would be willing to help, too," he continued. "He's about fifteen, only a year or so older than Steph is. Scott thinks—and I think he's right about this, too—that having someone closer to her own age involved would probably help. Besides," he grinned, "I gather young Karl thinks Fisher is a marvelous invention. I wouldn't be a bit surprised if part of what he has in mind is, um, *inveigling* our Stephanie into eventually introducing him to the rest of Lionheart's family."

"Oh, I *see*," Marjorie murmured with a smile of her own.

"Anyway, that's what he called about," Richard said.

Marjorie nodded, then frowned in pensive silence while her flashing knife finished sectioning carrots and slicing tomato wedges. She paused to hand a celery stalk to Lionheart before she began cutting the rest of the head of celery into neat lengths. In fact, she cut considerably more than even two humans and a treecat were likely to polish off. Finally, though, she finished the celery, inhaled deeply, turned to face Stephanie, and put her hands on her hips.

"I suppose you think this would be a *marvelous* idea, don't you?" Her tone was severe, yet she also smiled—slightly, and reluctantly, but smiled.

"I don't know if I'd say it was a 'marvelous' idea," Stephanie replied cautiously. "I do think it makes sense, though. And I *would* like to learn to shoot. For that matter, you know you and Dad promised I could start the junior marksmanship program in Twin Forks next year."

"We promised you you could do that when you turned *fifteen*," her mother corrected gently but firmly, and Stephanie wiggled slightly. "Still," her mother continued, "you're right that we did agree you could learn to shoot, at least eventually. And even though I'm not real crazy about the thought of killing anything myself, I have to say Scott probably does have a point about you and me learning to shoot, too, Richard," she admitted, glancing at her husband.

Stephanie contented herself with a gravely thoughtful expression, experience having taught her this would not be a moment to rush in enthusiastically.

"If—and I said *if*, Stephanie—we agree to this, I want your word you'll do *exactly* what Ranger Lethbridge tells you to do. I know you probably would anyway, but we're talking about weapons powerful enough to stop a hexapuma. Those aren't toys, and if they can stop hexa-pumas, they can do a lot of damage to anything *else* they hit . . . and it won't make any difference to the target if what they hit gets hit on purpose or by accident."

"Yes, ma'am," Stephanie replied very soberly.

"All right." Her mother drew another deep breath. "Your father and I will think about this. I promise we'll make our minds up as quickly as possible, and we'll be as fair about it as we can. But I expect you to accept our deci-sion, whatever it is. Deal?"

"Deal," Stephanie said firmly.

She managed to keep any glee out of her voice or her expression, but she knew that tone. It might not already be in the bag, but it was looking good, she thought. Looking very good.

"All *right!*" Karl Zivonik said, peering through the spotting scope at the target. "Five for five in the ten-ring with that group, Steph! Looks like one big hole from here. Good shooting!"

Stephanie grinned hugely, then made sure the bolt had locked back the way it was supposed to, laid the rifle in the rack with its muzzle pointed downrange the way she'd been taught, and removed her ear protectors. The old-fashioned, muff-style protectors covered her entire ear (which was why Frank Lethbridge liked them so much) but were fitted with microphones which let her hear nor-mal sounds even though they protected her hearing from the high-decibel sound of gunshots. Despite that, she still didn't like the way they seemed to . . . close in on her. Of course, if there'd been anyone else on the shooting line, she would have left them in place anyway. The one time she'd started to take them off when she hadn't noticed another shooter's arrival, Ranger Lethbridge had peeled a strip right off her. She'd wanted to die on the spot as he relentlessly dissected the earthworm-level IQ involved in doing something like that. Even more effectively, he'd banned her from the range for two full days.

Somewhat to her surprise, Stephanie had discovered she was a natural shot. So was her mother—which had surprised Marjorie even more. Her father, alas, was not. He was turning into what Ranger Lethbridge called a 'competent' rifleman, but he was never going to be his daughter's or his wife's equal as a marksman, and pistols clearly were not his forte. Fortunately, his ego seemed sufficiently robust to survive that shattering disappointment.

"Give me!" Stephanie commanded now, pointing at the powerful spotting scope Karl had been peering through. He turned his head and grinned at her, putting one hand possessively on the instrument.

"That," he pointed out, "wasn't exactly the polite way to ask. I think you left a word out, didn't you?"

Stephanie returned his grin. Scott MacDallan hadn't mentioned that Irina's nephew had been present for her confrontation with Trudy Franchitti and Stan Chang, but she'd recognized him instantly. Apparently he'd seen and heard even more of it than she'd realized, too, and his opinion of Trudy was (if possible) even lower than Stephanie's. She found that very satisfying, and if part of that was because he was so unimpressed by how...well-endowed Trudy was, that could just be her little secret.

Karl was also a woodsman and a hunter. In fact, it was already obvious to Stephanie that he was much better at both than Ralph Franchitti or his father would ever be. And unlike either of them, he wasn't interested in impressive trophies. He loved Sphinx's forests as much as Stephanie had come to love them, and he was fiercely protective where they were concerned. That was why Frank Lethbridge had arranged his visit to the Forestry Service

HQ in the first place. In another couple of T-years, Karl was going to meet the Forestry Service age requirements, and he knew exactly what he wanted to do with his life.

He was also tall for his age—taller than Scott MacDallan already, and closing in on her own father's height. The fact that his family's muscles hadn't been genetically modified for a heavy-gravity environment gave him an impressive muscle mass to go with that tall, strong-boned frame, but he didn't try to tower over Stephanie the way some guys did. There were times when he got a little quiet, when his eyes got a little...distant, or maybe the word she was looking for was "sad." She didn't know where that inner touch of darkness came from, but the quiet moments seldom lasted long and he never let them linger or spill over onto anybody else.

He also didn't seem particularly bothered by the fact that she was "only a kid," either. Of course, she was only one T-year—well, all right, one *and a half* T-years, since he was almost sixteen—younger than he was. He appeared to be pleasantly unaware of that differential, though. He had a working brain, too, and he didn't talk down to her because she was younger. He didn't appear to feel especially threatened when it turned out she knew more about something than he did, either.

Besides, he had a sense of humor.

"You're right," she said now, her expression thoughtful. "I *did* leave a word out, didn't I?" She smiled sweetly. "What I meant to say, Karl, was 'give me the spotting scope *now*.'"

"I thought that was it," he said with an answering grin, and moved so she could settle behind the scope and peer downrange herself.

The old-fashioned optical telescope was more powerful even than the telescopic sight fitted to the rifle she'd just been firing, and she felt a glow of pleasure as she looked at the target. Karl was right. She'd put all five rounds into the ten-ring at a range of a hundred and fifty meters. She'd been firing prone, off the sandbags, of course, but it looked to her as if all five holes could have been covered with a Manticoran quarter.

"Not *too* bad, I guess," she allowed.

"Hey, you're not going to goad *me* into telling you how great you are, so don't even go there," Karl replied, and she snorted.

"Can't blame me for trying, though," she pointed out.

"Can't say I'm *surprised* you tried, at least," he responded, and pressed the button to bring the standard bull's-eye target back to their shooting position.

Stephanie smiled at him and started policing up her brass. The gray-toned cartridge cases were actually made of a composite far stronger and tougher than any metallic alloy, but they were still called "brass" by a purist like Karl. It seemed pretty silly to Stephanie, but she'd come to the conclusion that there was something inherently anachronistic at the heart of those purists.

The cases were still warm, but the composite cooled quickly enough for her to handle without discomfort, and most shooters on Sphinx were thrifty souls. They reloaded their spent cases ("brass," she reminded herself with a mental grin)—or had someone else reload them—as a matter of course. Besides, leaving the range as clean as they'd found it was only good shooting etiquette.

"Well, I think we can pretty much take it as given that Frank—I mean, Ranger Lethbridge—is going to sign off on the rifle course when you shoot your qualification tomorrow," Karl said as he finished running a finger over the bullet holes. The holes vanished as the activated smart-paper regenerated itself, and he studied it critically for a moment, then nodded in satisfaction before he looked back up at Stephanie. "Want to go and shoot a few practice courses with the eleven-millimeter before we start cleaning guns?"

"As a matter of fact, I would." Stephanie's eyes lit, and Karl laughed.

"All right," he said. "Come on."

The two of them strolled across to the pistol range, carrying their ear protectors. One thing there was lots of on Sphinx was open space, and the handgun range had been set up for shooting out to fifty meters, which was a *long* range for any pistol shot. The qualification shoot for handgun wouldn't *require* Stephanie to shoot at any range in excess of twenty-five meters, but she'd discovered she liked to push herself at the longer ranges, as well.

She put her ear protectors back on while Karl hooked a silhouette target to the carrier and ran it out to seven meters. She waited patiently until he finished doing that, then stepped back and donned his own protectors.

"Present," he said in a much more sober and official tone, and she drew the heavy pistol from its holster.

The handgun Scott MacDallan and Frank Lethbridge had chosen for her was almost as long as her own forearm: a semi-automatic, chemical-propellant weapon directly descended from the firearms mankind had taken with him from Old Earth. Someone from those pre-Diaspora days would have called it an 11-millimeter magnum, and they probably would have been surprised that such weapons were still in common use. When it came down to it, though, any projectile weapon still depended on accelerating a bullet to high velocities very, very quickly, and chemical propellants (which had become even more efficient over the ensuing sixteen centuries) were still the easiest, cheapest, and most reliable way to do just that. More sophisticated weapons had been developed for specialized military and police uses, but old-fashioned firearms like Stephanie's pistol worked just fine for most civilian requirements, and you never had to worry about whether or not their power packs were charged.

They did tend to be good-sized, though, and some people might have been astonished that her mentors had chosen such a cannon for someone as small as Stephanie to pack about with her.

Well, they probably *would* have chosen a lighter weapon if their primary worry hadn't been stopping something like a hexapuma. As Ranger Lethbridge had pointed out, however, she could always use a heavier weapon to stop something *smaller* than a hexapuma, but a popgun wouldn't be much use if she and Lionheart found themselves reprising their original performance without the rest of his clan in attendance.

On the plus side, someone with Stephanie's genetic modifications was much stronger than an unmodified human of her size. Her bones were denser, as well, and her slender wrists were much more powerful than they looked. In addition, the heavy springs in the automatic's action soaked up a fair amount of recoil, and Lethbridge had fitted the massive handgun with a ported muzzle brake which reduced felt recoil by another thirty percent or so. Its sheer weight also helped to absorb recoil forces—Lethbridge carried a *13.5*-millimeter weapon built on the same frame—and it actually hadn't taken Stephanie long to get past her original discomfort with it.

Now, her expression as serious as Karl's, she drew the pistol, pulled back the slide until the action locked open to demonstrate that it was unloaded, and drew a magazine of fat, 11-millimeter rounds from the carrier on her belt.

"Ready," she said, holding the magazine in her left hand.

"Load," he told her, and she slid the magazine into place briskly enough to make sure it locked.

Karl watched her, then turned his head to survey the range. They were alone on it, but range procedure had been drilled into both of them.

"Ready on the right!" he announced. "Ready on the left!"

There was no response, since there was no one *to* respond, but he paused for a moment, anyway. Then he stepped back, putting himself well behind Stephanie.

"Range is ready," he told her, and she pressed the slide release.

The heavy slide slammed forward, stripping off and chambering the top round, and she settled into the shooting stance Lethbridge and Karl had taught her. It was something Lethbridge said had once been called a "Weaver stance," although he didn't know why. Stephanie didn't know, either, but she'd found it surprisingly comfortable once she'd actually adjusted to it, and the pistol leveled in her hands. The sight picture formed itself automatically, almost instinctually after so many hours on the range, and she squeezed the trigger.

Scott MacDallan stood on the upper-level deck outside Frank Lethbridge's Forestry Service office. They were far enough from the range that even the bellow of Stephanie's magnum was little more than a distant popping, and he shook his head with a smile. He'd expected Stephanie to enjoy herself, yet he'd been taken more than a little aback by how *much* she'd enjoyed the firearms training. She'd taken to it on an almost genetic level, and it hadn't hurt a bit for her and Lionheart to get so well acquainted with Frank and Ainsley Jedrusinski. Having two Forestry Service rangers—especially partners with Lethbridge and Jedrusinski's seniority—as friends and allies couldn't hurt.

"I didn't think she was going to be *moving in* here when you volunteered to teach her to shoot, Frank," he said wryly over his shoulder.

"Well, that's not exactly what happened, either," Lethbridge pointed out. "Unless I'm mistaken, she's actually been staying with Irina this week."

"In point of fact, she's been spending a lot of her time over at Aleksandr's and Evelina's," MacDallan corrected.

"Ah? Getting a little additional coaching from *Karl*, is she?" Lethbridge inquired with a smile.

"I would suspect so," MacDallan agreed. "Mind you, I don't think anything especially romantic has occurred to her at the moment, and I'm pretty sure it hasn't occurred to Karl, either. I could be wrong about that, but I doubt it." His expression saddened. "He's still hurting too much over Sumiko to be thinking that way about another girl yet. Especially one so much younger than he is."

The two men looked at one another, and Lethbridge nodded in silent understanding. The Uchida family's freehold shared a border with the Zinoviks... and Sumiko Uchida had been the only survivor when the last wave of the Plague swept over Sphinx and killed her parents and both of her older brothers. The loss had been especially bitter because it *had* been the last, unexpected wave of death—the same one which had claimed Irina Kasievna's husband, in fact—and the Uchidas and the Zinoviks had been close friends. There'd never been any question about who was going to adopt Sumiko when her family died.

She'd also been almost exactly Karl's age, not to mention smart and exotically pretty, and the two had been close even before her family's death. After it, they'd become almost inseparable, and no one had doubted that, in the fullness of time, Karl and she would marry and take over her parents' freehold. Things could still have changed, but people tended to marry young on frontier worlds like Sphinx, and the strength of their relationship had been obvious.

And then a crown oak branch, as big as a red spruce in its own right but weakened by a winter storm, had come crashing down from over a hundred meters in the air while Karl and Sumiko were keeping an eye on the younger Zinovik kids on a sledding expedition. Sumiko must have seen the branch splitting loose before it actually fell, because she'd flung herself forward and snatched Larisa, the youngest of the Zinovik girls, out of its path. She'd flung the younger girl to safety... only to be caught herself under two or three thousand kilos of plunging deadwood in a gravity well thirty-five percent higher than Old Terra's.

The fact that she'd been killed instantly had been no comfort at all, and her death had devastated Karl. It had seemed so totally unfair, so *senseless*, for her to die that way after all the death and dying they'd survived during the Plague Years, and it had taken the better part of six T-months for him to learn to smile again.

"You're probably right," Lethbridge agreed quietly. "Damned shame, but you're probably right."

"He'll get over it," MacDallan replied. "Or he'll recover, at least. In fact, I think he's doing exactly that. But even if he is, I'm pretty sure Aleksandr—and especially, Evelina—will make sure matters don't get out of hand. Besides, I think Karl's actually a little bit in awe of her."

"The girl's a heck of a shot," Lethbridge observed. "Smart as a whip, too. Cute, now that I think about it. And she's almost certainly the most famous fourteen-year-old on Sphinx." He shrugged. "What's there to be in awe of?"

"And Lionheart," MacDallan said. "Don't forget Lionheart—*Karl* certainly isn't going to!"

"Oh, I'm not forgetting *him*." Lethbridge smiled at the deck railing, where Fisher and Lionheart lay comfortably asleep in the sun. Normally, Lionheart and Stephanie were inseparable. Given the sensitivity of treecat hearing, the ranger was hardly surprised the shooting range was an exception to "normally."

"No, I'm not forgetting Lionheart," he said. "As near as I can tell, though, Lionheart seems to *approve* of young Master Karl."

"You're right, there," MacDallan agreed. "Which, to be honest, is one reason I'm not worrying the way I might where raging young hormones are concerned."

"Probably reasonable of you."

"Well, she's scheduled to go home tomorrow afternoon," MacDallan pointed out, listening to the steady crack of far-off pistol fire. "Should I take it you expect her to pass her qualifications shoots in the morning?"

"Oh," Lethbridge said, stepping up beside him and gazing off at the distant pistol range, "I think you can assume that."

21

"STEPHANIE," DR. HOBBARD SAID, "THIS IS DR. TENNES-
see Bolgeo. He holds the Kerry Gilley Distinguished Chair
of Xeno-Anthropology at Liberty University in the Chattanooga System, and he's come all the way from Chattanooga
on a Paulk Grant to study the treecats. The Ministry's asked
me to extend him every courtesy, and to introduce him to
you and Lionheart."

Stephanie looked at the man standing next to Hobbard.
He was of average height, with a round face and somewhat
thinning hair. He looked to be four or five T-years older
than her father and had a pleasant smile and eyes which
seemed to invite the rest of the world to smile with him,
yet there was something about him . . .

"Good afternoon, Dr. Bolgeo," she said, extending her
hand politely.

"And good afternoon to *you*, Miss Harrington." He actually bowed over her hand slightly, beaming at her. "And
please, call me 'Ten.'" His smile grew even broader. "I've

really always thought 'Tennessee' was a pretty silly first name, whatever my parents may have thought, and people have been calling me that as long as I can remember."

"I don't know if I'd feel comfortable doing that just yet, Dr. Bolgeo," she said, still politely. Then she smiled herself. "Maybe later."

"Well, I certainly hope you'll *start* feeling comfortable," he told her. "You've done something quite remarkable here, you know. Another sentient species? And one so much smaller than we've ever encountered before!" He shook his head admiringly. "I checked the literature before I headed out here to Manticore, and as far as I can tell, you're also the youngest person ever to discover another species of sapients. It's going to be one for the history books, young lady. You should be very proud of your accomplishment."

Lionheart stirred on her shoulder, and she heard a sound from him that she'd never heard before. It was almost too low to hear—in fact, she wasn't certain she was actually hearing it with her *ears*, at all—and it didn't sound very happy to her.

"Dr. Bolgeo comes with the highest recommendations, Stephanie," Dr. Hobbard said. "Paulk Grants are hard to come by, and the fact that he was able to secure one this quickly is a testimony to his stature in the field."

There was something a bit odd about Dr. Hobbard's tone, too, Stephanie thought.

"Spare my blushes!" Dr. Bolgeo laughed. "Dr. Hobbard, you know as well as I do that when it comes to securing grants it's *who* you know, as often as it is *what* you know." He shrugged modestly. "I won't deny it'll be a feather in my cap at the next Chattanooga Anthropology Conference to be the only person there who's actually met the galaxy's newest sentient species. And I'll admit Paulk Grants aren't exactly a centicred-a-dozen, either. But the bottom line is that all of us are simply following in this young lady's footsteps."

Stephanie smiled as politely as she could, and Dr. Bolgeo beamed at her all over again.

"What I'd like to ask you to do, Stephanie," Dr. Hobbard said after a moment, "is to go over firsthand for Dr. Bolgeo what you've already told me. He'd like to get... call it a general feel for the situation before he considers any fieldwork of his own."

"Of course, Dr. Hobbard," Stephanie said, although if the truth were known, it was last thing she wanted to do. "Where would you like me to start?"

"Well, Steph, what did you think of Dr. Bolgeo?"

"Honestly, Mom?" Stephanie looked up from the potatoes she was peeling. "I don't think I like him very much. Neither does Lionheart. For that matter, I'm not even sure Dr. Hobbard likes him."

"Really?" Marjorie Harrington looked over her shoulder at her daughter, garlic press paused in midair, and quirked an eyebrow. "Why not?"

"Why don't I like him?" Stephanie asked, and shrugged when her mother nodded.

"I can't really say," she said slowly. "Part of it, I think, is that he acts like somebody who thinks I'm just a kid but he's trying to treat me like a grown-up. Or the way he thinks a kid would expect a grown-up to be treated, maybe."

"I hate to say it, Steph," Marjorie said, inserting another peeled garlic clove into the press, "but you do tend to have that effect on people sometimes."

"Effect? What kind of 'effect'?"

"Well," Marjorie squeezed the press, crushing the garlic into the salad dressing she was making, "your dad and I wouldn't want you getting a swelled head, but some people—especially some adults—aren't sure how to react around someone who's both as bright and as young as you are. They try too hard, and they come off seeming, well, *phony*."

"I guess that could be part of it," Stephanie said slowly, her gaze thoughtful as she started peeling again. Now that her mother mentioned it, she had seen adults reacting that way around her, especially since she'd met Lionheart. And it had always irritated her, too. But she hadn't found herself actively *disliking* all of the others who'd done it.

"I don't think that's *all* of it, though," she continued out loud. "And I don't think that would cause Lionheart to dislike him."

"No, but it's possible that if *you* dislike him, *Lionheart* dislikes him," Marjorie pointed out, measuring olive oil and vinegar into the dressing. "We still don't really know all that much about how his empathy works. In fact, let's be honest and admit we're still trying to *guess* how his empathy works. I'm pretty sure you're right that he can read the emotions—generally, at least—of the people he meets. On the other hand, though, I'm *positive* he can read *your* emotions. So do you think it's possible he's picking up on the fact that this Bolgeo makes you uncomfortable and deciding he doesn't like Bolgeo because of that?"

"Maybe. It's possible, anyway," Stephanie conceded. But she didn't really think that was the answer, either. She thought it went deeper than that. And if she was right about Hobbard's not liking him, that might be additional evidence. After all, Dr. Hobbard didn't have any 'empathic sense' to be leading her judgment astray!

"Well, if you don't like him—and if Lionheart doesn't like him either, for whatever reason—I don't see any reason you have to have a lot to do with him," her mother said with a shrug. "You already told him pretty much everything you've told Dr. Hobbard, so unless he turns up something on his own and wants to discuss it with you, I think your father and I can be a little stingy about making your time available to him."

"Thanks, Mom!" Stephanie beamed appreciatively, and Marjorie shrugged.

"Hey, it's what parents are here for. That and reminding you to put your dirty socks in the hamper."

Dr. Tennessee Bolgeo sat in his hotel room and pondered.

The Harrington girl was smarter than he'd allowed for, and he'd already allowed for a pretty smart little cookie, considering what she'd accomplished. It was unfortunate he hadn't had more time—or at least more information—to study before catching the liner to Manticore. Of course, he admitted philosophically, it might not have helped in the girl's case. There was only so much one could do about people who persisted in being smarter than one found convenient. And then there was that dratted treecat.

Still, he'd recognized this was going to be an unusually complicated assignment. The fact that it looked like being even more complicated than he'd anticipated shouldn't come as all that great a surprise. And if it had been easy, they wouldn't have needed *him*, now would they?

He chuckled at the thought and took a sip from the glass in his hand.

It was a good thing his patrons were well-heeled, he reflected. Producing the papers he'd needed on such short notice hadn't been easy, and they hadn't come cheap. Fortunately, they really were on genuine, security-validated Liberty University computer chips. In fact, that was one of the reasons they'd been so expensive, since the forger had had to steal the blank chips from the university's offices without alerting the chip inventory system to his depredations. And the certification for his Paulk Grant was first rate, too. Even if anyone should come to suspect they might be forgeries, they ought to pass any test the authorities this far out in the Fringe could apply, and no one was likely to send all the way back to Chattanooga to check them at the source.

And if worse came to worst, the fact that he had a second set of patrons right in this microbe-sized "Star Kingdom" should come in handy. It was amazing how a man with the right contacts—and the right experience—could find the proper support team in almost any situation.

None of which got him any closer to solving his problems.

He took another sip of his drink and leaned further back in his chair.

In one way, this entire trip represented a speculative effort on the part of his immediate superior, Tamerlane Ustinov, president and CEO of Ustinov's Exotic Pets, Inc. One wouldn't have thought, perhaps, that the interstellar trade in *pets* could show enough return to send someone hustling all the way out to the boondocks this way, but it could. Oh, puppies and kittens and bunnies—or their alien equivalents—could never have paid for a trip like this, but those weren't the kinds of pets Ustinov's Exotics normally carried. And even if they had been, Tamerlane wouldn't have sent his top collector after such mundane prizes. No, the people who patronized Ustinov's Exotics wanted pets which were...out of the ordinary. Most of Ustinov's customers were incredibly wealthy, people who could truly say price didn't matter at all as long as they got what they wanted. And what they wanted were the additions to their collections which no one else—especially their equally wealthy rivals—could match. Or if someone else *had* beaten them to the latest "must have" pet, they had to have one, too, and as quickly as possible. There was no way to guess at this point how much those collectors would pay for something as adorably cute as that treecat of Harrington's, especially with the persistent reports that it was intelligent, but the price tag would be literally astronomical, that much he was sure of.

Then there were those fascinating rumors that the creatures might actually be telepathic. Bolgeo had been inclined to dismiss that particular claim as too fantastic, something obviously too good to be true. But the way that little beastie had reacted to him suggested there might really be something to it this time. And if there was, he could almost literally write his own ticket from any of half a dozen black-market genetic labs he could think of. Manpower, on Mesa, for example. They'd pay a fortune for live specimens of a possibly telepathic species! And they were only the tip of a very lucrative iceberg. In fact, he could probably clear enough for "Dr. Bolgeo" to disappear into a *very* well-off retirement, and all he'd have to do would be to skim a couple of dozen treecats off the top of his delivery to Ustinov's.

And, finally, there were those patrons of his right here in the Star Kingdom. They were a bit more problematical, he admitted. He didn't see a good way to squeeze a lot of money out of them at this point, but he knew he could count on them to smooth his path if it became necessary. They weren't interested in pets, or in laboratory specimens. *They* were interested in proving treecats weren't really sentient at all. If they couldn't prove that, Bolgeo never doubted that what they'd prefer as a fallback position would be another mysterious Plague...this time one that killed off treecats, not humans. He doubted he could provide any such epidemic, although he'd keep his eye out for possibilities. He always liked to make people happy, and once he had his own treecats safely tucked away, anything that reduced the supply his rivals might be able to tap would be all to the good. Scarcity always drove up prices. On the other hand, he thought regretfully, it wasn't really likely he'd be able to manage anything like that. Fortunately, most of his Manticoran patrons presumably realized that, in which case they'd probably settle for the best information he could give them, instead. If he could at least confirm the treecats' sentience for them before it became commonly known—and accepted—by everyone else, they might be able to unload their land options before the price started plummeting. They'd still lose money, but not as much.

But the problem was how one went about acquiring specimens of a species which certainly did appear, based on Lionheart's example, to be able to detect emotions, even if they weren't fully telepathic. Presumably that meant they'd be able to recognize the emotions of anyone hunting for them, and they were already irritatingly small, obviously fast, and well suited to disappearing like smoke in their native environment. So how did one sneak up on an empath? And if the little beasties really were telepathic, how did one keep the creatures from calling for help if someone did manage to grab one of them? That was a particularly pressing question, given the potentially messy consequences of such a call for help. Bolgeo wasn't certain he believed the story about them ripping a hexapuma apart. He'd checked the data on the hexapumas, and they seemed awfully formidable for something the size of a treecat to take down, even in a mass attack. But he wasn't about to assume it wasn't true, either. Much better to discover he'd been more cautious than he'd had to be than to do something careless and outstandingly stupid and find out he hadn't been cautious *enough*.

Especially when the consequences might be so . . . permanent.

He had time to think about it, he decided. Time to collect more information, insert himself into the "scientific community" looking into the treecats locally. For that matter, even though no one at Liberty University had actually ever heard of him, he probably did know more about xeno-anthropology—and he for darned sure knew more about xeno-*biology!*—than at least half the "genuine scientists" falling over their own feet here on Sphinx. He didn't anticipate any problem passing himself off as the xeno-anthropologist he claimed to be, and the letter from Idoya Vázquez was completely genuine. No one out here in Manticore had ever seen a *real* Paulk Grant, so it wasn't too surprising the Interior Minister had accepted his credentials without question.

That letter would open all sorts of official and semi-official doors for him—as long as he didn't overplay the card, at least. He didn't want to throw his weight around so much he irritated the locals into passive resistance; he'd seen that happen before, and the consequences were seldom good. It was even distinctly possible that someone who felt his toes had been stepped on by a pushy outsider might go to the trouble—and expense—of sending a query back to the Chattanooga System for a background report on one Dr. Tennessee Bolgeo. Sending messages over that kind of distance wasn't cheap, but it was amazing how much some people would spend if it offered the possibility of whacking somebody who'd irritated them sufficiently.

On the other hand, even if someone sent an inquiry off today, it would take literally months to reach Chattanooga. That was one reason he'd chosen Liberty University, although the fact that it was one of the most respected and prestigious institutions in the explored galaxy had also been a factor. And so had the fact that it was so *big*, had so many satellite campuses scattered about the Solarian League. With a faculty that large, someone like Dr. Hobbard probably wouldn't be all that surprised they'd never heard of some of its professors, no matter how good a reputation they had in the field. Like the aforementioned Dr. Tennessee Bolgeo. Of course the *university* knew who was on its faculty, and it would be astounded to learn it had a professor of that name. So it was, perhaps, fortunate all round that he'd have time to complete his operation here and depart, treecats in hand (figuratively speaking, at least; he wasn't going to actually risk his hand anywhere near something with those teeth and claws), long before any embarrassing responses from Chattanooga could reach the Star Kingdom.

Assuming he could get around that entire empathy angle somehow.

He hummed tunelessly, tapping one index finger against the rim of his glass while his agile brain revolved possibilities.

It all came down to range, he thought. How close could he get before they detected him? And, conversely, how far away could he be and successfully take one of them alive? But how did one go about determining the range of an invisible sense of a previously completely unknown species without already having one for examination and experimentation?

Indirection, he decided. He needed an *indirect* way to evaluate the treecats' range. Now how...?

He stopped whistling, and his eyes narrowed slowly. Could it really be that simple? Oh, it would probably be expensive, and it would take him at least a few days to set up, but still...

He began to chuckle, shaking his head, then snorted. Maybe it *would* be that simple! And if it was, it would actually be amusing to use that little creature's very dislike for him against it.

"I don't like him, Scott," Stephanie said, frowning at her bedroom com terminal. "And Lionheart doesn't like him, either. I talked to Mom about it, and she came up with two or three different explanations that could all be pretty harmless, I guess. But I still don't like him."

"Your mom *may* be right, Steph," Scott MacDallan said

from his Thunder River office. "On the other hand, smart as your mom is, she hasn't been adopted by a treecat. I have, and nothing I've ever seen out of Fisher suggests he takes a dislike to humans for no good reason. In fact, he seems to like some people I don't have much use for a lot more than *I* do. From what I've seen of Lionheart so far, I'd say it's pretty much the same for him."

A corner of MacDallan's mind was a little bemused by the fact that he was very seriously discussing this topic with a fourteen-year-old.

"That's what I think," Stephanie agreed now. "Still, I've got to admit he hasn't actually *done* anything I could object to. I mean, except for smiling too much and making me wonder when he's going to offer me a lollipop or jellybean, anyway." She grimaced with so much disgust MacDallan found it difficult not to chuckle. "By grown-up standards, he was just being polite, I guess. And I know I look even younger than I am to a lot of people, but I'm not exactly still in kindergarten, you know. *Blechhhh!*"

"Unfortunately, we can't go around shooting people for that," MacDallan pointed out. "Mind you, it sounds like he ought to come under the 'Needs Killing' rule, but I don't think the Star Kingdom's adopted that one yet."

"'Needs killing rule'?" Stephanie repeated, grinning as she heard the laugh he'd tried to keep out of his voice.

"Yeah, that's the one that says it's justifiable homicide if you can convince a jury of your neighbors that he was such a pain he needed killing," MacDallan explained, grinning back at her. "I always thought it was a good way to encourage good manners and common courtesy, personally. But like I say, I don't think Parliament's gotten around to passing that one locally."

"In that case, King Michael better get in gear and get it adopted quick. We need it on the books before he gets out of range again!" Stephanie said tartly.

"Why don't you drop him an e-mail with the suggestion?"

"People already think I'm weird enough, thank you."

"Yeah, I guess they do." It was his turn to grimace, obviously thinking about how "weird" some people had considered him over the years because of his psychic talent or whatever it was.

"But since we can't shoot him, what *do* we do about him?" Stephanie asked more seriously.

"I don't see anything we *can* do . . . yet. You say all he's done is basically ask the same questions Dr. Hobbard's asked. Oh, sure, he's been irritating, but he hasn't actually done anything out of line yet. And the truth is, we need to maintain at least some objectivity ourselves. We need to make sure we're not letting our own eagerness for the 'cats to be even more special than they really are lead us into leaping to conclusions that turn out later not to have been justified."

"You're saying that even if Lionheart doesn't like him, that may not really prove anything about *Dr. Bolgeo*," she said slowly. "That Lionheart might be wrong about him. Or that *I* might be wrong about the *reasons* Lionheart doesn't like him."

"That's *part* of what I'm saying," he agreed, nodding to her from the terminal. "Maybe he just wears a cologne that smells really disgusting to a treecat. Maybe he thinks on a 'frequency' that's like a ringing in the ears, or some kind of irritating background whine, as far as a 'cat is concerned. We don't really know yet how reliable a treecat's empathic sense is where human beings are concerned, and we need to find out. In fact, this might be an opportunity to do a little experimenting of our own."

"What do you mean?" Stephanie asked, eyes narrowing in sudden speculation.

"Well, if this Bolgeo's really serious about studying the treecats, he'll probably want to talk to me, too, which should give me a chance to size him up for myself. Then you and I will have something more definite in the way of impressions to compare. And if he comes back into range of Lionheart—or Fisher, for that matter—we watch how the treecats react to him. Let's try and get something a little more specific than just a feeling that they 'don't like him,' and let's see if he eventually does something that would justify their dislike. Until we can establish some more definite way to communicate with them, assuming we ever do, we can't just *ask* them why they're reacting this way. From where I sit, that means we need more observational data. And before we could get anyone to take us seriously about someone with credentials like Bolgeo's, we're going to have to understand what's happening ourselves well enough to be able to convince someone else to accept the treecats' judgment."

"You mean I have to go ahead and talk to him again," Stephanie said distastefully.

"'Fraid so, kid," he said sympathetically.

Scott MacDallan, Stephanie had discovered, was one of the few people who, like her parents, could call her "kid" without instantly irritating her. Normally, at least. At the moment, though, as she glowered sourly at his com image and thought about enduring more of Bolgeo's company, she wasn't inclined to cut him any slack. Especially since she realized he was right and she didn't want him to be.

Good thing for you Lionheart's asleep, she thought, glancing at the treecat sprawled along his perch beside her bed and snoring gently. *He'd give you one of those "Stop-being-such-a-crybaby" bleeks of his. And you'd deserve it.*

"All right," she sighed. "All right! I'll be good. But I'm telling you right now, Scott MacDallan, you *owe* me for this one. You owe me big. And I've got a feeling that one of these days, even if I don't get to shoot him, I'm at least going to be perfectly justified in kicking him right in the kneecap!"

22

DR. BOLGEO, STEPHANIE DECIDED, WASN'T ONE OF those people who got more likable the better you got to know them.

She still couldn't decide exactly why she disliked him so intensely. It wasn't just because he gave her that big smile while pretending he didn't think of her as just one more kid. And it wasn't—or shouldn't be, anyway—just because she had the distinct impression he was working on wheedling more information out of her, since it wasn't as if he was alone in *that*. Dr. Hobbard kept trying to get more out of her, and she actually liked Dr. Hobbard. It was almost as if the two of them were playing a game with rules they both understood, and Dr. Hobbard was an opponent Stephanie could respect. Of course, Dr. Hobbard played the game openly, without trying to sneak around and trick Stephanie into telling her things. She was quite sure Bolgeo would play any trick he could, but she could have lived with that. In fact, she would normally have taken a certain pleasure out of dropping false information on him while letting him think he was tricking her into revealing the truth, so *that* wasn't what she found so irritating. And she didn't dislike Bolgeo this much just because he wouldn't leave her alone, either.

No, there was more to it than any of that . . . she just wished she could figure out what that "more" was.

Scott MacDallan and Irina Kisaevna had both met the Chattanoogan now, and they didn't much care for him, either. Neither did Karl, for that matter. None of them could put a finger on exactly why they disliked him so much any more than Stephanie could, but they knew he wasn't high on their list of favorite people. And, interestingly, Fisher had reacted to him very much as Lionheart did.

Unfortunately, as MacDallan had pointed out, "We really, *really* don't like him" wasn't enough to get her out of being polite to him, which was why she currently found herself, to her considerable disgust, sitting at a checkerboard cloth-draped table in the Red Letter Café, an open-air sidewalk restaurant in what passed for Twin Forks' business district, waiting for yet another interview with him. She was pretty sure her parents would have found a way to politely decline the luncheon invitation if Bolgeo hadn't gotten Dr. Hobbard and Chief Ranger Shelton to front for him.

Stephanie didn't know how the Chattanoogan had found out about her campaign to secure an internship with the Forestry Service, although it probably hadn't been too hard, given how all the news stories had emphasized the "human interest" angle of her intention to eventually pursue a Forestry Service career. But the opportunity to eat lunch with Shelton and improve her relationship with him couldn't hurt, and she was actually eager to show the chief ranger more of her relationship with Lionheart. And she liked Dr. Hobbard too much to be impolite by refusing to have lunch with *her*. She knew her parents felt the same way about both of Bolgeo's other table guests, and she had to admit that inviting them along had been a shrewd move on his part.

The Harringtons had gotten to the café early in case the restaurant's proprietor and staff took a little convincing before they allowed an "animal" onto their premises. For that matter, Stephanie wasn't sure there wasn't something in the health code which would have prevented a restauranteur from allowing that. But Twin Forks really was a small town, one where everybody knew everybody else—or at least knew all *about* everyone else—and she and Lionheart had become celebrities. Besides, Eric Flint, the Red Letter's owner, was one of Stephanie's friends. Despite something of a reputation as a curmudgeon, he always spoke to her as an equal (which a lot of adults seemed constitutionally unable to do), and he'd pointed her towards some interesting sources for her history and economics classes. Not only that, he was from the planet of New Chicago, and New Chicago had been a dumping ground for radical anarchists, socialists, and—especially—every member of the Levelers' Association the government could round up after Old Earth's Final War. The descendants of those deportees had a zealously maintained reputation as scofflaws and rule-breakers, and it seemed pretty clear to Stephanie that Mr. Flint actually *hoped* some Public Health busybody would come and object to his decision to seat Lionheart.

No objections had been raised, however, and now she listened to the juicy crunching sound as Lionheart ecstatically devoured celery sticks.

"You know if you keep pigging up celery that way, we're going to have to start feeding you even more laxatives. And this time I think I'll ask Dad to find one you *don't* like," she said warningly. Lionheart, predictably, paid her no attention, and her father chuckled.

"Don't worry, Steph. I'm pretty sure I can come up

with one that tastes bad enough he won't be in a hurry to repeat the experience."

"Good," Stephanie said, grinning up at her father. "The *last* time he ate his weight in celery, he kept me up all night!"

"He *does* like it, doesn't he?" Marjorie Harrington observed, and her husband snorted.

"That's sort of like saying that *I* 'like' oxygen, Marge! I only wish I could figure out what it is about celery— *celery*, of all things!—that seems to generate such addictive behavior in every treecat."

"As long as it doesn't turn out to have any kind of long-term ill effects, I don't suppose it really matters," Marjorie said slowly. "Still, you're right. We really do need to figure out why they all seem to crave it so much. Among other things."

"Yeah, like why they don't—" Stephanie began, then paused as Lionheart abruptly stopped chewing on the current celery stick.

The treecat straightened, sitting bolt upright in the highchair Mr. Flint had provided. Treecat teeth and celery made for a messy meal, and the end of his current stalk hung down in wet, well-shredded ruins as he held it in his remaining true-hand, but he wasn't paying it any attention. Instead, he turned his head, ears more than half-flattened, and stared up the sidewalk on the other side of the low wall separating the Red Letter's tables from the pavement.

"Lionheart?" Stephanie asked, her eyes narrowing as she took in the treecat's stiffness. He seemed to be listening intently, focused on something human ears couldn't hear, and he obviously wasn't delighted with whatever had attracted his attention.

Stephanie looked up at her parents, both of whom were clearly as baffled as she was. Her father shrugged, and all three of them turned to look in the direction Lionheart was staring so fixedly.

Twin Forks was small enough for people to walk to most destinations, and the warm (for Sphinx) sunlight and deep, comfortable shade of the green belts the city planners had incorporated into the town made that the preferred mode of travel. Even a relatively small population could provide a lot of pedestrians under those conditions, especially during the lunch hour, and the sidewalks were crowded. Nothing about the various passersby seemed especially significant, though. Certainly not anything which should have fixed Lionheart's attention so firmly, and Stephanie frowned in perplexity as the seconds trickled past, turning slowly but steadily into minutes.

Finally, after what felt like half an hour but was probably closer to five minutes, max, just as she was about to start asking Lionheart questions in an effort to figure out what was bothering him, a trio of pedestrians strolled around the corner towards the restaurant. It wasn't hard for her to recognize Dr. Hobbard, Chief Ranger Shelton, and Dr. Bolgeo.

Lionheart saw them at the same instant she did, and again she heard that low, almost-snarl she'd heard the first time they met Dr. Bolgeo. She glanced at him quickly, then looked up at her parents.

"Do you hear that, Mom?" she asked her mother.

"Hear what, honey?" Marjorie asked, looking down at her with a frown, and Stephanie's curiosity sharpened. Now why was *she* able to hear it when clearly neither of her parents could?

"Never mind," she said quickly, lowering her voice slightly as Dr. Bolgeo and his other lunch guests came closer. "I'll explain later."

Her mother cocked an eyebrow, her expression curious, but she also nodded. That was one of the things Stephanie loved about her mother—she knew there were times when it was better not to ask questions. And she was willing to trust Stephanie's judgment about things like that, too.

Stephanie smiled across the table at her, then reached out and touched Lionheart gently. He looked at her, ears coming back up almost into their normal position, and made a soft sound all of them could hear.

"Time for us to behave—for *both* of us to behave," she warned him, simultaneously concentrating hard on the thought herself. He looked back at her for another moment, and she gazed into his green eyes, hoping he'd understand the message she was trying to get across. Then he blinked and nodded in the gesture he'd learned from his human family.

I don't think he understands why *we have to behave, though,* she reflected, *and I don't blame him. I'm starting to think treecats probably* do *have that "Needs Killing" rule of Scott's! They're obviously what Mom likes to call "direct personalities," anyway. So maybe it's just as well Dr. Bolgeo arranged for us to meet someplace nice and public where Lionheart's less likely to try to rip his eyeballs out.*

Somehow, she found the possibility of the Chattanoogan's suffering a certain degree of bruising and laceration at Lionheart's hands rather attractive. Then she made herself put that thought away and rose and to smile politely at her host as the three adults entered the restaurant.

Well, that worked rather well, actually, Dr. Tennessee Bolgeo congratulated himself later that same evening, as he sat studying the imagery on his hotel room's desk terminal.

He hadn't expected to learn very much from his afternoon's conversation, but he'd ended up garnering a few extra tidbits after all, not so much from anything the

Harringtons had offered as from interpreting comments Hobbard made. The xeno-anthropologist had obviously been putting things together for quite a while, and her contributions to the table conversation had clarified several points Bolgeo was pretty sure the close-mouthed Harringtons would have preferred to keep *un*-clarified.

That was nice, yet it wasn't what he'd actually been after, and he carefully considered the numbers displayed in the small windows opened in the imagery in front of him. The numbers in the window in the lower right corner of the terminal were a time display from the camera which had recorded the imagery; the numbers in the window in the lower *left* corner of the terminal were from his uni-link's GPS tracker. At the moment, that uni-link was networked to the terminal, and the computer was comparing the locator's time-stamped record of Bolgeo's movements to the timestamps on the video. From there, it was an easy matter for the computer to display his exact distance from the Red Letter Café at any instant.

Which was how he knew he'd been precisely one hundred and fourteen meters from the restaurant when Lionheart suddenly stopped chewing his celery and turned to stare in the very direction from which Bolgeo was approaching.

It had turned out to be less expensive than Bolgeo had anticipated. The immediate furor had died down a great deal, but the girl and her treecat remained figures of considerable interest both here on Sphinx and on Manticore, and it hadn't been hard to convince one of the local news stringers to let him have a copy of the imagery. It had been a straightforward *quid-pro-quo*, after all. Bolgeo had explained that he really wanted an opportunity to examine video of Lionheart when Lionheart didn't realize he was being recorded. Solely from the highest of scientific motives, of course. And the cameraman had been more than willing to let him have it in return for the advance tip about the Harrington family's luncheon engagement with the Sphinx Forestry Service's uniformed commander and the head of the Crown commission studying the newly discovered treecats. He'd been in place, carefully concealed at an upper-floor office window on the other side of the street, almost an hour before the Harringtons had arrived at the Red Letter, and he'd recorded every moment of their time in the restaurant.

Bolgeo had figured he'd probably have to retain a private investigator to follow the kid and the treecat to get that kind of footage, and he'd expected that to cost a pretty centicredit. There weren't many PIs on such newly settled colony worlds, as a rule, so he'd been afraid he'd have to recruit someone from the much more populous planet of Manticore, where there were now enough people to make finding someone to sneak around and spy on his neighbors fairly straightforward. He hadn't liked the prospect, though. The sort of PI who'd follow a fourteen-year-old girl around at the behest of an off-world stranger was also the sort who was likely to wonder why the off-worlder in question was interested in the kid. The possibility that he'd try to black-mail money out of Bolgeo in return for not mentioning his interest in Stephanie Harrington to the authorities—purely as a concerned citizen, of course!—had not seemed beyond the realm of possibility. And given most colonial planets' attitude towards child molesters, Bolgeo was pretty sure explaining his interest to those authorities would not have been the most enjoyable experience of his life.

Instead, he'd pulled it off for no more than the cost of lunch for six humans and one treecat, which made it one of the best bargains he'd ever managed.

He ran the imagery again, checking the moment at which Lionheart had become aware of his approach for the third time, then fast forwarding to when he took his own departure. He'd excused himself early in response to a previously arranged com call, but he'd urged his guests to finish their meals at their leisure and instructed their waiter to put whatever desserts they might choose to order on the credit voucher he'd already authorized. Then he'd left... and Lionheart's turned head had tracked him with unerring accuracy even after he'd vanished into the pedestrians. In fact, the treecat had looked after him until his GPS indicated he'd been one hundred and eleven meters from the restaurant.

So, he thought now, tipping back in his chair and clasping his hands on the back of his head as he gazed up at the ceiling, *the little critter picked me up at just over a hundred meters. And he tracked me* outbound *to just over a hundred meters. So I think we can probably take his...* "empathic detection range," *for want of a better term, as a hundred meters. Of course, that's here in town. Twin Forks may be a podunk little burg, but there's probably enough people around to produce a lot of... background noise.*

He frowned thoughtfully. There was no way to know just how distracting an empath might find the emotions of others. Would it be like trying to listen for a single voice in a roomful of talking people? Or could the treecats block out emotions they didn't want to hear? Could they listen for a single emotional... fingerprint, call it, without being distracted by the other humans in the area?

Best to assume his range is knocked back if there are a lot of other people in the vicinity, Bolgeo decided. *It'll be a lot smarter to operate on the assumption that he can* "hear" *me—or someone else—from a lot farther away out in the woods. On the other hand, let's not get too carried away with allowing for that. So if he could pick me up at a hundred meters here in town, let's assume he could pick me up at... oh, two* hundred *meters in the bush.*

His frown turned into a smile, and he chuckled.

I can work with that, he thought.

23

STEPHANIE WATCHED THE TREETOPS SLIDE BY BELOW AS she and Lionheart floated towards the heart of his clan's territory. Sphinx's slow, ongoing seasons were turning those treetops steadily denser and leafier, and a part of her still wanted to slip her glider through the nearest opening in that canopy and land so that she and her companion could explore the cool, green depths of the forest. She felt all those yet unseen trees and hills and streams and creatures calling to her, and someday she would answer that call. But not today. Today she was bound for yet another visit with Lionheart's relatives, and she'd found that the lengthy flight was a good time to think things through.

She banked slightly, compensating for a crosswind and felt Lionheart shifting his weight in tandem with her. Whatever else the link between them did, it had turned him into the ideal passenger. Maybe it was his arboreal evolution, but he seemed to possess an instinctive grasp of how to help control their flight...and to be aware of what she was going to do even before she was.

She smiled at the thought, but then the smile faded as she contemplated her problem. At least some of her and Scott's friends and allies were prepared to do what they could to hamper whatever Dr. Bolgeo might be up to, yet there really wasn't much they *could* do. Frank Lethbridge and Ainsley Jedrusinski had agreed to help keep an eye on him, but the Forestry Service wasn't giving them much time off lately. In fact, the Interior Ministry's pressure to provide guides for all the off-world scientists so eager for excursions into the bush in search of treecats had most of the rangers working overtime.

That could have worked for them, since having Lethbridge or Jedrusinski assigned as Bolgeo's guide would have been the perfect way to make sure he wasn't getting into anything he shouldn't. Unfortunately, Bolgeo wasn't venturing out into the bush anymore. In fact, he hadn't been for several weeks now. In a more reasonable world, the fact that he was staying peacefully in Yawata Crossing should have made her *less* suspicious, Stephanie supposed, but not in his case.

If he's really here to study treecats, then he ought to be out in the bush trying to study *them, not sitting on his butt in town,* she thought grimly. *But he's not even trying to get onto the request list for Forestry Service guides. Or hire a private guide, like Mr. Franchitti. For that matter, he's not even pestering Dr. Hobbard anymore! So if he's not going to be studying them, why doesn't he just buy himself a ticket back home and leave all of us alone?*

She squeezed the button on her right hand grip to bring up the holographic display from her glider's built-in GPS. The moving map popped into existence on her helmet's visor, transparent enough for her to see through but automatically kept centered in her field of vision as long as she held the button down, and she allowed herself a certain sense of smug satisfaction as the green icon tracked directly across the map towards her destination. Now if only the rest of her life could stay that firmly on track!

Her satisfaction faded and she released the button as her thoughts came back to Bolgeo yet again, like a bit of space debris sucked into a planetary gravity well. She wished she had some sort of proof that Lionheart and Fisher's antipathy for him was deserved, and not just so she could show it to other people. She hated this sense of distrust and suspicion when she couldn't prove it was justified even to herself.

And I can't *prove it—not really*, she admitted. *Sure, he's acting pretty strangely for a xeno-anthropologist, but there's not exactly a law against that. And at least he's not one of the "scientists" trying to insist on studying the BioNeering survivors. Idiots.* She grimaced. *As if anyone with any sense was going to let them stress those poor 'cats even harder after everything that's already happened to them! And as if studying a treecat clan as shattered as they are was going to tell them anything about* normal *treecat interactions, anyway.*

She shook her head in disgust, although part of her admitted (very unwillingly) that it had to be incredibly frustrating for any xeno-anthropologist to be denied the opportunity for first-hand observation of the only known clan. Not that it made her any more sympathetic with the effort some of them were mounting to treat Lionheart and Fisher like some kind of zoo specimens. There'd actually been talk of getting a court order to grant access to the two "captive treecats," but Chief Ranger Shelton had stepped on that one hard.

He'd done it very publicly, too, and despite her concern, Stephanie smiled broadly as her mind replayed the interview in which a local newsy had "just happened" to ask him about that. The newsy in question was a friend of Scott MacDallan's, but Shelton had seemed unaware of that as he explained in blistering terms that so far as he was aware, neither Lionheart nor Fisher had been consigned to any public zoo (or any other public institution) and that neither he nor the Star Kingdom's courts had any intention of infringing upon the Harringtons' or Dr. MacDallan's privacy. And, by the way, if anyone else cherished any thought of doing anything of the sort, he recommended they take a good long look at the stringent legal penalties for trespassing on private property and privacy violation. Which he, as an officer of the court, would of course be duty-bound to enforce...assuming the freeholders in question didn't simply shoot the tresspassers in question on sight.

He'd looked remarkably free of any dismay the thought of enforcing those penalties might have caused him, too, she thought.

At least he's on our side...some, at least. Or I think he is, anyway. I'm pretty sure he's not on the other *side, at least. I just wish I knew what he's really thinking. Especially about Bolgeo.*

"Dr. Hobbard," Chief Ranger Gary Shelton said as patiently as he could, "what, exactly, is it you want me to do? I mean, if you want me to *arrest* the man, I can think of at least a dozen homegrown scientists I'd rather lock up first!"

The Sphinx Forestry Service's commander leaned back in his desk chair and raised both hands in a gesture which mingled helplessness and frustration, and Sanura Hobbard sighed heavily.

"I understand, Chief Shelton," she said. "And I don't *know* what I want you to do, really. It's just...just that for someone from such a prestigious university, he's simply not a very good xeno-anthropologist. I mean, it's almost like he knows the theory but doesn't seem to have any practical field experience. And someone of his stature should be pretty well represented in the field's literature, too, but I've done an intensive search of our library records without finding a single published paper under his name."

"I'm as proud of the Star Kingdom as anyone, Doctor," Shelton said with a wry smile, "but we're not exactly the center of the explored universe out here. Is it really all that astonishing our library files—especially in a field as esoteric as yours—should be a little behind the curve?"

"Of course not," Hobbard agreed. "In fact, we're probably at least fifteen or twenty T-years—or more!—behind the Solarian League's mainstream scholarship in quite a few fields. That's inevitable when we're so far from the core worlds and the major universities and research centers."

"So the fact that you haven't found any books or papers of his doesn't mean none've been *published*," Shelton pointed out.

"No, it doesn't," she sighed. "I'm just not easy in my mind about it, though, Chief. And I suppose I'm feeling a little protective about the treecats myself. Maybe I've been hanging around with Stephanie too much!"

"Girl does have that effect, doesn't she?" Shelton grinned widely. "You've got to admire her, too. Even if she is keeping her mouth shut about half the things you and I would just love to know about the treecats!"

"I keep telling myself that sooner or later she's going to figure out she can trust me and open up," Hobbard said. "And when she does, I've got a feeling she'll be able to tell us plenty. Maybe that's one reason I'm so worried about Bolgeo, now that I think about it. I introduced him to her—not that I had much choice, given Minister Vázquez's letter—and if it turns out he's not who and what he claims to be, it's going to undercut a lot of the trust I've tried to establish. Not to mention the fact that if it turns out he's *used* me to get to her, I'm going to be royally pissed in my own right."

Sanura Hobbard seldom used that sort of language, Shelton reflected, which said quite a bit about just how seriously she took this entire thing.

"Well," he said out loud, "I'll try to keep as close an eye on him as my manpower permits. You know how strapped we are for warm bodies, though. I can't guarantee to make him a primary responsibility, Doctor. As you just pointed out, his papers from the Ministry are all in order, and so is all the rest of his documentation. I have exactly zero evidence to justify initiating some sort of criminal investigation at this point. So I'll do what I can, but to be perfectly honest, that's probably not going to be a lot."

Dr. Tennessee Bolgeo sat in his hotel room once more, watching a holographic display. It showed an overhead view of the Copperwall Mountains and their foothills, and he was watching a small green icon move slowly but steadily eastward, deeper into the mountains.

You know, he thought admiringly, *that really is one smart little cookie. And her parents have to be in on it, too.*

He'd wasted the better part of three local weeks tracking the location transponders he'd had planted on the Harringtons' air cars. He'd been positive from some of Stephanie's answers—and even more from some of the questions she'd carefully *not* answered—that she knew exactly where to find "her" treecats. Even without those clues, no one who'd spent fifteen minutes in the girl's company could've supposed for a moment that she *wouldn't* have found the other treecats by now.

At the same time, it was obvious from what other investigators (and newsies) had turned up that the treecats'

range wasn't actually on the Harrington freehold. It had
to be considerably farther away, or some of those search-
ing so assiduously for it would have found it by now. So
logic had suggested she was getting back and forth in her
parents' air cars. But after weeks of tracking every move
those air cars made, it had become obvious that whatever
else they were doing, they weren't going anywhere near
the heart of the Copperwalls.

Then it had hit him: hang gliding. That was what she'd
been doing the day the treecats rescued her from the
hexapuma! So was it possible she'd received her parents'
blessing to use her replacement glider to visit the "wild"
treecats no one else seemed able to locate?

The more he'd thought about it, the more logical it
had seemed, but what to do about it? Fortunately, every
planet, even a colony world this new, had its shady side,
its criminal elements. Finding them wasn't too difficult,
and it helped that three of his associates from Ustinov's
Exotics had arrived. They'd come in separately, on two
different starships, and none of them had had any contact with him. Not any *open* contact, anyway. But that
hadn't kept them from making a few quiet arrangements
for him, or from serving as his go-between with certain
of the less savory locals. None of the Manticorans knew
exactly what their new employers were after, but they
didn't really care, either, as long as the pay was good and
no one seemed to be getting hurt.

With their help, it hadn't been difficult to get a transponder planted on the girl's glider. Trying to get a bug
planted directly on *her* would have been a lot harder,
given her treecat's early warning system, but the glider
had been easy. He'd kept an eye on Dr. Hobbard's schedule so he'd known when she and both her parents would
be in town to meet with the xeno-anthropologist. From
there, it had been simple to use one of those locals to

visit their freehold in their absence and install the tiny, almost completely undetectable bug inside her glider's counter-grav generator's housing. Then all Bolgeo had had to do was sit back and wait until she led him directly to what he sought.

And speaking of leading me places, he thought, leaning forward slightly, eyes narrowing, *I do believe she's stopped moving. Which means she's landed.*

He tapped a query into the keyboard and smiled as a set of GPS coordinates came up.

24

<CLIMBS QUICKLY!>

Climbs Quickly's eyelids popped open as the mental shout disturbed his sleep. His two-leg slept quietly and deeply, her dreams a drowsy backdrop to her slumbering mind-glow, and he thought for a moment that the call which had awakened him had been a dream of his own. But then it came again.

<Climbs Quickly! Wake up!>

<Short Tail?> Climbs Quickly called back as he realized it was no dream. <What is it?>

<There is trouble!> The Bright Water scout's mind-voice was faint with distance, although Climbs Quickly could sense him moving steadily—and rapidly—closer. <Sings Truly and Broken Tooth have sent me to fetch you.>

Climbs Quickly started to ask what sort of trouble, and why his sister and Broken Tooth might think there was anything *he* could do about it. But then he paused. Short Tail was at the very limit of his mind-voice's range.

It would be difficult for him to hold any kind of detailed conversation at such a distance.

<*I come to meet you,*> he sent back, instead, and leapt down from the perch his person's father had constructed for him above her sleeping place.

He stood up on his true-feet, true-hand on the edge of his person's sleeping pad and nose perhaps a true-hand's width from her ear, and considered waking her. He knew she would be upset if she awoke and realized he'd ventured out in the middle of the night without her, but he also knew she would insist on accompanying him if he did wake her. And he had a shrewd notion of how her parents would react if they happened to awaken and discover he'd taken their daughter off into the night-struck forest without their permission or knowledge.

No, he thought. Better to go and discover what Short Tail was so bothered by. Besides, Death Fang's Bane's sire had made provision for him to go in and out of their nesting place without disturbing the two-legs with whom he shared it.

He turned and trotted down the hallway outside his person's room, turned left through the living room and crossed to the front door. The swinging panel his person's sire had installed in the door required Climbs Quickly to manipulate a small latch before he could open it. Climbs Quickly approved of that feature; there were several creatures, like the bark-chewers, who could have come in through that door and done much damage to his two-legs' possessions if not for the latch.

He pushed through the door and gave it a firm pat from the other side to make sure the latch had reengaged. Then he moved briskly across the cleared space around Death Fang's Bane Clan's nest place. With the loss of his right true-hand, he was no longer quite as quick as he'd been when Bright Water Clan first gave him his name, but he was still quicker than most as he swarmed up the net-wood trunk. He made his way to the lowest branch leading in the direction he wanted and went streaking along the aerial highway towards Short Tail.

<This is much better,> Short Tail said approvingly some time later, as he and Climbs Quickly finally met.

The senior scout had come a long way, and his fatigue was clear. For that matter, it was somewhat more risky for the People to travel by night than by day. Some predators—like the death-wings—saw better in darkness than the People did. They could actually spot one of the People from a range greater than that at which the People could detect their mind-glows, and a scout had to be alert and quick on his feet to avoid a death-wing's pounce under those circumstances.

<Yes, it is,> Climbs Quickly agreed. *<Now, tell me why you have come. What sort of "'trouble'" sends you out to fetch me at this time of night? And why do Sings Truly and Broken Tooth believe I could do anything about it?>*

<We do not know exactly what sort of trouble stalks the clan.> Short Tail's mind-voice was quieter, his mind-glow darker, than a moment before. *<And Sings Truly and Broken Tooth did not lightly send me to seek you. Indeed, there were some among the elders who felt the clan should simply move speedily deeper into the mountains without telling Death Fang's Bane or any other among the two-legs where we had gone.>*

<What?!> Climbs Quickly's ears came upright, and his whiskers bristled. *<What foolishness is this?>*

<I spoke against it, as did almost all of the other elders,> Short Tail said quickly. *<I do not think even those who made the suggestion truly meant it. It was just that...they are frightened, Climbs Quickly.>*

<Frightened? Frightened of what?>

<That is what we do not know.> Short Tail's ears flattened in mingled frustration, fear, and anger. <Over the last hand of days, three hands of the People have... disappeared.>

<'Disappeared'?> Climbs Quickly repeated.

<It is the only way I can describe it,> Short Tail replied. <They went out from their nesting places in the normal way—hunters, scouts, gatherers—and they did not return.>

A chill ran through Climbs Quickly, and his eyes narrowed intensely.

<I do not understand,> he said slowly. <You say they did not return. Did they not send even a mind call for help or in warning?>

<They did not,> Short Tail said flatly. <None of them did, and at least some of them were on errands which should not have taken them beyond their mind-voices' reach of the central nesting place.>

The chill in Climbs Quickly's blood grew more intense. It wasn't unheard of for one of the People to suffer an accident, or even to be pounced upon by one of the predators People normally evaded without undue difficulty. But it *was* highly unusual—in fact, Climbs Quickly couldn't remember a single case in which it had happened—for one of the People within mind-voice range to fail even to call out for help in such a case.

<Is there no clue as to what may have befallen them?> he asked.

<None that we understand,> Short Tail responded, and Climbs Quickly's ears pricked. The senior scout spoke more slowly, and there was an odd blend of hesitation, confusion, and unhappiness in his mind-glow. Obviously, he didn't look forward to explaining further, and Climbs Quickly wondered why.

<The reason some have suggested moving deeper into the mountains without telling any of the two-legs,> Short

Tail continued after a moment, <*is that they believe the two-legs are responsible for whatever is befalling the People. This is a new thing, Climbs Quickly. None of the memory songs tell us of People simply . . . vanishing this way, and some believe it must be related to the way in which we have revealed ourselves to the two-legs. You yourself have reported that some among the two-legs have pushed Death Fang's Bane to tell more about the People than she wishes, allow them to study you far more closely than she will permit, and Swift Striker has reported much the same thing about his two-leg. Some of the People have come to wonder if perhaps those two-legs who have been frustrated by Death Fang's Bane's and Darkness Foe's refusal to tell them what they wish to know or allow them to study you might not have decided to . . . take some of us for study. And now some of our scouts have reported hearing the two-legs' flying things moving quietly and carefully near our central nesting place. Some fear that those who have disappeared have been taken by the two-legs in those flying things.*>

Climbs Quickly's mind-glow had darkened as Short Tail explained. He wasn't surprised some People should feel that way. For that matter, he agreed with them. In fact, he suspected he could put a specific two-leg's face behind what had happened.

But how? Speaks Falsely didn't know where Bright Water's central nest place was. *No* two-leg knew that aside from Death Fang's Bane Clan, and Death Fang's Bane and her parents had taken careful precautions to keep it that way.

<*I do not know for certain, any more than you do, if the two-legs are responsible for these disappearances,*> he told Short Tail after a lengthy pause. <*But I believe it is indeed possible some among them are. I do not like thinking that, yet we have already learned much about the two-legs—including the fact that there are evil ones among them. I do know from the meetings Death Fang's Bane and*

her parents have had with the...elders of all the two-legs in the world that any who would steal away the People would do so only in defiance of their own elders and customs. That does not mean it could not happen, though.> His ears flattened, and his mind-glow was grim. *<I have told Sings Truly and the other elders of what I tasted in Speaks Falsely's mind-glow.>*

Short Tail looked back at him, then—in the gesture many of Bright Water's People were adopting from the two-legs—he nodded slowly.

There were times, Climbs Quickly thought feelingly, when his inability to communicate with Death Fang's Bane was particularly exasperating. He'd made strides in his ability to understand *her* as their bond matured and he learned to read more and more from her mind-glow. Either he was growing more sensitive to those echoes of thought which flowed through it, or else she was learning how to make them stronger, and he was learning to communicate simple messages back to her by gesture and body language. Sometimes he could even communicate a more complicated notion by acting out what he was trying to say. But so far, at least, he had no way to explain what he had seen in the mind-glow of the two-leg who had invited Death Fang's Bane Clan to the eating place in the vast two-leg settlement where Death Fang's Bane still went on occasion to fly with the other younglings.

The fact that he couldn't explain it was maddening. He knew Death Fang's Bane had sensed his own dislike for Speaks Falsely, and he knew she disliked him, as well. But there was no way for him to tell her every mouth-sound Speaks Falsely uttered carried its own freight of...falsity.

Matters weren't helped by the fact that until the People had met the two-legs it had never occurred to any of them that someone *could* speak falsely. There was no point in one of the People attempting to deceive another person in that way, since the other person was always able to sense the emotions and thoughts behind whatever was said. It was possible for the People to deceive or trick one another, but not by *telling* the other something which was untrue. Instead, the People had to arrange things so that the one they desired to trick had no clue of what was about to happen, and many of the younger People, especially among the scouts and hunters, delighted in contriving clever ways to do just that. It was good training, both for the one arranging the trick and for the trick's intended victim. On the one hand it taught the sort of forethought and cunning any hunter or scout might find useful one day, and on the other it taught the alertness and caution any hunter or scout most definitely *would* find useful one day.

But that was very different from what Climbs Quickly tasted behind Speaks Falsely's smile. There was something almost frightening about Speaks Falsely's concentration on Climbs Quickly whenever they met, yet Climbs Quickly had the strong impression (oh, how he *wished* he could read two-leg mind-glows as clearly as he could those of the People!) that Speaks Falsely was so deeply interested in him only because he was the two-leg's . . . doorway, perhaps, to the rest of the People.

He knew Speaks Falsely was deceiving all of the two-legs about him, and he knew Speaks Falsely was interested in the People in the same way the People were interested in particularly tasty ground-runners. But there was no way he could penetrate beyond that awareness, and no way he could warn Death Fang's Bane or her parents about even the little he did know.

Yet even if all that were true, how could Speaks Falsely have discovered the location of Bright Water Clan's central nesting place? Death Fang's Bane had been so *careful* to preserve that secret! And even if Speaks Falsely could have discovered that, how could anyone—even a two-leg, with all their marvelous tools—capture so many of the People without even one among the rest of the People hearing so much as a single mind-cry for aid?

You know what you do not really wish to think, Climbs Quickly, he told himself. *You believe Speaks Falsely wishes to* capture *some of the People for study, but you could be wrong. And if, instead, what he truly wishes is to* slay *the People and he has one of the two-legs' weapons, that might well explain why none of them have been able to call for help.*

Perhaps, yet his thought kept returning to the same question. How could anyone, even one as clearly cunning as Speaks Falsely, have found Bright Water in the first place? And having found it, how could he come close enough to do one of the People harm, even with one of the two-leg thunder-barkers, without one single other Person tasting even the tiniest trace of his mind-glow?

<Very well, Short Tail,> he said at last. <I *do not pretend I am glad to hear your news. And I do not know the best way to proceed from this point. If only I could truly* communicate *with Death Fang's Bane and her parents! But I am beginning to think the People will never be able to truly communicate with the two-legs as we communicate with one another, or even as they communicate with one another. Still, it seems clear to me that we must somehow make the good two-legs aware that something is happening to Bright Water. We know how they have aided and guarded Bright Heart Clan in its time of need, and I am certain they would aid* us, *if only they knew we needed their help.*>

<*That is the thinking of Sings Truly and Broken Tooth, as well,*> Short Tail said.

<*I thought it would be.*> Despite the gravity of the situation, Climbs Quickly's mind-voice was dryly amused,

and Short Tail bleeked a soft laugh. <*The problem is how we go about telling them.*>

<*Clear Singer and Walks in Moonlight Clan's scouts and hunters made Darkness Foe hear them,*> Short Tail pointed out, and Climbs Quickly flipped his ears in agreement.

<*That is true,*> he said. <*Yet it took all of them, and when Clear Singer made Darkness Foe hear, she had a very clear, very strong memory from True Stalker upon which to build. Even then, Darkness Foe clearly did not hear her full song. He understood much of what had happened, but until he went to Bright Heart Clan's range to see with his own eyes, he did not understand the details of what had occurred. Here we have no such strong, clear memory to begin with, only questions. I believe we could make Darkness Foe realize we are concerned, yet I fear explaining to him why we are concerned is beyond our power. Besides, Darkness Foe is far from Bright Water. It would take much time for us to contact Swift Striker and for Swift Striker to make him understand he must go to Clear Singer once more. And even if that were not so, Darkness Foe is . . . worried by the way Clear Singer made him hear her. It frightens him for some reason. Not because of the People, but because of how his own kind, the other two-legs, might react if they knew of it. Swift Striker and I do not understand why that should concern him so, yet we know he feels that way.*>

<*Yet if we do not go to Darkness Foe with this, then what?*> Short Tail asked, and it was Climbs Quickly's turn to bleek in soft, bittersweet laughter.

<*Sings Truly knows the answer to that question, whether she has yet shared it with you or not, brother,*> he replied. <*Indeed, it is the obvious answer . . . and the right one. I will bring Death Fang's Bane to visit Sings Truly and the other elders as quickly as I can. I do not think we will be able to explain things to her, but I feel confident that*

one as clever and as insightful as she will soon realize the People are worried, even frightened, by something. And she has many friends among the elder two-legs now—more than she realizes, I think. If she calls upon them to help her in understanding why the People are frightened, they will respond. Perhaps the time will come then for us to attempt to make Darkness Foe hear the People again, but I believe calling upon Death Fang's Bane's Clan ought to be our first step.>

25

STEPHANIE HARRINGTON WAS WORRIED AS SHE BANKED
her tiger-striped glider for the final approach to the treecat community.

She hadn't shared her anxiety with her parents before
setting out this morning, partly because she wasn't positive it was justified and partly because she was afraid
they might have objected to her going if they'd decided
it *was* justified. Yet it was painfully evident to her that
Lionheart was deeply worried about something. Indeed,
she could feel that worry simmering in her own emotions.

It was becoming clearer to her that while treecats might
be empaths and humans weren't, there was something
about her bond to Lionheart which made her at least
peripherally aware of his emotions. She couldn't feel a
single thing where any other treecat was concerned, but
she was positive she was feeling *his* emotions, however
imperfectly. That was the only explanation she could come
up with for the occasional "sounds" *she* detected from

him but no one else could hear at all. And because of that link to his emotions, she was only too well aware of his extreme...uneasiness.

Oh, I wish *you could talk,* she thought at Lionheart as the hang glider slowed still further and her feet found solid ground. She trotted forward for a few meters, absorbing the last of the glider's momentum, then came to a halt, pulled off her helmet, and began unbuckling both of them. *If you could just* explain *to me what's wrong, I'd fix it in a heartbeat!*

But Lionheart couldn't talk, and even if she was beginning to sense his emotions, she was no telepath. So the only thing she could do was go home with him the way he obviously wanted her to and hope she could somehow figure out what was wrong when she got there.

Tennessee Bolgeo stepped out of the warehouse door and closed it behind him with a sense of profound satisfaction.

The dozen treecats in the large, comfortable cages concealed within the warehouse looked decidedly woozy but appeared to be in excellent health otherwise. That was good. His research had suggested that the drug his assistants were slipping them in their food would keep them permanently disoriented without causing any long-term damage. Of course, calculating a safe maintenance dose to keep them that way had been a little tricky, but a man in Bolgeo's profession had to develop a good feel for xenobiology, and it seemed evident he'd gotten it just about right.

The question, he thought as he strolled across to the largish commercial-body air car, was how many more he could capture before the little creatures figured out what was happening. He wanted a minimum of, say, fifty or sixty before leaving Sphinx. In fact, he'd like more than that, since he figured the odds were against his being able to return for another haul, although he could be wrong about that. If he handled it right and no one actually bothered to check his credentials from Liberty University, he might very well be able to come back after all. If that proved possible, the fact that he'd been here before would actually work in his favor. He'd be a known quantity as far as the Sphinxians were concerned.

Best not to count on that happening, though. And that meant he needed as many as he could catch this time around. Besides, so far he'd managed to capture only males. In fact, he wasn't certain any human had ever actually met a *female* treecat, which led him to wonder why that was. It seemed unlikely there could be that huge a disparity between males and females in a clearly mammalian species. It wasn't like there could be a single egg-layer, like the queen bee in a hive. No, there had to be sufficient females to bear enough young for the species to sustain itself, yet apparently no one had ever encountered one.

He'd studied the available long-range imagery the Sphinx Forestry Service had recorded of the clan it had assisted after the BioNeering disaster, and he'd noticed that while all the males who'd been observed—and all the males he'd captured, for that matter—had the same gray coats and cream-colored belly fur, with dark bands around their tails, there were other treecats who had a different coloration. Whose coats were dappled brown and white—rather like an Old Terran fawn—and who seemed smaller, on average, than their gray-coated fellows. Obviously, he had to be cautious about making judgments about size, since all he had was the Forestry Service footage and it was always risky to draw hasty conclusions about size or body mass from something like that.

Despite that, he'd come to the conclusion that the treecats' coloration was as much linked to their genders as feather colors and patterns were among many species of Old Terran birds. The cardinal came to mind, for example. If he was correct, then the brown and white treecats were the females, and he really, *really* wanted at least a few of them. They would undoubtedly fetch a premium price from the pet fanciers, especially if they were available in only limited numbers. More to the point, it would be impossible for Ustinov's Exotics (or any of the genetic labs Bolgeo could think of) to maintain a useful population without females to bear additional young or at least provide ova for artificial breeding.

The problem was that they didn't seem to venture far from home. Or, if they did, it would appear the males took on the riskier tasks. Which would make sense. By and large, Nature seemed to assume males were more expendable than females, no matter the planet. Childbearers were always more important, ultimately, to the survival of the species, when all was said. Which was all very understandable but left Bolgeo frustrated and more than a little irritated.

His smile faded as he climbed into the air car and closed the hatch. The environmental systems came on, keeping the interior pleasantly cool, but he sat for several minutes, fingers drumming on the controls, while he pondered.

The traps he'd prepared had worked well, so far. In fact, he'd actually had to make fairly few modifications to a design he'd used several times in the past. He'd had to reprogram their chameleonlike "smart paint," but it hadn't been difficult to create an almost perfect camouflage, well suited to Sphinx's vegetation. Until they actually pounced, they were only small, compactly folded shapes, virtually impossible to see at any distance above a meter even if someone knew exactly what to look for.

On top of the camouflage, he'd chosen his sites very carefully. He'd used small remote platforms—the kind routinely used by surveyors and prospectors—to get a good look at the terrain within several kilometers of the GPS coordinates his transponder had given him. Getting them in under that kind of tree cover had been tricky, and he'd lost two of them, apparently to collisions with picketwood branches. He'd been afraid the treecats might hear them and be panicked into fleeing the area, but there'd been no sign of any such response. Just in case, though, he'd waited a full local week and a half after sending in the platforms before going anywhere near the treecats again.

The time hadn't been wasted. With the imagery from the agile platforms—especially the thermal imagery—he'd been able to identify the picketwood pathways the treecats used most heavily, then search for specific side branches, hollow trunks, and other natural hiding places near those pathways. He'd had exacting criteria for the spots he'd wanted, and only after he was satisfied he'd found them had he taken his traps out one night and put them into place.

His low-light vision contacts had made it daylight-bright, even under the enormously deep leaf canopy of the picketwood and crown oaks, and he'd worn a hostile environment suit. It had been heavy and clumsy, but it was a very special suit which had been treated to kill all external scent, and its sealed environment prevented him from leaving any scent of his own. The traps had been treated with the same scent-killing compound, and he'd baited each of them with celery juice.

He'd been careful not to use too much. The idea was to use just enough to send the tempting scent wafting out to where a treecat who passed within no more than a meter or two, possibly three, might detect it. Bolgeo wanted them close enough to smell it and go to investigate—make sure of what they were actually smelling—and walk into the trap before it occurred to them to call any of their friends to join them.

The Forestry Service footage of the BioNeering incident's

survivors suggested that treecats normally went about their routine tasks as individuals, not in pairs or groups. Perhaps because a race of telepaths had no need to remain in close physical proximity to communicate with one another? He didn't know about that, but it had meant it was unlikely another treecat would be within visual range at the instant one of them walked into one of his traps. He'd placed those traps far enough from the treecats' nests that (hopefully, at least) they would have had to do the telepathic equivalent of shouting loudly to be heard by anyone beyond visual range, as well. Unfortunately, he couldn't be positive of the distance at which they could make another of their own kind "hear" them, so he couldn't be positive he'd succeeded in that. But he could at least try to keep the traps far enough out that no one would simply "overhear" their thoughts when they detected the delectable scent of celery.

Once they came close enough, the proximity sensors built into the traps released a powerful, targeted spurt of gas. Bolgeo had tested the gas (carefully and very privately) on several types of Sphinxian wildlife first and lost quite a few test subjects in the process. In the end, though, he'd found one which knocked a treecat out almost instantly with no observable ill effects. And once the little creature had been rendered unconscious, the trap disconnected itself from the tree branch or the trunk or the interior of the hollow space to which it had been attached. It extruded mechanical legs, walked across to the sleeping treecat, and unfolded itself until it could very carefully and gently reconfigure into a cage around its captive. Then it sent out a coded radio pulse to announce it had fulfilled its mission and waited—monitoring the treecat and administering more of the gas whenever it showed signs of awakening—until it could be collected.

So far, the system seemed to be working fine. The unconscious treecats obviously weren't managing to call out for rescue, and Bolgeo or one of his assistants could collect the occupied traps with a simple air car trip. All they had to do was fly over the area where the trap lay waiting and trigger its counter-grav unit. The unit's endurance was no more than five minutes, but that was ample for it to rise above the canopy and for an air car pilot to put his vehicle into a hover, open a window, and collect the trap (and its contents) with a simple hand-held tractor beam like the ones used in any warehouse. Getting a trap back into place and reset was more complicated, requiring another nocturnal visit in the environmental suit, but even that was hardly an onerous task.

Except for the fact that he had yet to capture a single female, Bolgeo thought. There ought to be a way he could—

His thoughts broke off as his uni-link gave a soft, musical chime. Most people would have assumed it indicated someone had left him a voicemail, or possibly a text message. Most people, however, would have been wrong, and Bolgeo smiled at the confirmation that another of his traps had just collected its own treecat for him.

He entered a code, checking the tally, and frowned thoughtfully. That made three since the last collection flight the night before. Given the traps' locations and the weather, it was unlikely any of the captives were going to suffer from dehydration or starvation before they were collected. But the greater the number of traps sitting around with slumbering treecats, the greater the chance that an *un*-trapped treecat might happen along and spot one of them. And while he didn't like collecting them in daylight, he wouldn't have to land, anyway.

He thought about it for another several seconds, then shrugged. He didn't have anyplace he was scheduled to be, so he might as well fly over and collect them now. If he needed to land for any reason the environmental suit was ready and waiting in his air car's outsized cargo compartment, and so was the trank rifle. He didn't want to use it if he could avoid it, but the rifle's darts had an effective range of almost three hundred meters. They were guaranteed to knock out any treecat, and Tennessee Bolgeo was an excellent shot. Besides, who knew? He wasn't *planning* on using the trank rifle, but if it should happen he had to land and he happened to see one of those dappled brown-and-white coats, he wasn't going to pass up the opportunity to finally collect a female treecat.

"I don't understand what's wrong," Stephanie said, sitting on the picketwood branch fourteen meters above the ground, feet dangling in empty air. The slender, dappled treecat standing in her lap and staring intently into her eyes gave an audible "whuffle" of obvious frustration, and Stephanie stroked the delicate creature's silken pelt.

"I'm sorry, Morgana," she said humbly, projecting her regret as strongly as she could, "and I'm really trying. But I just don't understand what you're trying to tell me."

<*I see why you find this so frustrating, Climbs Quickly,*> Sings Truly said, turning to look at her brother. <*Death Fang's Bane is trying so* hard *to grasp what we are telling her, yet we cannot make her understand!*>

<*I know,*> Climbs Quickly replied, <*but the fault, if there is one, lies with us, not with her. She is very clever, Death Fang's Bane, yet she cannot hear our mind-voices, just as we cannot hear hers... if the two-legs truly have one, that is. I sometimes think from experience with Darkness Foe that they do, almost, but if so it is too different from that of the People for us to hear one another.*>

<*If only there were some way for us to make those moving images of the two-legs which you have described,*> Sings Truly grumbled.

<*Even that would not help in this case,*> Climbs Quickly

pointed out. *<To make the moving images, the two-legs require the thing Death Fang's Bane used the night we first met, and I believe they can only make moving images of something the picture-making thing has actually seen. And that is the problem here, is it not? No one has seen what happened to our missing People.>*

<You can be very irritating at times, my brother,> Sings Truly replied tartly, and Climbs Quickly bleeked a laugh.

<Perhaps, but better to be irritating and accurate than comforting and wrong. Besides—>

<Broken Tooth! Sings Truly! Climbs Quickly!>

The mental shout was actually all a single thought, but Sings Truly and Climbs Quickly snapped upright, heads swiveling automatically in the direction from which it had come.

<Come!> the distant mind-shout called. *<Come now! Something has happened to Twig Weaver!>*

It was obvious to Climbs Quickly that only a memory singer or a mated female could have projected her shout across the distance this one had clearly covered. And even as he thought that, he recognized the taste of Water Dancer, Twig Weaver's mate. But what was she doing that far from the central nest place? And what could have happened to Twig Weaver?

<I do not know what takes her so far from her nest and kittens, either,> Sings Truly said, clearly sensing his inner thoughts. *<Yet it would seem Water Dancer may have stumbled across whatever has been happening to the People.>*

<Indeed. And perhaps we do not need one of the two-legs' picture-makers after all!> Climbs Quickly flicked his head in his person's direction. *<Death Fang's Bane is here, Sings Truly. We must get her to come with us to rescue Twig Weaver and discover what has happened to him.>*

<Are you certain of that, Climbs Quickly? We do not know—yet—what has befallen Twig Weaver, and for all

her courage, Death Fang's Bane is still but a youngling. For all we know, those of the clan who respond to Water Dancer may be rushing into danger. Would you expose Death Fang's Bane to such?>

<She may be a youngling,> Climbs Quickly returned proudly, <but she is full of courage and she loves us. If we do not take her, and she later learns we did not, she will be angry. And if something terrible befalls Twig Weaver and we did not give her the chance to help us save him, her heart will be broken. I will not do that to her.>

Stephanie had no idea what was going on.

One moment, the female treecat she'd christened "Morgana"—the one she suspected might well be Lionheart's sister—had been staring into her eyes, almost vibrating with the intensity of her effort to make Stephanie understand whatever was of such concern to all the treecats. The next, Morgana and Lionheart had whipped around to stare at one another. And then, abruptly, Morgana leapt out of Stephanie's lap to crouch on the limb beside her.

"What is it? What's happening?" Stephanie asked sharply, looking back and forth between the two treecats.

They paid her absolutely no attention for several seconds. Not rudely, but because they were so obviously concentrating on something else. Then Lionheart looked back up at her, his huge green eyes as dark and almost...pleading as she had ever seen them. His remaining true-hand reached out and the slender, wiry fingers closed warmly around the little finger of her own right hand and tugged.

"Bleek," he said urgently. "*Bleek!*"

She looked down at him, trying to understand, and two more true-hands closed on the thumb and index finger of her left hand.

"*Bleek!*" Morgana seconded Lionheart. "Bleek! *Bleek!*"

They were both tugging her in the same direction, and she looked back and forth between them a moment longer, then nodded.

"All right, I'm coming!" she told them and activated her belt counter-grav unit and slid off the branch upon which she'd been sitting.

Climbs Quickly and Sings Clearly had become accustomed to the two-legs' marvelous tools, including the one which allowed Death Fang's Bane to apparently fly. They'd realized some time ago that the humming device on the two-leg youngling's belt didn't actually let her *fly*, since she seemed unable to move swiftly or control her direction without her personal flying thing, but it did allow her to float to the highest of branches. And because they realized that they were unsurprised when she pushed off the limb and started drifting gradually towards the ground so far below. Instead of panicking, they simply wrapped their arms and mid-limbs around her forearms and floated down with her.

Under most circumstances, both of them would have been bleeking madly in delight. Indeed, Death Fang's Bane sometimes gave armloads of kittens similar flights, and the entire clan enjoyed them immensely. This time, however, they were too worried—too well aware of Water Dancer's distant distress and the rising anxiety level of the rest of Bright Water's adults.

<*What do you intend, Sings Truly?*> Broken Tooth demanded as Death Fang's Bane's feet touched the ground.

<*Precisely what you* think *I intend,*> Sings Truly replied tartly.

<*No,*> Broken Tooth said firmly, sitting down on his haunches and folding both his arms and his mid-limbs. <*Not this time, Senior Memory Singer. There is no need—and no*

justification—for taking yourself or any of the other memory singers into what may be danger.>

Sings Truly stiffened angrily, but her brother quickly touched her on one shoulder. She looked at him, and he twitched his ears, his mind-glow radiating mingled understanding, sympathy, and amusement.

<Broken Tooth has a point, Sister,> Climbs Quickly told her. *<I think none of the clan will question this rescue mission. There is no need for you to lead them all to save your impetuous brother from his own folly this time! Besides,>* his amusement perked higher, *<given what happened the last time you led a rescue, they are probably terrified of what you might bring back from this one!>*

<I would not put it quite that way myself,> Broken Tooth said. *<On the other hand, I would not argue with the way Climbs Quickly has put it, Sings Truly. More, you know he is right. That we are right.>*

<Do not expect me to be pleased about it simply because you are right!> she told Broken Tooth and her brother in a fulminating tone.

<None of us are foolish enough to expect anything that reasonable,> Climbs Quickly assured her. *<We know you too well.>*

<I am glad one of us thinks you are humorous, Brother,> she said ominously, and he bleeked a half-laugh. *<But I will not argue. Only go—all of you! And be cautious!>*

26

STEPHANIE HURRIED THROUGH THE FOREST, SURROUNDED and accompanied by a flowing tide of gray and cream-colored treecats. She was half-tempted to use her counter-grav to join them on the picketwood branches along which they flowed, but treecats could fit through spaces and squirm around obstacles even a relatively small, frustratingly flat-chested fourteen-year-old human would have found impassable.

The forest floor was considerably more than ankle-deep in dead leaves and leaf mold, but it was clear of undergrowth, thanks to how little sunlight managed to penetrate the towering tree canopy, so the going was relatively easy. And at least, unlike most human interlopers into the Sphinxian bush, she didn't have to worry about things like hexapumas. Not with an entire clan of treecats filtering through the trees above her! Of course...

She paused for a moment to catch her breath and reached down, almost reflexively to pat the handgun at her hip. So far, she'd never even come close to needing that gun, and the truth was that she didn't expect to, not with the treecats to keep an eye on her. If she did run into another hexapuma, though, at least she might not have to get close enough to stick it with a vibro blade!

She grinned at the thought and, having caught her breath again, went jogging off with the treecats once more.

❖   ❖   ❖

<Water Dancer!> Climbs Quickly called. <We come— where are you? And where is Twig Weaver?>

Although Climbs Quickly was only a male, his mind-voice had grown so much stronger since his bonding to Death Fang's Bane that Water Dancer heard him easily.

<Up here, Climbs Quickly!> she called back. <Above the green-needle.>

Climbs Quickly turned, looking in the indicated direction, and spotted a small, distant brown and white shape on the high branch of a golden-leaf above what a human would have called a near-pine. Water Dancer was slender and delicate, even for a female, and normally presented a picture of gracefulness. Now, though, she was tense, frightened. Even without tasting her mind-glow, Climbs Quickly would have realized that simply from how rigidly she crouched on the branch.

<Is Twig Weaver there with you?> he asked.

<Yes! Oh, yes! But come—I cannot get him to wake!>

Climbs Quickly looked at Broken Tooth, who stood on his right side, then at Short Tail, on the other side, and saw their tense confusion mirroring his own. Then the three of them were moving again, climbing to the topmost branch of their net-wood tree and following it to Water Dancer's tree, then leaping across to the far taller golden-leaf and swarming quickly up to join her.

It didn't take them long to reach her, and her anxiety and

fear for her mate became steadily more obvious to them as they approached her. Then they were at her side, and she raised one slightly trembling true-hand and pointed.

<There.>

Her mind-voice was almost a whimper, and Climbs Quickly felt the fur rising along his spine, felt his tighly furled tail flattening out, as his eyes followed her gesture and he saw Twig Weaver.

Water Dancer's mate was one of Bright Water's most skilled hunters. Indeed, he took his name from the cleverness with which he wove branches and twigs together to create hiding spots from which he might pounce upon smaller game as it wandered carelessly past. But this time it was Twig Weaver who had been entrapped within someone else's weaving.

For a moment, Climbs Quickly thought someone had constructed a prison out of tree branches. That was what it looked like, at any rate. But then he realized it wasn't the case. The bars of the cage which had enclosed Twig Weaver *looked* like branches, yet they weren't. And as his nostrils flared, he caught the scent of cluster stalk . . . and something else.

<Cluster stalk?!> Broken Tooth said beside him. The elder's sense of smell had begun to decline with age, but he'd caught Climbs Quickly's recognition of the scent from the younger treecat's mind-glow. *<What is cluster stalk doing up here in the treetops?>*

<An excellent question,> Climbs Quickly agreed grimly. *<And one it would seem Twig Weaver might have asked himself before rushing to investigate.>*

<Bait in a trap, you think?> Short Tail said, and Climbs Quickly gave a two-leg nod.

<That is exactly what I think,> he replied, and tasted Short Tail's and Broken Tooth's understanding. The People were no strangers to traps for small prey animals, and

they had been known to use bait in their time. But until now, no one had ever set traps for *them*.

<*This is a two-leg thing,*> Climbs Quickly continued. <*I do not catch any two-leg scent on it, which is strange, yet I am certain of that.*>

Short Tail started forward, but Climbs Quickly reached out and stopped him.

<*Carefully, Short Tail! I do not catch any two-leg scent from it, but there is something besides the cluster stalk. Something I do not care for. Go no closer.*>

<*But we must go and help Twig Weaver,*> Short Tail argued.

<*Indeed we must, but with caution,*> Climbs Quickly responded. <*Taste carefully. Do you not taste his mind-glow?*>

<*From here?*> Short Tail snorted mentally. <*I am no memory singer, Climbs Quickly!*>

<*Neither am I,*> Climbs Quickly said. <*But I do taste Twig Weaver's mind-glow. Perhaps I have become more sensitive to that, as well, because of my bond with Death Fang's Bane. At any rate, he is alive, only asleep. So I think we need not rush forward and perhaps see more of us blunder into the same sort of trap.*>

<*I will take your word for the fact that he is only asleep,*> Short Tail said. <*As for your ability to taste his mind-glow, perhaps that is because you are getting more cluster stalk than any of the rest of us!*> There was a definite sparkle of laughter in that last sentence, tinged with relief that Twig Weaver was alive. But then the older scout's mind-voice sobered. <*Still, we cannot simply leave him there.*>

<*No, we cannot,*> Climbs Quickly agreed. <*But this is a two-leg thing. So perhaps it is fortunate we have a two-leg of our own to deal with it.*>

✧   ✧   ✧

Stephanie leaned against the crown oak's mighty trunk. As tall as an Old Earth sequoia (and even more massive, due to Sphinx's higher gravity), it towered over the lower growing picketwood like a titan, and she peered up at the massive branch a good fifty meters above her—five meters higher than the tallest branch of the surrounding picketwood but little more than halfway to the top of the crown oak—at Lionheart and the others. It was hard to make out details at such a distance, but they were obviously conferring with one another about something, and she wondered—again—what this was all about.

After a few minutes, Lionheart came swarming down the tree towards her. She held up her arms when he was within a couple of meters of the ground, and he launched himself into them, pressing close against her as she hugged him.

"Okay," she told him. "I'm here. Now what's this all about?"

"Bleek," Lionheart said, then raised his remaining true-hand and pointed up at the high perch from which he had descended.

"You know," she said, "this belt unit doesn't have anywhere near the power pack our glider does." She studied the branch in question, then shrugged. "Still, the charge looks pretty good so far. Okay, I'm coming."

Climbs Quickly moved around to the pads on his person's shoulder and back, clinging close as she adjusted the device on her belt and their weight seemed to magically disappear. When they weighed as little as one of the rotating gold-leaf seedpods that filled the air of leaf-turning season with flashing golden light, Death Fang's Bane reached out to the tree trunk and sent them bobbing up it at a speed few of the People could have matched.

They reached the limb where Broken Tooth and Short Tail waited, and she crouched on one knee beside the other two People while she adjusted a knob on her belt device. Their weight crept back up again, although not to anything approaching what it should have been, and Climbs Quickly pressed his nose against her ear, then pointed.

Stephanie Harrington followed Lionheart's pointing finger. For a moment, she didn't realize what she was seeing. Then she did, and said a word her parents would not have approved of.

The cream and gray shape of the treecat lay crumpled on its side in a small cage of some sort. She had no idea how it had gotten here, but she could tell it was a fairly sophisticated piece of engineering. It looked like it had articulated legs, ending in sharp, spurlike claws which were sunk into the limb's surface. It was a bit hard to make out the details, since whoever had left it here had very carefully camouflaged it, but it looked to her as if it might have its own much smaller built-in counter-grav unit, as well.

She looked up at the canopy above and instantly realized how the trapper, whoever he was, intended to retrieve his captive. The problem was what she did about it.

She started to hurry forward to rescue the treecat, then made herself stop. She didn't know enough about that trap. How had the treecat been rendered unconscious? Could the trap do the same thing to her if she got too close? What kind of security devices might be built into it? Could the person who had put it here be ruthless enough to include a self-destruct device, something that would blow up a trap and any treecat in it if someone tampered with it? And was there an alarm of some sort on it? Something which would tell the trapper her trap had been discovered if Stephanie tried to open it?

"Okay," she said, keeping her voice as confident as possible and speaking to herself as much as to the waiting treecats. "Okay. I see the problem. Now I think we probably need to get a little advice on how to deal with it."

The treecats looked up at her and she sensed their deep worry . . . and their confidence in her. She wondered if she was picking it up directly from the other treecats, or sensing it through her link to Lionheart. Or, for that matter, if she was simply reading their body language and the intensity of their huge green eyes.

She didn't know about that, but she reached for her uni-link.

"—so then Dad said I should com you, Scott. What do I do now?"

"Don't do *anything* for a minute, Steph," Scott MacDallan said firmly. "You may have a point about possible booby traps, and I don't want anything happening to *you!*"

"Well, I can't just *sit* here! I've got to get him out of there, somehow. Besides, what if the . . . *person*"—she'd been about to use another, much ruder word, but she stopped herself in time—"who set this trap comes back to collect it before I get him out of it?"

"A good point," he conceded. "But let me think for a minute first, okay?"

"Okay," she replied more than a little grudgingly, and he shook his head. He'd come to know "sweet little" Stephanie Harrington too well to expect her to sit there passively for very long.

Why, oh why did both her parents have to choose today of all days to be out on business? he asked himself.

Richard Harrington was even farther from his daughter at the moment than MacDallan was, and he was smack in the middle of a surgical procedure to save a genetically

modified Morgan horse's leg. And Marjorie Harrington
and her Forestry Service guide were half-buried (more or
less literally) in the root structure the picketwood network
the BioNeering release had contaminated, trying to figure
out how the rest of the picketwood had separated itself
from the dying portion before the contaminant spread
still further. She was at least as far from home as her
husband was, which meant neither of them could get to
Stephanie before—

"Look," he said, "Frank and Ainsley should both be
closer to you than your parents are. Can I go ahead and
give them your GPS coordinates? I know how hard we've
all been trying to keep Lionheart's clan's location a secret,
but it sounds like *someone's* figured it out, anyway. And
we need an official presence on-scene as quick as we can
get it there."

"Wellllll . . . all right." She knew he'd heard the unhap-
piness in her voice, but she'd already seen the suggestion
coming. And little though she liked the idea, she had to
admit it had to be done.

"Okay. I'll get them on their way as soon as you and I
are off the com," he said. " Now, what did your dad say
when you asked him about why the treecat's unconscious?"

"He says it's probably some kind of knockout gas. I've
been looking at the trap with my binoculars, and I see
what could be a kind of swivel-mounted dispenser in
the roof of the cage. At the moment, it's pointed at the
treecat. I guess it may be waiting to give him another
squirt if he starts to wake up before somebody gets here
to collect him."

"Which doesn't mean it won't turn itself around to
squirt *you*—or one of the other treecats—if you start
fooling around with it!" he said sharply.

"I'm not a *complete* null wit, Scott," she said testily. "I
already figured that out. But Dad says most of the gases

that would be most effective—and safe to use—against a native species with a treecat's body mass wouldn't be powerful enough, or effective enough against humans, to knock *me* out."

"Which is all fine and good, assuming whoever set this trap is as smart as your father and equally concerned about not harming the critters he's trying to trap," he pointed out.

"I *know* that. But if you don't want me to 'start fooling around with it,' what *do* you want me to do?"

"To be perfectly honest," he said, "what I'd *like* to do is order you to climb down out of that tree and get back to a safe distance before whoever set the trap comes along and realizes you're onto him. I don't know what kind of person we're dealing with here, Stephanie. I don't know how far he'd go to... eliminate any witnesses. Unfortunately, I *do* know it won't do me any good to tell you to back off, will it?"

"Not much," she admitted, lips twitching in a brief half-smile, and he chuckled.

"Well, in that case, I think the best thing you could do is probably to back off at least a little ways and keep an eye on things. If somebody turns up to collect that trap, try to get a look at the air car. Maybe you can identify it later. In the meantime, find yourself a good spot to keep a lookout while I get Frank and Ainsley. I'll be in the air, headed your direction myself by the time I get hold of them."

27

STEPHANIE HARRINGTON SAT ON THE CROWN OAK LIMB, her back braced against the trunk, with her knees drawn up under her chin and her arms wrapped around her shins.

Her expression was not a happy one.

She was willing to admit MacDallan might have a point, but that was one of her *friends* in that trap over there. It was almost certainly one of the treecats who had helped save her from the hexapuma. She owed him. More than that, he was part of her *family*, and she *hated* just sitting here doing nothing!

Lionheart shifted slightly on the branch beside her, and she made herself draw a deep breath, then unwrapped her arms from her shins. She stretched her legs out along the limb, making a lap, and held out her arms to him. He swarmed into them, cuddling against her, and she tucked her chin over the top of his head and hugged him.

Climbs Quickly pressed his nose more tightly against his two-leg's collarbone, buzzing with a bone-deep, reassuring purr. He felt her anxiety, her frustration, but he and Broken Tooth and Short Tail had listened to her conversations with her parents and with Darkness Foe. They hadn't understood any of the mouth-sounds, but they'd understood enough—at least in general—from Death Fang's Bane's mind-glow to know Darkness Foe, Swift Striker, and Darkness Foe's friends who had helped teach Death Fang's Bane the use of her weapon, were all on their way to Twig Weaver's rescue. They knew that, and it filled them with hope, but they also understood Death Fang's Bane's worry and burning desire to *do* something.

<*Well, at least we know what has been happening to the missing People,*> Broken Tooth said, sitting beside Death Fang's Bane and gazing much further down the tree where half a dozen other females were gathered around Water Dancer to comfort her.

<*And with Darkness Foe and the uniformed two-legs involved, I think there is an excellent chance all of them will be rescued,*> Climbs Quickly agreed.

<*If they can determine which of the evil two-legs did this thing,*> Short Tail objected. <*What if they cannot? And what if the evildoer responsible for this is like the one who destroyed Bright Heart Clan's range? What if he is prepared to slay his captives and conceal their bodies before the other two-legs can catch him? The two-legs are mind-blind, Climbs Quickly. They cannot simply taste his mind-glow and know he is the guilty one. I think that may be the reason there are evildoers among them—because unlike us, they cannot* know *what another of their kind is truly thinking or feeling. That is why they seem to insist so strongly on* proof *of evil doing. So what becomes of our missing brothers if the evildoer realizes what is happening and . . . disposes of them?*>

He kept his mind-voice low, but it was perhaps fortunate

Water Dancer was too far distant to overhear him anyway, Climbs Quickly reflected sourly. Not that Short Tail's
point wasn't valid.

<You may be right,> he acknowledged. *<Yet even if you
are, we and the good two-legs are in a far better position
to discover who has done this than we ever were before.>*

<Yes, we are,> Broken Tooth said. *<Although, if we
succeed in rescuing Twig Weaver, I think perhaps Water
Dancer will be hearing from him about this day.>*

<Not if Twig Weaver has any wisdom at all!> Climbs
Quickly retorted. *<Take it from a memory singer's brother—
and one who has bonded with a female* two-leg, *to boot—no
good* ever *came of trying to tell a female what she must or
must not do! And if he should be foolish enough to try that
in Water Dancer's case, she will only send him the mind
picture of him lying asleep in the two-leg trap.>*

Both of his companions' mind-glows radiated wry amusement at that. Water Dancer hadn't wanted her mate to go
off unaccompanied when so many of the People had been
disappearing. But he'd been confident in his ability to look
after himself, and with the clan so short of scouts and
hunters, he'd refused to ask another to go with him. And
when she'd threatened to follow him herself, he'd delivered
a tremendous scold, pointing out that their kittens were
scarcely weaned. Surely she had better things to do than
follow him about! And if there actually was any danger,
they had no business risking *both* of their kittens' parents!

In Climbs Quickly's opinion, any male—especially a
bonded male—should have known how useless it had been
to issue that sort of decree. In fact, Twig Weaver should
have realized it would only make Water Dancer even more
determined to keep him safe. Which was precisely why she
had asked one of the older females to keep watch over her
offspring while she went scuttling through the branches
behind Twig Weaver.

Climbs Quickly didn't know how she'd managed to keep him in sight without his detecting her familiar mind-glow, but it was obviously as well for Twig Weaver she'd done so. At least the clan knew where he was, and now Death Fang's Bane and Darkness Foe knew what had been happening. Now if only they could—

His head came up suddenly, ears pricking forward, and a faint snarl sounded deep in his throat as he recognized the sound of one of the two-leg flying things.

Stephanie saw Lionheart's head rise abruptly and sensed a sudden spike in his emotions. She didn't know what he'd heard, but she strained her own ears, trying to catch whatever sound had alerted him.

For several seconds, she heard nothing but wind sighing through foliage and the distant call of the Sphinxian equivalent of birds. But then she heard another sound, and her face went pale.

That can't be Scott or either of the rangers—not this quick! she thought. *But if it isn't any of* them ...

Her eyes darted back to the trapped treecat, and her stomach twisted into a sudden knot. Of course. Whoever had set that trap would have fitted it with some sort of signal to tell him when it had something in it. She wouldn't want to leave it sitting too long lest one of the other treecats come along, discover the victim, and realize what had been happening to the members of his clan. Which meant she was going to activate that counter-grav unit any second now and the only physical evidence of what she'd been doing would disappear ... along with yet another member of Stephanie's treecat family.

Her jaw clenched. No. No, that *wasn't* going to happen! Not to another of *her* treecats, it wasn't! But how—?

"Give me your net!" she told Lionheart, pointing at the

net wrapped about his middle. "All of you—give me your nets, now!"

Lionheart looked at her, his expression perplexed. For just a moment she thought he didn't understand. Then she realized he *did* . . . and that he didn't want her risking herself.

"Give me the *nets!*" she repeated harshly, holding out both hands and making grabbing motions. He looked at her for a second longer, and then his true-hand and hand-feet moved, unwrapping the cargo net he continued to carry with him everywhere he went.

He held it up to her, and by the time he had it unwrapped from around his torso, the other two treecats with him had unwrapped their nets, as well. Stephanie snatched them up, twitched her own counter-grav up to reduce her weight to no more than a kilo or two, and went racing along the branch.

Climbs Quickly watched Death Fang's Bane run along the branch towards Twig Weaver's prison and pride warred with fear in his heart.

He was terrified his two-leg was about to be rendered unconscious exactly as Twig Weaver had been. If that happened, there was nothing any of the People could do about it, for they would simply be put to sleep themselves if they came near the trap. And despite the magic device that so reduced Death Fang's Bane's weight, she would still fall from the tree, a triple hand and more of People-lengths above the forest floor. When she hit, especially if she was unconscious, what had happened to her when her flying thing crashed would probably seem minor compared to the hurts she would suffer.

Yet with the terror, and brighter by far, was his fierce, fresh pride in his youngling. She knew as well as he did what might happen—no, she knew *better* than he did. Yet it never even occurred to her to hesitate, and in the blazing corona of her mind-glow he tasted her unyielding determination to protect Twig Weaver and every member of Bright Water Clan, whatever the cost.

Yes, there are *evildoers among the two-legs*, he thought. *But there is also* my *two-leg, and her friends, and there is no evil in* them!

Stephanie flung herself to her knees beside the caged treecat.

The trap's motion sensor detected her and swivelled the gas dispenser in her direction. She heard it hiss, but whatever gas it had been loaded with had no effect on her. Not immediately, at least, and she looped the first treecat cargo net through the camouflaged bars.

It was long enough to go around two of the bars, then loop around a side branch of the main crown oak limb, and she knotted it tight. Then she flipped the second net through a bar on the other side of the cage, wrapped it around another side branch and tied it just as tightly. The third net went around a bar at one end, and it was just long enough to reach around the main limb and still leave her ten or twelve centimeters of slack. She knotted that one, as well, and then went running back along the limb toward Lionheart and his friends.

Part of her wanted to stay right there, hanging onto the trap with her own body weight as an added precaution. But if she'd been trapping treecats, she'd have brought along whatever sensors she could—thermal sensors for sure, if she could get a reading through the canopy—and if the trap failed to rise on its counter-grav the way it was supposed to, she'd take a really close look at it to see why.

She didn't know what the trapper would do if she realized there was another human being present, but she had a strong suspicion that whoever it was might be tempted to go ahead and remove the evidence anyway, especially if she had gone ahead and installed an explosive charge of some kind. And if an interfering human got in the way, too bad for the human in question.

Her main concern, though, was to keep whoever it was from making off with his captive. She was confident the three cargo nets between them were enough to overcome the maximum lift capacity of a counter-grav unit small enough to fit into that trap. So unless the trapper wanted to come down after it, it wasn't going anywhere. And if the trapper *did* come down after it...

Climbs Quickly's ears flattened as Death Fang's Bane dropped from the golden-leaf tree to the upper branches of the net-wood and drew the thunder-barker from its holder on her belt. He'd enjoyed her training sessions as much as she had, watching (from an ear-saving distance) as she mastered the weapon and tasting her delight as she felled target after target. And he'd been glad she had it when they flew back and forth to Bright Water. He wasn't certain if it would slay a death fang with a single bark the way the longer, more powerful weapons did, but its bite would certainly make any death fang back off. He was in favor of that. He was in favor of *anything* that didn't require him to face another death fang or the rest of his clan to come swarming to their rescue!

But now, as he tasted Death Fang's Bane's mind-glow, watched her moving cautiously along the net-wood branch until she had a clear line of sight to both Twig Weaver's cage and the forest floor below, delight was the last thing he felt. There was a cold lump at his person's center—a knot of fear and dread. Not fear of whoever might be hovering overhead in the flying thing but of what she might be about to do in the next few moments. There was no hesitation in her. If it came to it, if it was the only way to protect herself or the People with her, she *would* use the weapon; Climbs Quickly knew that just as surely as he knew the sun would rise in the morning. But she didn't want to. She wanted to do *anything* else... except allow an evildoer to harm the People.

Stephanie threw herself prone on the broad picket-wood limb and spread her elbows in the solid isosceles triangle Frank Lethbridge and Karl Zivonik had taught her, holding the heavy pistol in both hands. She figured she was far enough from the trap to be beyond the reach of most thermal scanners, especially in such dense leaf cover, but she could see it quite clearly. In fact, she was almost perfectly positioned, not that realizing that made her feel any calmer. Her heart thundered—harder, she suspected, than it had when she and Lionheart had faced the hexapuma—and her mouth felt dry.

Tennessee Bolgeo opened the air car window as he hovered thirty meters above the tallest portion of the leaf canopy. He'd have liked to get a little lower, but he should be close enough, and staying out of the trees struck him as a very good idea.

He glanced at the trap's position transponder one more time, fixing its location relative to the air car firmly, so he could be ready when it broke free of the branches, then pressed the recall button.

Stephanie's breath caught as the trap suddenly twitched. It jerked in place, snatching her tied nets suddenly taut. It rose perhaps a centimeter from the branch, then stopped, quivering, unable to break free of its anchors, and she felt herself smiling as she imagined the reaction of the person who'd left it here.

Bolgeo muttered a curse.

The trap should have cleared the tree cover by now. According to the signal from it, its counter-grav was on full force, which should have shot it into the clear like a cork from a champagne bottle. But there was no sign of it, and the transponder showed it wasn't moving at all.

It had to be stuck on something. That was the biggest potential drawback of this technique, especially in such heavy timber. He'd been lucky none of the other traps had jammed, but now he had to figure out what to do about *this* one.

He was tempted to just go away and come back later that night when he could collect this one and also the other occupied traps while the treecats were hopefully huddled in their nests wondering what had happened to their friends and relations. The downside of that was that by now any treecats in the vicinity must have heard his air car. If they came scampering to investigate, they'd probably find their trapped relative. Whether they'd be able to tell anyone—like that pestiferous Harrington family—about it was problematical, but they'd know what had been happening, and the likelihood of his catching any more of them would plummet. On the other hand...

He pulled out his thermal scanner, trying to get a reading on the trap and its vicinity. For all he knew there were already a dozen treecats down there. From what he'd been able to learn of them, they'd certainly rally around to guard one of their own in a situation like this, and the thought of tangling with something which had managed—allegedly—to pull down a hexapuma wasn't high on Tennessee Bolgeo's to-do list.

The sheer vertical depth of the dense leaves defeated his scanner, however. He couldn't make out a thing through them, which left him in an unpalatable position.

Well, he thought, *the enviro suit's made for some pretty nasty hostile environments. I kind of doubt anything the size of a treecat's going to manage to get a claw through it! Besides, even if all the stories about them killing the hexapuma are accurate, it took* dozens *of them.*

He hesitated for a few more moments, then shook his head with a sigh.

If you want the big bucks, you've got to suck it up and do what it takes to earn them, he told himself, and turned the air car towards the riverbank where he'd landed the night he distributed his traps.

The trap stopped quivering and smacked back down on the branch as its counter-grav exhausted its power supply. Stephanie felt a cautious glow of optimism, which strengthened quickly when the air car turned and moved off.

She was actually surprised the trapper had given up so easily, but just as she was about to sit up and return her pistol to its holster, she heard the pitch of the air car's noise shift. It was coming lower. It was landing!

She cocked her head, eyes closed, trying to follow its flightpath by hearing alone, and her jaw muscles tightened. Whoever it was, she was heading for the river which supplied Lionheart's clan with fresh water. It also opened a break in the otherwise solid tree canopy, and a good air car pilot could get in under the picketwood that way if she was careful. Which meant—

She started to reach for her uni-link, then stopped herself, brown eyes hard. Scott and the rangers were already coming as quickly as they possibly could. Telling them what was happening wouldn't get them here any sooner, but it would give them the opportunity to tell her little girls had no business facing unknown numbers of illegal poachers with a gun. She *knew* what they'd say...and a part of her suspected they'd be right. But knowing what they *would* say was very different from actually hearing them say it.

She sat up, looking around with narrow, calculating eyes. If the air car was landing near the river, the poachers would be coming from about... *that* direction, she decided. They'd probably come straight across to the base of this tree, then use their own counter-grav to reach the trap. If they did that, then they'd take off from just about... there.

Stephanie had never tried to fire a weapon while hovering on counter-grav, but she suspected it wouldn't be the easiest thing in the galaxy to do. Or the most accurate. So *her* best move would be to let whoever it was get off the ground but not onto the crown oak limb. Catch the bad guys in midair, when she'd have all the advantages.

Of course, even if I do, she's likely to figure a "little kid" like me wouldn't really squeeze the trigger, she thought grimly. *If she does, she may try to ignore me or even come right at me, figuring I'll freeze.*

She remembered something Ainsley Jedrusinski had said to her. The ranger's expression had been very serious, her voice level.

"Never draw a weapon unless you intend to use it, Stephanie," she'd said. "Never aim a weapon at another person unless you intend to shoot her. And never shoot at another person unless you intend to kill her."

Stephanie had felt her eyes go wide, felt Lionheart sitting very still on her shoulder, and Ainsley had shaken her head slowly.

"If you aim a weapon at someone else, you raise the stakes. Whoever it is has to assume you will—or may, at least—pull the trigger. If she's willing to back down, well and good. If she's not, and some people won't be, she may decide to go for broke, instead. If she's got a weapon of her own, she'll use it. If she doesn't, she'll try to take *your* weapon, and if that happens, she'll probably use it against *you*. So never think for a moment that simply waving a gun at someone is going to magically make them do whatever it is you want them to do.

"But the flip side of that is that you'd better be sure—*damned* sure—the stakes are worth escalating a confrontation that way. If there's *any* question in your mind that stopping the other person justifies killing her, then it doesn't. Because the truth is that once you shoot someone, you can never put that bullet back into the gun. It's going to hit them, Stephanie, and if it comes out of something as powerful as the pistol we've been teaching you to use, the odds are that it *will* kill whoever you shoot, whether that's what you want or not. So make up your mind. If you decide to aim your weapon at someone else, then you aim—and you *shoot*, if it comes to that—to kill. Not to wound your opponent like some holo drama hero. To *kill*. Because you've decided it's better they be dead than that you or someone else be dead. If you're justified in shooting at all, then your sole object should be to neutralize the other person as quickly as possible, and the fastest way to do that is to shoot to kill. And if you deliberately shoot to kill, at least you'll never know you killed someone by *accident*."

Stephanie had thought then that at least part of it had been Ainsley making sure she'd be scared spitless at the thought of actually shooting another human being. But she'd also realized that what Ainsley was telling her was the grim truth, the consequences of picking up a weapon.

That her friend and teacher was telling her that now so it wouldn't come at her cold and unconsidered if the moment ever arrived.

I hope it hasn't arrived now, she thought, climbing up one branch and working her way several meters further out from the main picketwood trunk to get the best angle. *I hope it hasn't. But if it* has, *Ainsley, I'll remember.*

TENNESSEE BOLGEO FINISHED WIGGLING INTO THE
environmental suit and sealed the closures. He checked
the heads-up display on the inside of the transparent
plastic face shield and nodded in satisfaction. Everything
in the green. He had fourteen hours worth of air, which
certainly ought to be plenty, since he was no more than
two or three hundred meters from his trap.

He picked up the trank rifle and checked it for readiness. It was a selective-fire weapon, capable of single shots
or full automatic. Its magazine contained forty darts, each
guaranteed to knock a treecat off its feet instantly, and he
had two more mags on his belt. He didn't expect to need
them, but between the armor of his environmental suit
and the firepower of the trank gun, he wasn't especially
worried about meeting up with a handful of treecats.

He looked at his GPS tracker, which showed the position
of the trap's transponder, and started trudging through
the drifts of ancient leaves.

✧   ✧   ✧

<It is Speaks Falsely!> Climbs Quickly said suddenly as he recognized the approaching mind-glow, then wondered why he felt surprised. Certainly Speaks Falsely's emotions had made it amply clear how *he* regarded the People!

<What shall we do, Climbs Quickly?> Broken Tooth asked urgently. Four or five hands of scouts and hunters had followed them out to rescue Twig Weaver. Now all of them sat silently in the branches, following the approaching mind-glow, and anger rose off of them like smoke.

Climbs Quickly glanced at Broken Tooth, faintly amused that the elder who had been so adamantly against closer contact with the two-legs was asking *him* what to do in this situation. But the amusement faded quickly, and he looked at Death Fang's Bane.

She was lying very still, once again in the position her weapons teachers had taught her, and he tasted the absolute intensity of her focus.

<I am not sure, Broken Tooth,> he admitted. *<Death Fang's Bane has decided what she is going to do. I fear that anything we might do could interfere with that, confuse her or startle her at exactly the wrong moment.>*

<She is only a youngling, Climbs Quickly. It is not right that the weight of this should fall only on her.>

Climbs Quickly tasted the sincerity in Broken Tooth's mind-glow and sent back a quick, warm wash of gratitude. But—

<A youngling, yes, Broken Tooth. But never "only" a youngling. It is true the weight of defending our clan should not fall only on her, but it is a weight she has chosen to bear. All we can do is wait and see what chances.>

✧   ✧   ✧

Bolgeo found himself breathing heavily as he forged through the thick drifts of leaves. It was like wading through mud, he thought. The upper layers were dry and crisp, but as the leaf mold got deeper, it got moister and more crumbly. There had to be a good forty or fifty centimeters of... *mulch,* for want of a better word, under those upper layers. And in Sphinx's dratted heavy gravity, his feet sank deeply into it with every stride.

Still, it wasn't that much further. Every picketwood trunk looked the same to him—he imagined it was easy for even the locals to get badly disoriented in a thicket like this one—but the tracker kept him on course and he caught fairly frequent glimpses of his target crown oak through breaks in the foliage.

Catching these little beggars is hard work, he reflected. *Next time, I'll send one of the boys out here instead of coming myself!*

<*Climbs Quickly!*> Short Tail said suddenly. <*Do you taste what I taste?*>

The senior scout had suddenly come upright, gazing intently off into the forest. But unlike everyone else, he wasn't looking in Speaks Falsely's direction. Climbs Quickly looked at him, ears pricked in question, then reached out in the direction Short Tail was looking.

<*Yes, I do!*> he said, snapping fully upright himself.

<*Are you thinking what I am thinking?*> Short Tail asked, and Climbs Quickly nodded.

<*Oh, indeed I am, Short Tail,*> he replied, his mind-glow dancing with evil delight. <*Indeed I am!*>

Stephanie caught a flicker of movement out of the corner of her eye. She glanced sideways, and her eyes widened as she saw Lionheart and half a dozen other treecats go scampering off through the picketwood. For just a moment, she thought they were running away, but she knew instantly that that couldn't be what was happening. There was too much focus and determination in Lionheart's body language. No, he and his friends were up to something—something they believed would help—and she found herself hoping they were right.

They might not be, though, and she settled back into her waiting position.

It was a very young death fang.

An older, wiser death fang would have realized it was drawing perilously near to the central range of a clan of the People, at which point it would have turned and gone someplace else. Quickly.

But this death fang was in no more than its first turning of adulthood, so Climbs Quickly supposed he shouldn't be too quick to judge. In fact, it wasn't all that unusual for a youthful death fang to blunder into even closer proximity than this. The People tended to locate near rivers and streams, and death fangs needed water as much as anyone else. So every so often a particularly incautious death fang was likely to stray into forbidden territory.

As a general rule, the People preferred to herd young death fangs back out into the forest rather than attacking them in earnest. There was always the possibility—as Climbs Quickly knew better than most—that one or more People might be badly hurt or killed in a death struggle against a death fang. Besides, it made more sense to teach them when they were young to fear the People. That way when they were older they would know better, and some of them at least might teach their mates or their own young to stay clear of the People's range, as well.

Now Climbs Quickly and his fellows looked down on the death fang ambling steadily along as if it had not a care in the world.

<*A very young death fang,*> Short Tail thought dryly.

<*Yes,*> Climbs Quickly agreed. <*It is well grown, though.*>

Short Tail radiated silent agreement. Although young, the creature was very nearly two-thirds the size of the one Climbs Quickly and Death Fang's Bane had faced. No wonder it seemed so unconcerned. It was big, powerful, dangerous... and too young to realize there might be things abroad in the world which were even more dangerous than *it* was.

<*I realize we are all angry at Speaks Falsely, and rightly so,*> Broken Tooth said. <*Still, are we certain we wish to do this thing?*> Climbs Quickly and Short Tail looked at him, and the elder flipped his tail. <*I am simply saying that so far as we know, Twig Weaver has not been injured. Now that we have seen the manner in which he was trapped, I think it likely* none *of our vanished People have been. And now that we know who is responsible, I believe the good two-legs should have a far better chance of restoring them to us. If we do this, though, it is highly likely Speaks Falsely will be slain. Do we wish that outcome? And perhaps even more importantly, how will the other two-legs react if they realize what we have done?*>

Climbs Quickly and Short Tail exchanged glances. Intellectually, they could understand what Broken Tooth was asking, and the People never killed for the sheer pleasure of killing. Unnecessary deaths were to be avoided whenever possible. Yet true though that might be, it was also true that for the People, those who had chosen to make themselves enemies came in two categories: those who had been properly dealt with, and those who were still alive.

<*If Speaks Falsely... suffers a misfortune on our range,*>

he has no one to blame but himself,> Climbs Quickly said, tasting Short Tail's emphatic agreement. *<Besides, he undoubtedly has one of the two-leg flying things, like the one Death Fang's Bane wears. If he is quick enough, he will be able to get out of harm's way before anything unfortunate happens. And if he is* not—>

He flipped his ears in a shrug, and Short Tail—and two or three other scouts and hunters—bleeked in amusement.

<I did not precisely object, *you know,>* Broken Tooth replied. *<As a clan elder, however, it is my responsibility to ask such questions. Now that you have answered me, how do we wish to do this thing?>*

Bolgeo was more than two-thirds of the way to the crown oak when his suit's external microphones picked up the sounds.

He paused, turning in the direction they seemed to be coming from, trying to figure out what they might be. He'd never heard anything quite like them, and something inside him turned cold as he heard them now.

The snarling, yowling ruckus was headed his direction, and it was coming fast. It seemed to be emanating from several distinct sources, as well, and his expression tightened as he realized they were the voices of treecats. Obviously the little beasties *had* spotted the trap. In fact, it was entirely possible they'd had something to do with the failure of its counter-grav, although he couldn't imagine how they'd been able to get close enough without being gassed. At the moment, though, they were clearly headed his way, and they didn't sound any too happy.

Don't panic, Ten! he told himself sharply. *If they're really as intelligent as all their champions've been claiming, they're certainly smart enough to try to run a bluff to scare you off. In fact, they're probably smart enough to realize that killing a human being wouldn't be a very good idea, whatever the provocation!*

It was, perhaps, unfortunate that Scott MacDallan and the Forestry Service had never gotten around to publicizing the fact that a treecat named Fisher had ripped out the throat of a human murderer named Mariel Ubel. True, Ubel had already been dying from two bullets fired by MacDallan, and under the circumstances, MacDallan and the rangers had agreed there was nothing to be gained by emphasizing Fisher's part in her demise. But Fisher hadn't known his person had already killed her before he hit her...and he'd been perfectly willing to take responsibility for her death.

Still, even if Bolgeo had known about that incident, he probably wouldn't have panicked. He did have the protective suit, after all. And he had the trank gun. In fact, the more he thought about it, the more pleased he was by the treecats' noisy approach. If they'd found the trap, it was possible they *would* manage to share their discovery with the Harringtons, and from that point, the Forestry Service would be thoroughly on guard. He'd already accepted that he probably wasn't going to trap many more of them, anyway. But if they were prepared to come out into the open to scare him off, they'd also come out where he could get at them with the trank gun. He might be able to take as many as fifty or sixty of them under those circumstances!

He grinned at the thought and brought the trank gun to his shoulder, gazing through the electronic sights towards the steadily growing ruckus.

The trapper's sudden pause puzzled Stephanie.

Unable to taste Bolgeo's mind-glow, all she could see was a sealed, completely anonymous environmental suit.

It could have been anyone, although she would hardly have been surprised to discover who it actually was. But she couldn't understand why whoever it was had stopped. For that matter, she had no idea what Lionheart and the other treecats were up to. They were certainly making plenty of noise, though, and—

Her thoughts broke off and her eyes went suddenly round in astonishment.

Tennessee Bolgeo was expecting treecats.

What he got was something rather different.

His mouth dropped open in horrified astonishment as four meters of enraged, panicky hexapuma came bounding out of the forest straight at him. A Sphinxian might have recognized the huge creature's adolescent clumsiness. One of the Forestry Service's rangers would certainly have realized it was as frightened as it was angry—not that that made it any less dangerous. But Bolgeo was neither a Sphinxian or an experienced ranger. What he saw was a night-black monster charging right at him. He didn't even notice the treecats bounding from limb to limb behind it, or the dozens of deep, bleeding cuts and scratches on the hexapuma's hindquarters.

The trank gun was already up and ready. His thumb automatically switched it from semiauto to full automatic, and he pulled the trigger frantically.

Panic is not a helpful thing where accuracy is concerned, and he managed to miss with his first dozen darts. The trank gun's rate of fire at full auto was in excess of four hundred rounds per minute, however, and he emptied the entire magazine in just under six seconds. Most of the other darts didn't miss, either.

Unfortunately, what would have dropped an eight or nine-kilo treecat instantly only made an enraged, *650-kilo* hexapuma even angrier, and this one's priorities shifted from simply getting away from the tiny demons goading it along to the much larger threat which had just stung its tough hide so painfully. In its present mood, it would have been prepared to tear almost anything apart. The fact that the bipedal tormentor in front of it was bigger—and obviously far slower—than the treecats only moved it to the very top of the hexapuma's "to eat" list.

Bolgeo yelled in terror as the hexapuma headed right for him, totally unfazed by the tranquilizer darts. He threw the trank gun at it butt-first, turned to run, and slapped at the controls for his backpack-mounted counter-grav unit, all in one movement.

The trank gun—hurled with far more force than careful aim—flew straight into the hexapuma's mouth with freakish accuracy. It drove a twenty cetimeters of its length directly into that fang-studded maw, and the hexapuma hacked painfully at the sudden obstruction blocking its airway. It shook its head and slowed, but it didn't quite stop, and Bolgeo had risen no more than a meter into the air when a huge, taloned paw ripped into his backpack.

The counter-grav unit kept the claws out of his flesh, but it had never been designed to stand that sort of abuse. It stopped functioning abruptly, and the power of the hexapuma's strike hurled Bolgeo through the air. His arms windmilled wildly, fighting for balance, and then he slammed into a picketwood trunk headfirst.

He slid down it, stunned, less than half-conscious despite the enviro suit's protective headpiece, and the only thing that saved him was the irate hexapuma's frantic efforts to get his trank gun out of its gullet.

Stephanie stared in disbelief at the scene below her.

The hexapuma—coughing, choking, spitting—batted at

the rifle stuck in its mouth with all four of its forward limbs. She didn't think the weapon was going to be stuck there long, though, and when the creature finally got it unjammed...

There was no doubt in her mind how the hexapuma came to have arrived at such an opportune moment. Well, that wasn't quite true. She had no clue how it had come to be in the vicinity in the first place, but she knew *exactly* why it had come thundering right past the base of her tree. The tidal wave of treecats flowing through the picketwood behind it made that crystal clear.

For a moment, all she was aware of was just how unnecessary to defending her treecats she'd suddenly become. They'd managed quite well for themselves, thank you, although even then the back of her brain realized it was only because the hexapuma had happened along. Still, they *did* seem to have found a solution to their problem.

That was her first thought. Her second was that the hexapuma was definitely going to tear the treecat trapper limb from limb as soon as it got its mouth unclogged. And however angry she might be, the thought of watching another human being—even one willing to trap *her* treecats—being shredded the way *she'd* almost been shredded wasn't something to be looked forward to.

It was odd, she thought later, but it never occurred to her even once to blame the treecats for what they'd done. As far as she was concerned, they were simply defending themselves. That didn't mean she wanted to see anyone *killed*, but she wasn't going to pretend the trapper hadn't brought whatever happened to her upon herself.

Still...

Tennessee Bolgeo shook his head dazedly, blinking hard, trying to get his eyes to focus. They didn't seem very interested in cooperating with him on that. Then, abruptly, they did, and he gave another fully understandable squall of terror as the hexapuma flung its head to the side one last time and the badly battered trank gun went spinning away.

He managed to flop over and go scooting backwards on the seat of his environmental suit while the hexapuma coughed and sucked in fresh air. His movement only served to attract the monster's attention afresh, however, and it cocked its head, looking at him much the way a hungry robin might have regarded the first worm of spring.

It opened its mouth again, snarling.

Bolgeo's right hand scrabbled frantically at his belt, trying to find his bush knife in hopes of at least selling his life dearly. But the bush knife wasn't there. It had gone flying when he slammed into the tree trunk, and his hand found only the empty spot where it was supposed to be.

The hexapuma crouched to spring, and Bolgeo squeezed his eyes shut. It was going to—

CRRRAAAAAACCCCCK!

His eyes flew open again as the thunderclap echoed through the forest. The hexapuma yowled in agony, rising up on its rearmost limbs, twisting its body, forelimbs and mid-limbs flailing as it tried to reach the source of its sudden pain.

CRRRAAAAAACCCCCK!

A second shot ripped out, slamming into the hexapuma's back two centimeters from the first. It screamed even more loudly, but it *still* didn't go down.

CRRRAAAAAACCCCCK!

The third shot finally found the target it had sought, and the beleaguered monster collapsed with a final bubbling moan as a 17.8-gram, 11-millimeter jacketed hollow point slug travelling at 490 meters per second shattered its spine just below its shoulders.

Bolgeo stared incredulously at the monster as it slammed to the ground and lay twitching. He was still trying to grasp the fact that he was alive when something else smacked into him.

He looked down to find a much smaller, one-armed version of the hexapuma apparently glued to his chest and snarling up at him through his transparent face plate. He reached automatically to pull the treecat loose, then yelled in pain as twenty needle-sharp claws dug into his chest.

His mind registered the observation that he'd been wrong about the environmental suit's ability to resist treecat claws. A point which was drawn even more forcibly to his attention as two more treecats bounded out of the trees above him. One of them pounced on each of his arms, wrapping their own limbs around them, and he yelled again—even louder—as their claws ripped at the environmental suit and the far more fragile human skin underneath it.

Then there were dozens of the little demons, falling out of the branches like a furry waterfall, bearing him down under their combined weight, and he flailed desperately—uselessly—suddenly wondering if he'd just discovered an even worse fate than being killed by a hexapuma.

SCOTT MACDALLAN'S AIR CAR CAME HURTLING OUT of the sky at an insanely reckless velocity. He knew he was flying far faster than was safe, but he didn't really care, and neither did the young man in the passenger seat. In fact, Karl Zivonik had spent most of the flight trying to make the air car move even more rapidly by sheer force of will.

MacDallan's radar had picked up the transponder of Frank Lethbridge and Ainsley Jedrusinski's official Forestry Service air car coming up fast from astern, but they were at least fifteen minutes behind him, and he had no intention of waiting for them. As a matter of fact, at the moment an official presence was the last thing he wanted getting between him and whoever had been trapping treecats and threatening Stephanie Harrington. Lethbridge and Jedrusinski could have whatever was left when *he* was done.

The air car grounded in a marginally clear space on

the bank of a small river, considerably less boisterous than Thunder River. It wasn't his best landing, not that he cared under the circumstances, and a corner of his mind noticed the commercial-style air car sixty or seventy meters farther down the river.

"Where is she? Where *is* she?" Karl demanded, already flinging open the passenger side hatch and pulling his 10-millimeter Gerain Express from the rifle rack.

"That way!" MacDallan replied, pointing in the direction of the emergency beacon from Stephanie's uni-link. "About three hundred meters!"

Karl didn't bother to answer. He was already almost as tall as his father, with legs which were not only longer but younger than MacDallan's, and he went bounding into the bush like a treecat with its tail on fire. MacDallan paused just long enough to grab his own rifle, then went thrashing off after the younger man.

He was running hard when he heard a sudden shout from Karl. For a moment, his heart leapt into his throat, but then he exhaled explosively as he realized Karl wasn't yelling in despair or even anger. He was ... *laughing?*

MacDallan couldn't imagine what could have produced *that* reaction, and he redoubled his pace, only to slither to a halt, feet sliding in the thick leaves and mouth falling open in astonishment.

Dr. Tennessee Bolgeo sat very, very still in the shredded remains of what looked like some sort of environmental suit. It was going to take a forensic reconstruction to be positive about that, given the smallness of the pieces to which it had been reduced. Bolgeo's epidermis seemed to have suffered quite a bit of surface damage of its own in the process, which might explain why he was sitting so carefully motionless, given the dozens of obviously unhappy treecats clustered in the branches above him.

Or the explanation might be even simpler than that,

MacDallan reflected, taking in the dead hexapuma sprawled untidily ten or twelve meters short of Bolgeo...and the fourteen-year-old girl sitting on a limb all her own, ten meters up, with a handgun that looked as big as she was resting ready on her knee.

"*Stephanie!*"

"Oh, hi, Scott! And you too, Karl!" Stephanie replied, taking her eyes off Bolgeo at last and waving cheerfully with her free hand. "Glad you got here. Say, could you kind of take charge of Dr. Bolgeo? It's been all I could manage to keep Lionheart's family from eating him."

"Well, that was certainly exciting," Dr. Sanura Hobbard said, looking around the table.

She and Chief Ranger Shelton had joined MacDallan, Irina, Karl, Lethbridge, and Jedrusinski as the Harringtons' dinner guests. Fortunately, the Harrington freehold boasted a very large dining room, with a table sized to match. The wreckage of a delicious supper lay strewn across that table, and everyone seemed to be settling back into a comfortable post-dinner sort of mood.

"Yes, it was," Marjorie Harrington agreed. There was the very slightest edge of frost in her voice, and she gave her daughter a very direct look across the table. "As a matter of fact, your father and I would appreciate it if you could manage to find something just a little *less* exciting to do with your time, Steph."

"It wasn't *my* fault, Mom. Besides," Stephanie added virtuously, "Lionheart and I told anybody who'd listen from the beginning that Bolgeo was a bas—" She paused and looked demurely at her mother. "I mean a *stinker*, of course!"

"You'd *better*, young lady!" her mother said sternly, but her lips twitched, and Stephanie grinned.

"While I might quibble with your choice of nouns,"

MacDallan said with a smile of his own, "you *did* make the point fairly strongly, at that. We should've listened harder." His expression turned more sober. "I'm just glad things worked out as well as they did and nobody else got seriously hurt."

There was a general murmur of agreement, and Richard Harrington raised his wine glass in Shelton's direction.

Despite the chief ranger's conversation with Hobbard, he'd shared the xeno-anthropologist's suspicion about Bolgeo's official credentials to the full. And despite how terribly shorthanded he was, he'd arranged to keep tabs on the Chattanoogan. He hadn't had the manpower to do it himself, but he'd discussed the situation with the Twin Forks chief of police, and the cops had kept an eye on Bolgeo for him. They hadn't managed to actually spot any of the treecats being transported into the warehouse holding facility, but they'd been watching one of Bolgeo's assistants when he leased the warehouse in the first place. So the instant Shelton got Frank Lethbridge's com message about Bolgeo's apprehension, he and the police had moved on the warehouse.

As a result, all of the missing treecats had been found, rescued, and restored to their clan. It was unlikely Bolgeo and his cronies were going to serve a lot of time, given the treecats' unresolved legal status, but they'd probably get at least half a local year or so for poaching, if nothing else, during which Shelton would be sending out their biometric data to see if there happened to be any outstanding warrants floating about the galaxy. Everyone would have preferred something a bit more forceful, yet the important thing was that the treecats were safe.

Richard Harrington had monitored their condition until they were fully recovered from the tranquilizers Bolgeo and his partners had been feeding them, and a couple of them had seemed a little slower to snap back than the others. Those two had become semi-permanent fixtures at the Harrington freehold, and one of them was currently perched on the back of Karl's chair, next to Stephanie and Lionheart. The two treecats looked like matching bookends, both clutching celery stalks extorted—without any particular difficulty—from the two young people. Fisher sat on the back of MacDallan's chair, facing them across the table, and now Hobbard let her eyes circle the three treecats before they came back to Stephanie.

"Stephanie," she said quietly, "I know how protective of the treecats you are. I understand that, and I don't blame you a bit. Or you, Scott. I think I even know what it is you're worried about, and I promise you I have absolutely no desire to see what happened on Barstool repeated here on Sphinx."

Stephanie's smile had disappeared. She looked seriously back at Hobbard for several seconds, then nodded slowly.

"We've never been afraid that was what *you* wanted, Dr. Hobbard," she said quietly.

"I'm glad to hear that. And I have to confess I was a little surprised—as well as disturbed—by what Bolgeo had to say about 'backers' right here in the Star Kingdom." Hobbard shook her head. "It doesn't sound like there are very many of them yet, and they don't seem to have themselves well organized, but the fact that there are *any* of them this early in the process is worrisome. I'll admit that. But in a lot of ways, it really only strengthens my belief that we have to get some sort of official protective status in place for the treecats. And for me to do that, I need...well, I need more cooperation than I've been getting."

"Dr. Hobbard," MacDallan said, "Stephanie and I have never disagreed with you about the need to protect the treecats. What we're worried about is how those protections are structured. How good they are—and how solid. You're right, we haven't been cooperating with you as fully as we could have. And Steph is right that our lack of cooperation was never aimed at *you* in the first place. We understand your commission has to look into the question of treecat intelligence, look at the whole question of whether or not they're really telepathic. It's just—"

"Just that we'd rather go slow than rush ahead too quickly and make mistakes we can't fix later," Stephanie said.

"Exactly!" MacDallan nodded firmly.

"Would it help any," Hobbard said slowly, "if I admitted I share some of your concerns? Or, for that matter, that I'd be prepared to . . . shave my final report, let's say, in the treecats' favor?"

"Is this something official representatives of the Forestry Service should be hearing?" Shelton wondered.

"I don't see why not." Hobbard smiled. "I'm not going to get away with any 'shaving' without the Forestry Service's active connivance, you know."

" 'Connivance' is such an unpleasant word," Shelton said, gazing down into his own wine glass. "I'd prefer to think of it as *cooperation.*"

"Excuse me," Lethbridge said, looking back and forth between Hobbard and his superior, "but do my ears deceive me, or am I hearing something that sounds suspiciously like the birth of a pro-treecat conspiracy?"

"I don't know if I'd call it a conspiracy," Hobbard said, her tone considerably more serious than Lethbridge's had been, "but that might be moving in the right direction. The main thing is that we've got to get some sort of support structure in place before more of those 'backers' of Bolgeo's wake up to the threat the treecats represent to those land options. And we've got to—at least *some* of us have to—really understand what the treecats are. How we can coexist with them on this planet without doing them irreparable harm even if we have absolutely no intention of doing so. We have to figure them *out,* Stephanie."

She looked earnestly across the table into Stephanie's eyes.

"We have to know how to avoid hurting them, and to be honest, I think you, even more than Scott or anybody else who winds up adopted, are going to have to be our point person on that. You and Lionheart were the first to establish your bond, and in some ways I think yours is stronger even than Scott and Fisher's. I promise you that anything I learn from you will remain confidential until and unless you and I *both* agree the time has come to go public with it, but please, let me in. Let me learn enough about the treecats to keep them safe."

Stephanie gazed at her for two or three heartbeats, then turned and looked into Lionheart's eyes. Those green, slit-pupilled eyes. They gazed back at her, and she felt an odd sensation, one that hovered on the very edge of clarity, like a memory she could *almost* recall. That wasn't a good description of it—only as good a one as she could come up with—and yet she was certain that Lionheart understood at least the heart of her concerns, her worry. There was no way he could possibly have understood *all* of it, but he knew what she longed to ask him. She could never have explained to another human how she knew that, but she did, and she realized she was almost holding her breath. Then he reached out and touched her cheek very gently...and nodded.

"All right, Dr. Hobbard," she sighed. "I won't say I don't have some reservations, and I don't promise Lionheart and I may not decide there's something we don't want to tell even you. But we'll *try* to cooperate."

"Thank you," Hobbard said simply.

"Well," Shelton said brusquely into the short silence which followed, "this is all well and good I suppose, but there's still that question of the *cooperation* you wanted, Dr. Hobbard. It's obvious to me that you've already co-opted at least two of my officers"—he glowered at Lethbridge and Jedrusinski—"but it's equally clear you're going to expect me to cooperate with *that* young woman, as well." He jabbed an index finger in Stephanie's direction. "In fact, it sounds to me as if you're about to start leaning on me to cave in on that 'junior internship' nonsense of hers, and I'm here to tell you it isn't going to happen. No way, no how."

Stephanie's face fell, and Shelton folded his arms across his chest and sat back from the table, his own expression a model of mulishness.

"Don't try that woebegone look on *me*, young woman," he said firmly. "Unlike some people, *I* don't go around changing my mind at the drop of a hat! I said I'm not having any 'junior interns,' and I'm not. Which is why the Sphinx Forestry Service has just instituted the rank of probationary ranger."

"'Probationary ranger?'" Stephanie repeated in a puzzled tone. "I'm not sure what that is, Chief Ranger."

"What it is," Shelton told her, "is the lowest of the low. The bottom rung on the Forestry Service ladder. The equivalent of junior assistant bottle-washer. However, it does have a few perks. For example, it has this."

He reached into his breast pocket, extracted a small leather folder, and slid it across to Stephanie. She picked it up, her expression still puzzled, and opened it. For a moment or two, she just looked confused. Then her eyes widened suddenly.

"But this is—!" she began.

"*That*," Shelton interrupted her, "is a badge. It is, in fact, *your* badge, and that and a nickel will get you a cup of coffee in Twin Forks. Of course," he smiled suddenly, "it *may* get you a few other things, as well. Like assigned as the Forestry Service's official treecat expert. I've got one around here somewhere for your buddy with the big grin, too," he added, grimacing down the length of the table at Karl. "Hopefully he'll be able to supply at least a *little* restraint to the equation. Not that I hold out much hope of *that*, of course! Still, since I don't seem able to keep you out of the bush no matter what I do, and since you and that little monster on the back of your chair seem determined to litter the forests with slain hexapumas wherever you go, it seems to me that the only way I can possibly hope to limit the carnage is to give you official status so you bloody well *have* to take orders. Is that *understood*, Ranger Harrington?"

"Yes, sir!" Stephanie said, grinning hugely. "I always take orders if they make sense!"

"Oh my God." Shelton put one hand over his eyes. "I can see I'm going to have my work cut out for me."

"Well, that's only fair, sir," Stephanie said. "I mean, it's a big planet, and you *are* the Senior Chief Ranger. Why, I can't even begin to imagine what Lionheart and I are going to find out there for you!"

"Are you *sure* this is a good idea, Chief Shelton?" Marjorie Harrington asked in a very serious voice, although it was obvious she was fighting hard not to smile herself.

"Of course I'm not sure it's a *good* idea," Shelton replied. "I'm just sure all the others that have occurred to me are even worse." He shuddered delicately. "Your daughter and her friend are a menace, Dr. Harrington. This is simply the best way I could come up with to minimize the damage. I hope."

"Don't worry, sir," Stephanie reassured him, grinning even more hugely and reaching out to catch a double armful of treecat as it leapt down from the back of her chair. "Lionheart and I'll be good—promise! Won't we, Lionheart?"

"*Bleek!*" Lionheart agreed joyfully, and the table dissolved into laughter.

GLOSSARY

Ante Diaspora—the notation Ante Diaspora (or AD) indicates the T-year counting backwards from 2103 CE, Year One of the Diaspora. That is, the year 2102 CE would be the T-year 01 AD.

bark-chewer—treecat term for wood rat.

burrow runner—treecat name for a Sphinxian chipmunk.

cluster stalk—treecat name for terrestrial celery.

condor owl—a nocturnal flying predator of the planet Sphinx. An average adult condor owl's body is 1.4 meters (4.5 feet) long, with a wingspan of 2.9 meters (9.5 feet) and a body weight of 5.4 to 6.35 kilos (12–14 pounds). Despite the name assigned to it by the Sphinxian colonists, it is actually mammalian and is covered with fine down, not feathers. It has very acute vision and is fully capable of taking even an adult treecat if it can surprise it. Indeed, it has been known to take considerably larger game and is considered a dangerous threat even to humans. Unlike Sphinxian "birds," it has only a single set of wings but four sturdy legs, each ending in a set of powerful talons.

crown oak—a deciduous hardwood tree which looks much like a *really* big white oak but has large, arrowhead-shaped leaves. It also sheds its leaves *twice* in the course of a planetary year, once shortly after the end of spring and again at the end of autumn. The summer-autumn foliage turns a bright, deep gold, rather like terrestrial maples, before falling, hence the treecat name for it. The spring-summer foliage does *not* change colors before it falls. Average height of a mature crown oak is 80 meters (263 feet), although some as tall as 102 meters (335 feet) have been reported.

death fang—treecat name for hexapuma.

death-wing—treecat term for condor owl.

Diaspora—humanity's expansion to the stars, dated from September 30, 2103 C.E. and the departure of the first manned interstellar vessel from the Sol System. Therefore, 2103 became officially Year One of the Diaspora.

golden ear—treecat name for range barley.

golden-leaf—treecat name for crown oak.

grass runner—treecat name for a Sphinxian range bunny.

gray-bark—treecat name for red spruce.

green-needle—treecat name for near-pine.

ground runner—a generic treecat term for small, non-arboreal prey animals.

Gryphon—Manticore B-V, the fifth planet of Manticore B, a G2-class star which is the secondary component of the Manticore Binary System. The planet of Gryphon is the sole habitable planet of Manticore B and has an orbital radius of 11.37 LM and a gravity of 1.19 Old Earth standard gravities.

hexapuma—a six-limbed Sphinxian predator. Hexapumas are very quick for something their size and extremely territorial. There are several subspecies of hexapuma, which vary in coloration depending on the season and the climatic zone in which they are found. The largest species are located in Sphinx's temperate zones, and adults of those species can be as much as five meters (16.4 feet) long with tails 250 centimeters (8.2 feet) long and weigh as much as 800 kilograms (1,763 pounds), more than most terrestrial horses.

ice potatoes—a Sphinxian tuber, about twice the size of a terrestrial Irish potato, edible by humans. It is a winter-growing root with a rather nuttier taste than potatoes.

lace willow—a willow-like tree found mainly along waterways or in marshy territory. It is relatively low growing and bushy, with very long, streamer-like leaves. The leaves have a pierced look, because they form insect-trapping openings (thus the name "lace willow").

lace leaf—treecat name for near-lettuce.

lake builders—treecat name for near-beavers.

Manticore—Manticore A-III, the third planet of Manticore A, a G0-class star which is the primary component of the Manticore Binary System. The planet of Manticore is the inner habitable planet of Manticore A (orbital radius of 11.4 LM) and the capital world of the Star Kingdom of Manticore. Manticore has a gravity of 1.01 Old Earth standard gravities.

Manticore Binary System—the home star system of the Star Kingdom of Manticore, consisting of Manticore A, the G0 primary component of the system, and Manticore B, its G2-class companion star.

mountain eagle—a bird analogue of the planet Sphinx. It has two sets of wings and a single pair of powerful, talon-tipped legs. An average adult mountain eagle's body is 1.0 meters (3.2 feet) in length, with a wingspan of 2.4 meters (7.9 feet) and a body weight of 4.1–5 kilos (9–11 pounds). The mountain eagle is a very efficient hunter, but prefers small prey and seldom attacks treecats.

near-beavers—a Sphinxian mammal approximately 51 centimeters (20 inches) long. Although the colonists have named it the near-*beaver*, it is actually closer to a six-legged otter in basic body form. Unlike terrestrial otters, however, the near-beaver is an industrious dam-builder. Various species of near-beaver are found in virtually every Sphinxian climate zone except the high arctic.

near-lettuce—a native Sphinxian plant very similar in size and shape to terrestrial head lettuce, although its leaves are perforated in a lacey pattern. It is edible by humans and is quite popular in salads, with a flavor which combines that of terrestrial lettuce and onions.

near-otter—a Sphinxian mammal approximately the same size as a treecat. Although they look very similar to the Sphinxian near-beaver, they have clearly carnivore teeth without the tree-gnawing incisors which gave the near-beaver its name. They do not build dams, but they are very fast, strong swimmers and skilled hunters and fishers.

near-pine—an evergreen tree with tough "hairy" seedpods and a rough, deeply furrowed bark. The seeds are about the size of peanuts and have a strong, nutty flavor. They can also be crushed for oil. Average height of a fully mature near-pine is 62 meters (203 feet) although at least one specimen 76 meters (249 feet) has been recorded. After the crown oak, near-pine is the tallest Sphinxian tree. Mature trees are branchless for the lowermost third of their height.

net-wood—treecat name for picket wood.

peak bear—a six-limbed omnivore found primarily in mountainous territory. It stands about a meter (3.3 feet) tall at the shoulder and can be up to 2.5 meters (8.2 feet) in length and weighs up to 550 kilograms (1,212 pounds). Although not as territorial as the hexapuma and not a pure carnivore, the peak bear is a ferocious hunter and is considered the second most dangerous land animal of Sphinx.

peak-wing—treecat term for Sphinxian mountain eagle.

picket wood—a deciduous tree which spreads by sending down runners from its lower branches. Each runner eventually becomes its own nodal trunk, sending out branches of its own to form huge, extensive networks of branches and trunks which are all technically the same tree. Picket wood has very straight, very rough-barked trunks which are a deep gray and black. Leaves are long and splayed, with four distinct lobes. They turn a deep, rich red before falling at the end of the year. The average height of a mature tree is 35–45 meters (114–148 feet)

Post Diaspora—the notation Post Diaspora (or PD) indicates the T-year counting from 2103 CE, Year One of the Diaspora. That is, Year 2103 CE is considered Year 01 PD.

purple thorn—the treecat name for a low, densely growing, thorned plant which is nearly impenetrable and almost impossible to eradicate. It has small, very bitter-tasting berries, but it is a necessary component of treecat diets, since the berries provide critical trace elements required for full development of their empathic abilities.

quick heal—a family of therapies which accelerate healing and recovery times. It reduces tissue healing times by a factor of four but is only about half that efficient at speeding the knitting of broken bones.

range barley—a native Sphinxian grain. Range barley is an alpine grass with a bearded head. While edible by humans, it has a rather astringent taste which is not widely popular. It can be ground into flour and baked or be more coarsely ground and made into a porridge.

range bunny—human name for a small, ground dwelling Sphinxian animal, approximately two thirds the size of a treecat. It runs with a distinctive "two-stage" leaping motion, hence the name, despite the fact that it doesn't really look very much like a terrestrial rabbit.

red spruce—another evergreen, this one with scaled, very dark blue-green leaves and a pyramidal form. Its seedpods are smoother than the near-pine's, but the seeds themselves are bitter tasting (to humans, at least; Sphinxian critters like them just fine). It is called "red spruce" more because of the almost russet color of its wood, which is prized for decorative woodwork. Average height of a mature red spruce is about 17 meters (56 feet).

ribbon-leaf—treecat name for lace willow.

rock tree—a Sphinxian hardwood, so called because of the extreme hardness and density of its wood. A mature rock tree stands about 13 meters (42 feet) in height. It has long, slender, sword-shaped leaves of a particularly rich bright green which turn dark purple in the fall. It is noted for its very straight trunk. The brown rock tree is the most common species, named for its light-brown, rather rough bark. The next most common species is the yellow rock tree, named for the deep golden yellow natural color of its timber. Various species of rock tree can be found in almost every Sphinxian climate zone, although it does not like mountains.

snow hunter—treecat name for peak bear.

Sphinx—Manticore A-IV, the fourth planet of Manticore A, a G0-class star which is the primary component of the Manticore Binary System. The planet of Sphinx is the outer habitable planet of Manticore A (orbital radius of 21.15 LM) and has a gravity of 1.35 Old Earth standard gravities.

Sphinx Forestry Service—The Sphinx Forestry Service (SFS) is a Sphinxian planetary agency charged with the combined functions of wildlife and natural resources protection, exploration, environmental conservancy, and law enforcement. It is an arm of the planetary government, not the Crown, and consists of a very small cadre of full-time professional Rangers assisted by a larger force of part-time sworn volunteers.

spike thorn—a native Sphinxian flowering shrub which fills much the same niche as azaleas or laurels, attaining a maximum height of about 3.6 meters (12 feet). Its leaves are dark green and spade-shaped, and it produces very sharp thorns up to 10 centimeters (4 inches) in length. Its blossoms, which come in many different colors, are vaguely tulip-shaped and are prized for the flavor their pollen gives to honey produced by imported terrestrial honeybees.

Star Kingdom of Manticore—a star nation consisting of
the three habitable planets of the Manticore Binary
System. Those planets are Manticore (the capital world)
and Sphinx, which both orbit the primary stellar component of the Manticore System, and Gryphon, the sole
habitable planet orbiting the secondary component of
the star system.

T-Day—Terrestrial-Day; the standard day used to keep
track of all dates for interstellar purposes.

T-Month—Terrestrial-Month; the standard month used to
keep track of all dates for interstellar purposes.

T-Week—Terrestrial-Week; the standard week used to keep
track of all dates for interstellar purposes.

T-Year—Terrestrial-Year; the standard year used to keep
track of all dates for interstellar purposes. It is one
Old Earth year in length. Because the Star Kingdom
of Manticore has three separate planets, each with its
own local year, Manticorans tend to use T-years in
all of their dating conventions. The planet Manticore's
year is the "official" year of the Star Kingdom but is
seldom used (except by a handful of diehard purists)
outside purely official documents.

tanapple—a native Sphinxian fruit, so named because it
looks very much like a bright green, somewhat outsized
terrestrial apple with a thick, easily peeled skin rather
like a terrestrial tangerine. It is sweet tasting but tart.

tongue-leaf—treecat name for rock tree.

uni-link—an all-purpose, multifunction device. It combines the functions of timepiece, communicator, GPS
navigator, data net interface, data storage device, and
emergency locator beacon. Although it is commonly

worn as a wrist bracelet, it also comes in pocket versions, which tend to be larger and even more capable.

white-root—treecat name for ice potatoes.

Wildlife Management Service (WMS)—Meyerdahl equivalent of the Sphinx Forestry Service.

wood rat—a Sphinxian rodent-like, marsupial arboreal, about a third the size of a treecat. They are small and fast-moving creatures which live primarily on the bark and leaves of the crown oak, although they also infest other types of trees when no crown oak is available. They are also very fond of finished timber products, such as lawn furniture or wooden paneling. Enough of them can do significant damage to or even kill any tree, but such concentrated infestations are rare.

ABOUT THE AUTHOR

David Weber is the *New York Times* best-selling author of the Honor Harrington science fiction series. His novels range from epic fantasy (*Oath of Swords, The War God's Own, Wind Rider's Oath*) to breathtaking space opera (*In Fury Born, Empire from the Ashes*) to military science fiction with in-depth characterization (the celebrated and awesomely popular Honor Harrington series). Reviewers call Weber "highly entertaining" (*Booklist*), "outstanding... superb... excellent" (*Wilson Library Bulletin*), "remarkable" (*Kliatt*), "worth shouting about" (*Philadelphia Weekly Press*) and "great" (*Locus*). Weber lives with his wife and three children in South Carolina.

The following is an excerpt from:

FIRE SEASON

DAVID WEBER & JANE LINDSKOLD

Available from Baen Books
October 2012
hardcover

1

CLIMBS QUICKLY'S TWO-LEG WAS UP TO SOMETHING she shouldn't be doing... again.

The emotions surging through her mind-glow made *that* perfectly clear. And it was just as clear that she knew her elders would have disapproved strongly. But Death Fang's Bane had a true gift for bending rules, and she was having a grand time.

Her friend, Shadowed Sunlight or possibly "Karl" (if indeed the single sound most usually applied to this two-legs was a name, not some other designation), was less delighted. Climbs Quickly couldn't read Shadowed Sunlight's mind-glow as easily as he could that of Death Fang's Bane, but the basics were present. Shadowed Sunlight's mind-glow overflowed with determination, watchfulness, alertness, and apprehension.

Climbs Quickly leaned forward in his seat, watching intently as the "air car" (or "car"—a sound so very like "Karl" that the similarity had confused him for quite a time) sped along a complex path through the maze of tree trunks among which they traveled.

Climbs Quickly couldn't quite figure out what precisely was the source of Death Fang's Bane's excitement. True, the air car in which they were traveling was moving very quickly—and sometimes rather erratically—but that didn't seem to be excuse enough for the surges of excitement and dread coming to him through their shared link.

The folding flying thing in which they had more routinely traveled before this new fascination had gripped his two-leg was far more erratic. Yet, unless the weather was particularly bad, Death Fang's Bane didn't react this strongly to piloting her folding flying thing.

The treecat thought a bit wistfully about the folding flying thing. He preferred it to the air car in which they were now traveling. The feeling of the wind on his fur was delightful and the winds carried such interesting scents. Also, the glider *felt* faster somehow. He'd figured out that the air car actually covered distances more quickly, but with the winds closed away, the sensation of speed simply wasn't the same.

A touch forlornly, Climbs Quickly pressed his remaining true hand against Death Fang's Bane's shoulder, then used his left hand-foot to indicate the air car's closed side. From past experience, he knew the transparent panels here could open—although he hadn't quite figured out how to manage the opening himself.

To emphasize his request, Climbs Quickly made a small sound of pleading protest. In the time that he'd lived with Death Fang's Bane and her family, he'd learned how much emphasis humans placed on mouth noises. The People relied on mind-speech, using sound and gesture to provide emphasis. These alien two-legs, by contrast, seemed to have no equivalent to mind-speech, relying instead on complex mouth noises augmented by a bewildering variety of gestures—gestures that didn't seem to mean the same thing from occasion to occasion and could be eliminated completely.

He pitied them, for their mind-glows were brilliant and warm. It seemed sad that even two good friends like Death Fang's Bane and Shadowed Sunlight could not share them.

"Bleek!" Climbs Quickly repeated. Then, when Death Fang's Bane didn't acknowledge him, he extended his claws and struck them against the clear panel, making a noise like hail hitting rock. "Bleek! Bleek!"

When he felt Death Fang's Bane gust out her breath, then chuckle, Climbs Quickly tapped the transparent panel again, just in case she'd missed the point.

"Bleek!"

"Bleek!" Tap! Tap! "Bleek! Bleek!"

Stephanie Harrington gingerly began to remove one hand from the air car's stick. Immediately, the car swerved alarmingly.

"Hands on the controls!" snapped Karl Zivonik. "Stephanie! I'm taking enough of a risk letting you fly without a permit. You want to wreck us and get my license pulled?"

"Sorry," Stephanie replied with uncharacteristic meekness. She knew perfectly well the risk Karl was taking. If they were found out, losing his license would be the least of the penalties. "Lionheart wants a window open. Since I'm flying low and pretty slow, I think it's okay."

She couldn't see Karl rolling his eyes, but she guessed at the expression even as he emitted a gusty sigh and turned to address the treecat directly.

"Back window," he said to Lionheart, pointing for emphasis. "Stephanie has enough distractions without you leaning over her shoulder and the wind blowing her hair in her face."

One of the things Stephanie liked about Karl Zivonik was that he was among the small handful of humans who addressed Lionheart as if the treecat was intelligent enough to understand him. Most humans either didn't bother to talk to the treecat or, if they did, they adopted the syrupy tones they used to address very small children—or pets. More annoying were the handful who seemed to think that if they spoke very slowly and used very simple phrases the treecat would understand.

Stephanie supposed this last bothered her so much because it was actually probably the best approach, but those who used it didn't employ a consistent and scientific approach.

Karl pushed a button. As the back left side window slid down, the air car swerved slightly. Stephanie corrected, but overdid it—in part because Lionheart had just removed his weight from her shoulder—and she was off-balance.

"Steph!" Karl turned the single syllable into reprimand and protest in one.

"Sorry," Stephanie repeated.

She scanned the control panel: direction indicator, elevation, engine temperature, fluid levels. There was so much to keep track of. Worse, unlike with the hang glider, where an accident meant some busted struts and fabric (and if she wasn't careful some busted Stephanie, as she remembered all too vividly), here she might damage expensive equipment.

Worse, Karl didn't own this air car. At sixteen T-years, he had dreams of owning one, had even admitted that he was saving towards a used model, but this air car was "his" only because he needed to get to his job as a provisional ranger with the Sphinxian Forestry Service. His parents considered use of the car fairly compensated by the time they saved shuttling Karl back and forth from Thunder River, which was about a thousand kilometers away—an investment of a couple hours each way, even at the speeds an air car traveled.

Since Karl and Stephanie were the only probationary rangers in the Sphinxian Forestry Service, they were regularly assigned to work as a team, allowing only one ranger's time to be taken up with supervising them. Since Stephanie couldn't pilot, this meant that usually they worked in the vicinity of Twin Forks, the town nearest to the Harrington freehold and where Richard Harrington had his veterinary clinic. There was plenty of room in the Harringtons' sprawling stone house, since Stephanie's parents definitely planned on additional children. That was one of the reasons they'd emigrated from their heavily populated homeworld of Meyerdahl, and Stephanie was looking forward (guardedly) to the novel experience of siblings. In the meantime, Karl often stayed with the Harrington family, taking advantage of all that currently unoccupied space, although sometimes he stayed with friends in Twin Forks.

They were coming into an area where the forest giants were more widely spaced, so Stephanie hazarded talking in addition to piloting.

"I think I'm getting better," she said, "but I'll admit, I never thought handling an actual air car on 'manual' would be so hard. I mean, I was getting perfect scores on the simulator, even in the 'auto-pilot-off' setting.'"

"Wonder-girl," Karl retorted with a grin. "You always get perfect scores on everything. If you hadn't, I would never have let you try this. Reality is different than a simulator. What I don't understand is why you can't wait until you have a learner's permit like every one else. Your fifteenth birthday isn't that far off."

Stephanie was glad that concentrating on piloting gave her an excuse to pause before answering. She knew she tended to "push." Only lately had she tried to figure out why. It wasn't as if her parents didn't love her or expected her to win their approval. If anything, Richard and Margery Harrington were almost too approving, too fair, too balanced.

They'd let Stephanie know, gently and in small increments, that she had advantages most people did not. For one, although they'd tried to hide this from her lest she get either lazy or smug, Stephanie knew her IQ scored nearly off the charts. Karl's statement that she always got perfect scores on everything was only a slight exaggeration.

For another, Stephanie was a "genie,"—her genetic mutations making her stronger and tougher than average. She paid for these advantages with a higher than usual metabolism, but given that Mom and Dad always made certain there was ample interesting stuff to eat—they shared her metabolism, after all—she never suffered for this. What she did suffer from was the flashes of hot temper that came with the package. She simply didn't get along easily with most people—especially people her own age. They seemed dumb, fascinated with things she wasn't in the least interested in.

Karl Zivonik—who was over a T-year and a half older than her—was the closest Stephanie had to a friend her own age, the first she had made since her family emigrated to Sphinx from Meyrdahl a bit over four T-years ago. Even Karl was more like a big brother than a friend, watching over her, scolding her, teasing her, practicing target shooting with her, and, well, letting her fly his car, even though it was against the rules.

However, despite the amount of time they spent together, Stephanie still felt there was a lot she didn't know about Karl. At times he'd fall into a brooding silence or snap at something she didn't think was all that bad. From Karl's aunt, Irina Kisaevna, Stephanie had learned that much of Karl's family and many of his friends had died during the Plague. Stephanie guessed that probably had something to do with his moods, but she sensed there was more. Occasionally, someone named "Sumiko" would get mentioned—usually by one of Karl's host of younger siblings—and there would be this uncomfortable quiet.

Anyhow, despite the amount of time she'd been spending with Karl, Stephanie's best friend was Lionheart.

I mean, look at him, now, she thought affectionately, glancing into the rearview mirror to do so, *hanging out the window like some cross between a grey and cream floppy toy and a six-legged weasel. No one would ever guess how smart he is....*

At long last, Stephanie answered Karl's question, "I don't want just a learner's permit. You know as well as I do that you can qualify for a provisional license at fifteen."

"At need," Karl said. "You can get a provisional license 'at need.'"

"My family does live pretty far from Twin Forks," Stephanie was beginning, when an overwhelming sensation of alarm surged into her from Lionheart. The strong wave of emotion was far stronger than the normally faint, elusive sensations she received, yet its very strength made it hard to define: apprehension, anxiety, yet somewhat removed.

"Bleek!" Lionheart spilled the meter and a half of his furry length over into the front seat, landing in Karl's lap, rather than Stephanie's as would have been his more usual choice. "Bleek!"

Showing Lionheart understands more about operating machinery than most would grant a treecat, Stephanie thought, but the thought was fleeting. Lionheart was pointing off to the southwest. Every line of his body was tight with urgency.

Stephanie immediately shifted course. Karl didn't protest.

"What's bothering Lionheart?" he said, stroking the thick grey fur along the treecat's spine in a effort to soothe him.

"I don't know," Stephanie admitted, "but whatever it is is over that way. Let's go find out!"

✧   ✧   ✧

Pleased when the clear side panel was opened, Climbs Quickly immediately poked his head out the opening. Again, he was reminded that the air car moved more quickly than did the folding flying thing. His fur flattened against his face and his inner eyelids dropped into place. Even so, this was an infinitely better experience.

During the seasons he had lived with Death Fang's Bane and her parents, he had come to the conclusion that two-legs and the People did not use their senses in the same fashion. Two-legs were so sight-oriented that, as in this wonderful fast-traveling vehicle—they would actually eliminate signals from scent or sound. Taste—except when eating—did not enter into their experience of the world. The importance of touch was harder for him to judge.

By contrast, the People relied on sight, scent, and hearing about equivalently. As hunters—especially when moving through the treetops—they were very aware of the usefulness of touch, including signals carried by vibration. He had *no* idea how two-legs managed without whiskers! Taste was also important, especially in how it could add dimension to the sense of smell. And in the pleasure it brought to food...

At this speed, Climbs Quickly found himself relying primarily on scent for his assessment. He caught a variety of tantalizing odors: bark-chewer mingled with the sap of the golden-leaf it had been sampling; the tangy scent of purple thorn; the musky perfume of tongue-leaf in summer flower. At one point his fur bristled when an upward eddy brought him the rank odor of death fang, liberally associated with the blood of some unlucky ground runner.

Climbs Quickly wondered how the two-legs could think they knew anything of a world most of them merely saw as they passed over faster than a winter wind, glimpsing what lay below only as a blur of green and brown. Perhaps the two-legs had senses he couldn't guess at, just as most of them had no idea how the People used mind-speech.

In any case, today, Death Fang's Bane and Shadowed Sunlight were traveling below the canopy—and not at too great a speed. Climbs Quickly, for one, was going to make the most of it.

Drawing in a luxuriously deep breath of the warm, late summer air, Climbs Quickly caught a new scent, one that shocked and appalled him as even that of the death fang had not... The scent of smoke and, behind it, the hot, brain-snapping odor of freshly burning fire.

Arboreal as they were, the People were all too aware of the danger brought by forest fire. It offered a danger to them greater than any death fang or snow hunter. Those could be escaped by flight into the upper branches or even—with cooperation—fought and killed—although rarely without injury, as his own scars attested. However, even the greatest cooperation could not fight a forest fire. The best the united strength of an entire clan could hope to achieve was to forestall the fire's spread while the weak and young got away.

Climbs Quickly shivered inside his skin and breathed in the scent again. It was hard to pinpoint where it was coming from with so many conflicting winds, but he was a trained scout.

The course on which Death Fang's Bane was taking the vehicle was erratic, but it did not seem to be going in the direction of the smoke and fire. For a moment, Climbs Quickly almost gave into the impulse to ignore what he had smelled. After all, he was far away and this was nowhere near the range of his own Bright Water Clan.

However, his own natural curiosity had not been dulled by his seasons with the two-legs. Moreover, the songs of the memory singers—of whom his own sister was one— provided a connection to clans that would never meet, even if that connection was attenuated by distance.

Usually, Climbs Quickly's first impulse would have been to get Death Fang's Bane's attention, but he knew

that not only was she responsible for the vehicle's movement, she was not handling this chore with her usual
ease. Therefore, although his alarm was growing as the
scent of smoke became more intense, he leapt over the
seat and into Shadowed Sunlight's lap.

"Bleek!" he said, pointing in the direction in which the
smell of smoke was strongest. "Bleek! Bleek!"

His faith in these two-legs had not been misplaced. Almost
immediately, he felt the vehicle change direction. Nor was the
impulse entirely that of Death Fang's Bane. Shadowed Sunlight's mind-glow was less easy for Climbs Quickly to read,
but he could feel in it acceptance that he had some reason
for his urgency—even if the reason was as of yet a mystery.

"What's in that direction?" Stephanie asked, trying to
increase the speed while not losing control of the air car.
"Let me know if Lionheart seems to think we're going the
wrong way."

"He's still pointing southwest," Karl said. "Let me call
up the area map. We're within a Forestry Service district,
but I'm pretty sure it's close to private holdings near here."

Stephanie knew Karl wasn't being in the least slow,
but she felt an intense sense of impatience—or urgency.
Not for the first time, she wondered if her feelings were
always entirely her own. For example, she could always
locate Lionheart, no matter how far away he was. She
knew he could do the same with her. However, she felt
certain Lionheart knew what she felt sometimes even
better than she herself did. However, how much did the
link work the other way? Might the urgency she felt now
not be her own impatience, but Lionheart's?

"Oh, Steph," Karl said with a chuckle. "You're going to
love this. The private lands we're heading toward belong
to the Franchitti family."

Stephanie made a rude noise. The Franchittis were not among her favorite people on Sphinx. In fact, it wasn't stretching the point too much to say that they were among her least favorite. Certainly Trudy Franchitti, who was roughly a year older than Stephanie, was on Stephanie's "Most To Be Avoided" list.

"Well," Stephanie said. "Maybe we don't need to go that far. I wonder what has Lionheart so riled. If it was something on the ground, we should have flown over it already. I mean, we're not moving all that fast."

"I've been thinking the same thing," Karl said. "Which means it's something he could smell from a long way off. Take the car up, Steph. Maybe we can see what he can smell."

Unspoken between them was that they both had guessed what this threat might be. The season was very late summer—on Sphinx the seasons lasted for approximately fifteen T-months. This summer had started out normally enough, but as it had progressed, conditions had grown increasingly dry. Drought status had been declared. Fire warnings were posted everywhere.

Very carefully, Stephanie brought the air car up above the canopy. The gigantic crown oaks and near-pines that dominated this area were so widely spaced that it was possible to steer between them. Since steering without the autopilot and radar assistance was something Stephanie had wanted to practice, they had stayed at trunk-level. This choice had the added advantage of keeping Stephanie's more erratic maneuvers away from casual observation.

"Steph!" Karl was pointing southwest, his gesture unconsciously mimicking that of the treecat who rested in his lap. "Smoke!"

Looking in the direction indicated, Stephanie saw the faintest wispy greyish-white traces threading through the thick arboreal canopy.

Karl was already on his uni-link, comming the SFS

fire alert number. "This is Karl Zivonik. We're at..." He rattled off coordinates. "We've spotted smoke. It's pretty faint and might be coming from private land, but we thought we'd better report it."

The voice of Ranger Ainsley Jedrusinski came back over the com. "We've got it, Karl, and one of the weather-watch birds is just clearing the horizon. Give me a sec."

There was a brief delay while she queried the weather satellite for a downlook. Then her voice came back. "*Definitely* a hot spot over accepted limits, especially given wind direction. We're going to send in a crew. Good work. Out!"

Stephanie had set the air car to hover and now she glanced over at Karl. "So, do we go to help?"

Karl considered. "Well, Ainsley didn't say we shouldn't, and it *is* our fire, sort of. But if we go, pilot."

"No problem," Stephanie said, setting the auto-pilot to hover and sliding so they could change places. "No problem at all."

Climbs Quickly hadn't exactly relaxed when Shadowed Sunlight and Death Fang's Bane had demonstrated that they understood his warning about the fire. From past experience, he knew that two-legs took fire at least as seriously as did the People. Moreover, being what they were, the two-legs would likely deal with the fire in some fashion—rather than merely running from it. He had witnessed such actions in the past and seen Shadowed Sunlight and Death Fang's Bane being trained to fight fire. While he was still uncertain why some fires were put out promptly while others were permitted to burn in a contained area, he had come to trust that any danger this fire offered would not be ignored.

Now, settled comfortably across the back of Death Fang's Bane's seat Climbs Quickly decided that it couldn't hurt to spread the warning a bit further. He was no memory singer to send his mind voice out between clans, but he knew his mind voice—especially since he had bonded with Death Fang's Bane—was stronger than that of most males. Moreover, his sister Sings Truly was considered one of the most remarkable memory singers of this generation. Even at this distance, he might be able to reach her. She could spread the word to other memory singers and so alert the clans. At the very least, he might reach some scout or hunter who would relay the warning.

Climbs Quickly sent out a call, then opened his mind to "listen" for a reply. One came almost immediately, but it was not his sister's voice he heard. This was an unfamiliar voice, male and much closer.

<Help!> it cried. <*My brother and I are trapped by the fire. Help!*>

There was a desperation to the cry, as if the one who gave it had been calling for some time and had lost hope that any would hear. The mind-speech included information not included in the simple message. The two treecats were high in a green-needle, within a grove of such trees.

This was not good for several reasons. Unlike the net-wood groves in which clans tended to make their central nesting places, green-needle trees did not have interconnected branches. Instead, branches tended to taper off, ending in needles that would not bear an infant bark-chewer, much less a full-grown Person. To make matters worse, green-needle trees burned fast and hot. These brothers must have been hard-pressed to take refuge here.

The fire had not yet reached their refuge.

<*Can you get down? To another tree?*> Climbs Quickly asked.

<No,> the speaker—he called himself Left-Striped—replied. < *The ground is very hot. We tried. My brother—he insisted he could run fast enough—badly burned the pads of his hand-feet and true-feet. We made our way up into*

a green needle and hoped the winds would carry the fire elsewhere, but...>

Climbs Quickly knew then what this call really was. It was not so much a call for help—for what help could come in such a situation? It was Left-Striped's last attempt to make certain that the clan to which these brothers belonged would learn of their deaths and so not be left to empty mourning.

So the situation must have been in the days before the coming of the two-legs, the tragedy accepted as something to be sung of in sorrow, but now...

Climbs Quickly's "conversation" with the stranded treecat had taken only breaths. Now he rose onto his true-feet and began pointing. He tried to show that he was indicating a specific portion of the fire effected area by angling his gestures precisely along the lines where he could "feel" the other treecat's mind-glow.

Death Fang's Bane made mouth noises at him. One of these was the one she used as his name; the rest was only noise. Yet Climbs Quickly sensed concern in her mind glow, a desire to comfort, to reassure.

She made more mouth noises. Climbs Quickly felt fairly certain that she understood he was not merely repeating his warning about the fire, but a frustration that matched his own indicated that his new message was not reaching her.

"Bleek!" he said desperately, wishing the sound carried different meanings the way mouth noises seemed to do. "Bleek!"

—end excerpt—

from *Fire Season*
available in hardcover,
October 2012, from Baen Books